BRIGHT
MIDNIGHTS

Book 2
The Limerent Series

LS Delorme

This book is dedicated to my loved ones,
alive and dead, seen and unseen. I love you always.

* * *

Prologue

Infestation

It was 10 a.m. on October 31, and the day was knife-sharp and bright in the way that only happens on sunny days in autumn. The sky was Carolina-blue and dotted with puffy white clouds. A cool wind carried both red maple leaves and a distant smell of firewood.

A bell rang from the grounds of a school which was laid out in a small patch of green in the middle of a forest, sheltered on all sides by old hardwood trees. In an earlier time, it might have been a meadow filled with goldenrods, sundrops, milkweeds, and stinging nettles. Now it was mostly cut grass with an occasional weed interloper, but something of the wild still clung to it. Perhaps it was the cottonwood seeds and dandelion tufts blowing in the wind or the low hum of cicadas that could be heard from the trees in the distance. It had a lushness that was both seductive and vaguely nauseating.

The main road to the school led through the woods to the front of the building, where it ended in a horseshoe-shaped drive and a mini parking lot for dropping children off. At the entrance, a large sign in royal blue read *Pineville— Home of the Bobcats* in italicized gold letters.

The school consisted of three buildings arranged in a U formation with the largest building in front, making up the bottom of the U. This red-brick building housed administrative offices and the library. The two other buildings were painted white and housed classrooms. Children were visible through the windows, sitting quietly at their desks. It was how school should be, with children studying and nature outside waiting to be explored. Maybe it would be that way again someday ... but that wasn't what was on the agenda for today.

A teenager was standing still in the parking lot, sniffing the air. He was handsome, bronze-haired, and athletic. Almost no one would have guessed that he was ill. Even fewer would have suspected that he was plagued by both pain and voices in his head, surviving each day only by taking increasing levels of pain-killers and antipsychotic drugs. Maybe one person in ten million would have been able to see that the boy was not alone. He was accompanied by wisps and shadows. Some of these had a humanoid form, but others looked more like scraps of spiderweb or clumps of dark cotton. A few looked like bloody balls that rolled in, over and around his body with movements that looked purpose-ful. Others would have defied description using anything as carbon-based as shape or color. He knew that these shadows were doing more than making him sick. They were shredding his soul in a way that would last far beyond his mere death.

As one particularly large shadow pushed through him, the boy stopped and winced. After a moment, he sighed, and shook his head. Moving from the park-ing lot toward one of the classroom buildings, he passed by the administrative building, where a few of the staff glanced at him from the window and smiled. He was well known and liked, and no one would think twice about his coming to school a bit late.

He walked quickly toward the classroom building on the far right but didn't enter it. Instead, he walked to the other side of the building, toward the end that was facing away from the office. Here he found a single exit door. He opened his backpack and pulled out a chain and master lock, which he attached around the handles of this door. It wasn't perfect, but it didn't need to hold for long. After securing the lock, he went back around the building to the front entrance and pulled the door open. The noise echoed on the tiles of the hallway that connected the classrooms. There were only the two exits, one at each end. It would have been enough in case of a fire—but this was not a fire.

He closed the door behind him. His head was pounding now, as his heart sped blood to his body, completely ignoring the sedative effects of the drugs he had taken. The voices in his head were unusually silent but in the deep recesses of his mind, he heard another voice. It was a deeper voice, sad but certain.

"Save them from this pain," was all it said.

As he came to the first room on his right, his teacher from a previous year caught sight of him and smiled. As she did so, a small ball of blood dropped from her nose, landing on the floor and skittering toward him. The boy smiled and nodded back.

Without hesitation, he pulled a handgun from his bag and shot her in the head.

Chapter One

Coffee Grinders and Charms Speak

"Brains. Don't. Explode." Her mother's voice didn't so much creep up the stairs as stomp, bouncing and gaining volume with each step.

Amelie pulled the covers up over her head, trying to block out both her mother's voice and the harsh light of morning. She had fallen asleep "flying" inside her head last night and awakened this morning doing the same thing. Thinking about flying, some of the soft feeling of those moments returned to her, causing her limbs to tingle and her forehead to throb in a sensual way. Sadly, such memories were always fleeting and couldn't survive the light of day, or a morning with her family.

"It's what the paper says!" her father yelled back to her mother.

They would continue at this volume all morning, even though they were in the same room. She would have thought that they were both partially deaf, if her mother didn't have the ability to hear every single snarky comment that Amelie made under her breath.

Without warning, the shrieking sound of her father's coffee grinder assaulted her ears. Why her parents continued to use that old, secondhand coffee grinder was another one of her family's great mysteries. Her father had found it at a garage sale, and it was love at first sight. She counted the grinds until the magic number of sixteen had been reached and it became mercifully silent.

Amelie rolled herself out of bed and into a sitting position on the hideous dark blue shag carpet that covered the floor of her room. Like every morning, the sensation of the rug bothered her skin. It was an industrial grade, so it was course and spiky. The light from the window next to her bed felt too bright and the noise of her family making breakfast bordered on intolerable, even after the coffee grinder stopped shrieking. The smell of her father's Polo aftershave drifted up the stairs, assaulting her nostrils.

Bedtime was Amelie's favorite time of day. Her stomach, always sensitive and prone to distress, had settled down for the day. The glow of twilight streamed through her window, accompanied by the songs of cicadas and tree frogs. Bedtime meant flying inside her head, exploring other worlds and other galaxies. It was her bliss time. Morning, on the other hand, sucked. Morning meant having a headache every day until about 10 a.m., and a stomachache for the remainder. Morning meant school, teachers and frenemies. Morning meant breakfast with her redneck family. Morning meant being awakened by that piece-of-shit coffee grinder.

And thus she began her morning ritual, as it had been taught to her at the Cone Mental Health Facility, by someone who wasn't a nurse.

Amelie closed her eyes and dug her fingers into the carpet. She took deep breaths as she imagined herself being surrounded by a layer of clear Plexiglas. She envisioned it surrounding her body, starting at her head and then dripping down until it reached her feet. After one layer was completed, she began another. Sometimes she wondered if this was how a turkey felt as it was being basted. Basting or no, the noise around her started to become less jarring, the rug less scratchy, and the light less harsh. With each layer of mental plastic that she draped over herself, the sharpness of the world around her became dulled. Of course, everything else was dulled too, but life had taught her that this was the price she was required and willing to pay for some semblance of normalcy.

The only thing that the plastic shields didn't seem to dull was the internal physical discomfort which had always plagued her, but Amelie was used to this. There was always something not quite right in her body and it could take multiple forms. Headache, stomachache, indigestion, nerve pain, tonsilitis, cystitis, colitis ... pretty much anything that ended in -*itis* was always on the menu. When she had been young, her mother had taken her to the doctor's office. The doctor had attributed all this to Amelie being "high strung", which her mother translated into "Amelie's fault". So she had learned to accept these things as a part of her day-to-day life, and to ignore them as much as possible. By age seventeen, she was already an expert at both pain management and mother avoidance.

When she was finally able to open her eyes without squinting, and the noise had subsided to a reasonable level, Amelie got up and went to sit at her powder-pink-and-white dressing table. While it was usually tidy, today it had a copy of the SAT results that she had printed off at school yesterday. This paper stood out amid the normal residents of her dresser such as her brush, comb, and jewelry. If someone in her family saw these results, it might result in discussion, but no one ever came into her room. That was partially from a lack of interest, and partially from a pointed directive given by a social worker years earlier.

4

Amelie brushed her curly, wheat-colored hair upward and into a ponytail, as she began the second part of her ritual. She imagined a second set of eyes behind her actual eyelids and firmly shut them. She then surveyed her pale face in the mirror and put a little powder on for the shine. She didn't bother with makeup. In fact, the very thought of makeup was darkly amusing to her. She wondered what it would be like to have a need for that, a desire for that kind of attention. It gave her that "rabbit running over a grave" feeling. Shaking it off, she got up and grabbed clothes from a random hanger in her closet.

The rest of her family was in full motion by the time she got to the kitchen. Their kitchen was small enough, but with her brother joining both her parents in it, there was room for little else. Her father was leaning against the kitchen counter waiting for her mother to pour him his cereal, while he read his newspaper. This wasn't nearly as highbrow as it sounded. The newspaper was really a magazine filled largely with celebrity gossip. For a grown man, he was weirdly addicted to what celebrities had been doing over the weekend.

"Hey Amelie, you hear about what happened in Virginia?" her father said. "Boy went crazy and shot up a school. Then after all that, one of the cops went crazy in the parking lot and shot up the crowd that was waiting."

Amelie's mother responded before Amelie was required to do so.

"A cop? Again? Who the fuck are they letting into cop school?" Opal snapped, as she banged around in the kitchen looking for something. "And what the hell is wrong with the schools? There was a school shooting in Arizona not two weeks ago."

"Yeah, well the paper says it happened 'cause they was both sick with something. It says the shooter boy's brain exploded."

"Like I said, no one's brains explode," her mother said with authority.

"Says right here," her father said, pointing to the paper. "Doctors say his brain looks as if it just exploded. And the doctor here says what made the kid crazy could be contagious, and the cop caught it."

"That's dumb. If the cop went crazy, it was from stress."

"Well, that don't explain his exploded brain," her father muttered.

"BRAINS DON'T EXPLODE," yelled her mother. "I work for a doctor and—"

This was the beginning of her mother's recurring rant about how much more she knew about medicine than everyone in the house—nay, in the world. Amelie tuned her out.

Her brother Will was digging in the fridge for raw eggs, which he had recently decided constituted a healthy breakfast. Amelie didn't know from what friend, or movie, he had picked up this little piece of propaganda and didn't

5

care. Nor did she bother to inform him of the dangers of salmonella. It would serve him right if he got sick, but he never did. He had the intestinal fortitude of a cockroach. She squeezed by him for long enough to grab a cereal bar from the cupboard and some ham from the fridge. After a moment's hesitation, she also grabbed a can of Red Bull. She could feel her brother smirk behind her back.

"Hey, isn't that like three days in a row for you with the Red Bull?" he asked, with over-the-top sweetness. "Your SAT's done, you ain't got no good reason for it anymore."

"So you're saying I have a good reason," Amelie muttered under her breath. Then quickly clamped her mouth shut, annoyed with herself. She had broken her golden rule with her family—say as little as possible and avoid all physical contact.

Will lunged at her in a pretend play fight, but she ducked quickly under his arm and edged into the foyer where she collected her books from the side table, shoving them, along with her breakfast, into a backpack.

As she had finished packing her bag and was turning toward the door, a brighter version of her brother's voice stopped her.

"Hey, Ame, wait up. You workin' tonight?" her brother asked as he rounded the corner into the foyer with a glass of yellow goop in one hand and a box of Lucky Charms in the other.

"Yes." She responded through clenched teeth, turning toward the door. She knew what was coming. It was a well-rehearsed scene that got played out at least a couple of times a month. What he wanted was for Amelie to provide him and his friends with free drinks.

"I thought my buddies and I could come by the steakhouse and say hi." He grinned at her.

She knew that this very grin got him laid more often than was good for him. Actually, as he was 6'2", blond, and athletic, he didn't even have to grin to get laid—breathing was usually enough. But when he grinned at her this way, it always made her feel nauseated. She suspected he knew this, though she was fairly sure he didn't remember why.

"Probably not a great idea. I'll be too busy to talk to you," she said, putting her hand on the doorknob and hoping to make a quick escape.

"For god's sake, Amelie. He's your brother. Would it hurt you to help him out a little?" her mother snapped from the kitchen.

Yeah, Will's my brother. I'm well aware of that, but are you?

She almost said it but bit her tongue in time.

6

This was not like her. Life had made her an expert at feeling nothing and expressing even less. She mentally slammed a cage down on those thoughts as hard as she could. Before she could completely lock down, she felt her inner eye open wide. Several of the words on the Lucky Charms box Will was holding began to glow, and not just a little. The word *calories* was lit up like solar flares. When he turned the box slightly, the word *sugar* flashed like neon from several spots on the ingredient list along with the words *bad* and *low*.

Damn. Not today, she thought.

"I've got to go, I'm going to be late," she muttered as she pushed through the screen door.

She was letting her family get to her more than usual today. None of their behavior was unusual. Her family was being typical of her family. Her reaction to this incident was what was unusual. She could usually keep her visions at bay fairly easily. This made the visions her "simple" issue. If she kept her shields up and her inner eyelid closed, she didn't see them, and yet they had slipped through this morning. There was no reason for it, unless she was reacting to something yet to happen. Great. She would have to watch carefully today.

Despite her uneasiness, the sight of her old green Toyota Corolla made her smile. It was old but it was in good condition, and she loved it. She opened the door, threw her books in the passenger seat and started the engine. It didn't purr, it growled, but that was fine with her. Her smile got broader as she backed out, knowing she had twenty minutes of alone time before she got to school. This was her second favorite time of the day.

She didn't see the wispy shadow that raced from the bushes and toward her car as she drove away ... or notice that her heart was beating off rhythm.

Chapter Two

Longing, Lust and Other Learning

Vice Principal Phillip Sawyer pulled into the Mt. Morris School parking lot several hours before the start of the school day, as was his habit. He didn't get there early because he had any great love for his job, but because he had even less love for his family. Having a few hours to himself in the morning, under the guise of being dedicated to his job, was something he had grown to depend on for his psychological well-being.

There was another, more important, reason for him to get to school early. He liked to sit in his office, at his desk next to the window, so that he could watch the students as they entered the building. Of course, he didn't get his ass out of bed to watch a typical bunch of pimply sixteen- to eighteen-year-olds, even if he did enjoy watching them torture each other. No, that wouldn't have been enough, but every few years there were a few special enough to be worthy of his attention. Every five or six years there would be an extraordinary one. In that sense, it had been a spectacular few years at Mt. Morris, because there were two in the school right now.

Before getting out of his car, he ran his hands over the top of his head, smoothing the eight to ten long, thick strands of hair that he had grown specifically to cover his baldness. It was difficult to keep these strands in place throughout the day, so he had to resort to keeping hairspray on hand. He opened his glove compartment and pulled out a small spray bottle of John Frieda. As an afterthought, he also grabbed the bottle of Lexapro that was sitting next to it, opened it, and popped one into his mouth.

Roughly six months ago, he had contracted a nasty flu that lasted almost a month. Somehow, after this, he had found it harder to put on the brave face he needed to tolerate his life. His doctor had prescribed antidepressants for him after a visit during which Sawyer told him that he found his life increasingly miserable. He found it darkly amusing that the doctor didn't suggest making changes in his life. No, he was just supposed to suffer having an ugly wife and a sullen teenage girl, with a stiff upper lip, and it was fine to medicate himself to get through it. In truth, the drug only took the edge off things, but that was enough to keep him taking it daily.

As he got out of his car and started making his way up the stairs that led from the teachers' parking lot to the school, he felt his mood lift. His wife would be out with her girlfriends tonight. He suspected that that "girlfriends" really meant "lover". That might just be wishful thinking on his part, but the thought was enough to brighten his mood.

By the time he had reached his office, arranged his desk and put his lunch in the tiny refrigerator by the window, he was positively happy. It could've been a reaction to the drug, but it wasn't. He was anticipating. Usually, he didn't have to wait long because, like him, Amelie McCormick was an early starter.

Amelie was his secret little obsession. He lived for the moments that he saw her coming into school or managed to walk by her as she changed classes. Having her was not possible, of course, but he felt a desire for her unlike he had ever felt before. Just the thought of her made his groin ache. Seeing her bordered on unbearable, but he watched her anyway. He wished that he had some excuse to talk to her. Without a legitimate one, he feared that, somehow, she might be able to read his thoughts.

What if she knew that I fantasize about her constantly? Or that visualizing her face and body is what makes sex with Lisa bearable? Or that I get erect just watching her walk into the school building every morning?

"Good morning, Phil. Here early as usual?" sang Ms. Hartness as she swished into the outer office, startling him from his reverie.

"Yes, just getting my day in order," he replied brightly.

"Did you see the reported SAT results yet?" she called.

"I was just getting to those."

"Well, I stopped by Krispy Kreme on the way in. The Hot Donuts Now sign was on," she chirped. "You should get one before they're all gone. The early bird and all."

"Indeed," he muttered.

Phil got up from his desk and dutifully went to Ms. Hartness's desk to procure some deep-fried dough. She had also picked up a latte for him at Starbucks. She got him coffee every morning. His wife, Lisa, had once referred to Dawn as his "work wife". Looking at Dawn, packed like a sausage into her bright pink shift dress, it was hard to keep from shuddering.

"Do you know what I heard?" Ms. Hartness asked, just as Phil was turning to go back to his office.

"What's that?" he replied, a bit too crisply, but Ms. Hartness didn't notice.

"That Charlie Danos boy, you know, the kid in the band? He got another DUI. There's also a rumor that he has a girlfriend in high school. He's got to be twenty-three or twenty-four now. That's just not right," she said, with an exaggerated shudder.

"It's scary, is what it is," Phil responded, making a point to look directly into Ms. Hartness's eyes. "That's why we always have to pay attention. We need to *know* our students, so we will know if someone starts acting differently. Kids can change quickly. We grown-ups have to keep up."

He said this with a smile and a little wink in her direction. While Principal Scales would have found that wink inappropriate considering the subject matter, Ms. Hartness giggled. Sawyer couldn't get away from her fast enough.

#

He had just settled back down at his desk with his coffee and doughnut, when she called after him.

"About those SAT results, we have a dark horse in the top ten. Apparently, Amelie McCormick is quite a bit smarter than we all thought. I mean, of course, we know she's the smartest of Jack's crowd, but I hardly thought she was the 1400 SAT-type, right? I suppose we should talk to the college counselor ..."

She rambled on but Sawyer had stopped listening.

His heart was hammering in his chest and his vision had narrowed to a pinpoint. He focused on the smudge of his own fingerprint on his window. This information could open the door to some legitimate interaction with Amelie. He wasn't sure how to set it up, and as he heard Ms. Hartness's heavy footsteps approaching, he knew he couldn't think on it now. He closed his eyes and when he opened them, the world had broadened again. At the same moment, he heard the sound of scraping from across the room, coming from the top of his bookcase. A book fell to the floor, just as Ms. Hartness entered his office.

"I think we may have rats," he said quickly, to divert the conversation.

"Ooooh," Ms. Hartness squealed, pulling up her hands to her face and standing on her toes. He cringed. Seeing a fifty-something woman respond to a mouse like a *Tom and Jerry* cartoon was singularly unattractive. But it was a distraction, and he used those extra seconds to come up with an idea reasonable enough to pass the laugh test.

"Can you call an exterminator to come in?"

She nodded, scampering from the room.

"And can you bring me Ms. McCormick's information? I'll want to take it to the guidance counselor." He waited for her to balk, explanation prepared, but no resistance was forthcoming.

"Of course." She was too freaked out by the possible mouse to question the need for him to *personally* take information about *one* student to the guidance counselor. Of course, he would need to go to the guidance counselor about the other scores as well, to make it seem legit. He would need to craft that scenario carefully, but not now. For the moment he simply closed his eyes. Whatever illicit, immoral or depraved images played on the red screen of his inner eyelids were for his brain only—and this was a good thing.

He would arrange to have a conversation with Amelie, under the guise of discussing her college applications. It wasn't much, but as it was confidential, it could happen behind closed doors. A small reptilian smile played at his cracked lips.

He couldn't see the pale gray, misty figure sitting on top of his bookshelf. He didn't see it jump down and glide in his direction, sniffing with its eyeless face. It moved toward him, but as it got closer, Sawyer coughed. As he did so, droplets of saliva sprayed the shadow. It halted, trembled, and then exploded, bathing the room in millions of tiny particles.

Mr. Sawyer took a deep breath in and sighed. He then stood and moved across the room to pick up the book that had fallen to the floor.

It was Goethe's *Faust*.

Chapter Three

Cresting the Chemical Wave

As Amelie rounded the first corner of the school auditorium, she felt a wave of slimy energy. She knew that Mr. Sawyer, their creepy vice principal, watched her every morning. He had been obsessed with her since she first arrived at the school, having been transferred in from a different middle school. Amelie had recognized this as potential trouble the first time she saw him staring at her with *the look*. Ever since then, he had gone out of his way to find ways to be close to her. She mitigated this as much as possible but as school was basically a caged environment, there was only so much she could do.

Amelie came into full view of Sawyer's office when she turned the second corner of the auditorium, but she waited to put her shields back up in defiance. The car, and her brief walk into school, was one of the few times she could relax and let her guards down, and today she was very resentful about having to put them back in place.

She *was* in a dangerous mood today.

Of course, Amelie was used to stares. They had started when she was nine years old. In the beginning it was just staring, but as time went by, the comments started. First there were the statements made out loud, often to her parents. "Your daughter sure is pretty." "She's quite a looker." And the ever-popular, "She should be a model." Even at that tender age, Amelie knew this was not true. She was pretty enough, but she was no beauty. Her face was too soft, so she generally photographed badly. Her deep-set eyes, although a lovely mixture of blue and gold, were small in her face. Her mouth was not full enough. Her hair was a blah wheat color. Yet men didn't see her with the critical eye with which she saw herself.

Her mother finally gave in to people's comments and sent her photo off to a local modeling agency. The agency sent a very nice letter back that said, in gentler terms, "Are you fucking kidding?" This was when her family realized what she had always known. This thing was not about her looks. It was something else. Maybe smell, or chemicals, or movement triggered it. She didn't know, but she had pondered this often, the way a chronically ill person ponders the pathology of their disease. The one thing she knew for sure was that a person had to be in her physical proximity to be affected by it. The more time spent with her, the less a person was able to control their behavior. If she had not learned some control on her end, it might have panned out even worse than it did.

The visions had started about the same time as the staring, but they started more subtly. She would see one word lit up in a paper someone was reading. Sometimes it was nothing more than a change in the underlying color of her environment. Eventually, it progressed to the point that she could predict events if she concentrated on the connection between these words, colors, sounds, and symbols. At the time, she had been very excited by this and had made the mistake of mentioning it to her mother. Her mother responded by telling her that she was either pretending or she was possessed by demons and needed to see a priest. At such a young age, Amelie had found it hard to tell if her mother was joking. Even now, it could be hard for her. So she quickly learned to shut up about the visions. Besides, they were small potatoes compared with the other things, which had gone to hell in the proverbial handbasket shortly thereafter.

Amelie shook her head gently. It was best not to think of these things, particularly when the school day was just starting, and she needed her mask firmly in place. She adjusted her gait and step and concentrated on her plastic shields. For a moment, she actually felt Sawyer's disappointment, but she blocked that out as well. She sat down on the wall of the landing and waited for her "friends" to show up.

The school was ostentatious, snobby, and built in a ditch. The "landing" was the bridge that traversed the grass moat surrounding the school and led to the school's main entrance. What was called ground level was actually the third floor of the building. Who knew what architect had decided that it was a good idea to build a school in a hole, but it was the same architect who had thought it was a good idea to build the auditorium facing backward away from the main road.

Loitering on the landing was a status symbol. Only the most popular groups would have such nerve, and Amelie was a member of such a group. While she didn't want to wait for her friends, she was expected to do so. It wasn't long before she saw two of her clique walking across the parking lot toward her. Sophie and Elodie tended to show up together, as they carpooled. As they approached the landing, Amelie thought for the hundredth time that they looked

13

like chiral bookends. Both were tall and slim, with athletic builds. Both had long hair, parted on opposite sides. Both wore cashmere sweaters and skirts. But while Elodie had dark hair and a Mediterranean skin tone, Sophie was pale blonde and white-skinned in a Nordic sort of way. Both were pretty, in a bland, catalog-model sort of way. Neither was beautiful, although one would be hard put to convince either of them of that fact.

They were whispering to each other as they walked up. Sophie plopped herself down next to Amelie with a dramatic sigh.

"Is something wrong?" she asked, as Elodie sat down on the other side of her. The dramatic entrance had been her cue to inquire.

"Judith told Sophie that Jack was going to ask her out today," Elodie responded.

Her vocal tone was neutral. This was as close as Elodie came to voicing actual disapproval. Amelie felt her skin begin to crawl. She knew that some sort of tirade was coming.

"And that's a good thing?" Amelie asked noncommittally.

"Am, you've known Jack for, what, five years? Have you not *seen* him?" Sophie widened and rolled her eyes with all the subtlety of a silent screen actress.

"Yeah, I've seen him. I assume you think he's good-looking?" Amelie asked, as she pulled out her Latin notebook. It gave her something to concentrate on during the upcoming rant and helped keep her nausea at bay.

"No, I don't think he is good-looking. I think he is gorgeous," Sophie replied. "In fact, he is about as close to perfect as a boy can get. Every girl he has dated has—"

"Lost her virginity on the first date," Elodie interjected. Elodie was a devout Christian and saving her technical virginity for marriage … or maybe god.

"And your point being?" Sophie asked. She turned to Amelie. "Elodie refuses to acknowledge that the virginity ship sailed for me, and most other people, long ago."

Amelie put on her best "let's all be friends" smile, as more students began to appear around them. Some variation on this little exchange happened every two or three months, with different boys. It was as excruciatingly boring in its repetition as it was predictable in its content.

Elodie had just started to respond when Judith appeared and pushed in next to Amelie. Judith had an unnatural ability to approach unnoticed, which had nothing to do with her appearance. She was much closer to beautiful than either Sophie or Elodie, but in a sharp, unsettling way. She was tiny, in height *and* bone structure but she had dark skin coming from Greek ancestry. Her eyes were

14

enormous in her small face and bright green. Her jawline was square, almost like a man, but her lips were full and feminine.

"Ladies, can't you see that you're making our Amelie uncomfortable?" Judith said, draping an arm around Amelie's shoulder in a chummy fashion. Amelie forced herself to relax into this. Judith was smarter than the others, both in the academic and the Machiavellian sense. Flinching would show weakness.

"You know she hasn't had as much experience with this as, well, *some* of us … for whatever psychological reason." Judith looked pointedly at Sophie, while patting Amelie on the shoulder. There it went. Sophie looked confused for a moment, unsure of who had been insulted. Multipurpose insults were one of Judith's particular gifts.

"Amelie, you should just ignore them when they start up with that shit. On a different topic, did anyone finish the calculus sheet that was due today?"

Sophie visibly blanched.

"I did the sheet," said Amelie, as she pulled it out of her notebook and handed it to Sophie.

The girls huddled around the paper and began scribbling quickly onto their virgin worksheets. All of this was done without any pomp and circumstance. This was the true reason Amelie was allowed into this inner circle of rich kids. Her lack of social standing, money or known breeding was never openly discussed, just as her intelligence was depended on and never questioned.

Amelie looked at the girls in front of her, scribbling away. These girls had no concern about how they would pay for anything. If they could get in to a good university, their parents would pay. If they couldn't get in on grades, it's likely their parents would pay their way in.

Amelie didn't have that kind of luxury. Her parents didn't have the money to pay for a public university, let alone a private one. So she would need some scholarship money. She needed stellar grades for this, so she had made every grade count from the moment she stepped foot into this place. That, plus her SAT scores, should put her in good position to get at least some money. Whatever costs scholarships didn't cover, student loans would.

The problem was that Amelie wanted a gap year to go to Europe. It was actually more of a need than a want. It was her escape from her life and her past, and she had planned it with military precision. Deep inside, she hoped to find a place in the world where she wouldn't stick out so easily—even if she slipped up. A place where she could relax just a bit and let down the mask she always wore. She was afraid that, as the days and years rolled by, there might be nothing left of the real her left beneath the mask.

Sophie finished her worksheet, came over and slid in next to Amelie.

"Ready for another fun, fun day with Pryll?" she smirked.

Oh god. Amelie had forgotten that she had English Lit first thing. At the thought of that, a small knot formed in the pit of her stomach and her intestines gurgled in a threatening manner. Normally, she was more stoic about this, after all, she had this class every other day, but she started today off kilter and jangly. She would just have to batten down.

At that moment the bell rang and the torment that was high school began in earnest.

#

English Literature class was one of Amelie's least favorite classes, but it had nothing to do with the subject. It had been Amelie's observation that any subject could be interesting with the right teacher. The problem was that, at least at the high school level, you rarely had the right teacher. A disturbingly high percentage of people teaching in high schools seemed to be there to work out psychological issues from their own high school experiences. This was played out to terrible effect in front of classes around the country year after year. Amelie had not one, not two, but three teachers with obvious past high school issues. Her Latin teacher was a closet gay man desperate to be considered cool by the athletes and popular boys. Her Math teacher was an ex-class clown, who couldn't seem to make the distinction between teaching and being a comedian. The worst was her English Lit teacher. It was bad enough that the woman insisted on flirting outrageously with boys less than half her age, she was also threatened by the girls in the class, no matter their appearance or social standing. This resulted in a supremely uncomfortable hour for everyone except the teacher, and the boys with a mama complex.

It wasn't really surprising Ms. Pryll had a problem with Amelie. Amelie knew it was the flip side of her issue. She always tried to keep things very low-key in Pryll's class, but sometimes she still had issues. It started out simply, with nasty looks and lower grades, but it became more pronounced when they were asked to keep a journal of their private thoughts for class. Of course, this personal journal would then be turned in to the teacher for grading, making the "personal" aspect of it laughable. Most of the kids crafted their journal entries with the same sort of stoic resignation with which they ate cafeteria lunches, and initially this was the route Amelie took. But the teacher made such scathing comments on everything Amelie wrote that she began to write things to amuse herself. She composed dreadful Rousseauian poetry. She wrote short stories where the heroine tried to kill herself. She read and reviewed not only the book *Lolita*, but also the movie and songs that had been inspired by the book and movie. She would never have done this if her teacher might have been concerned, but Pryll wasn't. She usually just wrote sarcastic comments in the margins such as "how very insightful" or "was this supposed to rhyme?"

Amelie had just made it to her seat when Ms. Pryll entered the room with a crisp clap of her hands.

"Good morning everyone, I hope you remembered your journals," she chirped. The class groaned.

By this time most of the class was in their seats, but there were still a few stragglers trickling in. Hudson, the quiet blond boy who sat behind her, was noticeably absent. Well, it was noticeable to Amelie. Hudson was in the unenviable position of being smart, but not smart enough to use it as a weapon. This meant he was easily picked out as a victim. Amelie guessed it was for this reason that he was always on time. He was probably just sick today, but there was something niggling at her about his absence.

Jack, the virgin slayer, was sitting at the back of the class with Ryan, another member of her clique. They both had their feet up on their desks and were snickering. They were friends of her brother's and were similar to him in many ways: size, coloring, universal appeal, and lowball IQ.

"Now, get those feet down, you knaves. Tsk tsk," Ms. Pryll said when she caught sight of them. The "tsk tsk" thing was one of her flirting mechanisms. She always put all five fingers up to her own cheek when she did this, as if she were giving herself a kiss with her hand. Ryan gave her a big smile and Jack winked as Pryll laughed and blushed. Sophie looked at Amelie and sniggered. Amelie tried not to roll her eyes. Lately, that gesture had been getting away from her.

"Everyone, could you pass your weekly journals forward," Ms. Pryll announced. "And I think, perhaps, today I will pick a few of you to read your entries to the rest of the class. Ms. McCormick, you always have such *interesting* entries. How about we begin with you?"

Ms. Pryll motioned her forward. Ah, the eye rolling had been noticed. Amelie really wasn't off to a good start today. On top of her intestinal grumbling, she was feeling the beginnings of a tension headache creeping up the back of her neck.

Just as she was standing up to assume the position at the front of the classroom, someone stumbled through the door. It was Hudson. He was slumping, holding on to the doorframe. Hudson wouldn't be drawing attention to himself in normal circumstances. Something was wrong. Ms. Pryll was finally pulled from her flirting by the fact that the rest of the class was staring at the doorway. As they watched, Hudson slid down the doorframe into a huddled position.

17

"Now Mr. Crowe, please come in and sit down," said Ms. Pryll, with exasperation.

Hudson managed to hold up a small blue object, before slumping forward.

"Dude's been drinking?" Ryan laughed from the back.

Hudson tried one more time to raise his head and lift the thing in his hands. Everyone in the class just stared at him. The front of Amelie's forehead suddenly exploded with images, and the lighted words from the cereal box this morning made sense.

Low. Sugar. Bad.

"He's not drunk," Amelie snapped. "That's a glucose meter. He's diabetic."

Amelie dropped her notebook and ran to the door, falling to her knees beside Hudson. She had a vague notion that this hurt and she would be bruised later, before she grabbed Hudson's head. She didn't know if people in insulin shock had seizures or not, but that didn't matter. She knew what to do. She had been told by something more reliable than memory. Low blood sugar was bad.

What to do? Okay, Elodie had her phone. What else? Jack, he always ate breakfast at his desk. Today it was a bottle of orange juice. Thank god.

"Elodie, call 911—now! Jack, throw me your OJ," Amelie snapped.

Jack just smirked at her, completely disengaged in the fact that another human being was in crisis. A wave of fury replaced the images in Amelie's head, making everything around her look shiny, sharp, and red. The world began to move in slow motion. She turned, her eyes met Jack's, and she let her well-constructed shields drop … just drop. The energy that flowed out of her felt glorious.

"Jack, throw me your OJ, now," she said, softly this time. She saw the shocked look on Jack's face, but he immediately grabbed the OJ and tossed it to her. The chemical wave that seemed to be her birthright rolled over him, through him, past him and across the class … person by person, face by face.

Amelie turned to Hudson. She held his head gently. His eyes were open but unfocused, still she managed to get some of the OJ into his mouth. He swallowed without much trouble. She waited a couple of minutes, and then gave him another sip. After a few rounds of this, Hudson's eyes regained some clarity. She waited another three or four minutes before she gave him another sip, just to make sure that he wouldn't vomit it back up.

She heard the clump of boots in the hall. Paramedics arrived at the door. Ah, so Elodie had managed the brainpower to dial 911 after all.

Damn, these guys are fast.

"What's happened?" asked the paramedic as he knelt beside Hudson.

18

"I think he's diabetic. He had an insulin monitor, and it was reading low," Amelie lied. She handed the meter to the paramedic. She had no idea if the insulin monitor had read low. She knew in other ways that his sugar was low.

"I gave him some OJ. I hope that's right," she said. As she was talking, she could feel the eyes of the class on her.

She instinctively began to rebuild the shields she had dropped, when she felt someone take the bottle of OJ away from her. Hudson had propped himself up on one arm. He began drinking on his own.

"You did just right," the paramedic said, flashing her a smile and patting her on the shoulder. "Now can you go over to my partner there and tell him exactly what happened."

Oh, that would be the partner that was now talking to Ms. Pryll, and the principal, who had just appeared. Great. As Amelie got up, she felt a hand on her leg. Hudson looked up at her shyly.

"Thanks," he said. Amelie felt relief, but only for a second. Then the full knowledge of what she had just done hit her.

Shit. Shit. Shit. Shit.

True, she had hastily re-established her shields but, looking around her, she knew the damage had been done. Jack was looking at her with a scary manic gleam in his eyes and, from Pryll's expression, she suspected that her days of being even remotely low-key were extinct. Other kids in the class were looking at her with a mixture of intrigue and confusion. She stood for a second, unsure of exactly what she should do. She didn't want to be anywhere near Pryll at the moment. But, as the paramedics attended to Hudson on a stretcher, Principal Scales motioned her over.

"You did a great thing for your classmate, Amelie," he smiled. Principal Scales was one of the good ones. He seemed to actually like kids, which was rare in his line of work. At that moment, the paramedic who had been speaking to Pryll appeared at her side.

"Well, it's a good thing that someone in this class had the wits to understand what this young man was trying to tell them by holding up his glucose meter. It's a shame that person wasn't the teacher," he said this to Amelie, but he made pointed eye contact with the principal. This guy was furious. He had a name tag on his coat that read "Grayson", but the "son" part was lit up like a spotlight. It wasn't hard to catch the meaning. His son was diabetic as well, and he wanted Pryll's head on a platter.

Shit. Close it down. Close it down.

Wasn't she in enough trouble without all these little cracks in her defenses? She looked over at Ms. Pryll, whose mouth was hanging open like a trout. Oh god. Well, on the positive side, her headache seemed to be gone.

"Thank you, Amelie," the paramedic said, as the bell rang. "If it's okay with your principal, you can go on to your next class, while I have a few more questions for your teacher."

There was a threat in that statement, but it was not directed at her. Scales nodded his head at her.

Amelie couldn't get out fast enough.

Chapter Four

Principals and Pedophiles

Amelie had only made it through fifteen minutes of her next class when Mr. Sawyer showed up in the doorway.

"May I borrow Ms. McCormick please?" Mr. Sawyer asked.

The class made a low "ooooohhhhh" sound as Amelie got up to leave. She feigned indifference, but her heart was hammering.

Nothing to be afraid of, they just want to know what happened.

Nope, nothing to be scared of at all. She just had to walk to the office … with Sawyer. Her headache came flaring back with a vengeance.

"Ms. McCormick, it seems there has been quite a bit of activity this morning," Sawyer said as they started down the hall together.

"Is that what this is about, sir?" Amelie asked. She was suppressing a gag reflex because she could feel his words on her skin, touching her, probing her. "Am I in trouble?"

"No, no, of course not," Sawyer said. "The principal would just like to get a little more information from you. There seems to be some sort of discrepancy about what you said to Ms. Pryll when you were trying to help Hudson."

"I don't recall saying anything to her," she responded shortly.

"Well, that's the interesting thing, you see." He moved a bit closer and tried for a conspiratorial tone. "I probably shouldn't be telling you this, but your teacher and a few other students seem to be under the strong impression that you called her a 'stupid bitch'. On the other hand, some seem to think you were the proverbial Florence Nightingale running to the aid of a fallen soldier."

Oh god, he's going for romantic.

"I didn't call her a stupid bitch," she said.

"Perhaps one of your friends said that during the heat of the moment?" he asked, moving closer still. They were almost at the office, just a few more feet

21

to walk. She felt him brush up against her gently as they walked, and the surge of sexual energy coming from him was sickening. With his touch came visions of a sexual nature—and herself front and center in them. She shuddered and slammed down her inner eyelid.

"Well, I just realized I forgot something," Sawyer said, as he opened the door to the office for her. With the door open, it was easy to hear Lila Pryll crying in Mr. Scales's office.

As Sawyer turned and scuttled away, a graphic mental image snuck past Amelie's shields—of him masturbating in the bathroom. She could have done without that.

But for now, she had more pressing problems. She went into the office as unobtrusively as possible, nodding to Ms. Hartness to let her know she was there. She sat down quietly on the couch and pulled in every ounce of energy she had. The conversation in Mr. Scales's office was not hard to hear, but she tried to pretend like she wasn't listening.

"I will not have students disrespect me in that manner." Pryll's voice was sharp and shrill.

"Lila," Scales was using his "reasonable" voice. "The boy was having a diabetic incident. If she had not stepped in, things might have been much worse for him, and for the school, and for *you*."

In the last part of this sentence, he seemed to be losing some control of his vocal tone. Amelie knew and respected this man. He was normally sedative-calm and smooth as silk. But now he was on the edge of losing his temper.

"I don't know how a sassy teenager backtalking me helps me in any way," Pryll snapped.

"Because, if something had happened to that boy, then it would have been your neck on the chopping block, worse than it already is. Seriously, Lila. What were you thinking? A child comes into your class in obvious physical distress, and a student is the one who recognized the problem and called an ambulance. It makes you, me, and the whole school system look negligent."

"What did you just say to me?" Pryll virtually shrieked. "Did you just call me negligent? I will call a lawyer—"

Scales cut her off. "That's not a bad idea, and you'll have plenty of time to do it, as you're now on leave until there's been an investigation into the situation. The paramedic on duty happened to be not only the son of the school superintendent, but also the father of a diabetic boy. He made a call to his father within minutes of getting Hudson in the ambulance. It's rolling downhill now, and I have been asked to suspend you until we can find out what happened. I think it would be best for all if you said as little as possible and just went home."

22

Silence followed, then talking, but softer and indiscernible.

Amelie pulled a novel from her backpack and tried to read. Her head was throbbing behind her eyes, and her mind was reconstructing the events of the day, looking for holes in her story, mistakes that could further unravel into nightmares, trying to catch problems before they started.

She had known from the moment she felt the chemical wave leave her body that she would have little control over the ripples that would come from it. She was also ninety-nine percent sure that the conflict over what she did or did not say to Ms. Pryll would be split down sexuality lines—not gender but sexuality. Those who liked girls would have seen her in the form of sexual archetype that they found most exciting or compelling. Those who were not attracted to girls would have found something offensive in her behavior. It would be difficult for her friends as there would be serious conflict between the persona she adopted within their group and the chemical message they just received. She would have to overdo her nerd girl persona in the coming months.

The door to Mr. Scales's office opened and Ms. Pryll came out, wiping her nose with a tissue. The woman was not attractive to begin with, but crying had made her nose more bulbous, her acne scars stand out red against her face, and had left little mascara rivers running down the sides of her nose, collecting in her marionette lines. She glared at Amelie as she passed her on the couch, purposely running into one of her legs. Great. That relationship had gone from bad to physical violence fast. Amelie was feeling the beginnings of full-fledged panic set in, when Mr. Scales appeared at the door to his office and motioned her in.

"Please sit." He motioned to the old, brown leather couch next to his desk rather than the padded chair in front of it. Amelie nodded and sat down quietly. Mr. Scales looked at her for a moment, then nodded, pulled out a slip of paper and scribbled something on it. He called Ms. Hartness and handed it to her. Hartness then nodded with a tight smile and left the room.

"Ms. McCormick," he began. Amelie didn't mind his use of her last name. It sounded quaint when Principal Scales said it, as opposed to smarmy when Mr. Sawyer did.

"First, let me thank you for having the presence of mind to recognize the problem with Mr. Crowe. It was a good thing you knew what the glucose meter was. Just out of curiosity, how *did* you know, as apparently our staff did not?"

Amelie was not expecting this question, although she should have been, and hesitated for just a moment. But she thought up a lie and she thought it up quick.

"A friend of my parents had one when they came over to the house one time. I was curious about it, and he showed me how it worked," she lied.

"You knew his blood sugar was registering low?" he asked.

"Yes, sir. It seemed low to me. Am I in trouble?" she asked, redirecting the conversation.

"No. No. Of course not. I'm thanking you. I was just curious about the circumstances. But there is one thing I need to clear up. Ms. Pryll was extremely upset because she said that you called her, and I quote, a 'stupid bitch'. Did you say this?"

"No, I did not," she said simply. No point overstating this, it was the truth.

"Any idea why several of the members of the class seemed to think you said something like this?"

"Does that mean that other members of the class think that I didn't?" she asked.

"Just so," he responded, with a small smile. "That seems quite odd to me. The ones that think they heard you call your teacher a bitch are quite adamant about it. The ones who think you didn't say that are just as adamant. Of course, I haven't had time to talk to many people yet."

"I would never say something like that," Amelie said. "Ms. Pryll hates me enough as it is. I wouldn't want to do anything to make things worse."

"Why would you say that she hates you?" he asked.

"I've read her comments in my journal."

"Actually, I would like to see that, if you don't mind. It might be illuminating for me."

Amelie pulled out her notebook and handed it to the principal.

"As to what you did or did not say, I wouldn't actually hold it against you if you had said something of the sort. It was an emergency situation, and people often don't have time for social niceties in such circumstances. So, if you did say something, you will not have any trouble about it. I just want to check the stories on all sides."

"I didn't say anything. At least not out loud," she repeated.

"Very well. I believe you. However, I think you might have had enough stimulation for one day, so I have asked Ms. Hartness to call your parents and tell them I'm sending you home for the rest of the day. Do you have your car with you?"

"Yes."

"And you can drive yourself?"

"Yes."

"Then you can be excused for the day. Take a break and try to relax this afternoon. These sorts of events can be very taxing. Particularly for kids like you."

"Like me?" she asked. The hairs on the back of her neck were standing up, but Principal Scales's smile was warm and genuine as he stood up from behind his desk.

"Yes. Smart and sensitive. Go on now."

"Thanks." She smiled, collecting her books. The principal escorted her to the door. As she was just about to leave, Mr. Scales took her arm, leaned into her and said very softly, "And Amelie, try not to talk to anyone on the way out." As he said this, he patted her arm gently.

He feels something.

"Yes sir," she managed to squeak before fleeing from the office, both strangely comforted and confused.

#

Amelie had seven texts from Jack by the time she got home from school. She had just walked in the door and turned her phone back on so she could send her mom a text when it began pinging. She got texts from Elodie, Sophie, and Judith—confused, excited and sardonic in said order. But it was the texts from Jack, whom she had hit so hard in class today, that got her full attention.

The first one was innocuous enough. Hey, it's Jack. I just wanted to say that what you did for that diabetic kid in English Lit today was cool. Ciao, Jack.

The second was a little more intense.

Hey Amelie, it's Jack. Didn't see u in PE. Elodie said you were sent home early. Hope u aren't in trouble. Some girl said u called Pryll a bitch, I told her that was bullshit. Let me know if u want me to grab ur homework. I was gonna come see Will anyway. Ciao Baby, Jack.

The cutesy sign off was a danger sign. He was trying to sound cool and distant but it's hard to be cool and distant when this was your second text in one day to a girl you've barely acknowledged for four years.

The third, fourth, fifth, and sixth texts were in the same vein, but the tone had intensified to the point that he sounded desperate by the last one.

Hey Ame, it's Jack. Hey, I haven't heard back from u. Getting worried. Hope u aren't taking that bitch Pryll too seriously. I heard she's getting suspended, so there'll be a sub until Xmas. Gonna come by after practice to drop off your homework. I stopped by your classes to pick it up. The teachers didn't want to give it to me at first, but I have ways of persuasion. ;) See you this afternoon, Ciao Jack.

That last text didn't bother with the pretense of dropping by to see her brother. It was all about her.

Shit.

25

Closing these things down when she was forced to be close to the person affected was difficult in the extreme. She would need to find some way to get out of seeing him. Maybe she would go to the library later to avoid a confrontation.

But for the moment she had the house to herself. It had been a stressful day and she wanted nothing more than to fly herself away to that beautiful world in her mind. With that thought, she dropped her phone and books by the side of her bed, lay back and let her eyes go soft in her head.

Chapter Five

Breathing Saki

Amelie's breath began to quicken and grow shallow as she focused all her energy into the center of her forehead. Within seconds, the darkness behind her eyes became lighter. On this rose-colored screen, faint, blurry images began to appear: a hillside, a dark cave lined with mother-of-pearl, an opal the size of a cable car with tall, giraffe-like creatures chanting around it. A heartbeat later, she was no longer watching images, but part of them.

Today, Amelie found herself above a vast forest. Pollen and spores filled the skies, and the air smelled like dirt and chlorophyll. The wind was cool and moist against her skin as she spun in the air. She had not been over this particular forest before, but she had seen thousands like it in her nightly travels. The sky above her was impossibly black behind a blazing sun. Almost as soon as she turned her attention to the sky, she shot upward and through it, toward the stars.

Space curved around her as she flew. This part was always a bit uncomfortable, but not long-lasting. When she slowed down, she found herself surrounded not by the blackness of space, but by a velvet darkness that was filled with images and glowing symbols. There were planets, bits of scenery, holes of light, currents of gas, and cosmic waves breaking against sands of stars. Most of these images were new, but there were a few recurring images and scenes. She could travel to any of these places if she wanted.

Somewhere, back in her body, she could feel pressure building up behind her eyes, but she brushed that feeling aside. Her body would be fine. She was not asleep. She was just away.

Just beneath her one of her recurring images appeared ... a hallway filled with doors.

27

This hallway wasn't a favorite, as it didn't do anything besides occasionally change its look. Usually, she just flew through it and back out. Today, as she dropped down into it, it looked like a hospital corridor, clean and sterile, with white-tiled flooring and walls. Amelie waited to speed up and rush through it as she usually did. Instead, she felt herself slowing down, drifting past steel doors.

Suddenly her forward motion stopped, and her feet touched the floor of the hallway. This had never happened before. As her feet touched the floor, the appearance of the doors changed. They were now circular, made of dull silver with engraved markings that connected and intertwined in a way that was both elegant and meaningless. There was something sort of creepy about them. She moved closer to one and put her hand against it, only to immediately yank it back. The door was so cold that she checked her hand for frost burn.

"Don't be ridiculous," she told herself. "You're in your bed at home."

This wasn't turning out to be a pleasant experience. She was about to leave and fly again, when she noticed that a door in the distance was giving off a slight glow. She had never seen a door in the hallway glow before. She walked toward it, and as she did so, a cool breeze caressed her skin. It smelled of cedar.

As Amelie approached the door, she saw that it was indeed shining. The door itself was made of jade-green stone with rivulets of silvery blue running in patterns like water across it. Slowly, she reached out, wary of another unpleasant sensation … but not this time. Instead, the door felt cool and solid. Almost immediately, a crack appeared underneath her hand, running the length of the door until it split and opened inward onto a field of manicured grass. Amelie felt a strange tugging sensation in her gut … and then a world opened up all around her.

#

Amelie whirled to look behind her, but the door that had been there was gone, along with the hallway. She was now standing on a grassy hill. At its top sat an English manor, complete with topiary sporting splashes of yellow, white, and purple. When she looked down the hill, she saw a field of long grass. Further down the hill was a small but dense clump of trees, which ended at the edge of a large lake. The water of the lake was glass-still, reflecting the blue sky and streaky white clouds above. The scene was nothing short of breathtaking. It was more like a song than an actual place. Looking down at herself, Amelie found that she was wearing a long dress with numerous undergarments that made it hard to breathe, let alone move. As she was alone, she removed these undergarments and dropped them on the ground in disgust.

Relieved of her burden, Amelie walked down the hill toward the lake. The long grass pulled at her clothes as she passed. She approached the copse of trees growing by the lake. The growth was so thick that she couldn't see through it.

Walking to the edge of the trees, Amelie took a few tentative steps out of the sunlight. The air was fresh, and the bubbling sound of water told her that she hadn't been wrong about its proximity to the lake, so she moved toward the sound of the water. The trees around her were old and beautiful. Just as she had made her way through a patch of willow trees, she came upon a large pool in their midst. It took her a second to notice an odd outcropping of rock jutting over the pool. It took a half second more to notice something even more out of place.

Lying outstretched on a smooth portion of the rock, head resting upon a lazy arm, was a young man. He was dark haired and lean, dressed in the tattered remains of what was a probably once-white shirt and black trousers. His black hair fell to the nape of his neck and was probably straight, but wildly unkempt. His skin was pale but not sickly so. She would have guessed him to be about her age, or at most a couple of years older, but it was hard to tell because he was so beautiful as to seem ageless. So beautiful that Amelie found herself holding her breath. He looked more like a painting or a mythological being than a real human. In fact, with goat legs he could have been a satyr. He rolled over in his sleep, throwing his arm over his eyes. He had a heart-shaped face with just a slight amount of scruff to it, like he was too young to grow a proper beard. Amelie smiled at that. She moved to the water's edge and sank into a crouching position.

The boy was motionless now, having fallen back into a deep sleep. Overhead, the wind rustled in the trees, and golden leaves danced in the air around her. The sunlight that was able to pierce the trees made dappled patterns on the boy's pale skin. She watched his chest move up and down. Her own breath was coming faster, and as it did, she became aware that she was feeling something, something strong. Feeling much of anything besides caution was an anomaly for her but feeling something this strong happened ... never. Just to watch this boy was more engrossing that any play she had seen, any song she had heard, any book she had read. He did nothing but breathe and occasionally move his head ever so slightly—and she was riveted.

Amelie was startled out of this reverie by the sound of a twig snapping. Starting, she found herself not ten feet from a stag, staring back at her with wide black eyes. She heard a splash, and the stag was gone. When she turned, so was the boy.

A cloud covered the sun, and the wind came up. The air around her crackled with energy. Something felt wrong. She scrambled to her feet and was beginning to back away when the boy leaped from the water and onto the bank just a few feet in front of her. He was crouched and when his black eyes met hers, she felt her blood run cold. His form was human, but there was nothing human about his movements, or what was behind those eyes. He smiled and uttered a low growl.

Her body had her running before her brain—which was trying to tell her all this was unreal—could stop her. She sprinted toward the manor house, pulling up her wretched skirts as she forced her way through the long grass. Behind her she could hear the sounds of pursuit, but it sounded wrong. The cadence of the running didn't sound like someone on two feet, but on four. She couldn't see anyone, but she could see the grass being bent as something came at her. The manicured grounds of the manor house were only a few feet away.

She had just thought she might make it, and be seen by someone, when she was hit hard from behind. Thrown onto the short grass, she rolled, with someone on her back. Something ripped across her arm, causing a flash of pain. She landed face down on the grass but was roughly turned over. That boy she had found so beautiful was now on top of her. He had the same tousled hair, ripped clothes and beautiful face, but his black eyes were reflective. When he smiled at her, she thought she saw fangs, but his form was fuzzy, out of focus. His nose was inches from hers, his mouth moving toward her throat, when he stopped and sniffed. His eyes then changed, cleared, and he threw himself backward away from her.

"You're not—wait. Hold it. You're not from here, are you?" he gasped.

She wasn't sure if this was a question or a comment, but it gave her the chance to scramble to her feet.

"Are you from here?" he yelled this time.

"No," she yelled back. She wanted to run, but her skirts were tangled between her legs.

He rocked back onto his heels, put his head down and started taking deep breaths, hands clenched on thighs. His form shifted, becoming more clearly defined. He now looked simply like the young man with the tattered white poet's shirt and trousers. When he looked up, clear black eyes regarded her cautiously, as he raised his hands, palms up toward her.

"God, I'm so sorry. I won't hurt you. Really. I won't. Promise." He moved forward ever so slightly, and she scrambled backward, tripping over her skirts and falling on her butt in the process.

"Easy. Easy. Can we start again? I promise I won't move an inch until you're comfortable. Not an inch. Okay?"

She nodded but glanced to her side. The house was just there, she could make it there in two minutes at a fast run. If this was a dream, she wasn't sure what laws of physics would or wouldn't apply.

But was this really a dream? She had been flying and had dropped into the hallway and come through one of its doors. Did that mean she fell asleep? Most likely she would just wake up before anything too bad happened. And yet, her arm was bleeding. Had she ever bled in a dream before? No.

All this went through her head in a crazy jumbled fashion as she eyed the boy in front of her.

Then, without more thought, she jumped up, grabbed her skirts, and raced for the house. She listened for the sound of pursuit, but as her heart slammed and the house got closer, she heard nothing. She made it up the hill and into the topiary garden. Still she heard nothing behind her. Glancing over her shoulder, she saw nothing. She slowed and crouched behind a hedgerow, but still nothing.

She was in the manicured English garden behind the manor house. In the field below her, she heard the normal sounds of wind in grass and birds in trees, but no sound of movement. Amelie backed slowly toward the house. When she reached a large patio offering a door to the house, she stopped. She couldn't see anyone in the house, but this angle gave her a better view of the meadow below and the path in the grass made by her recent flight. It looked invasive, like a rape of some sort.

Bending over her knees, she took some deep breaths. She was still trembling with both fear and exertion—but with something else as well. She felt completely, unnaturally alive. Her senses were heightened. The cold air kissed her skin, the rough cloth of her garments caught the hairs on her arms, and her heart beat in a staccato rhythm. It was odd to have this level of sensation in a dream, or even a vision.

She could also feel the pain in her arm. Lifting it up, she saw a large bloody rip in her clothing. The red stain on the white fabric was spreading. So her arm was bleeding quite a bit, probably as a result of the running.

Keeping an eye on the field, she grabbed the torn part of her sleeve and ripped it off, awkwardly tying it around her forearm, using her teeth to pull it taut. Once done, she sat down with her back against the house and closed her eyes. She concentrated on her room. In her mind's eye, she could see herself,

31

lying on her side in her bed. With this came a tugging sensation behind her eyes as she felt herself drift toward that image.

She was startled back by a voice.

"Hello. It's me. Look I know I promised that I wouldn't move, but I just wanted to make sure you were okay. You were running pretty hard, and I smelled—sorry, I mean I noticed you were cut. I just want to make sure you aren't bleeding to death or anything."

The vision of herself on her bed disappeared and she was back in whatever world this was.

"Stay back," she called. This was useless and impotent, but at least she could break the glass of the door and get into the house if she had to. Surely, there must be someone inside a place this large.

An arm stuck out from the nearest hedgerow, waving a strip of white cloth. It looked like piece of his tattered white shirt.

"Truce!" he called. Then he stuck his head out from around the bush and smiled, a beautiful smile to be sure. He didn't look dangerous anymore, but looks could be deceiving.

What nice teeth you have.

All the better to eat you with, my dear.

"Look, I'm really sorry," he said, walking out slowly from behind the bush. She jumped and turned for the house, but he stopped and held his hands up.

"Easy. I'm not going to hurt you. I should have recognized that you weren't from here. Jeez, I should have seen that immediately." He ran his hand through his hair, where it promptly encountered some leaves and stems and got stuck. Absurdly, Amelie had to suppress the urge to giggle.

"Well, this is a terrible start, isn't it?" he said, yanking his hand out of his hair. "I didn't react fast enough."

Then, contradicting himself, he moved forward so quickly that she didn't have time to run. He had her arm in his hands and was examining the makeshift bandage, which was now quite red.

"You're bleeding a lot. We should get you inside and sit you down." As he said this, he opened the patio door, which wasn't even locked, and gingerly helped her inside.

"Uh, maybe we should knock, or tell someone we're here," Amelie said.

Safety in numbers and all that.

"Oh, don't worry. It's empty at this point," he said.

Why should she worry? She was only alone with a potential werewolf. And "at this point"? What odd phrasing.

The boy led her to an ornate burgundy Victorian settee. She sat down and he gingerly put her wounded arm up on the arm of the couch. He then left for less than a minute, returning with some scissors, a gauze bandage and some tape. He undid her makeshift bandage, and let out a sigh.

"Thank god, it's clotting already. You got slashed by a rock and I was afraid, because it was in your forearm. There are lots of veins there, but the cut isn't that deep. It's probably just bloodier because you were running."

At this point he actually made a "tsk tsk" sort of noise.

"YOU TRIED TO EAT ME!" she yelled, surprising herself, not only by the words that came unbidden, but by the force of her voice. "What did you expect me to do? Lie back and make it easier for you?"

He pulled back and put his hands up again.

"It's okay. It's okay. I'm not judging … or eating. I promise, okay?"

"Okay," she said, trying for calm, but her voice was jittery. "What are you, some sort of werewolf?"

"Is that what I look like to you?" was the odd response.

"No, well not really." The oddness of the question took the proverbial wind out of her sails.

"What do I look like, exactly?" he asked, his head cocked to the side, not unlike a dog, despite the fact she had just said that he didn't look like a werewolf. Perhaps a were-dog. She found herself giggling at that. He smiled in return but was obviously waiting for an answer.

"Oh, I don't know. You look like a guy."

He rolled his hand.

"Okay, black hair, a bit messy. White skin. Black eyes. Maybe a bit in need of a bath …"

As she spoke, his black eyes got wider and wider, and began to get that wild look again. Her apprehension level went back up.

"You never told me if you were a werewolf or not?"

The question seemed to pull his mind back from wherever it had gone.

"Oh me, no. I'm not a werewolf. Well, not exactly. Here, let's start this more formally, shall we?"

He smiled and stuck out his hand. "I'm Clovis. And you are?"

"Amelie," she replied, taking his hand. It was unusually warm.

"That's a lovely name. Amelie."

"It's a mistake. My mother meant to name me Amelia, but didn't spell it right for the birth certificate," she blurted out, then winced. But he laughed.

"Well, Amelie is much nicer than Amelia … to my taste at least," he replied, smiling. She found herself smiling too, and miraculously relaxing. Surely, if he were planning to kill her, he wouldn't be so concerned about her bleeding. But still …

"So, if you aren't a werewolf, what are you? And why were you attacking me?"

"She comes up with that question, right out of the box," he muttered to himself before turning his gaze to her.

"The short answer is that I have to act in a certain way with people who are from this story. But as you aren't from here, I can be myself. I know that isn't much of an answer, but I can't really give you much more than that."

"Are you going to turn *back* into whatever you were if someone else comes around?"

"Well, it might happen IF someone were to come around, because this is a major character here, but they won't. At least not here and now. Either way, you won't have to worry. I won't hurt you, and I won't let anyone else hurt you. Okay?"

She nodded.

"Where are you from?" he asked as he re-dressed her arm.

"Ummm, North Carolina? Is that what you're looking for?"

"Is it pretty there?" he asked, applying something that seemed like salve to her skin. It smelled like menthol and went on cold and tingly.

"Yes, sometimes. Particularly at dusk," she replied.

Clovis looked up at her and smiled again, although a bit awkwardly.

"Oh shit," he said suddenly as he lifted up her other arm. "I got you here."

He was looking at four nasty scratches on her other arm. She hadn't noticed them and didn't remember getting them, but they looked disturbingly like scratches from claws.

"Let me just put some salve on these too," he said. "Look, I'm really sorry. I know I keep saying that."

He sat back and looked at her.

"I guess I should say I'm sorry that I tried to eat you, as you so succinctly put it. But I'm not sorry you're here."

He looked at her, smiling.

She said nothing. As the fear of being eaten, molested, or worse, was fading, she was beginning to feel strange. The feeling was tingly, uncomfortable, and a bit scary … like the emotional equivalent of how your arm feels as it is waking up from being asleep for too long.

Clovis ran his hand through his hair and coughed.

"Well, this is a bit awkward. I know you're probably just waiting for me to turn my back so you can run, or you want me to leave at the very minimum. Right?"

She said nothing. Somehow, she couldn't find words.

"No? Really? Okay, then that's fantastic," he said with a grin. "And in my own defense, I thought you might have been someone else. Someone against whom it's much better to make the first move."

"There is a girl out there that hates you enough to make it reasonable to defend yourself by biting her throat out?"

She didn't mean to say this out loud, but he didn't take offense, in fact he looked relieved and even laughed a bit.

"Oh, I'm sure there are many girls out there who hate me enough to want to rip *my* throat out. But not many who would be a danger to me."

Okay, he was a cocky bastard. Fair enough.

"Listen, I'm not sure when someone else might show up, so I really need to ask you a couple of questions before I leave you alone. Just to make sure you're safe. 'S okay?"

She nodded. "Okay."

"How did you get here?" he asked.

"I came through the hallway," she said matter-of-factly.

For a split second his eyes widened again, and his mouth opened, before he composed it and put on a smile. Did she see fangs in that split second?

"What hallway?" he asked.

She felt like she was on shaky ground now. She wasn't sure if the wrong answer would turn him back into whatever he had been before.

"There is a hallway. With lots of doors. I picked a door and went through."

"You were dreaming then?"

"No, I'm not really asleep."

"But you have a body somewhere else?" he asked, with something like incredulity.

"Yes, I'm lying on my bed at home. Maybe half asleep by now."

He moved forward quickly, taking her arm in his hand and holding it up to his nose.

"But you're bleeding," he whispered. She was not sure if it was to her or to himself.

He was even closer to her now, the top of his head almost at her nose. He smelled of grass and wind and something else. Something sweet. It was a strange, heady smell. He still held her arm next to his nose. She wondered if she had picked the wrong supernatural being, maybe he was a vampire … but this was daylight.

Neither of them was speaking, but the moment was not a calm one. There was a buzzing, like an electrical current, building between them, getting stronger by the second.

"AMELIE!" a voice called from the distance and Amelie jerked. She felt a tugging sensation in her forehead. Clovis had opened his eyes and was looking at her intensely. She felt his hand on her arm began to lose substance.

"No, wait!" he said, eyes wide. "What city do you live in? Where do you spend most of your time? What is the name of any guy you know?"

It was such a weird collection of questions, but she didn't have time to think about it much. She seemed to be slipping away and he was getting fainter. But he looked so distressed that she called out the first answers that came to her head as he disappeared in front of her.

#

When Amelie opened her eyes, she was in her room, and it was dark outside. She sat up quickly and looked at her right arm. There was no bandage there.

Of course not, how silly of her to even check.

"Lady, you better git down here for supper right now!" her mother yelled from downstairs.

Amelie flipped on the bedside lamp and headed down the narrow stairs toward the kitchen. She felt a bit heady and had to steady herself on the handrail.

In their living room, Amelie's mom had put some TV dinners on each person's plate. Despite her mother's palpable impatience, Amelie was the first one at the table, which meant she got to pick the turkey TV dinner, always the best of the lot. The men were camped out in front of the TV, which was placed strategically to show off the deer head that was mounted on the wall. This might have been somewhat less offensive to her if it had been a stag. But no, it was a doe. It was like having Bambi's mother watch you eat your dinner every night, with accusing eyes.

Amelie was having a hard time aligning where she had just been to where she was now. She sat down and pulled the aluminum foil cover off her turkey with dressing and cranberry sauce, and began to eat.

"Your brother's friend Jack dropped by earlier to drop off some of your homework. I called up for you, but you didn't answer. I don't like being ignored," snapped her mother, sitting down in front of the country-fried steak dinner.

"I didn't hear you," Amelie responded shortly.

36

While she found this odd, because she was usually pulled out of her reveries quite easily, she was not displeased. It meant that she did not have to deal with Jack post-incident. If she could avoid him for a few days, then the chemical stuff would probably calm down.

"Don't snap at me girl!"

Her mother's tone was moving into the danger zone. It had been years since Opal had actually hit her, but there was no love lost between them, even in the best of times.

"I wasn't snapping. I was just saying. I don't know why I didn't—" but her mother interrupted her.

"What the hell you done to your arm?" Amelie was shocked and looked down at her right arm. It was normal.

"Nothing, see?" she said, holding out her right arm.

"Not that one, the other one," said her mother, pointing.

Amelie looked, and sure enough, there on her left arm were several long gashes, as if she had been jumped on by a dog. It was then that the nausea hit her, and with it the world suddenly went sideways.

Chapter Six

"It's Rabies"

When Amelie opened her eyes, she was in her bed. The morning sun was streaming through her curtains, and it was acutely painful to her eyes. She sat up slowly, but even this small movement made her head pound. Looking down at herself, she noticed that she was still wearing the clothes she wore to school. She had a vague memory of her father carrying her to her room and leaving quickly. Her head felt like someone was trying to drive an ice pick up one nostril and into her eye socket. She swung her legs over the side of the bed to the floor, but this caused a stabbing pain to shoot through her left arm. She looked down and saw four angry red scratches on her left inner forearm. They were raised a bit and tender to the touch. Her head felt sore and stuffed with cotton. That, combined with her arm, made her suspect that she had a fever.

Suddenly, she remembered how she had gotten these scratches and her head reeled. The grass, the pool, the boy, the attack, the recovery, the boy.

Amelie quickly lay back down on the bed.

How was this possible? Bringing something back from a dream was like some horror movie plot line, except she hadn't technically been dreaming ... had she? She sat up again and waited for the head rush to subside. It was then that she noticed a piece of paper taped to her mirror. Gingerly, she retrieved it and returned to her bed.

It was her mother's handwriting.

You had a fever last night. This morning you still seemed hot, so no one woke you. Call Dr. Payne if you're still hot when you wake up. 669-0798. – O.

Her mother always signed "O" for Opal. She never wrote "Mom", at least not with Amelie. Amelie slowly made her way to the bathroom to check her temperature. The thermometer read 101.5. It wasn't super high, but it was a fever. Given the circumstances of her injury, it was probably a good idea to get it checked out, but to do so she would need a believable story in case the troll picked up the phone at her doctor's office. The nurse, Gary, who was a very chirpy Haitian man, was great and sometimes picked up. But Joan, the receptionist, was a troll of the Billy Goats Gruff variety.

Amelie thought for a moment. She would say that she saw a dog as she was leaving school. The dog jumped up on her. She didn't know who owned it, as she had never seen it before. She didn't see where it went. Due to the circumstances of her life, Amelie was an accomplished liar and knew that it was always best to keep one's lies simple and unadulterated.

She got up and made her way gently down the stairs. She went to the living room where the phone was sitting next to their old, gray vinyl couch.

She dialed Dr. Payne's number with some trepidation. As the phone rang, she murmured, "Let it be Gary. Let it be Gary. Let it be Gary." A woman's voice answered the phone.

"Dr. Payne's office."

Damn, it was Joan.

"Good morning Joan, this is Amelie McCormick," Amelie began, going for uber politeness. "My mom thought I should call and get an appointment to come in today."

"And why would that be? The roster is full today and the waiting room is packed with people." Joan sniffed. Amelie shouldn't have mentioned her mother. Joan hated Amelie's mother for some reason that seemed to be rooted in ancient history.

"Well, I passed out last night, with a fever. I wouldn't think anything about it, but I got scratched by a dog yesterday so ..." Amelie heard Gary in the background.

"Who's on the phone?"

"Amelie McCormick, fever, scratched by a dog," she heard Joan yell, across the waiting room full of people. Great. Suddenly she heard the phone bang down hard. A second later Gary picked up.

"Hi there, Amelie," he said brightly. "What's this about getting scratched by a dog?"

"Oh, it was stupid. I was going to my car yesterday and this large dog came up. It was very friendly, so I petted it. Then it jumped up on me. It got me with its claws. I wouldn't be calling except that the scratches are red and swollen and I have a fever."

The line was silent for a moment.

"Are you there?" she asked.

"Oh yes, sorry, Amelie," Gary said brightly. Then, more quietly, "The thing Joan failed to mention is that Dr. Payne is out today. We have another doctor taking his patients, but that means he has his caseload plus Dr. Payne's caseload. So we won't be able to squeeze you in today."

"Oh. That's okay. It can probably wait," Amelie said quickly, a bit relieved in spite of herself.

"No, actually it can't," Gary responded with unusual bluntness. "Any animal bite or scratch has to be seen immediately. Let me make some calls and I'll call you back. Are you at home right now?"

"Yes, I think I'm here for the day."

"Good. Just stay put and I will call you back in ten minutes at the most," he said, and then hung up. That was a bit abrupt for Gary, but whatever.

Amelie looked down at her arm. She was pretty sure it was starting to look better. It wasn't quite as red, but it was still inflamed and very tender to the touch. She got up and went to the downstairs bathroom to wash it. As she was running water over it, the scab on one of the scratches opened up. When she pulled it off, pus came out of the open cut and immediately that particular scratch felt better. She put her arm back in the sink, but under slightly warmer water this time. The scabs on the remaining three scratches softened and loosened. Sure enough, when she took her arm out from under the water and wiped it with a towel, these cuts came open as well. She pushed on them, even though it was a bit painful, and a surprising amount of pus came out of all of them. It was a good thing she had never been squeamish. She used a paper towel to wipe her arm. She then pushed a bit more, and more pus came out, mixed with blood. She cleaned this and wiped it away as well. When she pushed for a third time, blood was all that came out. All four scratches felt much better.

She got some Rawleigh's salve down from her mother's cabinet. The stuff was originally designed for cow udders and was basically liquefied phenol. Her mother used it for all cuts, abrasions, and blisters. She stopped short of using it for fevers and vomiting, but Amelie wasn't sure that she hadn't tried that when they had been smaller.

"If anything can kill alien-world bacteria, it's Rawleigh's salve," she giggled to herself.

She applied the salve to her arm and then covered it with cotton gauze and some medical tape. As her mother worked for a doctor, she brought this sort of thing home on a regular basis. Their apartment was better stocked with medical supplies than some doctors' offices.

Just then the phone rang.

"Hello?"

"Amelie?" a male voice asked. It wasn't Gary.

"Yes?"

"Hi, it's Jack."

Shit! Shit! Shit! Shit!

"Oh, hi Jack," she said in as bland a tone as she could manage.

"I didn't see you at school today, and Elodie said she thought you were sick. I hope it didn't have anything to do with what happened yesterday." He said this in a rush, as if he were nervous.

Nervousness was a bad sign.

"No. It's stupid but when I was leaving yesterday, this big friendly dog jumped up on me as I was getting into my car. It scratched my arm and now it seems to be infected. So Mom wanted me to go to the doctor."

"Do you need me to come give you a ride?" he asked quickly.

Damn, she should have seen that coming. She was getting careless.

"No, you're at school. You would get in trouble if you left."

Even worse, she knew that was a mistake just as it came out of her mouth. What followed was predictable.

"Oh, I don't mind getting in a little trouble for you," Jack replied softly.

Gross. The impact of yesterday was still firmly in place.

"Thanks Jack. But I don't even know where I'm going yet, or when. I'm waiting for a call back from the doctor. So I really should get off the phone."

"Oh right," he said. "Well, just let me know if you need something later. Your homework, or a ride, or anything really."

"Thanks, Jack."

Thank the merciful stars, the call-waiting beeped.

"Hey, I have to go, it's the doctor's office."

"Sure," he said. Amelie hung up before he had the chance to say anything else.

"Amelie?" It was Gary this time.

"I found a doctor for you to see. He works at one of the Urgent Care clinics near your apartment, the one just at the corner of Balsam and Kenwick. Do you know where that is?"

"Yes," Amelie said. It was less than five minutes' drive.

"The doctor's name is Dr. Diasil. I have already called and alerted him to your condition. Are you okay to drive? What is your temperature? I should have asked you that before."

"It was 101.5 this morning when I woke up, but it feels like it has gone down. I should be fine to drive," she said.

41

"Well, don't if you have any hesitation. I can always call one of your parents to come home and drive you."

"No, no. That's not necessary," Amelie said quickly. Her father was unreachable at his construction site and the last thing she wanted was having to sit with a pissed-off Opal in a doctor's waiting room for two hours. This might create a situation where she actually had to have a conversation with her mother, something she religiously avoided.

"Well, I'll tell him that you're on your way," Gary said, back to his bright self.

Amelie didn't want to go, but given not only the temperature but the pus, she thought it was better to be safe than sorry. She got dressed quickly, grabbed a cereal bar and a soda, and headed out to her car. It was around 12:30. She hoped that things might have slowed down a bit at the clinic now that the morning rush was over.

#

When she got to the Urgent Care clinic and assessed the waiting room, she decided that she had only been partially right. There weren't that many people in the waiting room but the ones who were there looked ensconced. There was a little boy playing video games on his mom's phone, while his mother was across the room having a heated conversation with the receptionist. A young man in an old, brown leather jacket, and with a fedora over his face, appeared to be sleeping in the corner. There was an older-looking redneck woman who was about seventy pounds too heavy and twenty years too old for the frayed, pink cut-off top that she was wearing, not to mention the tight jeans that left nothing to the imagination. In the far corner of the room there was a college-age couple huddled close together. They both had the look of guilt/panic that comes with waiting for results about pregnancy, a sexually transmitted disease, or both.

In other words, this was a typical Urgent Care day. Amelie walked to the receptionist window.

"We. Have. Been. Waiting. Here. For. Two. Hours," the mother was saying. She was punctuating each word in a manner that suggested that she thought the sixty-something-year-old receptionist didn't speak English.

"Ma'am, this is a walk-in clinic. The doctor will see your son as soon as he can. Now, will you please take a seat until you're called," the receptionist said with a voice of exaggerated patience. She handed Amelie a clipboard without much more than a glance.

Amelie took the clipboard to a seat as far away from the vidiot child as she could. This put her closer to the redneck woman, but still far enough away to avoid conversation. She began filling out the requisite paperwork.

"What happened to your arm there?" the redneck woman asked, pointing to Amelie's bandaged arm.

Oh no, Amelie had misjudged the distance thing.

"Nothing really, it's just a scratch," she said, bending her head down toward the clipboard, as she suddenly developed a keen interest in writing her own name with absolute precision. Unfortunately, the woman took this antisocial action as an invitation to converse, and moved closer.

"You're lucky. I haven't taken a shit in ten days. I'm so swollen I feel like I'm gonna bust," the woman said, in a stage whisper.

Swollen? How can you tell? Amelie thought to herself but chose to just nod and remain quiet. Maybe the woman would go away. She was feeling a bit light-headed again.

"How'dyu get the scratch?" the woman asked.

From a possible werewolf in a dream I had the other night, but I brought it back with me. Oh, and the werewolf was super hot, she thought, and was immediately shocked at herself. She looked up. The woman was clearly waiting for a reply.

"I just got scratched by a dog," she said curtly.

"Oh, they gonna want to give you rabies shots then, ain't they?" the woman said, and moved back a seat, like Amelie was contagious.

"It's not a bite, just a scratch," she said.

"Still could have rabies," the woman said knowingly.

"I don't have rabies," Amelie said firmly, hoping that would shut down the conversation.

"How'dju know?" the woman asked. Amelie said nothing. The woman then stood up.

"I'm gonna get me a glass of water, you want some?" she asked, walking to the water cooler.

"No thank you."

"You know, gettin' scared of water is one of the first signs of rabies. You should have them check you for that," she called across the room.

"I don't have rabies!" Amelie said, louder than she intended. The remainder of the people in the waiting room turned to stare at her. Even the guy in the leather jacket and hat stirred. The receptionist stood up quickly.

"Are you Amelie McCormick?" she asked.

"Yes."

"You should have told me the moment you came in. The doctor is waiting for you. Come this way please," she indicated to a swing door to her left. As Amelie walked through, she heard pink-shirt woman say, "I bet she got rabies."

A nurse showed Amelie to an examining room. No one took her temperature, her weight or her height. She was not asked to change into any sort of embarrassing backless dressing gown. Rather than waiting twenty-five minutes alone in a cold examining room, a nurse immediately came in with a syringe for blood samples. To Amelie's surprise, they took out eight vials of blood. She didn't recall ever having a blood sample taken at an Urgent Care before.

The nurse was curt and businesslike. After taking the samples she left briskly, saying, "The doctor will be right with you."

The doctor was with her in *less* than five minutes, which had to be some sort of world record for a Doc in a Box. The nurse came in with him, wheeling a tray with some syringes, a couple of vials, scissors, gauze and tape. She then promptly left the room, leaving Amelie alone in the room with the male doctor, which was unheard of, and probably prohibited by the AMA.

"Hi Amelie," he said, as he sat down on a rolling stool.

The doctor wore a badge that said Dr. Diasil. He was tall and thin, with dark, graying hair and an accent that indicated Hispanic ancestry. He sat just looking at her for a minute, silently. It was a bit unnerving.

"How did you say you got those scratches?" he finally asked.

Amelie repeated her whole friendly dog story.

"What kind of dog was it?" he asked.

"It just looked like a big mutt to me," she lied.

"Can you give me an exact description of it?" he said. Luckily Amelie had over-prepared on this point. She rattled off color, potential breed mix, and size. She also made sure she used the word "friendly" at least three times.

"Was there anything at all strange in the behavior of the dog?"

It started out as a gorgeous boy …

What was her brain thinking?!

"No."

"No increased spittle, or foam in its mouth?"

"No. Is there a problem? Should I be worried about something?" she asked, a bit more bluntly than she intended. The doctor's eyes widened, and he pushed his stool back a bit.

"I looked at your blood and you seem to have an infection. But it's an interesting one. I worked at the CDC for quite a few years before moving here."

He sighed ever so slightly before continuing.

"My specialty was infectious diseases. However, I can't identify the bacteria that I see in your blood. That has never happened to me before. I don't mean to scare you, of course. It may just be some mutation I'm not familiar with, but I think we should treat this aggressively."

"What does 'aggressively' mean?"

"Well, first I'm going to vaccinate you against rabies, just in case."

Oh my god, the redneck woman was right!

"Don't worry, this isn't the horrible shot in the stomach that they used to do."

He took a syringe off the tray. He swabbed down her upper arm with alcohol and then, with no foreplay at all, jabbed the needle into her deltoid. He then pulled out a vial of liquid and began swabbing down her scratches.

"Did these have pus in them?" he asked.

"Yes, but I cleaned it out. I thought that is what I should do."

"That's fine," he said, but his eyes flashed with a weird hostility. After finishing, Dr. Diasil re-wrapped her wound and disposed of gloves, pads, shot, and gauze in the biohazard bin.

"The shot I just gave you should be given again on days three, seven and fourteen. You will need to make appointments to come back here on those days. I will make sure that I'm here to check you myself. I'm also going to send samples of your blood to some friends at the CDC, just to make sure it's nothing we should be concerned about."

He smiled at her, but only with his mouth. Behind him, on a poster, the word *avoid* began glowing.

"Okay," she said politely. "Is there anything else I should do? Do I need to miss school?"

"No, no," he said briskly, writing in his paper. "You just need to sign a consent form for us to send your blood to Atlanta and you need to schedule your appointments. Of course, if there is any change in your condition whatsoever, you should contact me immediately. Do not wait, no matter if it is day or night."

He leaned forward and handed her a business card; it had his office and home number on it.

"Okay," she said.

"I'm also prescribing you two different antibiotics. One is Flagyl and another is Fosfomycin. Between the two of these, it should kick out anything you might have contracted. Take them exactly as prescribed," he said.

To her surprise, Amelie found that the receptionist not only had the bill for her but also both her prescription drugs. Once again, this was a first for an Urgent Care center.

Amelie drove home slowly. Her arm was much less painful now, and she guessed she had no fever, but she would take the medicine anyway. The doctor's words made her nervous. She couldn't tell him what had really happened.

Hell, she didn't know what had really happened.

Chapter Seven

Mr. Roberts

Amelie spent a full month after her Urgent Care appointment being poked and prodded by Dr. Diasil on a weekly basis, and keeping her head down at school. The first of these things was infinitely easier to deal with than the second.

The wound on her arm had healed very quickly. In fact, by the end of the first day of antibiotics she had felt fine. Still, she kept her appointments as she suspected she might get some sort of call from state health services if she didn't. Heaven forbid anyone with any authority contact the McCormick household about Amelie. That would trigger too many memories for everyone involved. At her last appointment, Diasil told her that there was nothing to worry about and that she didn't need to come in again. She was very relieved to hear this, because something about the microscopic way he looked at her made her extremely uncomfortable.

However, that discomfort was nothing compared to the levels of discomfort at school. For the first few days after her return, people whispered and stared as she walked by. There were palpable levels of detestation from the girls who had been in Ms. Pryll's class during the Hudson incident. Even now, many of the boys who had been present now seemed to go out of their way to say hello to her, or to stand near her in group gatherings. Among her circle of friends, the effects were much shorter lived. Elodie avoided her for a few days. Sophie made nasty and not-so-subtle remarks about her basic "plainness", but this only started after she had noticed how Jack was treating Amelie.

Jack was the biggest problem. That issue did not seem to be going away as quickly as she might have hoped. While he didn't call the house anymore, he made a point of hanging out with all of them on the landing before school started. This meant that Amelie had to time her arrival to give her friends enough time to copy her homework, but to minimize the time she spent with

Jack. The scheduling alone was hard enough but with Jack constantly trying to stand next to her and brush up against her, it was downright exhausting keeping her shields thick enough to avoid sending him any energy at all. On top of all of this, Mr. Sawyer seemed to be everywhere she turned these days. And any interaction with him, however brief, always made her feel like she was covered in slime, or worse.

Despite all of this, Amelie had almost enjoyed the last few weeks. The reason for it was absurd. It was the boy who had scratched her. She found herself thinking of him often. He had been the strangest creature. Of course, he was a figment of her imagination, and she was now pretty sure that the whole scratch incident some sort of bizarre stigmata-type thing, but still, he had felt so real to her. Even now she could remember the low tone of his voice and his occasional odd choice of words. Or the way he was shockingly feral one minute, and completely cultured the next. She had found herself wanting to look for him again, but she had been unable to focus her mind enough to fly in the past few weeks.

One morning, a couple of weeks into the month of December, she woke to the typical grinding of the coffee maker but with a slightly different headache than usual. This one was placed in the center of her head. On her way out the door that morning her brother blocked her path.

"What's up with you and Jack?" he said.

"Nothing," she said, trying to sidestep him.

"Then why have three people already asked me if you're dating? Three people at the university," Will said, with a smile that bordered on a leer.

"Don't know. But I'm hardly his type," Amelie said, ducking past him and out the door.

"Give yourself some credit," he called after her, making her shudder. She pushed that out of her mind as she got in her car and started it up.

#

When she got to school, she got out of her car and walked as quickly as possible into the building. She was very early, which was an excuse to go straight to class, as no one was on the landing yet. However, just to prevent a potential scene, she sent text messages to her friends telling them she would be in English Lit if they were looking for her. She had occasionally missed English Lit in the previous weeks, because it tended to conflict with her doctor's appointments. After Pryll's departure, there had been a series of different substitutes who were mainly babysitters, but the new permanent replacement for Ms. Pryll showed up for the last class. Amelie had missed it due to her last doctor's appointment, but Jack had texted her saying that the guy was weird and messing things up.

Amelie took this as a good sign.

When she walked into the English Lit class, she understood Jack's statement about the teacher messing things up. The nice neat rows of desks had been rearranged to something resembling a messy, overcrowded circle, a bit like theater in the round. She had no idea where her seat was.

"Ah, so this is Lady McCormick?" a bright voice said.

She jumped. She had thought she was alone. A man stepped out from behind the open door of a steel cabinet. He was probably in his forties, with olive skin and full, dark hair, graying at the temples. But what struck her was his eyes—they were almost golden and skipped across her face and body with a speed that was unsettling. He moved toward her and stuck out his hand for her to shake. She rearranged her books in her arms so that she could comply.

"Colin Roberts," he said. His hands were cool and dry to the touch. He had what might have been the faint trace of an Irish accent and he smelled like aftershave. "As you weren't here last class, I didn't have the pleasure of your acquaintance."

"Nice to meet you." She felt the ridiculous urge to curtsy.

"So I'll be your permanent substitute teacher for the rest of the year. I hear I have you to thank for my new position," he said with a half-smile. She barely had time to be startled by that statement before he changed gears.

"Jack, I told you last class, just take any seat," he called, without even looking around. Jack jumped and whirled.

"There are no assigned seats in my class. In fact, I order you to take a different seat every day."

Jack glowered at him before noticing Amelie in front of him. At the sight of her, he lit up like a sun and did a little wave.

Great. Just great.

Mr. Roberts turned back to Amelie.

"You missed my first day, so you didn't get the five class rules. No assigned seats. No food in the class. No toilet breaks. I believe you should learn bladder control. It might help you more than anything else you learn in high school. No excuses for missed assignments. If you didn't do it, you didn't do it. I don't want to deal with listening to pained excuses."

He stopped and counted on his fingers. "One two three four—oh yes. No overly short skirts or low-cut blouses for the girls. It's difficult enough trying to teach teenage boys without having to compete with pubescent lust."

Amelie's mouth dropped open ever so slightly, but she caught herself and shut it immediately.

"To be honest, it's a bit distracting for the teacher as well, but I didn't say that out loud. You can take a seat now," he said this last bit quickly and blandly, making her wonder if she had heard the first part right.

The class was filing in. Rather than the usual dull, flat expressions, they all looked expectant, almost excited. Well, the girls did. The boys in the class looked sullen. It was likely due to the fact that Mr. Roberts was attractive, intelligent, and in possession of a scalpel-sharp tongue.

"Good morning class," Mr. Roberts said. "As I have a few administrative details to finish up regarding your upcoming assignments, I would appreciate it greatly if you work independently, or at least quietly, for the next thirty or so minutes. Work on homework, read a book or stare into space and think about whatever it is that teens think about in those moments ... just don't let that go too far."

Did he mean what she thought he meant by that?

Sophie caught her eye and suggestively bit her lip. Seems Amelie wasn't the only one who took it that way.

Mr. Roberts sat down at his desk and began furiously scribbling on Post-it notes. Amelie pulled out her Latin homework for review but found it hard to concentrate. She could feel Jack's eyes on her, and this was confirmed the few times she quickly glanced his way. Eventually she gave up and pulled out the novel she always carried in her purse, for just such uncomfortable moments. After what felt like an eternity in the spotlight, Mr. Roberts finally stood up.

"Right, then," he said, striding into the center of the room like an actor stepping onto a stage. "Okay. Now, what were we talking about at the end of the last class?"

"The fact that Ms. Pryll will not be back for the rest of the semester," offered Heidi Stack, resident class gunner.

"Hmmmm, yes. And that would be because ..." he held his palms open waiting for answers.

"She was a crap teacher."

"She's incompetent."

"She has a medical problem."

"She had sex with one of the students?" came a flat voice from the back. Amelie just about choked when she saw that this statement had come from none other than Hudson. He gave her the strangest look, then dropped his eyes. Amelie expected the teacher to freak ... but no.

"All interesting answers," he replied, "but none of them are correct as far as I know. The truth is that she will be gone for the rest of the semester because it was decided by *the powers that be*."

He stressed those last four words.

"This is another important life lesson, kids. In any situation you always need to know exactly who has the power. If you don't, you won't know whose face to slap and whose ass to kiss."

"He just said ass," Heidi whispered to Charlotte Ives, her best friend. Mr. Roberts whirled on her.

"Ms. Stack, no swearing in my class please," Mr. Roberts snapped.

Sophie caught Amelie's eye, pointed at the teacher, and made a fist by her cheek while pushing her tongue in the other direction.

"And I assure you that there will be no engaging in any activity in my class that could have legal ramifications for me. So Ms. Chappell can drop her hand now."

Sophie dropped her jaw instead.

"So back to the idea of the powers that be. Those dictate that I teach you certain subjects this year. You must have some Shakespeare, as well as a nineteenth- or early twentieth-century English writer, poet or playwright. You must read a modern dramatist. And you must read a whole collection of dismal self-absorbed poets. What was Ms. Pryll's itinerary in regard to that glorious agenda?"

"We were supposed to keep journals," Jack offered.

"You can take those home. It's not required, and I have no desire to read any of your personal thoughts," Mr. Roberts said.

This statement was met with cheers, clapping, and an occasional "yesssss".

"What about your reading requirements?" he asked.

"We were going to read *Death of a Salesman*," Heidi responded, probably trying to redeem herself in the eyes of the teacher.

"Death of consciousness," muttered Mr. Roberts. "What else?"

"*Wuthering Heights*." This was Sophie, who normally considered herself above class participation.

"Teenage girl histrionics. Next."

"*Hamlet*," Norman Iggleston said. Norman was an African American boy with a slight lisp who, as far as the class was aware, had never spoken outside of saying the word "here".

"Gee, how unexpected," Mr. Roberts said dryly. "Well, that all sounds terribly boring. So I'm going to try to shake it up just a bit, within the confines of the rules."

He walked to his desk and came back with a stack of papers that he began to hand out.

51

"This is part one of your first assignment. On each of these papers there is the name of a nineteenth- or twentieth-century English writer. You are to read what is written on the paper and prepare a written report and presentation by next week."

The class groaned.

"Make the presentation less than five minutes. I want to get through all of you in two days and I doubt you will have more than five minutes' worth of interesting insights anyway. Also, let it be known that I won't be pleased if you show up with a forty-page PowerPoint deck," he said, making direct eye contact with Heidi, who developed a sudden interest in the grain patterns on her desktop.

He came to Amelie's desk and handed her a sheet of paper. On it was written *Amelie—Saki* and that was all. She had never heard of a writer called Saki, and it sounded Japanese, not English.

After handing out all the slips of paper, Mr. Roberts returned to the center of the circle.

"For your second assignment, if we must read Arthur Miller, then we will read *The Crucible*. I think its message is more pertinent to the teenage experience."

"Yeah, right," Ryan muttered.

"Excellent. Mr. Spoon has honored us with an opinion. And why, precisely, do you take issue with *The Crucible*?"

"I don't see how it has anything to do with our world. Why do I care about a story about a bunch of witches who were burned?" Ryan said, looking quite proud of himself. Amelie guessed this was for knowing what *The Crucible* was about.

"From your comment, and attitude, I will assume that you have never actually read it before, or listened when it has come up in history classes," replied Mr. Roberts.

Ryan's face grew cloudy and he began to glare at his desk.

"I see Mr. Spoon is checking out," said Mr. Roberts, "but for the rest of you, as it was brought up, let's think this through. *The Crucible* is based, roughly, on the Salem witch trials. In Salem, a bunch of little girls turned a town upside down with accusation based on little to nothing, insinuation, fear, and by creating a momentum toward insanity."

Heidi raised her hand.

"We studied the witch trials in American History. I just don't understand how adults could be convinced to burn innocent people because some little girls called them witches. Wouldn't that have been murder and been illegal?"

52

She looked smug. Amelie focused on keeping a placid facial expression, resisting the overwhelming desire to roll her eyes.

"Would it?" Mr. Roberts asked.

He walked to the whiteboard and drew a bell curve on it, with a line down the middle and the standard deviations for sixty-eight percent, ninety-five percent, and ninety-nine percent. He pointed to the middle section of the curve and circled it.

"This group, the ninety-five percent, dictates the rules of society. If ninety-five percent of people think it's okay to sleep with your sibling, as they did in Egypt, then it will be considered okay. Laws will be written in keeping with these beliefs. Remember, beliefs come first. Laws are only statements of societal beliefs. So, if ninety-five percent of people believe that witches exist and that witches are evil, then the behaviors and laws will follow suit. At that time, it wasn't illegal to kill a witch. It was lauded."

He paced in the center of the circle.

"The saddest part of this is that the greatest minds and the most extraordinary people on our planet are those at the tail ends of this bell curve. Therefore, they will always be at risk for being persecuted. I, personally, think our society is actually becoming narrower and less open to people that are truly unique."

"How about gays?" Jack ventured. "They used to really, I don't know, like give gay people a really hard time and now …"

"And now they don't? Really? Has that been your experience?" Mr. Roberts asked. Jack looked panicked for a moment.

"I'm not gay, so I wouldn't know, but I'm okay with people being gay. I mean, whatever anyone wants to be," he finished uncomfortably.

"Yes. That's the current attitude, but once again, it's limited. Gay is okay now, but only in certain places and with certain people. It's not universally accepted yet. But there are other quite amazing people, with extraordinary gifts, that I have no doubt you would consider crazy."

"Like X-men?" Hudson asked softly.

"Maybe something like that, but most likely much subtler," Mr. Roberts said, sitting down cross-legged on top of an empty desk.

"Let me tell you a story. When I was younger, I did a fair bit of traveling. One of the things that started to fascinate me on my travels was comparative religion. How there were certain common themes, ideas, images that appear over and over again in a variety of religions. Of course, there are the obvious ones, like the great flood, which is present in many religions. But there are also more obtuse ones. For example, I saw two different 'seers' during my travels. One was in the Xinjiang province of China. The other was in Peru. Neither of these men had ever traveled outside of their own villages, yet, while in a trance, both described exactly the same image to me."

"I bet lots of people think of the same thing," Ryan muttered.

"What did they describe?" Amelie asked. She couldn't help herself. He was sucking her in along with everyone else. Mr. Roberts smiled at her.

"While in a trance, both described flying over the world as they knew it before being led to a long hallway filled with doors. When I asked them what was behind the doors, they both said, 'stories from the library'. Well, they said something like this, but I had to translate from the language and regional dialect."

For a moment, Amelie stopped breathing.

Just at that moment the bell rang. The class sat in stasis for a moment. Then they began to file out quietly, without the usual teen banter. Even Sophie left on her own, thoughtful. As Amelie was collecting her books, Mr. Roberts came over to her with a strange smile. He leaned forward, put his hands on her desktop and looked into her eyes. Suddenly his eyes changed color. They went from gold to jet-black.

"You should read 'Gabriel-Ernest'. I think you'll find that interesting," he said with a little half smile.

Amelie felt herself go numb. She had seen those eyes and that smile before, but not in the real world. Her heart started to hammer in her chest with a mix of shock, fear, and excitement. Just then Mr. Robert's eyes changed back to their normal golden color, and he shook his head.

"Yes, that's quite a well-written story," he said, but he looked a bit confused.

"Remember, your report is due Monday," he said as he swiftly collected his papers and headed for the door, leaving Amelie feeling like she had just been sideswiped.

Chapter Eight

Carter's Change of Heart

It took Amelie five minutes to pull herself together well enough to leave the classroom. Her shields had been badly fractured, and she needed a few minutes to re-establish them and collect herself. She pretended to rearrange her books and look for things in her desk, as she reimagined the layers of plastic around her. More time alone would have been better, but she still had Latin class to sit through between now and her 11 a.m. study hall. On top of that, her Latin teacher didn't like her much. She had just finished restoring her shields, and was collecting her books, when a familiar face appeared in the doorway.

"Hey Amelie, you heading to Latin now?" asked Carter Grimes.

"Yes. I was just getting my stuff together," she said, feeling vague irritation, but plastering it over with a docile smile.

Carter was Elodie's on-again, off-again boyfriend. The on/off part was a result of her refusal to have sex with him. Or to be more precise, her refusal to have intercourse with him—they did almost everything else. Amelie couldn't understand what his problem was. As far as she could tell, they had more sex, and more varied sex, than any other couple in the school. This was an attempt on Elodie's part to placate him. It usually worked for a couple of months and then they would break up when he realized that he wasn't going to change her mind about parting with her technical virginity. During the next month or so, Amelie suspected that Carter was reminded that intercourse in and of itself wasn't nearly as interesting as all the other things that he got from Elodie. So he would come back to her and act like it was because he loved her, so he was willing to sacrifice. It all sounded a bit worse than it probably was.

In truth, Carter wasn't as bad as some of the others. He was fairly smart, and he wasn't too vain, probably because he was built like a cross between a teddy bear and a line-backer. He tolerated Elodie's constant attempt to convert him to Christianity with much more grace than Amelie could have mustered. He was also civil with Amelie, although he clearly thought that she was kept around for her homework assistance value. That was actually a relief for her, as once this idea was established it was unlikely to be broken by a slip, like the one the other day.

No, the annoying thing about Carter was that he was horrifically lazy. This meant he was always trying to hit her up for her Latin homework. She didn't mind this if he did it in the morning, but more often than not he did it on their way to Latin class. This meant that they had to run into the locker area next to the class, where he hurriedly copied her paper. About every fourth time, they would make it to class just as the bell rang. This left the door open for the teacher to comment about exactly why they were always coming into class late, together. But, as this was her raison d'être in their group, Amelie complied.

She walked to the door where Carter was waiting.

"Hey, you hear anything more about what happened with Pryll? Is she coming back?" he asked. He always tried to have a short conversation with her before directly asking for her homework. It was a bit like foreplay.

"I don't know," she said. "But everything is fine now. It's no problem."

"I hear the new teacher is weird," he said.

"I think he's good. He's just a bit more eccentric than Pryll. Plus, he has kind of a dramatic style."

"Is he gay?" Carter asked. She knew he meant it innocently, but the implications annoyed her nonetheless.

"I don't think so, and I don't really care," she said, hiding the bite of the words with an overly sweet affectation. Carter didn't notice either way.

"Hey, did you happen to do your Latin homework?" he asked. "I was gonna do it, but you know, I got back together with Elodie last night and we had a lot to talk about."

He winked at her and she inwardly cringed.

"You want to take a look at mine?" she asked with dutiful perkiness, as she started shuffling through her papers to find it.

"Thanks Amelie, you're a lifesaver. Let's just stop here while I look at it," he said, indicating the lockers across from the Latin class. She didn't know why he even bothered to mention that. This was a well-known, well-rehearsed scenario. Still, perhaps on some level, he needed to convince himself that it was a novelty.

She sat on the deep window ledge, shuffling quickly through her papers as he waited. Just at the moment she managed to locate the correct sheet of paper, all of her other books and notebooks slipped from her hands and fell to the floor. She thrust the paper out toward Carter and was leaning to pick up her books, but he didn't take the paper from her. Instead, he bent down to retrieve her books, saying, "No, no. Let me get these for you. After all, it's my fault that you dropped them." He looked up at her. His normally light-brown eyes were now black. Instinctively she backed further up into the deep windowsill.

"Are you okay?" he asked, standing up, still smiling. His eyes were glued to her face.

"Yes, I'm fine," she replied.

I just don't know who I'm talking to, she thought.

"It took me a while to find you. I have to admit I was quite worried about you, after your injury. Of course, you wouldn't bring an injury back, but I was worried anyway. ," he said, cocking his head sideways.

Her heart felt like it was going to burst out of her chest, but she wasn't afraid. Well, not as much as she should have been.

"No, I'm fine, but thank you for asking. You know, Carter, you're quite a bit more attentive than you usually are," she said, with a tiny smile.

"Well, if I haven't been attentive in the past, then I must be blisteringly stupid," he said, as he leaned against the wall, still holding her books and papers.

"Do you want this?" she asked a bit shakily, holding the paper out to him.

"No, today I'm contemplating accepting the responsibility for not doing my homework. I think I would rather spend a few minutes just talking to you, rather than rushing to copy someone else's work in a frenzy."

"Is there anything in particular that you would like to talk about?" Amelie asked. She was breathless. This was not the normal Carter Grimes. Nor was it Carter Grimes being affected by what happened the other day. He hadn't even been in that class. And anyway, it wouldn't have changed his speech pattern, eye color, and body stance. To top it all off, he wouldn't have known the real circumstances of her arm injury.

"I'm happy to talk about whatever you want," he said, smiling. "Or you can just tell me more about yourself. Your favorite books, movies, colors, flowers …"

He moved closer to her. Suddenly around them there was the smell of grass, water and trees. The smells of that other world. She started to feel a bit dizzy.

"Oh, I don't like flowers. I'm allergic to most of them," she blurted, pushing her hair behind her ear and looking at his chest, arms, anything but his face. She pushed herself up on the ledge in the windowsill just to have something to do with her hands. "But, you know, only cut ones put in vases. I like wildflowers. Even if I wasn't allergic, I wouldn't like the idea of something dying so that I can put it in a vase. I'd rather just see it in nature."

She was babbling and she couldn't make herself stop. "And you?"

He looked surprised.

"Do I have a favorite flower? No, not really. Wait, girls don't give boys flowers here now, do they?" he asked. She looked back at his face, and he had a look of genuine shock.

"They can," Amelie replied. "But I thought this was just a question about what we liked—just a theoretical conversation."

She was really babbling now. She needed to pull herself together.

A couple of people walked by and gave them an odd look. It must have looked like she was flirting with Carter. A moment later, Mr. Sawyer walked by and actually stopped for a moment and gawked. But for the moment she couldn't bring herself to care. She felt fluttery and she was breathing fast, but she felt good. Really good. Maybe this was what happiness felt like.

"What's theoretical anyway?" he shrugged slightly.

"Theoretical means—" she began, but he stopped her by rolling his eyes.

"I know what it means. What I was suggesting is that I'm not sure that people ever really operate in the realm of theory. Everything said, everything done, from words to deeds, are all done for a reason. Why would I want to know your favorite flower if I hadn't at least considered the prospect of getting them for you?" he said, raising one eyebrow just a tiny bit.

Nope, not Carter, definitely not Carter. She wasn't quite sure why, but clearly he was flirting with her. He reached out slowly and took the paper that she had in her hand. He looked at it for a second and smiled.

"I guess Carter won't have his homework today then," she said softly.

"Then that's Carter's problem for not getting his work done last night. Isn't that why they call it homework? You do it at home," he said, looking back down at the paper. "Besides, this doesn't look very hard."

"No?" she asked. "You must be good at Latin then. This is fourth year Latin, so it's not beginner stuff."

Clovis smiled at her from Carter's body. He stepped a bit closer still. She was sitting in the windowsill, and he was way too close to being positioned right against her legs. If he got much closer, it would be kissing distance. She wondered what he would look like if he were really here. If he would look the same as she saw him in that other place. He was silent in front of her, his black eyes studying her face intently.

Suddenly a couple of people rushed by them, opening lockers, grabbing books last minute and slamming doors. The noise was jarring, and it brought her back to her world for a second.

"Class is going to start in a minute," she whispered. Funny, she could hear the disappointment in her own voice.

58

"Let me walk you to the door then," he said, stepping back for her to climb down from the window. He still had her books and papers in his arms. As they walked slowly to the door of her Latin class, people were openly staring. He stopped just at the threshold and handed her the books. "Enjoy your class and remember—"

He then said something quickly, but with such a strong Italian accent that it took her a minute to recognize the Latin, then she laughed.

"This too shall pass," she laughed. He smiled and closed his eyes.

And suddenly Carter was back. He looked at Amelie in a puzzled way.

"Did I get your homework?" he asked as they entered the classroom.

"You said there wasn't enough time to write it down, but you did look at it," she lied. "Did you get amnesia in the past five minutes or something?" she added, because if it had happened like that, she would be shocked.

"Oh yeah, no I remember," he said, as he walked to his seat in a daze, but just as the bell rang he turned and looked back at her with a confused expression.

"Okay. Mr. Grimes and Ms. McCormick, do try to get out of your lovesick bubble and sit down," the Latin teacher snapped. "Now, everyone get out your homework for translation."

Amelie shoved her books into her desk and put her Latin book and translation on the desktop. She knew that the teacher would call on her today. When he started out by making fun of her, it usually meant that she was in line for some type of humiliation. But she just couldn't make herself care.

Nor could she keep the smile off her face.

Chapter Nine

Revisiting the Wild

"I heard that you and Carter were talking near the lockers today," Elodie whispered as she came and sat next to Amelie at the library.

Uh-oh.

Elodie was incredibly jealous and possessive. Amelie had headed to the library immediately after her Latin class ended, so it had been just over sixty minutes since she had been seen with Carter. It was amazing how quickly news traveled in high school circles.

Elodie was looking at her with fierce doe eyes, if there was such a thing. Amelie smiled and leaned in conspiratorially.

"Yeah, I don't think he wanted everyone to hear it," she whispered. "He told me that you guys had gotten back together and had a really long talk last night."

"Really? He said that? He didn't ask for your homework?" Elodie whispered back.

"Well, he did at first. But it was like when he thought of you, he felt guilty about doing it," Amelie lied. "All he wanted to talk about was you."

Elodie positively beamed.

"People were saying that you guys were flirting, but I knew that couldn't be true. You're not his type," she said.

It took about five seconds longer than it should have for her to realize that this could sound like an insult.

"I don't mean anything bad. He's just not into girls who are ... well ..."

"Bookish?" Amelie suggested innocently.

"Yes, bookish," Elodie smiled. "Of course, you're okay—pretty and all, but you spend so much time reading and doing homework that you always look tired."

Elodie should have left it at "bookish", but she didn't. Amelie didn't care. Elodie alone was harmless. She wasn't the sharpest tool in the shed, so she lacked the purposeful maliciousness of Sophie or Judith. Amelie interrupted Elodie's stream-of-consciousness rambling.

"Hey, speaking of bookish, I need to look up my assignment for English Lit," she said, getting up.

"Oh, the weird new guy. Sophie says he's really cute," Elodie sniffed disdainfully.

"Sophie thinks any male with working anatomy is cute," Amelie whispered back. Elodie giggled.

Amelie picked up her books and went to a reference computer. A quick search revealed that "Saki" was the pen name of an English author named H. H. Munroe. She wrote down the library reference number and turned, only to find Hudson standing behind her.

"Hi," he said shyly.

"Hi," she replied with a smile. Hudson had the look of a dog that expects to be beaten. "I'm looking up my English Lit piece."

"Me too," he said. "I got 'The Cantos' by Ezra Pound. I know the poet, he was an expat. He seems to be up to something with these assignments, but I have no idea what."

"I thought so too." She didn't want to have a long conversation with Hudson at the moment, but he was still standing there, looking embarrassed but determined.

"Listen, Amelie," he said. "I wanted to thank you for helping me a while back, you know, with the insulin problem. I heard that you might have gotten into trouble because of that, so I just wanted you to know that, you know, if the school ever gives you any trouble—well, my dad is a lawyer ..."

"Thanks Hudson, but I'm fine. It all blew over in less than a day, for me anyway," she said, starting to move away.

"I also wanted to warn you," he said.

"Warn me? About what?"

"About Jack."

Oh no.

"What about Jack?"

"So, you know most of the guys don't notice if I'm around, so I hear what they say. When they talk about girls,"—he was blushing bright pink—"well, normally they're crass."

"Who's 'they'?" Amelie asked.

"Jack, Carter, Hugh, Kevin, Ryan, Aidan ... you know the crowd."

61

Amelie nodded.

"Well, Ryan said something gross about you. He didn't mean anything, but Jack got super pissed off. He grabbed Ryan, threw him against a wall and said he should never say anything like that about you again. Then he said he was going to ask you out."

Amelie felt her stomach drop.

"I know you don't like him, so you should stay out of his way," Hudson continued quickly.

Okay, she knew it was bad, but this was worse. Hudson was right though, it was best to stay out of Jack's way. Maybe she would need to rethink her appearances on the landing.

"Thanks Hudson," she smiled and touched his arm. "I'll keep my eye on him."

Suddenly, Hudson assumed a very uncharacteristic pose. He leaned against a bookshelf, crossed his arms and crossed one foot over the other. He looked more like a bad boy hanging out by a pool hall than a nerdy school underling.

"The question is, who's going to keep an eye on you?" he said. For a flash, Hudson was not there. Standing in his place was Clovis, with his messy dark hair and knowing smile. And then, with the blink of her eye, he was gone.

Hudson didn't even seem to notice. He just stood up straighter and shook his head.

"Just don't be alone with him," he said.

"Uh-huh. Thanks Hudson," Amelie said, turning away quickly.

Her heart was beating fast again. She was beginning to suspect that she was having a breakdown. As much as she might like to pretend that Clovis was a real person, she knew he was in her head. Maybe, somehow, she made Carter act like him, which was bad enough. But now she was seeing things. This did not bode well for her mental health.

She needed to stop thinking about this. She could think about it later. At school she needed to stay calm and focused. She couldn't afford another slip up. She looked at the slip of paper in her hand. She would read. That would take her mind off things.

She found the Saki book easily enough. The library was empty except for those who had study hall, which meant the big fluffy chairs in the back corner of the library were available. Amelie snagged one, dropped her books, kicked off her shoes and curled up in the chair. She closed her eyes for a minute.

Her heart was slowing down. In her mind's eye, she could see the boy. He had said his name was Clovis, which was such an unusual name.

She opened the book and began flipping through its pages. Mr. Roberts had suggested she read "Gabriel-Ernest" ... or someone looking like him had suggested it.

As she was flipping through, her eyes scanned past a word and her heart began racing again. It took her brain a fraction of a second to understand why. She flipped back until she found the page. In the middle of the page, a sentence read:

"Do you mean that it's dead, or stampeded, or that you staked it at cards and lost it that way?" asked Clovis lazily.

Clovis. There was a character named Clovis in this. She looked up and when she did, her inner eye opened wide. The whole room went psychedelic. Colors and words were flashing everywhere. There was no way for her to even begin to translate this, there was just too much to take in. There was so much energy in her head that she felt like the top would blow off. She closed her eyes tight and took deep breaths.

It's a name. A coincidence, sure, but still just a name. Amelie started running multiplication and division tables in her head. She tried to remember the names of all of Shakespeare's plays. While doing this, she imagined the plastic dripping down around her. Finally, she could feel her energy subsiding.

She tentatively opened her eyes and opened the book. This time she flipped directly to the page with the title "Gabriel-Ernest". She had no idea what to expect, but she steeled herself. There could be no more outbursts.

For the next ten minutes, her resolve was severely tested. The story was short but by the time she finished it, she was perspiring and shaking.

"I'm having a nervous breakdown," she thought. "Well, at least my family can sue the school system or something."

The boy in the story was Clovis. In the story, his name was Gabriel-Ernest, and he was a werewolf. The story itself was similar to what she had experienced—but not exactly. The time frame was right. The character was close. Some of the plot was the same, but most was not. It was as if Clovis had been an actor playing the character of Gabriel-Ernest. But the similarities were occasionally heart-stopping.

On a shelf of smooth stone overhanging a deep pool in the hollow of an oak coppice a boy of about sixteen lay asprawl, drying his wet limbs luxuriously in the sun.

Or,

The boy turned like a flash, plunged into the pool, and in a moment had flung his wet and glistening body halfway up the bank.

She had experienced this, or lived some alternative version of it. And Clovis had found a way out of that story and into her world to flirt with her.

63

No, that was just too weird. She was going crazy. Amelie was trembling as she sat curled in her chair, but she was also smiling, against her will and better judgment.

Quit it, she told herself. *Get yourself together. You're at school.*

She closed her eyes and named all the popes she could remember. Once she was steady, she stood up. She needed to get off campus.

She shoved the book into her bag, along with all of her other books, then took two or three deep breaths to compose herself. As a precaution, she dropped another of layer of plastic over her.

How many times had she done this today?

Just as she was reaching the door to the library, she ran into Mr. Roberts.

"Ms. McCormick," he said, as he opened the door for her with an exaggerated wave of his arm.

"Thanks!" she said, hurrying past him.

"You okay there?" he called after her. She heard a smile in his voice.

"I'm fine," she called back, doing her perkiest Tinkerbell.

She was just about at the door to the landing, when she felt a hand on her shoulder and froze.

"Amelie, how are you?" asked Jack.

Shit.

"Hi Jack. Fine. Fine," she replied, imagining a steel box around herself, with spikes, and long, jagged shards of glass sticking out of it.

"How is all that?" he asked, as he ran his finger over the marks on her arm.

"Oh, my arm? That's fine now. They treated me with some heavy antibiotics, but I'm done with those now."

"You need a ride? You seem a bit out of breath," he asked, smiling broadly.

Oh no.

She was out of breath, and he had misinterpreted that.

"Thanks," she said. "But I can't leave my car at school. Mom would kill me." Amelie saw Judith coming out of the locker rooms.

"Judith!" she called. Judith looked her way and began walking over. This was a dangerous move, but Judith was the only person around.

Think of something to say ...

"Did you see Elodie today?" Amelie asked. "She and Carter are back together."

"Woohoo," Judith said in a voice dripping with acid. "I guess she is expecting us to be happy about that. Great. That means we get to take more of Elodie's online compatibility tests. Fun. But Jack, what's up with you and Amelie?"

Her words and delivery were classic for her, direct, pointed, and designed to draw blood. This was dangerous territory. Sophie had designs on Jack. Jack was glamoured with Amelie. And Judith liked other people's pain.

"Amelie!" a voice called.

She turned to see Hudson coming toward them. Normally, he would never approach their clique, but now he walked up in a relaxed manner that was completely unlike him. She held her breath for a second, wondering if this was actually Clovis.

"Hey Jack. Hey Judith," Hudson said with a casual wave. "Amelie, I was wondering if you could take a look at this poem for English Lit. The imagery is interesting but I'm not sure I'm getting all of it."

The shy, shrinking boy that had been in her classes for the past couple years was replaced by a boy much taller than she had ever noticed. His demeanor was cool and relaxed. A far cry from the victim stance he had exhibited just fifteen minutes earlier. It was almost as shocking as seeing him morph into Clovis. Everyone stared, jaws unhinged.

"Sure," Amelie said a bit shakily. "I'm heading out for lunch, but you can walk me to my car."

"Thanks," Hudson said. "Bye, guys."

What the hell was going on today?

As they passed over the landing Amelie turned to Hudson, who had a slight smile on his face.

"Are you okay, Hudson?" she said.

"Well, that's kind of an interesting question, isn't it?" he asked.

She looked at him carefully, but his blue eyes were still blue, and his face was his own. "I guess I'm not acting like you expect me too, am I?"

"You aren't acting like the person who has been in my class for the past two years, no," she said cautiously.

"Yeah, I know," he said. "Your car's in the lower parking lot, right?"

"Right."

They walked on in silence for a few moments.

"Did you know I'm an expat kid?" he asked out of the blue.

Amelie shook her head.

"Yeah. My parents have moved us every two years since I was born. I found it easier to change myself with every change of country. I don't know why, but it makes the moves more bearable. So I've been lots of different people in lots of different places. Back there, I became the kid I was in Singapore. We lived there just before we moved here. I was very popular there."

"Really? Do you miss that?" she asked, and then realized how it sounded and winced. She was getting as bad as some of her friends.

"I'm sorry, that was stupid, and not very nice," she said.

"No. It's fine. And no, I don't miss it. I didn't like the me that I was in Singapore. I wasn't always very compassionate, and I was a video game junkie," he said.

His demeanor had lost some of the confident charisma that he had exhibited minutes before, but the shyness had not returned.

"I decided that I wanted to be an observer here. It's less stress and I can conserve energy and actually study. I can focus on subjects that I like and am actually good at, like chemistry. I'd rather do that than waste my energy reacting to other people's perceptions of me," he said, kicking a stone. "I know all this sounds kind of messed up. But I am kind of messed up."

"I don't think it's messed up. I think it's smart and I think you have an impressive skill. You could be an actor," Amelie said. It wasn't a dangerous statement, but it came out before going through a filter. She needed to get control.

"Done that, too," Hudson replied. "But my messed-up life isn't the point. I stuck my nose in because Jack's a problem. He could be a big problem. I couldn't explain it well before because I was being my other self, but there's something psychologically wrong with him. And his reaction to you feels abnormal. Plus, you seemed scared just now. You were, right?"

Amelie nodded.

She was shocked at this Hudson. It was as if he possessed himself with himself. She could see how the person who had just helped her escape Jack would have been very popular. She regarded him out of the corner of her eye as they walked.

"About asking you out. He's gonna be pushy. He's not a guy who is used to hearing 'no' from girls. And then there's Judith—whoa—" he turned to look at Amelie, "you do know that she's a scorpion, right? And you do know she hates you? You don't actually trust her, do you?"

Amelie shook her head.

She had certainly never trusted Judith, but she had never really considered that Judith actively disliked her. She had always thought that she simply dismissed her, like she dismissed everyone else. There was food for thought here, and maybe concern.

"Good. She's the worst of a bad lot. I don't know why you hang with them. You must have your reasons, but they aren't actually your friends. You know that too, right?"

Amelie nodded.

By now they had made it to her car.

"You don't really need to talk about the poem, do you?" she asked.

"Nah. I've read it before. It's always on the reading list for International School kids."

"Okay," she said. She was so overwhelmed right now that she could feel actual cracks in her energy shields.

"Don't worry," Hudson said. "I'll be back to my old self tomorrow. I don't want to freak you out."

Amelie actually laughed out loud. She couldn't help herself.

"You're the least of my reasons for freaking out today," she said, then clamped her hand over her mouth.

Stop talking. Stop talking now.

"Really?" he smiled. "Well then, you have an interesting life. Maybe you and I should be friends."

Her brain told her to pull away, but there was something about this guy. His energy was different. Maybe he was gay. That would explain how he had escaped from her little accident a few weeks ago. He had been at ground zero and yet he had shown no signs of being glamoured. She still had to be careful, had to keep her walls up, but this was very unusual in her experience.

"You don't have to worry about me," he said, as if reading her thoughts. "Just friends, that's all."

"Friends," she said and stuck out her hand to shake his.

As she got in her car and drove away, she realized that she had had more actual human contact today than she had probably had in two years. Anxiety shot through her. She hoped that she wouldn't have to pay too dearly for this

Chapter Ten

Blossoming and Possession

Phil Sawyer moved quickly past Ms. Hartness in the outer office, and into his office. Here he dropped the papers he was carrying onto his file cabinet and sat down behind his desk with a lying smile plastered on his face and fists clenched in his lap, pressing hard against the tightness in his groin. The smile was there because he had had to pass Hartness on his way back to his office. The tightness came from the pictures in his head, the ones that were now swirling out of control.

"Did you find Carter Grimes?" Ms. Hartness chirped at him from the other room.

Oh, he had found him all right. He had been flirting with Amelie McCormick. She had been sitting in one of the windowsills in the locker room in front of the Latin class and everything about the situation had been wrong. Carter was Elodie's boyfriend. He was stupid and lazy. But the way Carter had been standing, and the way Amelie had smiled at him, left no doubt that something was going on. Just at the point that he had felt he would explode, he had seen Jack Turner on the other side of the locker room. The look on Jack's face had been a mirror of Sawyer's own feelings.

"Phil?" Ms. Hartness stuck her head into his office.

"Sorry Dawn, did you say something?"

"I asked if you had spoken with Carter about skipping class last week," she said, sighing in an "oh men" way.

"Oh no. He was just about to go into class, so I'll catch him later. But I did see Jack Turner. Do you know anything about his plans for next year?" he said, proud at how calm his voice sounded.

"No, I haven't heard anything about it. But I'm sure his family will make sure that he gets in to whatever university they want him to attend." Ms. Hartness sniffed.

"Well, that's exactly it, isn't it," he said. "I'm not sure that they may have considered what Jack wants. Can you try to set up some time for me to see him in the next couple of weeks?"

"You're so sweet," she said, beaming at him. "I'll set that up for you as soon as I can."

"Thanks Dawn, can you make sure I don't forget it?" he said, giving her what he thought to be his most charming smile. She smiled back and began patting her hair.

"Of course. Would you like me to get you some lunch? I was going out."

"That would be wonderful, Dawn, thank you," he said.

"What would you like then?" she asked, stepping further into the room. He didn't want to engage with her anymore. Her immovable red hair, pendulous breasts and odor of hairspray mixed with cheap perfume were repellent to him, but she was useful, so he handled her with care.

"Just get me whatever you're getting. You have the best taste in food. But fast is better, I guess. I didn't realize until you mentioned it but I'm much hungrier that I thought. I didn't have breakfast this morning. The wife was out with her friends last night."

Dawn's face grew stormy. She was of the opinion that his wife did not appreciate him enough and she told him this with a thousand little niceties every day.

"You're just too nice, Phil Sawyer," she said, shaking her finger at him. "I'll go right now. You should have told me earlier."

She turned and went to get her coat.

"You're my angel, Dawn," he called after her. It sounded so forced, but she obviously didn't notice as she called back.

"Flirt."

#

Then, mercifully, Dawn was gone. For the moment, he was alone. Soon he would have to go to the bathroom to relieve himself. Ever since he had escorted Amelie to the office after the incident involving Hudson Crowe, he had gotten an erection every time he saw her. In fact, in recent weeks he had gotten one every time he even thought of her. This meant he had been going around with an erection much of the time. It had required a change of his usual undergarment habits. He had assumed that this was just him, but after seeing how Carter

69

Grimes was interacting with Amelie and the jealousy that was apparent in Jack Turner's gaze, he was beginning to rethink this.

Something had definitely happened to Amelie McCormick in the past few weeks. He didn't know what it was, but it was affecting more people than just him. Maybe she was going into heat or something. He had always suspected that the reason that canine term "bitch" had come to be a derogatory term for woman was because women were indeed quite like dogs. They could be loyal but needed a master. They also seemed to have times when they went into sexual frenzy over some fairly uninteresting men. He suspected that this had more to do with some sort of fertility cycle than it had to do with the men in question. Maybe that was what was happening with Amelie. Maybe it was her time, and men were sensing it.

The thought of this both thrilled and horrified him. The thought of her having a sexual awakening was almost impossibly exciting. The thought that it would come at the hands of anyone but him was equally horrifying.

He sat at his desk staring into space, his mind beginning to weave dark fantasies of capture and surrender. From the corner of his eye, he seemed to see a red mist rise from his file cabinet in the corner of the room before taking on a humanoid/canine shape. But in his current state of mind, he barely acknowledged this before dismissing it completely as a trick of light. He didn't notice as it quickly advanced on him, wrapped itself around his body, melted into his skin.

He also didn't notice the beads of sweat that had broken out on his brow or the fact that his nose suddenly began to run.

Chapter Eleven

I Was a Fool

Despite her best efforts, it took another few weeks for Amelie to try another trip to the hallway. From Christmas through New Year's Day, she had been expected to cook, clean, and interact with her extended redneck family, as if her immediate family wasn't enough. Then her first full week back at school in January had been surprisingly difficult. Her mother had been working late every night. Apparently, not one but two different strains of flu were making the rounds at the moment and had already resulted in four deaths in their state. This meant that Opal was overworked, and Amelie was on call for all household duties. When she had added that to her regular homework, serving as emotional counselor for her friends, and the stress of trying to avoid Mr. Sawyer and Jack every day, she had been too exhausted at bedtime to do anything but sleep. She had tried, but the minute she closed her eyes, she drifted off.

It wasn't until the second Saturday of January that she finally got a chance. Her brother had gone out with friends. Her parents had said they were tired and went to bed very early, which was the euphemism for "we are going to have sex". So Amelie was free to go to her room by 8 p.m.

Now, sitting on her bed, she was nervous. What if she was wrong? What if she just made him up that one time and she couldn't do it again?

She lay down on her bed, closed her eyes, and focused on Clovis. On what she could remember of what he looked like, what he smelled like, the way he had looked at her when he was in Carter's body. This time, when her energy focused itself in the center of her forehead, she did not find herself flying. Instead, she found herself immediately standing in the hallway, which extended to infinity in either direction. Right in front of her was an old wooden door with iron symbols arranged like a horseshoe, and the door was glowing. When she

71

put her hand out and touched it, she was pulled toward it, with an accompanying stomach drop.

The first thing she saw was a dirt racetrack. Before she could notice much more, she was struck by the heat. As opposed to the winter environment she had come from in her real world, this place was in the middle of a hot summer. The air was so heavy with moisture that even breathing required more effort. For the moment, she was alone in a place meant for people. Just as this thought entered her head, streaks of light and color appeared around her. At first, they looked like smears of color, then like pointillism paintings of people, and then like ghosts.

Finally, with a crash of sound, everything came into sharp focus, and she was surrounded by people jostling her, yelling and clapping. On the track, horses with riders in carts behind them were thundering down the track toward the finish line. On her right were stands filled with people clapping and yelling. Most of these people were well dressed, and overdressed for the heat. Amelie wondered why some of these women weren't fainting in their long dresses, gloves, and hats.

On the bleachers, about midway up, a boy and girl were seated next to each other. The boy was dressed in a suit, but his clothes didn't sit easily on him. The girl, on the other hand, was completely comfortable in her uncomfortable finery. They weren't looking at each other but Amelie could see the rivers of energy running between them. Something very private going on there. Amelie looked away. In front of her, she saw a covered corridor leading away from the track, so she pushed her way through the crowds and into the shade.

Once out of the sun, Amelie could breathe again. On her left was a crowded area with betting windows. To her right, there was a corridor that led to the horse stables. This path was also covered and shaded but, as there were fewer people, she walked in that direction.

As Amelie walked down the row of stalls, she wondered why she had been drawn here. Maybe it had been silly of her to assume that she could just conjure the Clovis back into this dream, or whatever it was, through sheer force of will.

A glossy brown nose touched her arm and she jumped. The horse nickered and shook its head. Amelie didn't know much about horses, but it seemed friendly enough. She gently stroked him between the eyes.

Most of the people back here were boys mucking out the stables. Clean and dirty straw was flying in the air. Amelie peeked inside each stall she passed. She only took a brief look, and then quickly looked away. She told herself that this was because she didn't want to get hit with dirty straw, but that wasn't really true. The truth was that many of the boys mucking out the stalls had removed their shirts and were glistening with sweat. Amelie felt embarrassed watching them, and she was disgusted with herself for her own embarrassment. She saw boys without shirts at school all the time. She had never been one to care, but there was an energy here. With all the long dresses, gloves, and modesty, this place was buzzing with sexual tension.

To her left, she saw someone overshoot a wheelbarrow parked across the stable door and a pile of straw hit the floor a few feet in front of her.

She then heard a voice mutter, "Shit!"

Her heart began beating erratically when she saw a dark head appear at the stable door. She recognized him immediately. Clovis used his leg to push the wheelbarrow out of his way as he glared at the floor. He was holding a pitchfork and was dressed in overalls with no shirt. His skin was covered in sweat and his hair was a sight. He sighed and put his chin on the handle of the pitchfork.

"Mucking stables not really your thing?" Amelie asked in a voice that quivered just a little bit. His head jerked up and his face lit up like a thousand Julys before he could hide it with a forced cool.

"Oh, no. I'm much too patrician for stable-mucking," he said, and then cringed at himself. "Did I just say 'patrician'? Ugh."

"Why do you have to do it then?" she asked.

"Because of who I am here," he replied with a shrug and a smile. "Not very patrician after all, huh?"

Amelie laughed. Clovis pushed the wheelbarrow further aside. "I was just pissed off because I was almost done. That was literally the last pile of dirty straw. And I had to toss it halfway across the hall. Would you like to come in?" he bowed and ushered her in.

She stepped delicately over the dirty straw in front of her and entered the small stall. She understood why women walked so daintily in all those old movie clips. It was the shoes. They were excruciating.

The stable floor looked spotless, and clean straw was piled up against the stable walls. Several bales of straw were pushed against the far back wall. Another was in the center of the floor, untied and ready to be spread. Clovis motioned for her to sit on one of the bales against the wall. It was a smaller space than she had been expecting and she passed quite close to him. He smelled of sweat and straw—and horse shit, but it didn't bother her. How crazy. She was usually pretty phobic about excrement. She laughed to herself.

"What?" he smiled back at her.

"You smell like shit," she blurted out, then clamped her hand over her mouth.

"Well, that makes sense considering that I have been up to my thighs in it for the past hour," he said in a voice that was hard to read. Then he smiled.

"Should I change clothes?" he asked as he unhooked one of the straps of the overalls. It fell down, revealing the naked skin of his stomach. She quickly looked away.

"No, you can leave your clothes just as they are," she said quickly. He laughed.

"So you finally found me?" he said.

"I don't think I was the first to start looking," she said back.

He smiled broadly at this.

"I have no idea what you're talking about," he said, as he began raking the floor. She had remembered that he was beautiful, but she hadn't remembered he was this beautiful. Or maybe it was impossible to remember this level of beauty because it fries your senses.

Clovis was squatting on the ground arranging straw … and the straps of his overalls had fallen again.

"You know, I think I've figured out that this must be some sort of stigmata thing," she said quickly. He cocked his head at her.

"What are you talking about?" he asked, continuing to spread straw.

"Well, the last time I came back from seeing you, I got this infection. You know, from where you scratched me." Amelie said, as she looked away.

Clovis stood up quickly. She had his full attention now.

"You got an infection?"

"Yeah, it was at the spot where you scratched me. I went to see the doctor, who gave me lots of antibiotics, but it was almost gone by the second day."

Clovis sat down on the bale of straw in the center of the room. His face was noticeably paler, and he was staring at her. His gaze was intense, but unreadable.

"When you woke up, you had an actual wound?" he asked, leaning forward.

"Yeah, and—" she began, but he interrupted.

"And other people could see it—the wound and the infection, I mean?"

"Umm, yeah. I mean the doctor took blood samples and everything. He was afraid I had rabies."

"Rabies, which you get from dogs. He took blood. He found that?" Clovis's black eyes were glued to her face. If she looked at them too long, they seemed to spin. She looked away quickly.

"No, no rabies, but he found something he couldn't identify. I still had to go through the rabies treatments though."

Clovis got up and came to sit next to her on the bale of hay. His overalls had fallen off one shoulder. He still smelled of shit but something else as well, something sweet and salty. The already warm air got warmer with his proximity.

"When you came last time, you said you went into the hallway, right?"

"Yes."

"Was it the first time you had been there?"

"No. I have been a few times before, but I never stopped before. Oh, I touched a kind of creepy door that was so cold that it burned, but that was all."

"Okay. Let me get this straight. You've been in the hallway before but last time was the first time you had gone through a door, and that was where I scratched you? After seeing me, you woke up with actual scratches on your waking body? And you went to a doctor who was able to see bacteria?"

"Yesssss …"

"Okay." Clovis sighed, he put his cheeks on his fists, with eyes closed. When he raised his head and turned to face her, his eyes were burning.

"Two things. First, the hallway can be dangerous. Never, ever get near a door that feels off to you and certainly don't touch it!"

Amelie was surprised by the vehemence in his voice and his intense expression.

"Second. Don't go see that doctor again."

"Why?"

Clovis sighed.

"Let's just say that there are some people who would be *very* interested in everything you just told me. You don't want to be on their radar."

"But it's all in my head, right?"

"Is it? Is that what you think? You think the physical scratches that everyone could see was in your head?" Clovis asked, standing up again and picking up the pitchfork. In sharp strokes he began to push stray bits of hay to the corners of the stall. The sound of the metal hitting the floor made Amelie wince.

"I think it must be like stigmata," she replied, a bit defensively. "You know, where Christians bleed in their hands and feet like Christ on the cross. They believe it so much that they make it happen."

Clovis turned to her and then laughed out loud. The suffocating tension of the past moments broke.

"Are you comparing me to Christ?" he laughed. "Because that *would* be a first."

His laugh turned into a grin. She had to admit, with the grin, the hair and the pitchfork, he really looked a lot more like the other guy. She laughed as well.

"You like being compared to Christ? That's a bit vain of you," she said.

75

"Oh, I don't mind one way or another about Christ. But he hardly had a life that anyone would envy." For one second a darkness settled on his face but then it dissipated.

"However, I do like 'firsts'," he said, then paused. "Why are you so sure that none of this is real?"

"Because I'm in my own head," Amelie responded.

"And why would that make it not real?"

"Well, these visions are like dreams. Sort of. It's something my brain does to entertain itself," she said. The words sounded lame when she heard them aloud.

"What is your definition of 'real' then?" he asked quietly.

"I don't know," she answered. "Something that can be sensed with one of my five senses, I guess."

"Are you sensing this?"

"What do you mean?"

"Well, are you feeling the heat, or smelling the horses or seeing me?"

"Yes, but …"

"But what? You're sensing it."

"Yes, but it's happening in my head, not with my external body."

"But your head is part of your body," Clovis replied.

"Okay, well then what is your definition of real, if you have all the answers?" she asked. She was starting to get a strange, ground-tipping sort of feeling.

"All the answers? I'm afraid not," he said, laughing. "Sadly, I'm not quite that god-like."

As he pushed his hair off his face, the strap of his overalls fell down again, and he didn't bother to pull it back up. He just looked at her like he was waiting for something.

Amelie felt like her head was becoming a balloon. Clovis looked at her quizzically.

"You, okay?" he asked, coming over to sit next to her again.

"Yes, I think I'm just hot," she said.

"Maybe you should take off some clothes," he said, without suggestiveness.

"I don't think they allow that here."

"Oh yeah, you're probably right," he smiled. "Do you want to get out in the breeze?"

She felt that she should probably get some air, but she didn't really want to be around others. She wanted to be with just him.

"In a minute," she said. "Maybe this is all a bit much to take in."

"To talk about reality with a figment of your imagination?" he teased.

"Yeah, maybe," she said, looking down. "Or maybe the fear that the figment of my imagination might be smarter than me."

"Well, what would you need to experience to believe that I'm real?" he asked. His tone was no longer light. It sounded almost pained.

"Is it important to you that I think you're real?" she asked.

He was quiet for a moment. The sounds of the race outside seemed to get louder. The horses must be rounding the final corner. She could feel tiny puffs of air on the few exposed areas of her skin.

"It shouldn't be," he said finally. "But somehow it is important to me." His eyes were on the floor and for a second, he looked completely lost.

They were both quiet now. She could feel the sweat on her back, sticking her clothes to her skin. She could hear the beat of her own heart. Clovis was still looking down. He ran his hand through his hair and licked his lips. She felt like she was going to faint again, but it was a strangely pleasant feeling. Suddenly, Clovis lifted his head and smiled.

"I have an idea," he said. "If I'm part of your brain, then I can't know things that you don't know. What if I could take you somewhere? A real place, but somewhere you have never been and never seen. It can be a place that you can research later, so you would know that what we see is 'real'. Would that make this, and me, more real for you?"

He was watching her, waiting for an answer.

"If you can do that, then yes, I'll believe you're real," she said with a small smile.

Clovis beamed. "Cool," he said. "Okay, then for the next little while I won't see you, here or at your school. But exactly thirty-three days from now, you need to come and try to find me. I'll make sure that you can. Exactly thirty-three, okay?"

"Why won't I see you?" she asked.

"It'll take research and a lot of energy to do this," he said, but he was smiling. A piece of his hair got caught in one of his eyelashes. Amelie reached out to free it. She touched him for the briefest of seconds, but when she did, his large black eyes got significantly larger, and she became even more light-headed.

Clovis stood up quickly.

"Come on, we need to get you some air before you pass out. I have no idea how woman can stand wearing all those clothes in this heat."

Amelie stood up unsteadily. Clovis put his hand very gently to the low part of her back, touching her clothes but not her body.

They walked out of the stall and into the hallway with all the horses. A soft breeze hit the sweat on her body, and it felt like heaven. As they walked, the other grooms and handlers stared at them. Amelie wondered if they could see her body through her wet, clinging clothes, or if they were staring at Clovis. For his part, Clovis seemed to see no one but her.

"Where are we?" she asked.

"What story or what place?"

"Either, I guess."

"The place is Sandusky, Ohio."

"And the story?"

"It seems to be a story about a boy who falls in love with a girl he can't have," he said.

That made sense to her. It explained the energy of the place. The air was thick with more than moisture, it was pulsing with unrequited love and desire.

"Why can't he have her?" she asked, as they approached the ticket booths. A groom accidentally bumped into her and apologized. He had a strange little smile on his face.

"Hmmm. He thinks it's because he doesn't have money but really, it's because he lies to her about what he is," Clovis replied.

"Did you pick this story for us to meet in?" Amelie asked suddenly.

"No," he said, but he looked uncomfortable. "I didn't know you were coming. I mean, would I choose this place, looking like this if I had a choice?" He waved down at his shit-covered pants.

"Well, maybe not."

He had stopped walking and turned to her.

"I wonder if the places we go—" he started, when a voice froze him.

Chapter Twelve

The Devil With the Pink Dress On

"Clovis!" a loud female voice called. When Clovis caught sight of the owner of the voice, he shoved Amelie behind him, hard enough that she almost fell. He then walked away with an exaggeratedly cool gait. Amelie was so shocked that she just stood there staring.

The woman coming toward Clovis was not just any woman, she was a perfect specimen of female beauty. She was only slightly shorter than Clovis, but there was nothing masculine about her. Her figure was a perfect hourglass, with legs that Amelie's mother would have said "went on until Christmas". She couldn't see her facial features in great detail, but what she saw looked like something from a magazine, with pouty lips and a heart-shaped face. Her shiny red hair cascaded over flawless golden skin. What was most startling was what she was wearing—or not wearing. She was in a pale pink dress that looked like silk lingerie. On her feet were high heels, but not the torture devices that Amelie was wearing, they were modern, elegant sandals. Despite this, no one seemed to be staring at her.

The woman was now greeting Clovis with a hug and a kiss that did not look platonic. To make matters worse, she kept her hands on Clovis after the kiss was over, while she positively oozed sexuality.

Amelie stood rooted where she was, feeling foolish, plain, and awkward. She was out of earshot of their conversation, but she watched as the woman ran her hands through Clovis's hair and settled them on the back of his neck. His hands were in his pockets. A couple of obviously drunk men pushed past them, causing the woman to stumble for a second. She grabbed Clovis to keep herself from falling. When she looked up, her expression was murderous. The woman turned Clovis and pointed at the men who were now passing on Amelie's right. Clovis nodded but looked through Amelie like she wasn't there. The red-haired woman did not. She looked pointedly at Amelie, and then leaned forward to say something to Clovis. He shook his head. She then gestured to Amelie to come forward.

Amelie refused to move. She hated this woman. The woman took Clovis's arm and led him over to where Amelie stood. Clovis looked at her, and for a moment his eyes registered panic. Opening her inner eye, Amelie saw that yellow and black lights were dancing off the skin of the woman.

Caution.

"Hi honey," the woman said to Amelie. "You're staring at me like we know each other. Have we met?"

"No," Amelie said coldly.

"I'm here with her," Clovis said evenly.

"Oh, so the poor lamb is jealous. I understand," the woman said, giving her shoulders a little shrug and winking at Amelie. "Don't you worry sweetie, I won't take up much of his time. We're just very old friends and we meet so rarely."

Amelie glared at her.

"What's your name, lamb?" the woman asked her.

"Rose, you're pushing propriety," Clovis replied before Amelie could speak.

"Oh, since when are you all concerned with the rules?"

"Since I saw the impact of breaking too many of them," Clovis replied. Rose laughed, put her arms around Clovis's waist and leaned up to kiss him again.

"Baby, you smell awful," she chided him after the kiss.

"Well, I have been shoveling horse shit all day, so I probably have an excuse," Clovis responded coolly. "What are you doing here?"

"Besides just having a nice meal?" Rose purred. Clovis rolled his eyes.

"It's never a coincidence for you and I to be in the same place."

"Touché, darling," Rose laughed. "Well, given your friend, I don't think I will get what I was looking for from you."

"Seems not," Clovis replied.

"You know," she leaned in even closer to him—Amelie could see her breasts now actually brushing his arms—"we could always start some gossip. We did a good job of that once."

Clovis visibly stiffened, and stepped away from her.

"Yeah, and that was a mistake. I knew that then, and even you should know that by now."

"Oh baby, you didn't do anything wrong. I didn't do anything wrong. We were just doing what lovers do."

80

"Your definition of what lovers—" Clovis started, but Amelie had heard enough.

She walked away without a word, straight out to the racetrack. She was in the sunlight, but she didn't feel it. The crowd was yelling but she didn't hear them. She looked up at the stands. The boy and the girl she had seen before were still there, but now they were talking. Amelie wondered if these were the people Clovis had told her about. She wondered what would happen if she just pulled the boy aside and told him to tell the girl the truth. It probably wouldn't help.

She inched her way toward the racetrack, finding a space against the railing that had been vacated by a young boy. Her eyes were stinging in a way that meant tears were threatening, and she refused to cry. If Clovis had a girlfriend—no, a lover—that was his business. It's not like they were, what—dating. The very thought was ludicrous, which was why her reaction was embarrassing. She had only seen him a couple of times. And yet, suddenly, the question of his reality was no longer an issue. The existence of Rose was enough to crush any attempted denial. Rose was real. Amelie wouldn't have made her up by choice. She had detested the woman on sight.

The horses were coming down the stretch again. They pushed the air in front of them and that wind hit Amelie in the face. The smell of horseflesh and dirt assaulted her nostrils. The people in the crowd started to yell. That was probably why she didn't hear Clovis come up behind her, but she felt him as he moved in next to her against the railing. She turned to leave but he caught her arm.

"I need to talk to you about Rose," he yelled over the screaming of the crowd.

"No, you don't!" she yelled back. But the race was now over, and the noise had died down, so her words rang out in the void. Great, things *could* get more embarrassing. Amelie pushed her way through the crowd and back toward the stables.

"Amelie. Stop! I need to talk to you," Clovis came up beside her.

"I don't want to talk right now," she snapped. Clovis blew out a sharp breath in frustration that pushed his hair off his face. He grabbed her by the arm, firmly this time, and pulled her under the bleachers, banging against something in the process.

"Son of a bitch," he snarled, gritting his teeth. Then turned to her.

"You need to stop acting like a spoiled brat, and listen to me for a second," he growled at her. He had a look in his eyes that should have scared her, but didn't.

"I'm not acting like a spoiled brat. I just don't want to discuss the details of your love life with sex kitten bitch queen over there," she snarled back.

Clovis stepped back, then uttered a surprised little laugh.

"Sex kitten bitch queen, that's a bit colorful for you, but it's not bad— except you missed the sadistic part," he said with a dark smile. Amelie stood back with her arms crossed over her body.

"Okay. Maybe we're in this story because I'm supposed to be more honest with you. Maybe that's the message that drew me here," Clovis said quickly. This shocked her and piqued her interest. He shoved his hands in the pockets of his overalls and sighed.

"As you probably heard, Rose and I have been lovers in the past," he began. "But we are NOT lovers now."

"Okay," she said.

Clovis sighed again.

"Let me start another way. Do you remember last time we met, in that story?"

"You mean when you tried to eat me?" she replied. He smiled.

"Yeah, when I tried to eat you. Do you remember I said that I attacked you because I thought you might be someone else?"

"You thought I might be her?" she asked.

He nodded.

"But you said you were lovers," Amelie said.

"Yeah, saying we were lovers is a bit of a euphemism. What we did … well, it didn't have much to do with love, or even desire. It had more to do with other emotions."

"Like?"

Clovis cringed. Amelie could tell he didn't want to talk about this, but it made her feel a little better to see him uncomfortable.

"You're still very young," he said.

This might have felt like a slap in the face but for his vocal tone and facial expressions.

"Even as you get older, I hope you never have to understand some of the things that people do when they have forgotten how to have normal sensations. Rose likes taboos and violence. She has forgotten how to feel alive without it. She doesn't care if she's the aggressor or the victim. I think she actually prefers to play the victim with me. So if she meets me in a place where we are alone, she tries to—well, hurt me in order to get me to respond in kind."

82

Amelie was quiet. She was watching his face. His expression was intense but muscles on his face were relaxed. There were no tics, no tells. He was telling her the truth. She relaxed a little.

"I'm also telling you this for your safety. You obviously know now that there are more people like me in these places." He said the word "people" with slight hesitation, like it was a foreign word.

"Did Rose look different from the other people here to you?" he asked suddenly.

"Yes," Amelie said, "everyone else is dressed to cover themselves and she was wearing lingerie. Why weren't people staring?"

Clovis eyebrows went up.

"Because no one saw that but you," he said.

"But why would I see her differently?" Amelie asked.

"That must be your idealized form of feminine beauty," Clovis said. As he said this, he glanced down briefly, breaking eye contact.

"What did you see?" Amelie asked.

Clovis just shrugged before continuing. "That's not important. What is important is that you now know how Rose looks to you. If you see her when you're not with me, you need to run immediately. Don't wait for her to see you, and don't assume you can hide. You can't. If she remembers you, you're in danger. If you can't get away from her, try your best to kill her."

"That won't be hard," Amelie snorted.

"I'm not joking about this," Clovis said sternly. "You may only get one shot. Use whatever weapons are available in that world. It won't kill her permanently but it will temporarily remove her from the story you are in. So don't hesitate, okay?"

Amelie nodded.

Clovis stepped a bit closer to her. She could smell his breath, his skin. The energy coming off him felt like nothing she could describe. It made her feel dizzy and flushed. Her anger melted away, and with it much of her skepticism and control. Her eyes felt like they were melting into the back of her head. Clovis gave her a worried little smile.

"One more thing. So far, I'm the only one who has talked to you in your world in the way I do, right?"

"Yes, of course. Wait, are there going to be others? Like Rose?" she asked, shocked back into a semblance of focus.

"Most of my kind can't possess people in your space. Actually, *very* few can, but there are other things besides us, so it's better to play it safe," he said.

83

Amelie nodded, despite the fact that she had no idea what he was talking about.

"I need a way to let you know it is me when I'm in your world." Clovis said. "Just in case someone tries to impersonate me. Something only you and I know. A phrase or a name. No one else can know it or hear it."

Amelie closed her eyes and felt a tug in the pit of her stomach. He wanted a name for her. Somehow names were very important to her. Maybe it was the fact that her own name was a mistake that had never been corrected. A mistake that she chose to own and wear like a badge. The fact that he wanted to name her touched her. It felt like being touched by a god.

Chosen by a god ...

"Psyche," she said softly. "She's someone who went between worlds. No one else would call me that."

She heard him exhale deeply.

"That's perfect," he said, but he pulled back from her a bit, searching her face. "If I say that name, you know it's me. If you have any question, and I don't use it, early in the conversation, then you know it's not me."

She nodded.

"So, uh, was Rose right then?" he asked, his voice suddenly colder.

"About what?"

"About you being angry with me because you were jealous?"

Oh great.

She stood up straighter and squared her shoulders.

"I was angry with you for a lot of reasons. First, you pushed me. Then you looked through me like I wasn't even there. When you finally came over with her, you both treated me like I was some kind of insect. At the very least, that was rude. I don't like being pushed, hit, or grabbed. So, if she acts like a bitch, that is one thing, but you're different. I don't know about where you come from, but where I come from friends don't treat friends like that. Assuming we are friends ..."

She met his eyes levelly. Of course, these were not the only reasons she had been angry, but she wasn't going to think about that.

His face relaxed and he smiled. "Yeah, we're friends. And I'm sorry I pushed you. I hoped she wouldn't see you. I also thought it would be unwise to let her know—" he stopped suddenly.

"To let her know what?" Amelie asked.

"For her to see me paying too much attention to you," he finished, and ran his hands through his hair. "Rose doesn't respond well with people who have too much of my attention. But I can see how that would make you feel—well, it could look pretty shitty."

"Yes, it was shitty," Amelie said. "So, from now on, you don't have to shove me if you need me to fade back. Just give me a look. I can be pretty smart that way."

"I think you're a lot more than just pretty smart."

He smiled and she was smiling back. She noticed people walking by them were staring again, and whispering.

"What are they staring at?" Amelie asked Clovis.

"Us," he replied.

"I know that but why?"

"Well, what do I look like to you right now?" he asked.

"Like you did last time, maybe a bit dirtier," she responded. She didn't mention the missing shirt. He smiled again; it was a bewildered sort of smile.

"I love that," he said.

"What do you love?"

"That you see me like this."

"Well, what do you really look like?"

"What you see is what I really look like. Here, I suspect I look a bit like a fifteen-year-old boy. It probably looks odd to them that a pretty woman in her forties is hidden up behind the bleachers and acting the way you're acting with a fifteen-year-old boy."

"Wait, I look like a forty-year-old?"

"To the people here, yes."

"Well, that explains all the looks," she laughed a bit.

Suddenly, a yellow autumn leaf blew by her. It was incongruous with the summer weather. The people around her seemed to be slowing down, their colors bleeding out into the air around them. She was fading as well. Clovis tried to grab her but his hands went through her.

"Remember," he called, "thirty-three days! Find me in thirty-three days!" She nodded and he waved.

As the scene was becoming nothing a blur of color, she saw a streak of pink appear behind Clovis, and then Rose's face, with blue streaks for eyes. Amelie called to him, but then he was gone.

Amelie came to herself with her heart in her mouth, and her hands clenched around some small pieces of straw.

Chapter Thirteen

The Happiest Place on Earth

The next thirty-three days of Amelie's life were a horrible waiting game. When she had awakened from her last meeting with Clovis, she had been terrified. She had seen Rose coming for Clovis and since then she had heard nothing. Of course, he told her that she wouldn't see him during this time, but it had taken everything in her power NOT to go look for him in the hallway.

When the thirty-third day finally rolled around, Amelie could barely make it through the day. She realized, with a twisted amusement, that it was also the day of the Valentine dance. There were hearts and pink streamers up in the school, cards were exchanged, and flowers delivered. The Dance Committee had forced some poor kid to dress up as Cupid to deliver the flowers so, luckily for her, he had been easy to spot and avoid.

That night, Amelie ate her TV dinner as quickly as possible and excused herself immediately after finishing, saying she had a headache. Opal had frozen, fork hanging in midair, with a look on her face that might have been actual thought. Amelie had left the table quickly to avoid any conversation.

#

Lying on her bed, she had barely closed her eyes when she found herself flying in the hallway. She was once again drawn straight to a glowing door, but this time she did not slow down as she approached it. As she barreled toward it, she threw up her hands, covering her face for impact. Instead of feeling an impact, she felt warmth on her skin. When she opened her eyes, everything looked bright and blurry.

As Amelie's vision began to clear, she laughed out loud. She was standing on a wide walkway paved with multicolored concrete. Just above her was a green, wrought iron archway. In the middle of it was a giant waving mouse in red shorts, and the words *Hong Kong Disneyland Resort* in English and Chinese.

Amelie actually clapped her hands. As a young child, she had desperately wanted to go to Disneyland. At that time her family had neither the money nor the inclination for that sort of thing, so the dream had quickly died.

The people around her looked at her and smiled. Most of them looked Asian, but there were a few Caucasian people mixed in. Gauging from the pale blue color of the sky, Amelie calculated that it was early morning, but it was already hot. She could feel the heat of the sun on her skin. The air smelled of flowers, water, and sugar. She looked down to see that she was wearing a sparkly Minnie Mouse T-shirt with hearts all over it.

Amelie spotted Clovis when she was still only halfway down the walkway. He was sitting, one leg up, beneath a fountain of Mickey Mouse surfing on the spray of a whale. There was no way she could fail to recognize the physical stance and the mop of messy dark hair. She suddenly felt shy. She pretended to look at other things as she walked, the green mountains behind her, and palm trees lining the walkway.

When she looked back up, Clovis was walking toward her. He was wearing a T-shirt, dark khaki shorts, and black chucks. The T-shirt was a black-and-white sketch of Mickey, Donald and Goofy doing kung fu. He looked like your typical eighteen-year-old boy, and that should have made Amelie feel more comfortable, but didn't. When he was dressed like someone from another world, or another time period, she could think of him as imaginary. But now, with his hands shoved in the pockets of his shorts, dressed like any other boy, he looked like—well, like he could be something besides her made-up friend.

Shut up, she told herself.

Clovis made an exaggerated bow.

"Welcome to Hong Kong Disneyland. What do you think? Real enough?" he asked as he gestured around him.

"I guess I will know that when I get back," she laughed.

"Well, then, let me show you around so you'll have something to research," he said. He pointed toward a ticket booth and turnstiles.

"Okay. Just so I know. Do you look like you're twelve right now, or ninety? Are people going to think I'm a pervert?" Amelie asked as they walked toward the turnstiles.

Clovis laughed.

"You look about twenty-two or twenty-three. I probably look about twenty-four or twenty-five. We look Western, so people will speak to us in English.

People will probably see us as a couple," he said, throwing her a sideways glance with a sly smile.

"What happens when someone speaks to you in a language you don't speak?" she asked quickly, ignoring the other comment.

"There are no languages I don't speak," he said frankly. "So I'll take good care of you."

This last statement was said with a slightly self-conscious laugh. Once again, more like your average eighteen-year-old boy. Just at that moment, she noticed thick scabs on his neck, near his veins.

"What happened to you neck?" she asked.

"Well, just after you left last time, I had a little encounter with Rose." He shrugged, then added quickly, "No big deal. I got out of it pretty quick."

"I saw her coming for you," Amelie said. "I tried to warn you, but I didn't think you could hear me."

"I heard you. And thank you for that," he said, just as they got to the turnstiles.

He gave their tickets to the cast member.

"Congratulations!" she said with a smile. Clovis smiled and nodded, obviously trying not to laugh.

"What was that about?" Amelie asked him after they got past earshot of the woman. Now he laughed out loud.

"Put your hands on your head," he said. She did and found she had a hat on her head. When she took it off, she saw that it was white Mouse ears with a tiny white veil. She gasped.

"Oh my god," she said, and felt her face burning. Clovis laughed with delight, until he noticed her very real mortification. He stopped laughing but couldn't stop grinning.

"Don't worry, I'm wearing the male equivalent, apparently you just don't see it," he teased.

"So people think … we look like …" she found herself stammering.

"Newlyweds," he put his hands up as if warding off an evil eye. "Look, don't get mad at me. I was able to get us here, but I have no power over what roles we take.

"You want a Mickey waffle?" Clovis asked suddenly. "They have those here. Of course, I think they also have squid on a stick, if you prefer."

"No, no, a Mickey waffle is great," she smiled.

They walked beneath covered arches and on to Main Street USA, the Disney recreation of a small nineteenth-century town. At the end of the street was the famous Disney castle. It looked a bit smaller than she might have expected but it was beautiful nonetheless.

Clovis led her to a cart where they were making waffles. The air smelled like a pot of sugar and cream. They each got a waffle shaped like Mickey Mouse with whipped cream and strawberries. Behind the cart were some tables with umbrellas. Small birds were stalking the feet of the diners for scraps of sugary goodness.

As they sat down, Clovis pulled her chair out for her. He did this without thinking about it, but it surprised her. But then he sat down and immediately shoved about half the waffle in his mouth at once, and the chivalry vibe was gone.

"How did you get us here?" she asked. "Is this a dream?"

"No, it's a story," he replied, his mouth full of food.

"What's a story?" she asked but he interrupted her.

"You don't like the waffle? 'Cause if you don't, I'll eat it."

He hovered his fork over her waffle. She swatted his fork away with her own.

"No, I'm eating," she said.

A family with English accents and plates of waffles sat down at a table close to them. The woman had blonde hair with a few streaks of gray. Her face was beet-red from the heat. The man was wearing horrible dress shorts, black socks and trainers. His polo shirt was straining over his gut. With them was a little blonde girl dressed in a blue princess dress. She was probably about six years old.

"Are you getting married?" the little girl asked Amelie.

"So sorry," the mother said. "Hayley, you shouldn't bother people."

"Oh, it's okay," Clovis said to the woman, then turned to the little girl. "We already got married, sweetheart."

"Is this your honeymoon?" the mother asked.

"Yes. My wife never got to go to Disneyland when she was a little girl. So I brought her to the most exotic Disney I could think of. It's all part of my grand scheme to make sure she never leaves me," Clovis said, smiling. Amelie thought the woman might have blushed, but it would have been hard to tell.

"That's very romantic of you," the woman said. She fanned herself with a park map, as she pulled a chair out for her daughter to crawl onto. "I wish my husband were that thoughtful. He stopped that years ago."

"I got you, didn't I? Why do I have to keep trying?" The large man didn't quite snap, but it was close.

Amelie had just finished her waffle. Clovis got up and started clearing their trays away.

"It's never too late to lose her, you know," Clovis said with his back turned. The large man blinked quickly a couple of times. When Clovis turned around he had an odd smile and that weird animal look in his eyes. He then pulled Amelie's chair out for her. There was something off in this little exchange, but Amelie couldn't put her finger on it.

"That's the thing with women, they can surprise you," Clovis said, looking at the woman and not the man. The man now just snorted.

"Oh, she's too old and far too wide. She doesn't have the energy to run away anymore. Which is good because I don't have the energy to chase her. That's what happens when you get old, boy," the man said smugly.

"No, that's what happens when *you* get old. It never happened to me and I'm much older than you," Clovis snapped and then guided Amelie toward the street, as the English couple exchanged bemused looks.

"What was that all about?" Amelie asked as they got out on the street.

"That guy was an asshole," Clovis responded sharply.

"Yeah, but why did it set you off?" she asked.

"Because I hate stupidity," he responded without hesitation. "And that guy's attitude is the height of stupidity. If he thinks that his wife can't walk through this park and find at least a hundred men who are not only able but willing to treat her better than he does, then he's deluding himself."

"You think so? I don't mean to sound horrible, but she wasn't particularly pretty," Amelie replied, as a gorgeous Asian woman in short shorts sauntered by, as if to illustrate her point.

"So what? Beauty has little to do with what someone looks like," Clovis replied.

"Really? It must be nice in your world."

It came out a bit harsher than she intended. Clovis stopped in his tracks and looked at her very seriously.

"In my world we understand what beauty acts like, smells like, feels like, and tastes like—not just what it looks like," he said catching her eye and holding her gaze. At this moment, he looked worlds away from the teenage boy he was dressed as. Amelie felt her insides soften.

"Oh, and what was that bit about being older than him?" she asked quickly. "How old are you?"

"Do you want to get our photo taken in front of the castle?" Clovis interrupted. "There is a photographer right there." Before Amelie could respond one way or another the park photographer waved them over.

"Congratulations!" he said, smiling, and then waved them over to stand in front of the castle.

As they stood next to each other, Amelie smiled self-consciously. The photographer motioned for them to get closer together, and Clovis slipped his arm around her waist. This time, he didn't shy away from the contact, pulling her close to him. Her smile was now real, but she was getting that swoony feeling again, like she had felt sitting next to him in the hot stables.

When the picture was taken, the photographer gave them a piece of paper with number on it.

"You can see the photo at the photo shop on Main Street USA," the photographer said.

"So, do you want to start with Tomorrowland, Fantasyland, or Adventureland?" Clovis asked. Amelie shrugged. Her heart was racing, and she was suddenly out of breath.

"Hot again?" Clovis asked as he surveyed her face intently. "Let's get you somewhere cool."

#

He walked her across the bridge and through the castle. On the other side of the castle there was Fantasyland, the home of the under-three set. The area was full of toddlers, laughing, crying, yelling, and doing all the other things that toddlers do.

"There are air-conditioned shops this way," said Clovis, leading her down the bridge.

"How do you know where things are?" Amelie asked.

"I know everything," he said, with exaggerated cockiness, leading her toward a shop with a bubble machine in front. A group of young children had gathered there, running, shrieking, and chasing bubbles. As a result, they were outside of the shop, and not inside of it.

"Let's go in this one for a minute. It should be cooler."

He was right, the shop was gloriously shaded, cool, and empty. Amelie began to feel less dizzy. Looking around her, she saw that the store was stacked with shelf upon shelf of princess paraphernalia. Princess dresses, princess tiaras, princess pencils, princess paper. This must be the official Princess shop.

Her heart slowed down. The whole heat thing was odd, because she usually wasn't affected by heat. It only seemed to affect her in the hallway. She stopped and investigated a Sleeping Beauty art kit as Clovis wandered deeper into the store.

"Hey, they have adult princess dresses over here!" Clovis called. "You want one?"

Amelie rolled her eyes, but she walked over to where he was standing. There were various adult versions of Belle, Jasmine, Snow White, and even the wedding dress of Ariel.

"They have everything a princess needs," Clovis laughed, pointing to the wedding dress. "I wonder if they have Princess condoms, or maybe that would be Prince condoms. Anyway, it would make sense, it's supposed to be the Happiest Place on Earth, after all."

Amelie felt herself blushing again. Damn it, she was beginning to think he enjoyed watching her blush.

"You never answered the how old you are question," she said, quickly changing the subject.

"Oh, I hoped you had forgotten that one," he replied with a sigh.

"Nope," Amelie said, rolling her hand.

"Well, I don't really know, to be honest. I've been alive a long time," he said as they walked slowly up and down the rows filled with tiaras and wands.

"Long time meaning hundreds of years?" she asked. He shook his head.

"No, no. That's not very long at all. If you must know, long means since the birth of civilization."

"Shit," Amelie whispered, suddenly dizzy again, but not from heat. She sat down on the edge of a display case. If he was real, and she was now convinced he was, then what was he?

Clovis knelt next to her.

"Hey, look I didn't want to tell you. It's not that big a deal really."

"What do you mean, it's not a big deal? It's a huge deal," she said, and she put her head in her hands to steady herself. "Jeez, it makes me feel like a midge."

"What does that mean, 'feel like a midge'?"

"Like my life is short and insignificant."

"Listen," he said, sitting down next to her. "Your life is far from insignificant. Lives aren't less valuable because they're shorter. Besides it's just your bodies that are short-lived, not your spirit. The truth is that you and I are probably close to the same age. The difference is that your soul is particulate and mine isn't. That's all."

Amelie was about to ask what the hell that meant when a cast member appeared next to them.

"Is everything all right?" she asked in a thick Chinese accent.

"Yes," Clovis replied. "My wife isn't very used to the heat."

"Would she like a cool drink?"

"That would be very kind of you," Clovis responded with a smile. Then he said something quickly in Chinese that included the word "Coca-Cola". The woman gave him an odd look and scuttled off.

"What does 'particulate soul' mean?" Amelie whispered but Clovis shook his head and held up his hand, cutting his eyes to the back of the departing cast member.

"Not the time and place. Besides, I didn't bring you to Disneyland to freak you out or to talk philosophy."

"Then why did you bring me here?" she asked.

"To prove to you that I'm real, remember?" he said. "Also, I thought that, given your family, it might be something that you were missing from your childhood. Was I wrong?"

He looked at her with a shy smile. She smiled back.

"No," Amelie replied softly.

How did he know about her family?

The woman came back with a Coke in a Mickey Mouse cup. Clovis took it from her, handed her some money and sat back down next to Amelie. He held out the straw for her to sip.

"You're right, I don't want to talk about serious stuff," she said to him, then gave him a wicked grin. "You know what I *do* want?"

He narrowed his eyes suspiciously.

"I want to go on the 'It's a Small World' ride," she said. He laughed.

"Ugh. Does it have to be that one? You know we'll have that song stuck in our heads for the rest of the day?"

"Yes. It has to be that one," she said sternly. "And we have to sing."

#

They spent the next few hours riding rides and seeing shows. By early afternoon, she hadn't disappeared, and they were both hot and hungry, but she wasn't complaining.

"Let's grab some food in Adventureland," Clovis said as they crossed back through the castle and moved toward a richer, greener area on their right. "It's shaded, so it's cooler there."

Clovis headed off along the path toward a circle of large tikis. He motioned for her to follow him. As she entered the circle, all five tall statues sprayed her with water at the same time. It felt glorious. After a couple of minutes, they were both drenched.

"Well, I guess we are now appropriately attired for a restaurant in the jungle," Clovis laughed and jerked his head, motioning for her to follow him. She was about ten feet behind him when he turned back to her and gave her a small smile.

That was when it happened.

Amelie suddenly couldn't breathe. It wasn't heat. She wasn't dizzy. Instead, she felt a cramping deep in her pelvis. Warmth shot across her chest and her vision narrowed to a pinpoint. She could only see Clovis … everything else faded away.

Suddenly everything she had been experiencing fit neatly into place.

She wasn't attracted to Clovis. She wasn't grateful for his friendship. She wasn't thrilled to be able to let down her guards. Well, she was all of these things. But the full truth was much simpler. As fast, crazy, and inappropriate as it was, she was in love with Clovis. The thing she thought could never happen to her had just happened, in this tiny moment in the pulsing heat.

She had spent her whole life trying to discourage other people from having feelings for her. She had viewed love and attraction with a mixture of suspicion and disdain. So maybe she hadn't seen this coming because it was so completely out of her realm of personal experience … but here it was.

She didn't realize that she had been standing there like an idiot until Clovis started walking back toward her. His chucks were soaked and making ridiculous squishing noises as he walked.

"Come on, Am. Aren't you hungry? I'm starving," he said.

"Yeah. Okay," she squeaked out. He gave her a quizzical look as she ran past him toward the River View Cafe.

She stopped in front of the menu displayed at the entrance to the restaurant and stared at it, trying to focus her brain and slow her heart.

Clovis interrupted her chemical litany.

"This is the halal restaurant in Adventureland, but I don't suppose that matters to you?" he asked with a little smile.

She had no idea what "halal" meant, but she nodded. As they walked up the stairs that led to a dining area situated on a wooden dock, Clovis carried the conversation by telling her about the various types of food that they had here and about some of the stranger things he had eaten while in Asia—cat, dog, mouse embryo, and ox penis being just a few. Amelie was only able to nod. Her brain was on strike.

Once they were seated, Clovis ordered for them. Somehow, he seemed to know her tastes. It was little things like this, rather than the big things, that drove it home to her that he wasn't just an eighteen-year-old boy. He had the confidence of a man, and the manners of a man from an older time—when he felt like it.

He ordered spring rolls and when they came, he tried to teach her how to spin them using chopsticks. She failed that experiment, and Clovis ended up with a fair amount of spring roll on his shirt for his troubles.

"At least I can *use* chopsticks," she said defensively as a dim sum slipped away from her, skidding across the table and ending up in his lap.

"I know," he said with a smile, retrieving the dim sum. He then picked up his bowl of beef noodles and used his chopsticks to extract the last few noodles.

"What do you mean, you know?"

"I've seen them serving Chinese food at your school. They always give wooden chopsticks with the meals. Most people don't use them. You do."

"You've seen that?" she asked, shocked. "How often are you at my school?"

"I live in your story," he said shortly, as if that explained something.

"What does that mean?"

"Your world is my world, so I can see you if I can get physical enough," he said, then looked up at her suddenly. "Does it bother you? My watching your school?"

"No, I'm just surprised. Why would you want to watch my school? Nothing happens there. I can barely stand being there, and I have to be. Is there something particularly interesting about it?"

"Yes. You," he said without hesitation, looking at her. Amelie felt her face burn and she suddenly felt stupidly, giddily happy. She looked down. He nudged her foot with his under the table until she looked back up at him.

"So let me rephrase the question. Does it bother you to have me watching you? I guess it would probably bother some people."

"No," she said. "I don't mind."

Both of them were silent for a minute. His foot was still touching hers under the table. Amelie found herself obsessing over this little contact.

She didn't know how long they sat like that, but she could have stayed forever. Eventually Clovis sighed.

"We should go," he said, standing up and throwing money on the table.

"I want to get our picture before …" he trailed off, with a wan sort of smile.

She knew he had been about to say "before you disappear". She didn't want to think about that right now either. To be honest, she didn't want to think. She just wanted to be in his company.

Get ahold of yourself.

They started in the direction of Main Street USA, where the parade had just ended.

"I'm surprised you would want the picture," she said, aiming for a casual tone. "You don't really strike me as the Disney-type."

"Look, just because I don't want to get stuck singing 'It's a Small World' for the next seven days, which, by the way, isn't really as happy-go-lucky as it sounds, does not mean that I'm not a Disney fan. I'm a huge fan of their movies."

"Why come?" Amelie asked, horrified by hearing her mother's vernacular coming out of her mouth.

"Because, at some point, it becomes a physical necessity," Clovis replied with a grin. It took Amelie a moment to catch his meaning. She put her burning face in her hands.

"I assume you meant to ask why I'm a fan of the Disney movies?" he asked. She nodded, head still in hands.

"Well, mainly because they focus on improbable relationships. Laundry girl and prince. Mermaid and human. Beautiful brainy girl and giant buffalo. I love that."

"Why?" she asked.

"Because it's been my experience that improbable relationships, once they get past the initial hurdles, are the ones most likely to last. Maybe because it takes a great passion to get over those initial hurdles, and only great passion really lasts."

Amelie suddenly had the strongest sense that she had been here before, standing on Main Street USA, with Clovis explaining the value of difficult relationships.

He stopped in front of a shop modeled on an old-fashioned photo shop.

"We can get our photos here," he said as they entered the blissful air conditioning of the shop. Clovis pulled the paper with the photo number on it out of his pocket and scanned it into a machine. Amelie came up next to him and found that he was staring at the castle photo of them on the computer screen. For all the world, it looked like the two of them, standing in front of the castle. She was surprised.

"You look cute," he said, staring at the photo, but his voice sound further away. She tried to say something, but she couldn't speak. She was too thin. She felt a sense of panic about not being able to say goodbye to him. He looked up just as the world around her blurred.

#

Amelie came back to her bed feeling sicker than she had in a while. She ran to the bathroom and vomited violently. She spent the next thirty minutes locked in the bathroom, rocking back and forth until the cramping and vomiting finally stopped. After that she cried. She wasn't exactly sure why, but it came out of her the same way the sickness had. It had to be released. When her tears stopped, she put her head against the lid of the toilet. It felt unusually cool.

When she stood up, she caught a glimpse herself in the mirror. She was pink. She thought she might have a fever, but when she checked she was fine. It took a few moments to realize it was a sunburn—she had brought back the sun this time.

Outside, the sun was coming up. She sat down on her bed and picked up her phone. She had eight new text messages. Seven of them were from Jack.

Shit. The thing with Jack was not dissipating.

Still, she was fatigued enough from the vomiting that she felt herself drift back toward sleep. She failed to see the photograph hanging out of the notebook sitting on her bedside table.

Chapter Fourteen

Caught in the Act

After her night with Clovis, Amelie had no desire for any extended contact with her family. Her nerves felt raw and tender, and she had a difficult time erecting her shields when she woke up. The layers of clear plastic she visualized on top of her kept melting away. Maybe it was the sunburn, or maybe she resented having to do this. So she decided to leave early and drive to school the long way.

As she was putting on her clothes, little moments from the night before flitted through her brain, making her feel both giddy and scared. She would look up Hong Kong Disneyland today, but not to prove to herself that Clovis was real. She knew all of this was real. If she doubted it, she need only look at herself in the mirror. As for Clovis, he felt more real, more alive than anyone she had ever known, which was ironic because she suspected he was actually dead.

She had been considering the ghost thing for some time now. It made sense, given what she knew. He told her that he had been alive for thousands of years. She only saw him when she was in a dream-like state or when he was in someone else's body. Of course, demons were known to possess people as well, but she just couldn't see a demon mucking out stables or hanging out at Disneyland. A ghost made more sense.

When she heard the coffee machine downstairs, Amelie realized she was dawdling. So she ran down the stairs quickly, hoping to get out of the house without having to engage in any actual conversation with any family members.

No such luck.

Amelie was grabbing an apple from a bowl on the kitchen counter and shoving it into the front pocket of her book bag when she heard heavy footsteps in the hallway.

"Listen missy, I'm going to need to you to make dinner again tonight," Opal said as she stomped into the kitchen. "I gotta work late again. There's some new bug going around. I wish all of you would just stop getting so fucking sick."

"What's wrong now?" her father called, grabbing his newspaper and heading to the living room.

"Oh, some shit they're calling 'dog flu'—god-fucking-knows why. Maybe 'cause it makes people sick as a dog, but nurses been saying it makes people act like they been drinking. You know, swearing, fucking ... acting a fool."

"Don't sound bad to me," laughed her father.

"No? Vomiting up your guts don't sound bad? I guess cleaning up the waiting room after other folks vomited up their guts don't sound bad either?"

She glared around the kitchen and dining room, like her family was the cause of the recent viral plague.

Amelie nodded, looking down and letting her hair fall into her face, as she quickly pulled a Coke from the fridge and shoved it in with the apple and a cereal bar. Opal stood at the door of the kitchen and snorted.

As Amelie moved quickly past her and out the door, she heard her mother call from behind her.

"What's wrong with your face?"

Dodged a bullet, Amelie thought to herself almost giggling. Still, she would have to come up with some excuse for her sunburn, as her friends were bound to ask. But for now, she was free to feel happy.

The ride to school was beautiful. It was cold outside, but Amelie opened the windows anyway. The day was clear and crisp and there was a bit of wind that swept away the smell of death and decay that was ever present in the winter. Everything around her looked abnormally bright and alive. She opened her inner eye and watched for colors or patterns, but there was nothing unusual. There was just a good feeling all around. It made her want to wrap the world around her like a blanket. She wondered if this was what normal girls felt like after a date with a guy they liked.

That was not a date, and he isn't a "guy", she lectured herself, but she was still smiling at the thought.

She took the back roads to school. It didn't take much longer because they were devoid of traffic and she could drive fast. She had taken the apple out of her backpack and held the plastic bottle of Coke between her legs as she drove. She enjoyed taking turns a bit too fast and popping the clutch. There was such a freedom in driving like this. She turned on the radio and danced in her seat as she drove.

Amelie wondered if she would see Clovis today. She shouldn't get her hopes up. He had told her that it took a lot of energy to do "this". She wasn't exactly sure what "this" was, but it took him thirty-three days to set up their Disneyland encounter. So she suspected it might take him time to recover. She hoped not, but she had to prepare for it.

As she neared the school, she forced herself to pull her head out of the clouds and prepare for the day ahead. She would need a believable excuse for her sunburn.

Fell asleep under a sunlamp? Did anyone actually use those anymore?

Had a laser facial? None of her friends would believe she had the money or interest in that.

It's a side effect of an antiviral medicine that her mother gave her? That could get back to Opal, although it was unlikely.

Spent the night wandering around Hong Kong Disneyland with an amazing guy? That might be worth saying just to watch their faces—and to be able to say it out loud.

Fake tanner? But why would she have been trying this?

It was lame but it was the best she could come up with.

#

When she got to school, she pulled into the empty lower parking lot. All of the seniors usually parked in the upper parking lot, as was their privilege. Amelie preferred the lower one because it was bigger and more anonymous.

As she was gathering her books, she saw Hudson walking toward her car in her rearview mirror. He hadn't noticed her. He was carrying an old, rough-looking, brown leather backpack slung over one shoulder, but he wasn't walking in his normal slumped over fashion. His posture was straight, but he was looking at the tarmac, obviously lost in thought.

"Hi Hudson," Amelie called as she got out of her car. He started and immediately changed his gait.

"Hi Amelie," he mumbled as he walked past her. Then he stopped suddenly and turned around.

"Sorry. Old habits," he said, as he waited for her to catch up to him. He was looking at her directly, with no hint of the hangdog expression he usually wore. She supposed he had decided that he wasn't going to be that person around her. She was glad.

"I see you managed to avoid Jack for the Valentine dance. Well done!" he said, with a wry smile as they fell in step together.

"How do you know?"

"I went to the Valentine dance," he replied.

"Why?" she asked before she managed to stop herself. "Sorry, that sounded terrible."

Hudson laughed.

"No, why *is* the operative question. I didn't ask anyone, and no one asked me, of course. I went because I find it interesting to watch people. Watching people here is like watching a movie. Besides, there has been something strange about this place in the past few months, some strange energy or something."

Amelie had slowed her step and was looking at him closely.

"Sorry, too weird?" he asked.

"No. No. I think it would be impossible to weird me out these days," Amelie replied. It wasn't a serious slip, but she really should shut up. Hudson said nothing.

They were still on the auditorium side of the school, so they were out of sight of the people on the landing. Amelie felt the pull of dread that she always felt as she saw the corner of the auditorium approaching. Past that, she had to officially add acting to her shields in her balancing act.

"Hey, have you been okay recently?" Hudson asked suddenly.

"Sure, why?" she responded, shields once more tightening.

"Because you've been looking really tired … like you haven't been sleeping well," he said.

She couldn't exactly tell him why she looked tired, so she just shrugged.

At that moment, they turned the corner of the auditorium and Amelie saw that some of her friends were already on the landing. Sophie and Judith were there, along with Aidan and Jack. This was an odd combination to be at school early. Sophie was usually with Elodie, and Jack and Judith were almost never early.

Goody.

As if on cue, both she and Hudson changed their movements. Hudson went back to his more common hunched gait and Amelie stopped really smiling and plastered on the fake smile instead.

"Listen, I should tell you, I'm not the only one who's noticed that you look tired. I heard Mr. Sawyer talking to Jack about it in his office," Hudson said at a lower volume.

"Mr. Sawyer was talking about me with Jack?" Amelie whispered back.

"Yes. And not appropriately, at least from what I heard. Sawyer was asking whether you were dating Charlie Danos."

"Oh god," she muttered. "I don't even know Charlie Danos."

"Find me later," he said, as they got within earshot of her friends. He then stopped and unslung his sack and pulled out an orange. This allowed her to put some distance between them yet, even so, she saw Jack clock him with cold eyes.

"Amelie, what's up with your face?" Sophie asked at maximum volume as Amelie stepped onto the landing. She felt herself blush and was grateful for this natural reaction.

"It's nothing," she said as she came to stand next to Aidan. Judith was looking at her quizzically.

"It looks like you either took a vacation you didn't tell us about, or you have been experimenting with fake tanning," Judith said. Without meaning to, Judith had thrown her a softball. Amelie relaxed a bit.

"Okay. I tried the fake tan on my face, and it didn't work out so well," she said.

"What do you mean 'it didn't work'?" Sophie said. "It looks completely natural. It's even pink on your cheeks! What brand did you use? 'Cause I want it."

Think fast. Think fast.

"I don't remember. I'm just going to be interviewing with some schools soon and wanted to look a little less …"

"Goth pale?" Judith asked.

Amelie nodded.

"But you should have already submitted applications and interviews should be over," Judith said.

"Amelie is taking a gap year," Jack suddenly volunteered. Amelie stared at him.

How did he know that? Oh—Sawyer.

"She has asked for deferred entry, so she's applying for courses during her gap year," he continued, staring intently at Amelie's face.

Goddamn it, what didn't Sawyer know?

"Jack's right," Amelie said, refusing to make eye contact with him. "I'm applying to take some courses overseas. So I have interviews for that."

This was a lie as most of what she had to fill out was online.

"Going to Paris?" Judith asked, looking between her and Jack. Amelie nodded, willing Judith to shut up.

"Who would want to go to France?" Aidan snorted.

"What's wrong with you this morning?" Sophie asked, running her hand up Aidan's arm.

Amelie relaxed. She was no longer the center of attention, and there were only ten more minutes until the bell rang. She pulled her calculus notebook from her bag and began leafing through it.

"Carter borrowed my car last night, in exchange for some tickets to the State game," Aidan growled. "He went somewhere with Elodie and didn't return it. I got a text from him last night saying he'd bring it back this morning. He said they both got sick."

"I bet," Judith snorted.

"Check for stains on the seats," Jack laughed. "That flu is supposed to make people super horny."

"Thanks, Jack, I didn't need that visual first thing this morning," Judith said as Sophie pantomimed throwing up. Aidan's face became even stormier. He was very fond of his car.

"And you shouldn't talk that way in front of innocent little Amelie," Judith continued, putting her hands over Amelie's ears. As she did so, she accidentally knocked Amelie's notebook out of her hands and it fell to the ground at Judith's feet.

As it hit, a photo fell out of it onto the pavement. Amelie froze for just a fraction of a second, but it gave Judith enough time to snatch it from the concrete. Amelie just got a quick glance of two people wearing Mouse ears, standing in front of the castle at Disneyland, but it was enough to make her heart jump from her chest.

Oh god, the picture came back with me, she thought, followed quickly by, *How am I going to explain that?*

Judith was studying the photo.

"Interesting, who are these people?" Judith asked, as Sophie stuck her head over Judith's shoulder to look at it. Amelie took the photo from Judith. She felt relief flood her when she realized that, although the people in the picture might have borne a tiny resemblance to her and Clovis, it was not noticeable.

Think fast. This is a real photo from Disney. Can't be from a magazine. Isn't a computer printout. They are white, so probably not local. No date on the photo, that's good. Could be from a pen pal they know nothing about?

"Oh, it's from an Irish pen pal of mine living in Hong Kong," Amelie said, with a calm she didn't feel. She was hoping that would be the end of it, but the others were still looking at her.

"She sent me the photo because she wanted some advice about her boyfriend," she continued.

"That's the guy?" Sophie asked, taking the photo back and pointing at the young man who had been Clovis. "He's gorgeous. What sort of advice does she need? Fuck him, that's always the best advice."

"Don't be so tacky," Judith snapped. "What's the question? I'm good at relationships."

Jack snorted and Judith shot him a warning glance.

"She's in love with him. She thinks he may be in love with her, but she doesn't know for sure," Amelie found herself blurting out more truth than she intended.

"Are those Disney wedding hats?" Judith asked.

"Yes."

"But they are just dating?"

"Yes."

"Whose idea were the hats?"

"His, I think," Amelie replied.

"You wouldn't catch me dead wearing something like that," said Aidan, rolling his eyes.

"Exactly," said Judith. "Any guy who will do that, even if he is joking, is showing he's thinking of something long term. Love is long term. Crushes aren't. Guys don't do that sort of thing unless they are either in it for the long haul or they're desperate, pathetic losers. This guy doesn't look like a desperate pathetic loser. Is he?"

"No," Amelie said, finding herself being drawn into this dangerous conversation. It almost felt like getting advice from real friends—almost.

"So, good probability he loves her. Not a hundred percent but good probability."

Despite the fact that the words came from Judith, they still warmed her heart.

"But she said that he pulls away sometimes. He gets close and then he pulls back. Why would he do that if he loved her?"

"Oh, please." Judith said, rolling her eyes. "You're such a naive little thing. That's classic guy behavior. Love means commitment and commitment terrifies them. So they get in close, get scared, and then pull back. But if they keep coming back, it means they can't stay away, and that pretty much says it all."

"What makes you think you know so much about love?" Aidan snipped.

"Parents divorced when I was thirteen so my dad made me go see a shrink. The topic of love comes up a lot in therapy."

"You went to see a shrink?" Aidan laughed.

"Yeah, so what? I did my time, and I was done. I passed all my mental health exams with flying colors. We probably couldn't say the same for you, could we? So do you really want me to expound on that, Asperger's boy, or are we going to let it go?" Judith said sweetly leaning into Aidan and putting a hand on his face.

Aidan turned beet-red but shut up. He was outclassed and he knew it.

At that moment the bell rang; Judith fell in step with Amelie.

Goody.

"Jack was stag at the dance last night," Judith said quietly as they walked toward class. "I'm pretty sure that he wanted to go with you."

Careful.

"Oh. I had to work," she lied. "Plus, I'm not Jack's type."

"That's what you think? Really?" Judith asked, not smiling. She stopped at the door to English Lit class and turned to look at Amelie with an odd expression.

"You know, Jack's not used to not getting his way," she said softly.

Just at that moment, Jack and Sophie appeared behind her and entered the room together.

"Just remember that," Judith whispered.

What was that about?

Chapter Fifteen

Love and Obsession

As Amelie sat down in her seat, she took out the photo from Hong Kong Disneyland. There he was, although it was not him. And there she was, although it was not her.

At that moment, Mr. Roberts entered the room and clapped his hands to get their attention.

"Although it may seem like it's taken me an absurdly long time to grade these, I finally have your book reports."

Mr. Roberts handed back the papers swiftly.

"Hudson—*Now Sleeps the Crimson Petal*. Well done."

"Sophie—*Lady Susan*. Jack—*Madame Butterfly*. Heidi—*Jane Eyre*, because we couldn't avoid the Brontë sisters altogether."

Amelie noticed a smile forming on Mr. Robert's lips as he handed Ryan's paper back. Ryan, for his part, looked pale and drawn.

"For Mr. Spoon, yes, *The Little Mermaid*. But it seems you misunderstood the assignment. I expected you to actually read the Hans Christian Andersen story, not watch the Disney movie. The endings are quite different, you see. But we will discuss in more detail later."

For a moment Ryan just blinked and then glowered at his desk.

"Amelie—*Gabriel-Ernest*. I was curious as to which Saki short story you would choose, and I must say I was not disappointed," he said, looking at her intently for a moment before moving on.

As he read out the rest of the names in the class with the corresponding assignments, Amelie searched his face and movements for subtle changes, but she saw none. This was clearly only Mr. Roberts.

"Hey, how come some people got whole books and others just got a short story?" Ryan asked suddenly. He obviously wasn't well but that hadn't kept him from being pissed off about being singled out for humiliation.

"I'm not sure why you would find this upsetting, seeing as how you were one of the ones to get a short story, but to answer your question, I gave out very individualized assignments which I hoped would resonate with each of you. But as you watched the movie rather than reading the story, I'm afraid you missed the message of sacrifice and soul-searching that is implicit in *The Little Mermaid*."

"Mermaids aren't real, doesn't count," Ryan muttered, staring at his desk, but Mr. Roberts had turned his back on him and was addressing the class.

"For the rest of you, I read out all these titles aloud for a reason. Any guesses as to why?"

"To embarrass us," Jack said stiffly.

"Of course not, why would reading embarrass you? Any other ideas?"

"Because there's a theme," said Charlotte, Heidi's best friend and secondary class gunner. Apparently, Heidi was too busy reviewing her grade to be on her game.

"Precisely. And do you see a particular concept or theme that is running through all these works?" he asked.

"Love," Heidi said quickly, shooting a less-than-amicable glance at her friend.

"Yesssssss, but that's a bit simplistic. So, to expand it, how many of you found some theme of love in your assignment?"

Everyone in the class raised their hands—everyone except Amelie. She was thinking hard about the story, but it wasn't a love story.

"Ms. McCormick? Not you?"

"Gabriel-Ernest wasn't a love story," she replied, still thinking hard.

"Really? Are you telling me that you didn't find love in that story?" he asked, with a smile. Hudson developed a coughing fit across the room.

"It was more of a horror story," she began then she caught his look.

Found love.

She was suddenly hit with the smell of grass and flowers, sugar and salt. She had a flashing mental image of Clovis lying on the rock, exactly like Gabriel-Ernest. She looked down but not before she saw Mr. Roberts smile and nod.

What the hell was going on here? He wasn't Clovis, for sure, but how could he know? Is he a mind reader?

Amelie quickly visualized a blanket of steel covering her.

The rest of the class was looking at her, but Mr. Roberts walked to the center of the room and turned in a circle, addressing them all.

"Ms. Stack is essentially correct. These are all some form of love story, but there is more depth to it than that. Each of these works deals with a different aspect of love. There is narcissistic love, unrequited love, sexual love, repressed love, sacrificial love, infatuation, and forbidden love, just to name a few."

"I chose the theme of love because you are at the age where you'll begin to have your first experiences with it. Many adults dismiss these early experiences as frivolous or passing, but I'm here to tell you that early love will mark you for life. Therefore, I believe it is worth looking at it in some detail. I assigned the works that I did to send each of you a *particular* message. But the general message I would give is that you must be careful—no, not careful—you must be conscious of the choices you make. Love isn't a thing to be trifled with. It is life changing, and it can be soul crushing."

The class was quiet. Many had taken out their papers, as if searching for meaning in these solid objects.

"Most of these authors do a superb job of demonstrating a particular type of love within the confines of their story, but the best do something more profound. They bring you, the reader, into the story and make you love the characters as well, in a variety of different ways. Some of you will be more open and susceptible to this than others." He turned around in the circle slowly, once, twice, three times.

Amelie suddenly saw books lighting up around her. Turquoise and blue lights spun around him. He was glamouring them. She changed the steel sheets to a full set of armor around herself, allowing herself only small eyeholes to see through. The world narrowed to points.

"Did you not feel proud and protective of the plain, injured but strong Jane when she found out the truth about Mr. Rochester?" Mr. Roberts asked softly, looking at Heidi. Heidi's eyes brimmed with tears as she nodded. He then turned to Charlotte.

"Ms. Ives, I was impressed that you saw the element of love gone wrong in *We Need to Talk About Kevin* and the way love can be perverted by repression."

Charlotte nodded, her eyes suddenly unfocused.

"Jack, in Long's short story, did you resonate with Pinkerton or Cho Cho San?" he continued. "Or did your allegiance change over the course of the book and the past few weeks of your life? Did you find yourself wanting to believe in love, against all odds, like Cho Cho San?"

Jack's face flushed red, and he shot a look at Amelie. She did not like the dark red glow she saw in his eyes. Where the hell was Mr. Roberts going with all this?

She looked down at the paper she had been handed in order to refocus. At the top was a large red A. There was a small note under her grade. It read:

A well-written and insightful analysis but strangely passionless, all things considered.

The last half of the sentence seemed to be in a slightly different handwriting than the first.

Amelie felt her world began to tip sideways yet again. She chewed a small piece of flesh loose from the inside of her cheek, causing blood to leak into her mouth. Its taste was metallic, salty, comforting, and stabilizing. It helped her focus. She turned her eyes back to her teacher. He was looking around the circle at his students. All of them looked shell-shocked. Many were still staring down at their laps.

"Now you know how my class will run," he said curtly. "If you take the time and pay attention, this class could be transformational for you. If not—well, that's your loss."

To her surprise, Amelie saw heads nodding all around. Even the most jaded students were riveted.

"And speaking of loss …" Mr. Roberts said suddenly, opening his arms out to the sides like an actor preparing to take a bow, and turning to the doorway. Mr. Sawyer was standing there tapping his fingers on a notebook. Mr. Roberts looked at him for just a moment before turning his head to Amelie.

"Ms. McCormick, I think our dear vice principal is here to take you away."

#

As Amelie sat on a folding chair in front of Mr. Sawyer's desk, she had a vision of herself as a prisoner awaiting interrogation.

What would it be? Caning? Water boarding? Revelations about his sex life?

She hated being in the presence of this man, even in a large crowd. Spending time with him alone felt like rolling in the energy version of snail slime.

"I'm afraid that Mr. Lawson, our guidance counselor, has been out sick for the past few weeks," Sawyer began. "We got a phone call today from his wife telling us he caught the flu that has been going around and it aggravated a chronic problem. Therefore, he will need a bit more recovery time. Given some of the side effects of this particular flu, this might make his wife happy."

Oh, no. He went there.

Mr. Sawyer leaned back in his swivel chair, smiling.

"As a result, we are short-staffed, and I have taken on the role of guidance counselor until his return," Sawyer said, pushing his chair back from his desk and placing his foot on the top of his knee in a well-known crotch-exposure move.

Amelie tried to look at him impassively but was finding it hard. The sunshine streaming through the window made the hairs of his comb-over look shiny and oily. He smelled of McDonald's coffee, doughnuts and unneeded Pantene conditioner. She suppressed a shudder.

"I understand that you have been accepted by some very prestigious universities: UNC, UVA, UC Berkeley, and Ann Arbor, but you are looking for deferred entry. I also had a letter requesting a personal recommendation for gap year study at Oxford, Princeton, and the Sorbonne. Apparently, you will need recommendations from teachers and staff for those programs."

Amelie groaned inwardly. With the excitement and insanity of her world in the past few months, she had forgotten to get the recommendations for all the gap year study programs.

"Thank you for reminding me, Mr. Sawyer. I'll get those out as soon as possible."

"Yes. It is a bit surprising that you forgot … which brings me to my concern. This is a personal issue, perhaps I should close the door?" he asked, getting up and walking toward the door.

Uh-oh.

"That won't be necessary," she said quickly. "Mr. Scales is in his office, and I know Ms. Hartness is trustworthy."

She said this for Ms. Hartness's benefit, as she was loitering just outside the office door, pretending to arrange magazines in the waiting area. Mr. Sawyer stopped in his tracks and shot her a viperous look.

"Very well," he said, returning to his chair. There was a sheen of perspiration on his upper lip. For just a moment, Amelie saw mental flashes of a red room, and whips—and someone crying.

This guy was even more twisted than she had suspected.

"One of your friends, Jack, came to see me," he began. "He was quite concerned about you."

"Really?" she said with as little inflection as possible.

Mr. Sawyer waited for her to say something, but she remained quiet. At this point, it was unwise to give him anything he could twist. She had way too much experience of the insides of administrative offices, and people with sexual problems, not to know this.

"You have missed, let me see, nine days of school this year due to illness. That's unusually high for you. In the past two years, you hadn't even missed more than two in an entire year. You apparently had the flu in September?"

He stopped and waited, looking at her.

"Yes. I had quite a high fever for a few days," she replied.

"Yes. And then there was the incident with the dog. But you have also had other days here and there."

This wasn't true, but she said nothing. She waited, all her shields in place.

"So," he continued, leaning forward in his chair, folding his hands into a church steeple position and resting them on his lips. "Is everything okay with you?"

"I'm fine," she replied. She stopped but then decided to elaborate to make him feel he was getting somewhere.

"I'm a bit tired from the testing process. I spent a lot of time studying for the SATs."

"Yes. You did admirably on the SATs but that was some time ago, and most of your absences happened more recently. Is there something else going on that you want to talk about?"

"No. I'm probably just a bit run down. I work a lot too, you know," she replied.

"Your friend Jack was particularly concerned that perhaps you were staying out a bit too late with friends," Mr. Sawyer continued. "I know this is none of my business, but I just wouldn't want you doing anything that might jeopardize things at this late stage of your application processes. You will need to be healthy and free of distractions if you want to compete in schools like Oxford or the Sorbonne."

Is this a threat? she thought. *He thinks I'm dating someone, and I should stop, or he'll mess up my applications? And he's drawn Jack into this.*

Amelie was starting to feel hemmed in. This situation was worse than she thought. She was trying to find a verbal exit when Principal Scales stuck his head in the office door.

"Mr. Sawyer, I see you found Amelie. If you're finished with your discussion, I would like to see her for a couple of minutes," he said. His tone was light, but his gaze was not. He and Mr. Sawyer locked eyes.

Finally, Mr. Sawyer nodded tightly.

"Yes, I believe we are done for now. I can speak with Amelie about her university applications later."

Amelie stood up, and Mr. Sawyer stood as well, moving toward her, and extending his hand, as if to shake hands.

He's sick. Don't touch him.

She pretended not to see Mr. Sawyer's extended hand and exited his office, putting Scales between herself and him.

"Oh, not to worry on that account, I will personally handle Amelie's university applications from the school side," Mr. Scales said to Mr. Sawyer in a cheery but firm voice. "These are some very prestigious schools, and therefore deferred acceptance recommendations should come from the principal. I'll get Ms. Hartness to collect whatever information you have, and I will sort that out myself today."

"As you like," said Mr. Sawyer through clenched teeth.

"You have so much additional work on your plate these days, that we really should split the load on transcript and recommendation requests for seniors," Scales said brightly. Mr. Sawyer barely managed a nod.

Mr. Scales then turned to Amelie and ushered her further into the sitting area.

"You may go on to your next class," he said gently. Mr. Sawyer was standing behind him and his face was map of rage.

Amelie left the office quickly, closing the door behind her. Even though she now knew that Mr. Scales was shielding her from this guy, it was apparent that she would have to come up with some sort of strategy for dealing with him if she was going to survive the next few months.

#

Amelie's meeting with Sawyer was awful but mercifully short. She was on the way to the library for study hall when Hudson caught up with her.

"Hey, can I talk you into driving me to Krispy Kreme for some doughnuts?" he asked.

"Absolutely, I need to get off campus," Amelie replied.

"You were in the office … what happened?" he asked.

"Sawyer dragged me into his office to grill me about my dating habits," she whispered.

"Fuck! He isn't allowed to do that shit."

"Well, apparently no one told him."

They had just stepped onto the landing when they were accosted by Heidi Stack.

"Have you seen Charlotte?" she asked. Her face was blotchy and red.

"No," Hudson said.

"She's my ride." Heidi sniffled.

"You okay?" Hudson asked.

Hudson apparently hadn't bothered to re-adopt the persona yet, and Heidi looked up at him startled.

"Yes. I'm fine. But they are sending me home," she snapped.

"Then why are they sending you home?" Hudson asked.

"Because Ryan vomited on me. Now everyone is treating me like I have the plague or something. They didn't even let me turn in my Biology paper that's due. What if I get marks taken off because it's late?"

She was breathing heavily.

"Oh, no one is going to do that to you," Hudson said. "If you were slack, maybe, but not you. Besides, better safe than sorry."

Heidi gave him a sharp look. At first, Amelie had thought that Heidi had been crying, and that might still be the case, but her eyes had another look to them as well. They looked glassy and slightly unfocused. She now turned these eyes to Amelie with a manic level of focus.

"I'm NOT sick. Look at me, do I look sick?" she demanded.

Yes, you do.

"No," Hudson replied, catching Amelie's eye as he did so.

"So they are sending you home just because you were vomited on?" Amelie asked, trying to avoid both Heidi's eyes and the now-obvious rust-colored stain on the front of her sweater.

"No, not just that. Apparently getting a rash is one of the symptoms of some nasty virus that is going around, and Charlotte just had to tell Mr. Roberts that I had a rash. It's so no big deal. It's tiny and it's only on my arm," she said, her voice trembling.

At that moment, Amelie saw Jack appear on the landing behind Heidi. His eyes widened when he caught sight of her and Hudson. He immediately turned and went back into the building.

Shit.

Suddenly, lights began to flash around Amelie, and she felt this strange, strong sensation pulling at her insides, near her navel.

"They're calling it 'dog flu', of all the stupid names," Heidi continued as she pulled her sleeve up to reveal a small rash on her left inner forearm. She shoved her arm up inappropriately close to Amelie's face. So close that she had to pull back and refocus her eyes.

Amelie felt her heart skip a beat.

The rash was in the shape of four long scratches down her arm.

Chapter Sixteen

Stepping Into Judith's Parlour

During the next two weeks, the subject of dog flu came up a lot in the McCormick household, mainly in the form of Opal bitching about it.

"It's a fucking epidemic," she said in some form or another virtually every night. "Just make sure none of you go and git it, as I don't want to deal with that shit at home."

By "that shit" she meant more than just the basic flu symptoms of fever, diarrhea, vomiting, and an unusual rash on the arms. She was referring to some of the behavioral aspects of this particular flu that had the media in an absolute froth. Apparently, this flu caused a "suppression of inhibition" in its initial stages that was comparable to consuming large quantities of alcohol. So during the first twenty-four to forty-eight hours of infection, a person was more likely to be more angry, testy, weepy, and horny.

Amelie was just relieved that no one in her family noticed a similarity between the type of rashes that people were getting on their arms and the scratches she had supposedly gotten from a dog last fall. It was probably just a weird coincidence, but she couldn't help but worry about it a bit. It would be nice to run it past Clovis.

She hadn't really seen Clovis since Disneyland, and it had been twelve days. Still, she wasn't panicked because he had found little ways to let her know he was around. One day she found a few pieces of straw on her desk in English Lit class. On another, a cafeteria worker had handed her chopsticks with which to eat her spaghetti at lunch with a sly smile, a wink, and momentarily black eyes. Norman Iggleston had walked by her in the hall one day singing the chorus of "It's a Small World" in a clear, crisp voice and had sent a pleasurable jolt of energy up her arm by momentarily taking her hand.

All this made Amelie feel like Clovis's eyes were on her throughout the day, and this made her stupidly happy. The thought that he might be somewhere in the crisp wind that kissed her skin as she walked to and from the school building made her feel delicious. For the first few days after her return from Disneyland, she'd found herself subconsciously drawing little hearts in her notebook, until she noticed Sophie eyeballing her in class. At that moment it dawned on her, with mortification, that if Clovis was watching her he could see this too. After that, she tried to keep a closer eye on herself.

This particular morning had started out uneventfully. She had dragged herself out of bed early, thereby escaping any family interaction by being out of the door before they got up. Her morning classes had been surprisingly low-key. Mr. Roberts had been glassy-eyed that morning, saying he had been up late the night before, so he allowed them time to work on their next book assignment. So her day had gone relatively smoothly, until she ran into Judith, Sophie, and Elodie as she was leaving study hall.

"Hey, meet us at Wendy's for lunch," Sophie singsonged. Amelie wanted to say no, but knew she couldn't.

"Sure. But I don't have study hall after lunch like you guys, so I'll have to leave early."

"No problem," Sophie said. Elodie was not looking at her. Her eyes were downcast, and her face looked swollen and blotchy.

"Are you okay?" Amelie asked her.

"There's trouble in paradise," Judith snorted. "We can fill you in over lunch. See you there in ten minutes?"

Amelie nodded as she made her way to the car.

"If you make it before us, order me a chili and grab us some seats," Judith called.

Amelie got in her car and sighed. She didn't relish spending an hour listening to the sordid details of Elodie's sex life. But the day had gone well so far, so maybe it wouldn't be so bad.

Wrong.

She had barely made it to Wendy's, purchased food, and grabbed seats when Judith pulled up in her car, followed by Sophie and Elodie—in Jack's car.

Damn.

Jack and Judith came over and sat down on either side of her, as Sophie and Elodie got into the food line. Jack called across the restaurant. "Sophie, get me a double cheeseburger with everything."

Sophie raised her hand in agreement.

"So, Amelie, I wanted to tell you that I have a phone interview with Cambridge next week," Jack said, eyes crawling over her face.

"That's great, Jack," she replied, plastering on a fake smile.

"What's great is having a dad who can buy you into anywhere you want to go," Judith said. Jack gave her a nasty look, but Judith just shrugged.

"Oh, no offense Jack. That's a good thing. I plan to use my dad's long arm of influence to its full extent to get where I want to go. It's just that some of us don't have the money advantage," she said, smiling at Amelie, showing lots of teeth.

"Besides, I need to get Amelie up to speed quickly on the Elodie situation, so I don't have to listen to her repeat it," Judith continued.

"She's going to anyway," Jack said, with his eyes still on Amelie.

"Well, maybe we can get the shortened version if I give Amelie the details now," Judith replied, turning to Amelie.

"The day that Elodie and Carter borrowed Aidan's car, they both got that flu that was going around—and fucked in the car. Oops, I meant had sex. Or made love. Is that better?" Judith said, patting Amelie on the arm.

It felt like being jabbed with a knife.

"Well, ever since she thinks he's been pulling away from her. In the past week, he's barely spoken to her."

"According to her," Jack interrupted. "He might just be busy."

"Maybe," Judith said curtly before continuing, "but she seems to think that now he's managed to fuck her, he's lost interest."

"What do you think?" Amelie asked quickly, as Sophie and Elodie were approaching.

"Elodie's sexual inventiveness might be the only thing that's really interesting about her, so I don't think it's that," Judith said with a little smile.

Elodie and Sophie sat down, next to Judith and in front of Jack.

"Did Judith tell you?" Elodie asked, her voice quavering.

Amelie nodded.

"Elodie, dear, why don't we talk about something else to take your mind off things? For example …" Judith turned her flat green eyes on Amelie.

"Sophie tells us that Amelie might have a boyfriend," Judith began.

"What?" Amelie said, caught off guard.

Jack's eyes got wide for a moment, then narrowed dangerously.

"Sophie says you have been scribbling little hearts on your notebooks. That's not really like you. So who's the guy?"

Sophie was smiling at her in a knowing manner.

Damn you.

"I don't have a boyfriend. I mean, you guys would know if I did," she said, too fast, too defensive.

Slow down. Judith's not going to let this go. Think of something. Can't be anyone we know. Can't be anything they wouldn't believe. No celebrity crushes, they wouldn't buy that. As close to the truth as I can get.

"Okay, maybe not a boyfriend, but a crush. Anyway, Sophie says that you were writing the letter C with lots of hearts around it. Anyone we know?"

Shit shit shit.

She heard Jack made a noise that sounded like a growl. He was holding his burger so tight that ketchup, mustard, and even a few pickles were beginning to get squished out of the back of it.

Elodie's red eyes got wide.

"Carter's name begins with a C," she said in a raw voice.

"Wow. It takes her more than thirty seconds to realize her boyfriend's name begins with a C. No wonder you got shit scores on the SATs," Judith said.

Elodie's eyes filled with tears again. Apparently, Judith had no issue with kicking someone while they were down.

"It's not Carter," Jack growled as he got up and grabbed his tray with such force that a slew of fries flew in all directions.

"Hmmm. Interesting," Judith said, watching him stomp off. Amelie was using this time to frantically try to come up with possible saves.

"Sooooo, Amelie, have you got a crush on Carter? Or, even worse, do you have a mutual crush? I know that would be devastating for Elodie," Judith purred.

"No. I don't have a crush on Carter. That's ridiculous."

They all continued to stare. She was going to have to drop her nice persona a little bit on this one. Show her dark side, but one they would believe.

"Really? Carter? The guy who never does his own homework, and is proud of what he doesn't know? Don't take it badly, Elodie, but he and I would have nothing in common."

Elodie's shoulders relaxed a bit.

"So who's C, then?" asked Sophie.

Judith was watching her intently between bites of chili. She was the only one eating, so Amelie followed suit and took a bite of her burger.

"You guys are just going to make fun of me if I tell you," she said as she chewed.

"I'm sure we will, but would you rather have Elodie thinking you're after her boyfriend? That would be much more uncomfortable," Judith smiled.

Suddenly a thought crashed into Amelie's head like a wave.

117

Fiction. Go with fiction. They'll believe it but they won't get it, and it's not far off the truth.

She wasn't even sure this came from her, but the idea was perfect. She quickly ran through a list in her head and got one almost immediately.

Amelie let out an exaggerated sigh.

She looked over at Elodie, who was looking at her like a puppy waiting for scraps. Then at Judith, who looked like she had eaten all the scraps.

"C stands for Constantine," she said.

"There's no one at the school named Constantine, is there?" Sophie asked.

"Of course not," Judith rolled her eyes. "If you expect us to believe you have a crush on a Roman emperor … I'm not buying it."

"No. It's a character," Amelie said. Judith looked taken aback for a second. "From what?"

"It's a comic book character, okay? He's a DC comic book character. They did a movie about him."

"You have a crush on a comic book character?" Sophie asked, with a look that was a cross of disbelief and dismay.

"It's not the comic book part, it's the character part. I have a crush on that character."

"May I ask why?" Judith said.

Describe Clovis.

"He's mysterious and an antihero. He's wickedly smart. He's ambiguous, a bit like the character of Loki in Norse mythology. Constantine is like him. He's powerful and possibly very old, but no one is sure."

"Oh god. You actually *do* have a crush on a comic book character. Ugh," Judith rolled her eyes in an exaggerated fashion. "Well, I suppose that makes sense, given your total lack of interest in *actual* boys. But you're right, it *is* embarrassing, and pathetic."

Judith cut her eyes in the direction of Sophie, but Sophie wasn't paying attention. She was too busy staring at Jack, who was now outside, standing by his car talking to Aidan. Elodie looked at Amelie with relief and gratitude.

"It's okay if she wants to have a crush on some book person. At least she won't get her heart broken," Elodie said to Judith, but Judith was watching Sophie watch Jack.

"Well, it's been an interesting lunch," Judith said with a smile that would have unnerved an adder. "What have we learned? Let's see. Elodie is no longer a virgin, so if there is a god, he's probably pissed off. Carter really *was* after that one thing after all. Sophie has apparently been unsuccessful at pulling Jack out

118

of his weird obsession with Amelie, while Amelie seems to have a thing for imaginary guys. So much to process, so little time."

Elodie's eyes welled up yet again and Sophie turned crimson.

"You really are a bitch," Sophie spat at Judith, who just smiled. Sophie glared, got up and motioned to Elodie. Amelie felt a burning desire to slap the smile off Judith's face, but that wasn't an option. She settled for collecting her books. She sure as hell didn't want to be left sitting alone with Judith. Aidan came back inside the building while Jack was now pulling out of the parking lot, alone in his car.

"Jack said I should come ask if anyone needs a ride," Aidan muttered. Elodie and Sophie had come with Jack, but he apparently wasn't interested in their company on the way back.

"Oh, you're all planning to abandon me then? Just because I wanted to try to solve all of our problems. What's that movie phrase—'no one can handle the truth'," Judith said, taking another bite of chili.

"I guess that depends on whose version of the truth they're hearing," Aidan said suddenly.

Amelie jerked her head around just in time to see black eyes glaring at Judith, before they changed back to blue. Judith, for her part, looked momentarily shocked. Amelie found herself staring at Aidan openly, searching his face for remaining traces of Clovis. He turned and looked at her with as much puzzlement as his face was capable of registering. Nope, it was just Aidan now.

"Sorry, I need to get to my classes," Amelie said quickly, turning her back on them and moving toward the door.

She didn't trust herself to stay around Aidan if there was a possibility he might be a host for Clovis. She was still having to live down flirting with Carter, so she didn't need a repeat performance. She was in her car and out of the parking lot fast enough to get a few concerned looks from other patrons.

Chapter Seventeen

Foreplay

Amelie kept her head down for the rest of the day, avoiding friends and faculty alike. She was particularly on the lookout for Sawyer. In the beginning, she had discounted Sawyer as a perv, but a fairly harmless one. A few weeks ago, she came to the realization that he might be dangerous. But now, she might need to reclassify him as dangerous and possibly planning something.

Caught up in this train of thought, she had just stepped off the landing when she heard angry voices coming from the front of the auditorium. She picked up her pace. The last thing she wanted was to get involved in some altercation that might give Sawyer a reason to "talk" to her.

"Help!!!"

It was Hudson's voice. Amelie ran toward the front of the auditorium before she had time to think about what she was doing.

There she saw Jack holding Hudson over the railing that separated the front auditorium from the steep, rocky hill leading down to the baseball pitch. If Jack let go, Hudson would fall and be seriously injured.

The big three were present: Jack, Ryan, Aidan. There was also Kevin, one of their occasional minions. Amelie couldn't see Jack's face, but the faces of his friends were filled with that dark sort of glee that bullies have when picking on kids half their size.

"What's up, Jack?" she asked, aiming for casual. He turned to look at her. His face registered such a mix of emotions that it was difficult to watch. Hate. Passion. Insecurity. Fear. Love. Hope. Despair. Sometimes it hurt to know that she could do this to someone. But looking at Hudson's battered face, she decided that this was not one of those times.

"We're just having a talk with your boyfriend," Ryan snickered.

"Hudson's not my boyfriend," Amelie said flatly.

"Hudson Crowe. Crowe begins with a C. Do you think I'm stupid?" Jack snarled.

He pulled Hudson from the rail and threw him to the ground. They had obviously already worked him over, as his face was bleeding and he was breathing hard.

Now they all turned their eyes on her. It was probably a serious mistake to have spoken. She should have gone for help. Jack was at least a half a foot taller than she was and seventy pounds heavier—and he was the smallest in their group. Kevin was the tallest. Ryan the heaviest. But Aidan was the strongest. He was dark haired, fair skinned and missing anything resembling body fat. The muscles simply refused to allow fat in their neighborhood. He was also the only one, besides Jack, not smiling right now. Jack advanced on her menacingly.

"If he isn't your boyfriend, then who is? You seem to be flirting with a lot of people these days … except for me. All the girls think you're a prude, but I know better. I know you just play guys like me."

This sentence made little sense, but it didn't matter. Jack was not in a place where logic and reason spent a lot of time hanging out.

Amelie was backing up. If she could make a break to her left, she could run for the parking lot. Even if she didn't make it to her car, she would be where people leaving might see her. But for now she was surrounded, and they were backing her up the stairs and into the alcove in the auditorium entrance. Too soon she found herself with a wall at her back, and four very athletic assholes in front of her.

"Jack, look, I'm not dating anyone. I don't flirt with anyone. I don't have time for that. I'm trying to earn money for college. I know you guys don't have to worry about money, but some of us do!"

She was pointing out the class difference in the hope of making herself less desirable.

It didn't work.

"I know you have a white trash mom and dad. I know your brother, remember? You should be *honored* that I'm paying attention to you."

"Jack, you should test her out now," Kevin said. "No one's around."

She was in trouble now. She opened her mouth to scream but Jack grabbed her and clamped his hand over her mouth. As the fear gripped her, she struggled to pull away. When this didn't work, she bit Jack's hand. He pushed her back and slapped her across the face. He grabbed her again and covered her mouth. He used his body to pin her to the wall and started shoving his hand under her skirt. She was beginning to hyperventilate. She struggled, but physical force was not going to be enough. Her only hope was to push out at them with something

121

else. She knew that could backfire, but panic was welling up in her—and with panic came memory.

She was eleven. She was in her bedroom. There was a weight on top of her. She could hear her own screams, feel her own tears. In the equally horrible here and now, energy from the base of her spine was winding its way painfully up her organs, just as it had done when she was eleven. She knew that it would burst out in seconds and there would be hell to pay. She wouldn't stop it. She would let it. She hoped it would kill them all. It was about at her throat when suddenly Jack was yanked off her and thrown down the stairs. To her amazement, she saw Aidan advancing on him.

The other guys started forward, but Aidan turned on them and something in his look froze them. Amelie grabbed her books with trembling hands and started edging left. Aidan stopped, turned and locked eyes on her. His normally blue eyes were black.

"Amelie, would you mind waiting for a moment please? I'd like to speak with you. However, Jack and I need to have a little discussion about manners first," he said, as he hopped down the stairs and slammed his foot down in the middle of Jack's chest as he was trying to sit up. The air was audibly forced out of Jack's lungs, and he started gasping for breath. Aidan pulled him up with one hand, as if he were a child and not an athlete pushing two hundred pounds.

"Get your fucking hands off me, you asshole," Jack managed to squeak before Aidan punched him in the face. Jack fell backward. The others moved forward again but stopped when Aidan turned to them. His face was twisted with a red glee. He looked like a hungry lion raising its head from the neck of a gazelle.

Aidan leaned in close to Jack's ear and whispered something. Jack, who had been squirming to get up, suddenly went completely limp. For a moment, he seemed to be straining to breathe and then his body began to jump and twitch. Aidan stood up and turned to the others.

"It's so easy, you know," he said to the other boys, gently, like a lover.

"You're all so fragile. Your little brains are so dependent on just the right chemical mix for you to stay sane. One little change in that, and you end up in a straitjacket. All I have to do is slip a little something in your drink. Prick you with a pin. Hit you hard enough in just the right place. That's all it takes."

Aidan walked up the stairs toward the others. They all backed away from him. He had always been the strongest, and now he was definitely the scariest. Amelie herself was a bit frightened. A bit, but she was also feeling a fierce joy. She enjoyed watching Jack twitch on the ground. She was probably going to hell for feeling this.

"If I hear of any of you threatening Amelie, or her friend, ever again, I will make sure that you spend the rest of your miserable little lives in a padded room. Understand that?" he asked, making eye contact with each of the boys individually.

They all nodded. Jack had not moved from where he was on the ground. Aidan, who was now Clovis, turned to her.

"I should walk you and your friend to your car," he said. "Just in case one of these guys decides he has a death wish."

Amelie nodded. She saw the subterranean gleam in his eyes, and she had no doubt that the threats he just made were not idle ones.

Is he a demon after all? Would I care if he was?

He put his hand on the small of her back, and guided her down the stairs, past the gawking eyes of Ryan and Kevin. They didn't move a muscle. Clovis walked over to Hudson, who was now sitting up and rubbing his throat. He shrank back a bit as they approached.

"Don't worry," Clovis said. "You're fine now. But I think Amelie should drive you home, just to make sure. What do you think?"

Hudson nodded. His already wrinkled gray hoodie was now covered in dust and dirt. Clovis held out his hand to Hudson, but Hudson just shook his head.

"It's okay. I can do it," he said, as he got up. Clovis ushered them toward the upper parking lot, walking between them. Just as they were rounding the corner of the building, they heard talking resume from behind the auditorium. Clovis stopped.

"Go on to the car, I need to have a couple more words with the guys. I'll catch up."

"Okay," Amelie said.

She glanced at Hudson and both of them headed in the direction of her car. She was still out of breath, and her legs felt like overcooked noodles. Whatever energy had been building in her was now doing a little dance through her limbs. She was afraid to touch anything. She was also afraid she might fall down.

"Are you okay?" asked Hudson, rubbing his throat. "I saw what happened. I'm sorry, I shouldn't have let them catch me, but it all happened so fast. They jumped me before I saw them coming."

"I'm okay," Amelie said. "But I think you should have a doctor look at you."

Just at this moment Clovis ran up behind them. He put an arm around Amelie's waist. She leaned into him a little bit. She was grateful for his stability. But, if she was honest, his touch did nothing to calm her nerves. It made her all the more fluttery.

"Amelie's right," Clovis said to Hudson. "The throat is quite sensitive."

Amelie looked over and saw a strange smile on his lips. This was that other side of Clovis. The one she should be scared of, but that she found weirdly seductive.

At her car, Hudson moved quickly to the passenger side. Clovis leaned against her door as Amelie rummaged through her cluttered purse for her keys.

"Good thing you don't have to make a quick escape," he said, raising an eyebrow. She hit him on the arm, and this made him smile a bit.

"Seriously, though," he said, "that wasn't very smart of you."

"What wasn't?"

"Taking on four guys taller than you and almost twice your weight. It's not like you're some sort of ninja warrior, you know," he said sharply.

"I know. But—"

"No, no buts. Even if you were some martial arts expert, fighting isn't the way they show it in movies. People don't conveniently come at you one at a time, allowing you to fight each of them separately. No, they pile on you all at once. The truth is that humans fight ugly. You have no idea exactly how ugly, and I hope you never have to learn."

Amelie knew she was being lectured. Despite this, she had to fight to keep the smile off her face. What the fuck was wrong with her? She almost got raped by a gang of assholes, Hudson was injured, and Clovis was pissed at her … but he was here. He came.

"Would you stop smiling, and take this seriously," Clovis snapped. Shit, she thought she had managed to keep the smile off her face.

"I know. I know. You're right. It was stupid of me to go back there. I should have just gone for help."

"Then why didn't you?"

"I heard Hudson's voice. He, well, he …" Clovis turned to look at Hudson, appearing to really take him in for the first time. He nodded.

"Okay. But promise me that you won't take chances like that anymore. You of all people can't afford to."

She wondered what he meant by "of all people", but nodded. He reached out his hand and tipped her chin up so that she was looking directly into his black eyes. It was Aidan's face, but Aidan's coloring and facial structure was much more like Clovis's own than anyone else he had inhabited so far. And the black eyes were his own. She leaned against her car to keep herself upright. She wondered if he would kiss her.

"Promise me, Psyche. Say it," he said.

"I promise."

"Good," he said as he leaned back a bit.

He brushed a strand of hair off her face. She should have been getting in her car, but she was rooted in place. They just stood there, both beginning to breathe harder. A small cough near the passenger door brought them back to the present.

"Uh, right," Clovis said. "Your friend is right. I can't hold this guy forever, and as it is I will need to recuperate after all that. You probably won't see me here, or there, for a week or so."

This felt like a knife to her heart.

"That means you need to be extra careful, because I won't be able to help you. Okay?"

"Okay."

He stepped back as she opened her car door. She then turned quickly and gave him a quick hug.

"Thanks, Clovis."

He nodded but swallowed hard. That was not all that was hard. Amelie felt giddy.

She got in her car and rolled down the window. Clovis gave her a little wave as she pulled away. In her rearview mirror, she saw Aidan's body slump to the pavement.

She was happy to be in her car. She was happy to be alive. She jumped when Hudson coughed. She had forgotten he was there.

"I live off Reynolda," he said quietly. "Arbor Lane." She nodded and pulled out of the school parking lot.

"Who was that?" Hudson asked. She was happy she was driving, so she didn't have to look at him.

"Aidan Murphy," she replied.

"Nooooo," Hudson said slowly, as if he were speaking to an imbecile. "That was *not* Aidan Murphy. I believe you called him Clovis. So, who is he?"

She said nothing. Hudson waited. She had no idea how to answer that question. She couldn't remember how much she had said and didn't know how much he had heard.

"He's my friend," she said finally.

"Right," Hudson said. The air around him became tense. It was purply blue to her now-open inner eye, but with little streaks of yellow. There was a fight going on inside him somehow.

"It's just that—" Hudson began and then sighed. "Listen, I'm intuitive and I'm not stupid. So I'm nervous that I don't know who or, more disturbingly, *what* Clovis is. But the *most* disturbing thing is that I don't think you do either … and you're in deep."

125

Amelie snapped her head to look at him and almost drove them off the road before Hudson grabbed the wheel. She readjusted and put both hands on the wheel in the ten and two positions. Hudson sighed again.

They drove on in silence. Amelie didn't know what to say. She *didn't* know what Clovis was, and she thought it would give away too much to say she didn't care. He would ask why, and then she would have to explain the reasons she wasn't afraid. Silence was better.

She pulled onto Arbor Lane, a tree-lined road overrun with mansions. She looked again at Hudson, with his dirty jeans and crumpled hoodie. It was easy to forget that his father was a wealthy attorney.

"It's just there," he said pointing to a large Victorian home that was easily worth more than a few million dollars.

"You live *here*?" she asked. She didn't like the sound of amazement in her voice. But Hudson only laughed.

"Yep."

"Well, don't let any of my girlfriends know if you want to hold on to your virginity," she said before catching herself. "Shit, Hudson, I'm so sorry. That sounded really bad."

But he was smiling. It was a sad little smile, but still a smile.

"It's okay. Why do you think I dress like this? Why do you think I took on this persona?" he said. "I don't want assholes to target me. That's why I have always liked you."

Amelie felt a pang of guilt. Before this year, she had never paid too much attention to Hudson.

"It seems like I'm thanking you a lot this year. For saving my life in the fall. For being my friend after that. And for saving me today. When you see your friend, thank him too. I'm very grateful," Hudson said, then stopped for a second.

"You know, I may know some things about your Clovis you don't. He was in me, wasn't he?" he said suddenly. "That day in the library."

Amelie felt her jaw drop as she turned and stared at him. He raised both eyebrows at her.

"Yeah, I thought so," he said softly. "I don't remember what he did or said. I just remember feeling like I had never felt before."

"What do you know then?" Amelie asked.

"I know that having him inside me felt like living in a world on fire. It was like all of my nerve endings had been asleep and they were suddenly waking up all at the same time. Everything was so vivid. It felt like I could live in any moment for a thousand years."

"I also know that he is riveted by you. I couldn't really tell what he feels but I knew that I couldn't keep my eyes off you while he was in me. I don't know what that means, but you certainly have his attention."

Hudson stopped and looked away from her. When he spoke again, he was speaking to his front lawn rather than to her.

"Also, in the few seconds he was in me, I felt better than I have ever felt in my life. I've taken quite a few drugs over the years, but none of them compared to what I felt. It was absolutely amazing," he said softly to the grass outside. Then he turned to face her with the strangest look.

"So I need to ask you a favor. As much as I'm grateful for his help today and your friendship over the past few months,"—she looked back at him and the sadness was back on his face along with a forlorn sort of smile—"can you make me off limits for possession?"

"Don't worry, Hudson. I'll tell him. I don't think he would want to hurt you," she said.

"Really?" Hudson asked with a slow deliberation. "Are you so sure? Personally, I don't know what he would want, or what he would care about. He's not human. What's more, I suspect he never was. I don't know why I think that, but I do."

He never was ... but if he was a ghost?

Hudson looked at Amelie earnestly.

"Think about what that means, Amelie, what it *really* means," he continued. "Ever since I have been at this school, you have been nothing if not cautious. But how cautious can you be with something you can't begin to understand? How can you predict the behavior of something that doesn't operate by human rules? He may not have our same value system. He certainly doesn't have our same experiences. Getting stuck into something like this is a far cry from cautious."

Amelie looked away from him and to the trees lining the road. What he was saying was technically correct, but only technically.

"Maybe I'm tired of being cautious," she said, as much to herself as to him.

"I can understand that. I really can. But can't you just go out and get drunk? Or pick an inappropriate boyfriend? Or, hell, sleep with a teacher? Anything would be less risky than this."

"I can't explain this to you, Hudson. I'm really impressed with what you know and what you can see. But I can't ever explain to you why spending time with Clovis is actually one of my safer risk options."

"You can try," he said, gently putting his hand on her arm. She pulled her arm away. She didn't jerk it, but her movement was a clear statement.

127

"No, I can't. And I can't even explain why I can't explain," she said sharply.

She could feel tears forming in her eyes. She liked this guy. He was kind and sensitive. But she could so easily destroy him with just one little slip up. Now that she knew how very smart and aware he was, she liked him even more. She closed down her emotions, along with her face and her body. She felt him tense in his seat, as he picked up his bags and unbuckled his seatbelt.

"Okay. I know when I have gone too far. But I said all this just because I like you and I want you to stay safe. If you ever need to talk about this with someone, you can talk to me. I won't think you're crazy or weird—or demon-possessed. If you don't want to talk about it, there's always Krispy Kreme."

Amelie smiled at him, and he smiled back.

He pulled open the door and stepped out. Amelie leaned over and looked out the passenger door window.

"Hudson," she called, as he was starting up his walk. He turned and came back to the car. "Thank you for offering to listen. But I think, for right now, it's best for me not to say too much. I like you too and I don't want you to get hurt."

He smiled and gave a little shrug. "I wish I could argue with you about that, but you're probably right. He's shown that he's dangerous … but maybe you are too. I don't know what happens when you add those things together. So be careful, you."

They looked at each other and exchanged a small nod. Amelie rolled up the window on his side, and down on her side of the car.

"Yes, Hudson. We are both dangerous," she said to the wind as she began to drive. There were tears in her eyes, but a smile played on her lips.

Chapter Eighteen

Demonic Therapies

The day following her incident with Jack and his friends, all of Amelie's friends avoided her like the plague, but in strange ways. For the guys, this didn't feel intentional, it almost felt like none of them saw her. Her girlfriends, on the other hand, were intentionally avoiding her. Given the fact that the only conversations they could have at this point were uncomfortable and dangerous ones, she was fine with being ignored. It took another twenty-four hours to find out what was really going on.

When Sophie approached her and asked if she would be willing to put in a good word for Jack with the administration, she was floored. It took a few awkward exchanges for Amelie to discover that while Jack had confessed to having attacked Hudson, no mention had been made of him attacking her. She told Sophie that she would be willing to help out through gritted teeth. Later, after Jack approached her to thank her for her willingness to help, she realized that he really didn't remember anything, and that probably had something to do with Clovis.

As for Clovis, she had heard nothing from him since he saved her. At first, she put this down to him needing to regain his energy but as the days passed, she began to worry.

By the end of the day on Monday, she was becoming manic, which was causing her to ignore her usual shields and actions. She snapped at Sophie in one class. Later, she had to excuse herself from her last class of the day to cry in the toilet just because she happened to see Norman, which reminded her of him singing "It's a Small World" to her.

As she sat there on the toilet seat, sniffling pathetically into a ball of toilet paper, she mentally harangued herself.

You have to pull yourself together. Nothing bad has happened, but something bad will if you don't keep your emotions in check.

When the bell rang, she slunk back into the class. The teacher had left the room, but a folded piece of paper had been left on top of her books.

It read, *Come and find me tonight.*

She felt like the chemical floodgates opened up in her. The strength of her relief made her feel dizzy.

The rest of the day went by in a blur. She went through the motions of doing homework and having dinner with her family with her shields slammed down as hard as she possibly could, but it was all she could do to keep them there. That night, when she got into bed, she was so wired that she was afraid that she wouldn't be able to get to the hallway.

But when she closed her eyes, she immediately felt her consciousness pulled back into her own head through the middle of her forehead and she found herself in the hallway, standing in front of a glowing door made of soft stone. As she reached out to touch it, the whole thing crumbled in her hand like sand, and she was pulled through.

#

Amelie stepped through onto soft, pale sand. She was on a long stretch of beach. Behind her, running down the length of the beach, were cliffs. Rather than stark rock, these cliffs were covered in foliage and soft lavender blossoms. She could smell the sweetness of them as they mixed with the salty, fishy smell of the ocean. The beach itself was sparkling sand but for a few large boulders at the shoreline. Some looked like rough, primitive swords, others like the faces on Rapa Nui. It was still light, but the sun was beginning its descent across the sky, and it was long past noon. The vibrant blue sky was reflected in the wet sand at her feet.

Clovis was sitting close to the cliffs, on a medium-sized rock. She laughed self-consciously and started toward him, but it didn't take many steps to know something was wrong.

He was sitting with his arms wrapped around one of his legs, pulling it to his bare chest, as if for protection. His chin was resting on his knee. She didn't need symbols or colors to know a defensive stance when she saw one. As she came upon him, he raised his head and smiled, but it was not a smile of welcome.

"What's wrong?" she asked.

"Not bothering with social niceties today?" he asked, with a small smile. She felt stung.

130

"I didn't think we needed them."

"I know, that's part of the problem," Clovis said, jaw clenching as he looked away toward the water. "It would be easier if I could just hurt you. If I attacked you, scared you bad enough, you might never look for me again. The problem is that I can't do that, because it might actually injure you in your world."

He rubbed his forehead with one hand.

"Why would you want to hurt me? Why wouldn't you want me to look for you?" Amelie could hear the tremor begin in her voice, and she loathed it.

"What I want or don't want is irrelevant," Clovis replied coldly, still avoiding eye contact.

"What happened?" she asked. "The last time we saw each other it was great. We had fun at Disney, didn't we?"

That sounded lame, even in her own ears. It was also a half-truth—which he caught.

"Actually, the *last* time we saw each other I beat the living shit out of some idiot mortal because he was threatening you. I could have killed him!"

He said the word "you" with a familiarity that sounded like a curse.

"I'm sorry. I told you that I was sorry. I didn't ..." she began stammering, but he just shook his head.

"That's not what matters," he said. "What matters is that I have put both of us at risk. Not once, not twice, but continually. I can't keep doing that. It's dangerous for you and for me."

"Dangerous? You think I'm afraid?" She laughed. It was a real laugh. Sure, it had a tone that could mark the beginnings of hysteria, but it was real.

He leaped from the rock with a rough, animal grace and landed just inches in front of her. *Now* he was making eye contact.

"You aren't afraid of *me*?" he asked, eyes gleaming and spinning. His smile was like jagged glass. "You should be. Haven't you figured out what I am yet? No? I thought you were smart. Well, then let me spell it out for you. I am an incubus."

He pronounced each syllable of the word slowly, with emphasis. Pictures of demons sitting atop sleeping women flashed through her head. Her shock must have registered on her face because he laughed out loud.

"You've heard of us then. Then you know that most consider us demons, and that's probably not far from the truth. We are vain, and we are treacherous. We take advantage of innocents. We seduce people for pleasure. And that's it."

Each word felt like shrapnel digging into her heart. His eyes were locked on hers. She refused to look away and reined in her tears.

"But let me make this crystal clear for you, just in case there is some misunderstanding," he whispered, leaning closer still. "Incubi don't have relationships with humans—we have sex with humans. Only once, then we leave. So whatever schoolgirl notions you might have about me, you need to drop them right now. I'm an incubus. I'm not going to be your knight in shining armor. I'm not going to sacrifice myself for you. And god knows, I'm not 'boyfriend' material. Incubi are the real myth behind vampires, you know. We feed on you when we have sex with you."

"Well then, you should have done it already!" Amelie snapped back. "It's not like we haven't been together enough times, but you've barely even touched me."

He sighed with that cold smile and his breath kissed her face.

"That's what makes me the worst sort of incubus," he whispered, licking his lips. "I have a reputation for dragging out seduction. It's much more fun that way. So, when the human finally gives in to me, they give me everything, willingly. They would die for me. That's why Rose likes me so much. She sees me as a kindred soul. She's a sadistic sensation junkie. So am I."

Amelie took a couple of involuntary steps backward. Clovis stayed where he was, still smiling, but the smile had changed. For a fleeting moment, it was melancholy.

"Now you get it," he said. "I'm a monster."

When Amelie shook her head, Clovis moved quickly toward her again.

"This is what I am," he snarled, no longer smiling. "You need to get that through your pretty little head."

He rapped the top of her head with his knuckles as he spoke.

At that, her control snapped, and she pushed him away from her.

"STOP IT," she screamed. He looked taken aback but nodded and gave a little shrug. Like he had completed a dreaded chore.

"I don't know why you're saying all this," she said, trying to speak in a more rational voice, and standing straighter. "You may be an incubus, or you may be lying. But that doesn't matter. What matters is that I *know* monsters, and *you aren't one*."

"You just see me how you want to see me," he said, now really looking into her eyes. Was that pleading she was seeing?

"Even if you *looked* like a monster, I would know better. Like I said, I know monsters," she said, her voice breaking. Now it was her turn to turn away. She looked at the ocean.

"Real monsters don't look like monsters," she whispered. "They look like teachers and neighbors and friends. They wait where no one can see. They fondle you with their eyes, hungry for a moment alone with you. So you have to make sure you're never alone with another person. You have to plan every minute of your life, every step you take in your day. If not … they have … they have … they were …"

She couldn't keep it in anymore. Her whole lonely, restricted life came crashing down on her. She dropped to her knees in the sand and began to sob into her hands. All she could hear was the sound of her sobs and the surf.

After a time, her sobs subsided, and she realized that Clovis had come to sit next to her on the sand.

"Tell me everything," was all he said, and with his words her memories came flooding back.

Strangely, her pain receded, replaced by a thick numbness. She focused her eyes on the waves cresting. The way the foam gleamed silver in the late afternoon sun made everything seem unreal. Maybe this sense of unreality made it easier to talk about things she wished weren't real.

"I was eleven," she whispered. "It started when I was eleven years old … just after I got my first period. Suddenly everyone started … getting really weird. Homeless people would follow me. People at school, teachers, administrators were suddenly intensely interested in me.

"No, not everyone. Men. I was eleven. I had no figure. I didn't know anything about sex. It wasn't like I'd suddenly morphed into Marilyn Monroe overnight. But strangers would try to brush up against me when I was out with my family at the mall. At the school cafeteria, the servers would grab my hand as they were passing me my food. And whenever someone touched me, they would get the weirdest look on their faces. It's like they disappeared for a moment, like their humanity was gone and what was left was ugly."

Amelie's eyes were closed, but now a flood of faces washed through her brain. She opened her eyes and refocused on the ocean.

"One of my father's beer buddies offered to keep me and my brother for a couple of days so that my parents could have some 'alone time'," she whispered. "He acted like he was doing them a favor but, god, you should have seen the look in his eyes. I was eleven! It was like every pedophile, freak, or man having trouble with his wife within a hundred-mile radius could smell me.

"So, I started refusing to leave my room. My mother had to literally drag me out and beat me to get me to go to school. When I started showing up at school with bruises, it was just another excuse for people to touch me. I was called into principals' offices, counselors' offices, teachers' offices. All of it supposedly because they were concerned, but they weren't. Most were just trying to calculate what they could get away with, how far they could push propriety. My parents still probably wouldn't have done anything if something hadn't happened with my brother."

She stopped. She didn't want to say this, but at the same time, she did. She hadn't spoken of it to anyone since she was eleven, since …

"My brother raped me," she whispered, her own voice sounding far away.

"He came into my room one night, pinned me down and ripped my underwear off. He managed to get inside me a bit, but he didn't fit, and it hurt. He was so out of his mind that he didn't even think to cover my mouth. I started screaming and pushed him off. Then, I … I did something else to him too. I don't know what it was, and I've never done it again, but for about six hours after, he was like a zombie. My mother was frantic about him—HIM. I couldn't stop screaming, and she was worried about him. She was convinced that it was my fault. She called the cops, and they took me and my brother in. Even after the physical examination showed evidence of rape, she blamed me. She said I had provoked it and she wanted me away from my brother. She made up some lie at the hospital about me masturbating in public."

Amelie had been sitting completely still, looking hard at the shining bits of quartz in the sand. The world felt close and unwelcome. She sat back in the sand and pulled her knees up to her chest. Clovis was silent.

"They put me in an institution," she continued. "They diagnosed me as schizophrenic. They … they …" she started to stammer.

The memory was still so clear. The men, the drugs, the memory loss. Waking to find people touching her, fondling her. She reached out again for the numbness and found it still waiting for her, like a friend.

"They gave me electroconvulsive therapy," she whispered to the sea. "Just once, but enough to erase my memory for about a week. No one explained the procedure to me. When I came to my senses, a man was fondling me. I had no idea what was happening. When I think now about what could have happened to me if I'd stayed there longer … well, I don't want to think about it."

She shoved her fists to her forehead and bit the inside of her lip hard. The pain and the taste of the blood helped her focus.

The worst of the story is almost over, she told herself. She took a breath, turned her eyes back to the sea and continued.

"It could have been worse, but for once, I got lucky. One day this woman came in. She wasn't a doctor, but I could tell she was someone with power. She immediately told the staff that I was to be separated from everyone else. She demanded that no one be allowed to be in my room without someone else present. As she said these things, people began running around trying to make her demands happen. Phone calls were made. Doctors came in, took one look at her and signed whatever she put in front of them.

"When a doctor told her that I was receiving ECT, she slapped him. To this day, I don't know who or what she was, really, but I know she wasn't a doctor. I also know she wasn't normal."

Amelie could still remember how beautiful the woman had looked to her. She had looked like paintings of angels, with white-blonde hair, a petite frame and the bluest eyes she had ever seen. And she had radiated power, like Amelie thought an angel would.

"When she came to my room after they moved me, I tried to tell her that I was sorry, that I knew it was my fault … that I would try harder. You know, all the things a petrified little girl would say, but she just held me. She told me that what was happening was *not* my fault, but that it was coming from an energy inside me that I needed to learn to control. Over the next two weeks, she came in to see me every day. She taught me how to recognize my energy surges and to predict when they were coming. She also taught me how to build walls to keep it inside. Looking back, I think she used hypnosis to make it all stick.

"When I was sent home from the hospital, it was with a pile of official documents. The written terms of my medical release stated that I be given my own room in our house, separate and away from the family. There was also a court order that I be put in a different school from my brother. I was given a full scholarship at my current private school without ever applying, which paid my tuition until graduation. *She* did all that. I don't know how she managed to arrange it, but it saved my life. I wish I could thank her. Still, for me, every day is about keeping all this stuff inside me."

Clovis had remained silent through all of this. She was afraid to look at him. She knew he was there, but she was too far down her personal rabbit hole of memories to gauge his reaction at all. She took a deep breath. If she was going to tell it, she was going to tell it all.

"So I have … you know, kept everything inside and bottled up … until you. The times with you have been the only time I've been able to let go, to feel something without having to pay a terrible price for it. You don't seem to be affected by this thing that I do," she whispered, tears now trickling down her cheeks.

"You're the first real friend I have had since I was eleven … and I don't want to lose you."

She didn't know what exactly she was expecting him to say, but what he said was nowhere in the ballpark.

"You can't continue to live this way," he said softly. "Bottling that kind of energy up will poison you."

When she turned to look at him, his eyes were on the ocean. To her shock, she saw that his face was wet like hers, but his jaw was now clenched so tight that the muscles in his neck were standing out.

I bet if he were human, he would be a prime candidate for TMJ pain was her random thought. She let out a little laugh, but he didn't notice.

"What the woman told you was right," he said in a tight voice. "At that age, you were very vulnerable, so you had to learn to keep it inside. But as you get older, you *have* to learn how to let it out. Otherwise, one day you will find that your barriers don't work anymore. You will either end up crazy, dead, or a prostitute. I have seen it thousands of times."

"Thousands of times? You've known people like me?"

He nodded, eyes still on the ocean.

"Why didn't you tell me?" she asked.

"Because I didn't know *for sure* until just now. I suspected, and that's part of the reason that I thought I should leave you alone."

Before she could speak, he turned to face her. His black eyes were soft and warm. His expression was unreadable in intent but tender nonetheless. It was a look she had never seen before. She wasn't sure a human could produce such a look.

He took a deep breath and sighed sharply.

"Okay," he said. "Horribly painful it might have been. And since then, emotionally crippling, but we can fix it. You just need to learn a few things, and you can live a close to normal life."

"I thought you said you didn't want to see me anymore," she whispered. He visibly winced.

"I guessed who you might be, and—well, I thought that my presence might be making things worse, but I was wrong."

As he said this, she saw lights dancing around him. Blue and yellow. Truth and lies.

"I think I can help you," he said quickly. "I'm not a great teacher. Well to be honest, I haven't had much practice, but there are some basics I know. If you can master these, then life won't be so crippling."

"I would love to believe you," she whispered, "but I don't see how. If I don't bank this stuff, I can't see how I can ever get on a bus or walk on the street, let alone go to a class with the same people every day."

"You can, you just need a little knowledge and a bit of tutoring," he replied.

"What knowledge?"

He stood up and began pacing, running his hands through his hair. All of this information was swirling around her head like a tornado. She felt hope, excitement, fear, and the residue of sadness. These emotions fought for position in her throbbing, addled, post-tears brain. As she watched him, another emotion began to introduce itself unbidden. Her eyes were registering his beauty again. He was wearing loose fitting trousers and he was barechested. She had never seen him completely topless before. He was broad of shoulder, thin of waist, and lean.

She realized she was staring when he looked up at her suddenly.

"To start with you need to learn moderation ... but moderation isn't the best way to describe it," he said, misreading her expression as confusion. "Maybe you can think of it as intermittent excess. Rather than trying to hold the needle in the center, you let it swing back and forth to extremes, but quickly, so the average still ends up in the middle. Does that make sense? At least conceptually?" he asked.

Amelie managed a nod.

"Okay, listen carefully," he said, as he crouched down in front of her. "You need to learn to let your energy out in small bursts."

He flicked his hands open and closed in the air to demonstrate.

"This will hit most people for a nanosecond, and they will fall in love for the same amount of time. As long as you don't follow it up, as long as you don't stay in their presence, they'll associate it with someone or something else. You'll need to do this very often. Not as often as breathing, but the same idea. When you feel it build up, you let it out and move on. Eventually, you'll learn how to send out as much as you want, to whomever you want. You can learn to focus it from one person to another. You can not only make people fall in love with you, but with each other. Once you have it under control, it's not so bad. In fact, it can be quite fun. Of course, there will always be certain drawbacks, but your life will be very livable."

He gave her a small smile, meant to be reassuring but she thought but it looked more melancholy than happy. Still, to have this sort of hope. To be able to walk through the world with less fear. The air around her shone with pink and soft blue lights. Hope.

But how would she start learning? All of this made sense in the abstract but the likelihood of screwing up in the beginning was a hundred percent. And the impact of screwing up—well, she couldn't live through that again.

"I can't," she said, voice hitching slightly. "What if I mess up?"

"You *don't* have to worry," he said, kneeling in front of her. "I'll protect you while you're learning. No one will hurt you. I promise you that."

She felt a rush of energy coming from him and she was speechless again—how many times had that happened in the past few minutes?

"How? How can you protect me?" she asked.

A strange smile appeared on his face and his eyes glittered. It harkened back to their animalistic first meeting. Then his countenance lightened again, and he was again the Clovis she had come to know.

"Look, it's going to be okay. I—well, maybe I misunderstood some things. But from now on, it's going to get better. It's just a problem. We'll fix it. At least I can do that," he said. The last sentence was uttered through clenched jaws.

Amelie searched his face, but he quickly sighed and shook his shoulders.

"What I can't do is talk about this anymore right now. I feel like someone is pulling my guts like toffee." He stopped suddenly, and looked around as if noticing his surroundings for the first time.

"It's beautiful here, so let's enjoy it a bit. I, for one, am going to stop blathering and go for a swim."

He got up suddenly and, to her shock and embarrassment, pulled off his trousers. He ran for the waves and dove in. She had always thought that naked boys looked vulnerable and awkward, but not this boy. He was lean, but muscular and graceful, and he was completely lacking in self-consciousness, or the bravado often used to cover it. Maybe this was just because he was ridiculously beautiful. As he dove into the waves, she saw his muscles moving and flexing under his pale skin.

"Come on," he yelled as he pushed his wet hair from his face. "It's great."

She realized she had been staring. She quickly stood up and pulled off the dress she was wearing, standing in some sort of linen undergarment.

She ran for the water.

The sun was low on the horizon and the foam that kissed her skin looked lavender-pink in the light. He was right. The water was shockingly cold at first, but after a moment her body adjusted, and it felt glorious on her skin.

They spent their next hours playing, laughing, and talking about the perfectly inconsequential things that one talks about when one is playing and laughing. Stupid and silly things. Nothing serious. Nothing more emotionally treacherous than body surfing and water fights. Amelie felt her heart relax. The sense of impending doom and the dark memories were washed away by water and laughter.

"What about you and Hudson?" Clovis asked out of nowhere.

"What do you mean?" she asked.

138

"You said you don't have friends. But he seems to be something to you," he replied, as he studied a shell and then threw it across the waves with a sharp flick of his elbow.

"He's as close to a friend as I have ever had, I guess. Well, closest to a normal friend."

Clovis raised his eyebrows.

"I'm not normal?"

"You know what I mean. For some reason he seems less affected by me than most. I still have to be on guard but not as much. I've wondered if he's gay."

Clovis laughed.

"He's not, he's just less physical. That's part of his nature."

"In what way?"

"He's a shade."

"What's a shade?"

"A shade is someone who is part-ghost, so he's less physical by one-fourth at least," he said but stopped suddenly. He reached out for her hand, but his hand went right through her.

"Ah, it's time then," he said, his voice soft.

"Okay, before you go, look for me this week. I'll be around, I promise. Try what I told you. Think of it as a laser, but don't aim it at anyone you will be around very often. Pick a lower classmate, or, even better, a stranger in a store. Do it fast, and don't let the person see you if possible. Don't worry, I'll be there if things go wrong."

He was beginning to look thin, and she was feeling pressure in her head to hold the vision here. He did the little wave that he did whenever she was leaving. The one that she sensed would one day have the power to break her heart.

#

She came back to her room and her bed with a full brain and bladder. Dawn was a good hour away, but the birds were singing and the sky was beginning to lighten. She got up and made her way to the bathroom at the top of the stairs. She took care of the necessary bodily functions, and then threw up, but gently, if that was possible.

Once she had finished, she caught a blurry glimpse of herself in the mirror. Her hair looked wilder than usual, even for the morning. She reached up to touch it, and it was stiff. A thought entered her brain, and she took a strand of hair in her mouth. Salt. She tasted salt, and the grit of sand. Her heart began to

139

beat harder with excitement. This was yet more physical proof of the reality of her nighttime visits, not that she needed more proof.

She went back to her bed and lay there, reliving her interactions with Clovis. Her emotions were spinning in all directions. She was confused about what all this meant for whatever relationship they had. But she was happy that he had, in a weird way, acknowledged that they did have a relationship. He was friends with her. Even if what she felt was much more than that, being his friend was something rather than nothing.

She was also excited about what he told her about controlling her curse. If what he said was true, it could change her life completely. She rolled over on her bed and looked out the window. She could see light creeping up from the horizon.

She decided not to get a shower. She wanted to keep the salt and the sea with her for as long as she could. She decided that she would grab her food early and then spend some time in her car at school before everyone got there. So she dressed quickly and headed downstairs. She was just grabbing a breakfast bar and a soft drink when she heard her brother yawning. She moved quickly toward the front door, hoping to avoid him but her timing was off and instead she collided with him as he stumbled out of his room. He took one look at her, and grinned.

"I'm glad to see you loosening up a bit, little sis." He smirked. She was puzzled. What the hell was he talking about now? She raised her shoulders questioningly.

"Oh, come on," he smiled, taking a piece of her hair in his hands.

"I spent most of high school cutting class. And I know the look of a girl who spent the day lying in the sand by the lake rather than being cooped up in classes."

He saw it too. Her brother, her lowbrow, junk-food-obsessed brother saw this.

"Just a bit of advice," he said quietly. "Wash your hair before you go to bed. That way, Mom and Dad won't notice anything in the morning and they won't question."

He winked and it was the first time she didn't feel nausea at such a wink. Instead, she smiled at him. A real smile. Maybe the first one she had ever given him. She just couldn't help it.

"Thanks. I'll remember that," she said. She turned and left quickly but not before seeing a look of grateful pleasure on her brother's normally calculated facade. Perhaps she wasn't the only one keeping up shields.

Chapter Nineteen

Victims Aplenty at the Food Court

It was 8:30 a.m. on Saturday morning and Amelie sat curled up in a stuffed chair in her local library with a few books in front of her. But, for the moment, she was engrossed in her phone, searching the net. Of course, she could have done this bit at home, but ... her family.

She could also have gone to a bookstore or coffee shop, but Amelie liked her local library for the reason that she liked most libraries—they were often empty. She had a revulsion to places where large groups of people congregated. There was an inherent risk for her in such places but this library, like most small, local libraries, was still a safe haven from the crowd. This library had the added benefit of opening at 8 a.m. on Saturdays. Today there was only the seventy-year-old librarian sitting behind a round desk, and a girl who looked to be high school age walking up and down between the bookshelves. That was it, so she could relax her shields just a fraction.

She had started out her research into Clovis by looking up a couple of books. She looked up "incubus", wrote down the first few titles she found, located them and then deposited them on the table in front of her. After doing this, she began methodically looking up the basics on her phone. She started with a dictionary.

The dictionary definition of incubus was:

INCUBUS

1: an evil spirit that lies on persons in their sleep; especially one that has sexual intercourse with women while they are sleeping

2: nightmare

This was roughly what she had thought, and not very encouraging. That being said, it hardly described what had transpired between her and Clovis. On the other hand, this definition wasn't that far off what he had explicitly told her the last time they met.

Next, she turned to the *Encyclopedia Britannica*:

An incubus is a demon in male form that seeks to have sexual intercourse with sleeping women. In medieval Europe, union with an incubus was supposed by some to result in the birth of witches, demons, and deformed human offspring. The legendary magician Merlin was said to have been fathered by an incubus.

They hadn't had anything close to intercourse. The Merlin thing was interesting and made the top of her head tingle in a weird way. She shook it off and broadened her search.

After looking on various sites she realized that there was surprisingly little detailed information about incubi. For vampires, zombies, and werewolves there was a plethora of detailed mythology. Incubi, on the other hand, seemed to be lumped into a couple of categories with sparse information. The Church believed incubi to be angels who fell from grace due to their desire for human women. The Church also said that a person could identify an incubus because they had a penis that was abnormally large, made of steel or forked. Well, she had seen him naked, and while he seemed to have nothing to be ashamed of in that department, nothing she saw looked abnormal.

There were also more esoteric websites where people claimed to have had a sexual relationship with an incubus. These tended to fall into one of two categories. The first was the incubus as a demon lover, who were guilty of attacks and rapes. Many said that the incubus had fed off them and that they had been drained to the point of becoming sick. This part made Amelie uncomfortable. More than once she had been sick after being with Clovis.

But not every time, she told herself.

The second category was the "incubus as perfect lover". These people raved about the benefits of having an incubus lover. More exaggerated sites even offered to summon an incubus for you that would basically be your sex slave.

She was able to relate almost none of this to her experience, so she found herself skeptical.

She leaned back and closed her eyes for a moment. Could Clovis fit any of these descriptions? Could he be something evil? He clearly thought of himself as less than moral but with her, he had been nothing but kind, most of the time. He had acted like a friend. She felt herself set her jaw. Evil or not, he was her friend, so she would be his. Besides, she had been called evil before, too.

Amelie felt someone walk up. She opened her eyes to see that the old librarian was looking at the book she just put back on the table.

"That's a bit antiquated, isn't it?" he said. "Finding anything interesting?"

She looked into black eyes as he sat down next to her.

"Kind of scary stuff, no?"

"I guess so," she replied. "But it seems to be either all good or all bad. I don't believe anything is all good or all bad."

The old man with Clovis's eyes smiled at her. "That's very reasonable of you. Are you sure you're only seventeen?"

She wasn't sure if he was joking or not, so she just rolled her eyes at him. She wanted to keep things light after the other day.

"Is there somewhere really public that you can go in about an hour?" he asked.

"I could go to the mall," she said. "But why? I usually try to avoid 'really public'."

"Because I promised to help you and I'm going to," he replied. "I've been watching you this week and waiting for you to try out what we spoke of the other day, but you haven't."

"I've been scared," she replied.

"I know," he said with a smile. "So I'm going to lead you through it. Meet me at the mall in an hour."

And with that, he was gone. There was none of the extended banter of their previous meetings, and she was sad for it. Yet, if he could actually help her, she would be in his debt forever.

She realized that the librarian was still sitting next to her. He looked at her strangely.

"Thank you for explaining," she said to him, as she got up. He nodded in a confused way. She felt a pang of guilt about making this man question himself. At that age, he probably feared memory loss and dementia. She hoped his confusion would pass quickly and that, by the afternoon, he would have forgotten her.

She picked up her bags and purse and quickly left the library, not looking back.

#

Amelie was more than a little agitated by the time she got to the mall and found a parking space. By the time she actually got to the entrance, her heart was beating fast. She was nervous about what she was doing here. She was afraid that Clovis was going to suggest that she drop her shields. She had too much history of horror to even consider that. She was alone, what if it got out of control? That had happened before, even with her trying to control it. But just letting it go? What would that bring?

143

And let's not forget that I'm trusting this to a creature who has called himself a monster.

Stop being a coward. You're just going into the mall. Nothing has to happen, she told herself as she stood, seemingly stuck, at the Macy's entrance.

Amelie took a deep breath and forced herself to walk through the door. The air in the store was hot and dry on her face, in contrast to the cool, wet air outside. She stopped just inside the door, taking off her coat and folding it over her arm. A very large African American security guard eyed her for just a moment before looking off into space with a bored expression.

She wandered over toward a display of spring dresses and began looking through the racks. Clovis had said he would help her, but there were so many things that could go wrong. Just as she was about to give up, someone tapped her on the shoulder.

She turned quickly to look into the face of the security guard, the bored expression was gone. He was smiling at her softly with black, whirling eyes.

"Psyche," he said. She sighed. Her feelings of terror began to ebb away.

"You're here," she whispered, then winced at how that must have sounded.

"Of course, I promised I would help, didn't I?" he said. "Let's get started. I don't have unlimited energy for this sort of thing, so let's not waste it."

"What do I do?" she asked, taking a shaky breath.

"We are going to practice what I told you about," he said. "I will lead you to the people you should practice on, so we can be sure that you don't run into a freak or someone who is particularly susceptible. Then I will say something to you from that person. After that, you will breathe out and let some energy out toward the person I have spoken from. When you breathe back in, close the energy off, like you're turning off a faucet. That's the basics, but we can adjust as we go along."

"If I let it go at someone you're in, doesn't that mean it will hit you?" she asked.

"Your gift doesn't work on me," he replied.

She had suspected it, but hearing it said out loud brought a surge of happiness. Whatever was between them, whatever friendship they had, it had nothing to do with all of that.

"So you'll tell me who. And then I will let it out. Then what?" she asked.

"You walk away. Don't run. Don't do anything to draw attention to yourself. Just walk. And try not to blast the person. Just let out a little, with your breath. I will control the person and if there's too much impact, I'll redirect it."

"Okay," she said but she could hear a tremble in her own voice. He touched her arm slightly.

"This will work. It's a skill you'll need in order to survive your life. You just need a little practice. I promise. I *will* help you make this right," he said.

"Okay."

"Baby steps. Let's start now. Let it out at me. I have control of him so nothing will happen. I can help you get a feel for the intensity of the stream you need to produce before we move on."

"Okay," she said, but she still did nothing.

"Go on. It's okay. I can take it. Just let it out."

She closed her eyes … and then did what he said. She let a breath out and imagined a tiny crack in her shields with the energy flowing through it and toward Clovis. When she breathed back in, she closed it. Then she opened her eyes. Clovis was smiling at her.

"Good. Very controlled. But how do you feel? Do you feel any different?" he asked.

She took a few breaths and did a little self-scan. "No. Not really."

"That's what I thought. I barely felt anything. You need to let out more. Try again. Try to overdo it. We can tone it down from there, but you aren't used to letting go."

"I don't really know how to do that voluntarily," she said.

"Think of a moment when your guards weren't up. Go with that feeling and let it out. Try again."

Amelie closed her eyes. When had she felt free? She had felt free when she was with him. She thought of the time they were in Disneyland. She thought of how she felt at the restaurant, with her leg up against his, trying to use chopsticks. She hadn't even thought about her energy in that moment.

With this in her mind, she let out her breath and let her shields down. She felt them drop so hard she almost heard a metallic clank. When she breathed back in, she pulled them up, but it was hard. It took two breaths to get them all the way back up. Then she opened her eyes. Clovis's eyes were wide.

"Yeah, that was letting it out all right. Way too much, that one, unless you want a lifelong stalker. Still, it's a good start. How do you feel?"

To her surprise, Amelie found herself smiling in return. Really smiling. She should have found his statements concerning but somehow, she didn't.

"I feel lighter," she said, and laughed. It was a different laugh from her normal one. This laugh had no dark undertone. "I almost feel like someone gave me a happy drug."

"Not surprising really," Clovis said. "The release triggers endorphins and dopamine. So you *are* on happy drugs, but you can't let that make you sloppy or lazy. Try again. Think about half as much."

Amelie closed her eyes. Rather than visualizing her shields lifting, this time she tried making a door. She imagined a swinging door at a beach house. When she breathed out, she blew the door open gently with the energy, like it was a breeze. When she breathed back it closed, like a screen door flapping in the wind.

She opened her eyes and Clovis was smiling. "Good. Surprisingly good. Try it again."

They tried again three or four more times, and with each attempt she felt things become steadier. The door she visualized was more real, more under her control. After her fifth attempt, another security officer wandered by and gave them a questioning look.

"Okay, I need to vacate this guy now. You walk away first. He's going to get the effects of this, but I will direct it somewhere else, not at you. And I will make sure it's something that won't hurt him much."

"How would you do that?"

"I can focus it on a thing, and not a person. Like popcorn. I can make him obsessed with popcorn."

Amelie laughed out loud.

"Go on now. I'll see you inside the mall in a few minutes."

Amelie told her body to turn and leave, but it refused. She had never had to intentionally walk away from Clovis before. Usually, they were pulled apart by reality or exhaustion, or one of them disappeared. He reached out, put his hands on her shoulders and turned her around to face away from him. He then whispered in her ear.

"Give me five minutes, and then I will find you, I promise. Don't try anything until I'm there."

Amelie nodded, not looking back. She made her way through the rows of women's fashion. She felt giddy. What she had just done had been amazing. She hadn't even known that she could pull it in and out like that. For years, it had been about keeping it inside. The times it had escaped, it was accidental and uncontrolled. This felt different. She felt different. She felt better than she had in years. Her shields, although still in place, felt softer, more pliable and easier to manage. They didn't feel in danger of cracking.

She walked out of Macy's and toward the food court, where she ordered a small Coke at Chick-fil-A. She was expecting the gawky adolescent guy at the register to morph into Clovis, but he didn't. She took the Coke and sat down at one of the generic plastic tables set out in the center of a small convention of other plastic tables.

There were only a few people around her. It was 11 a.m., so the mall itself was still fairly quiet, the food court even more so. The lunch rush wouldn't start until 11:30 or later. Right now, there was an older woman sitting a few tables away from her. A couple of people, who looked like store employees, were standing at the Starbucks. There was also an older man who seemed to have mall janitorial duties, who was arranging chairs and picking up whatever scraps of garbage could be present at this time of the morning.

She had only been sitting for a couple of minutes when the janitor came down to sit next to her. His eyes were black. He smiled.

"Okay, now let's practice it a little bit," he said to her. "You go over to the guy you were just talking to at the Chick-fil-A. Ask for another Coke. As you're leaving, zap him quick and walk away immediately. Go to the Ralph Lauren store. I won't possess him, but I'll stay to make sure that nothing bad happens. Then I will find you wherever you are, and let you know how it went."

Amelie nodded and Clovis walked away.

She went back up to the Chick-fil-A window. The guy at the register smiled at her. He was red-haired, tall, painfully skinny and had both acne *and* glasses. Amelie definitely felt sorry for him, but she didn't feel afraid of him, which was a good start.

"Can I get another Coke?" she asked.

"You finished the other one already?" he asked, as he filled up a cup for her.

"Yeah. I don't drink coffee, so this is how I get my caffeine," she responded. "Do I owe you anything?"

"No, it's cool. Free refills," he said, handing her the drink. Amelie turned to walk away, and then turned back to him.

"Thanks," she said as she exhaled and let go. She saw his eyes widen, then she turned and walked away, inhaling and shutting down as she went. She heard the boy start to cough a bit, then a mother walked over with her stroller and grabbed his attention.

Amelie felt even better. She felt a little tired but also loose and relaxed. She couldn't remember the last time she felt this relaxed—well, not in her "real" world, anyway. As she walked around the balcony overlooking a makeshift gazebo and play area on the first floor, she moved in sync to the music being piped over the mall's speakers. She looked back at the food court, but the boy at Chick-fil-A had resumed his chicken-related duties. The janitor was now seated at a table, enjoying a coffee. No one was staring at her. No one was running after her because she "forgot" something, or "left this at the counter". Everything looked just—normal. Maybe all of this was what real life was supposed to feel like. Well, all of it except for the waiting-for-an-incubus part.

She threw away her drink and walked into the Ralph Lauren store, where she saw no one at first. These were not her type of clothes. It was an outlet store but still too expensive for her to afford, so it made her uncomfortable. For that reason, she had never once stepped foot in here. Now that she had, she didn't feel anymore comfortable. Everywhere she looked she saw cashmere. Cashmere sweaters, vests, scarves, gloves—even coats. She didn't even know they made coats out of cashmere.

A man stepped out from behind her. He must have been stocking the shelves on the near wall.

"Can I help you?" he asked in a clipped voice. This man was young, handsome, well dressed, and totally underwhelmed by Amelie's presence in his shop.

"No, I'm just looking," she said, as she self-consciously began flipping through the spring collection dresses.

"Um-hmmm," he said, turning back to his work.

Just at that moment, another employee appeared from behind the register. He, too, was meticulous-looking, with perfect, blond hair that could only have retained its shape with lots of gel. This guy walked straight over to her.

"Hi there," he said, smiling. The other employee looked at him questioningly, but Blondie just smiled and waved him off.

"Are you back to take another look at that dress from yesterday?" he asked, leading her to the back of the store. "Oh, here it is," he said, holding out a red silk floor-length dress. Amelie was about to start sputtering when he turned to her.

"Excellent. Really well done with the boy back there. I did have to redirect a little bit, but your intensity level was dead on," Clovis said. Amelie relaxed.

"I feel so weird. Just ... I don't know ... weird," she said.

"Good weird?" he asked.

"Really good weird." She smiled. "Like ... like ..."

"Like you aren't about to explode all the time?"

"Yeah, a bit like that, but more. My shields, my walls. They feel softer but stronger somehow. Does that make sense?"

"Of course. To survive you need to be flexible. If you get rigid, you die. That's true for all of us," he said with a shrug.

"Listen, there are a couple of tips I should give you," he continued. "It's better to do this when there is at least one other person around. That way the target can get confused about where the energy is coming from. In fact, it's better if you don't even talk to your target. And think of it as a laser, not a big wash of energy. Aim for one person and move out of the way. But make sure you aim at just the one, and don't get both of them."

148

"Why not?" she asked.

"Orgies are usually frowned upon in public places," he said. "And I don't want to get pulled into that."

It took her a second to get his inference, if not his exact meaning, and she blushed.

"I'm going to leave now. You should walk out slowly. If you see the sales guys start to talk to each other on the way out, then laser at the one and leave quickly. Can you do that?"

"Yes," she said. "I can do that." She realized with shock that she actually believed this.

Clovis smiled at her, and then the sales associate was back. He looked at her with confusion and then at the red dress he was holding and dismissively put it back on the rack before walking toward the front of the store.

As she walked out of the shop, she saw the two sales clerks chatting at the register. She exhaled and shot a fast laser of energy at the blond boy. She actually heard him gasp. When she looked back, he had his hand over his heart. But he wasn't looking at her. He was staring at his coworker. Ouch.

As she stepped out of the store, she felt that giddy rush hit her again, and clapped her hands.

Oh my god, she thought, *could it really be this easy? Could I have been doing this all these years?*

"A little excited, are we, Psyche?" said a boy as he approached her outside the store. He was dressed in loose jeans and a hoodie. He looked about her age.

"I'm fine. I feel great. It was so easy," she said to him as they were walking. "I can't believe how easy."

"Whoa. That's the dopamine talking," Clovis said. "It's not that easy, and you're far from a master yet. Those two guys back there are probably going to have an ill-fated love affair. That one was a bit too hard. But you're doing really well," he continued quickly. He must have seen some of the disappointment she felt at his words. She wasn't quite sure why she felt disappointed. What he said made sense, and yet she still felt a bit hurt. She was being stupid.

"Look. You *will* be able to do this. Just don't get cocky. You can play and take some chances because I'm here to cover any mistakes, but don't get full of yourself. I'd rather not have to defend you in a fight against some glamoured asshole."

"I know. I'm just happy. I never thought that I could feel like this." She realized what she was saying had double meaning, just as it was coming out of her mouth, but he didn't seem to notice. Then his last sentence registered with her, and she felt herself blushing again.

"Okay. Let's practice more while I still have energy to do this," he said.

During the next couple of hours Clovis taught her techniques to release, disperse, and redirect. He would give her a tip and then she would practice on three or four people. By late afternoon, when it was actually beginning to come fairly easily to her, Clovis asked her to meet him outside.

She went out of the main entrance to the mall, where a businessman walked up to her and winked.

"It's been a good day, right?" he asked. "You've done a great job. But now, I need to go and recover from all this."

"What do you mean 'recover'? Does this hurt you?" she asked, feeling concern creep into her chest. He had made several references to how he wouldn't be able to do this for long, and she hadn't even registered it.

"No. It doesn't hurt me, but it drains me a lot. It's really very hard to control someone completely, even if they are willing and it is for a short time. To do it if the host is not doing it voluntarily is—well, it would be impossible for most incubi."

Amelie felt guilt hot in her chest.

"I'm so sorry," she said. "I should have asked about it earlier when you said that you wouldn't be able to do it long. I guess I kind of suck as a friend. I'm not used to having a real friend."

"So, you still want to be my friend after what happened the last time we met? And after all the stuff you just read?" he asked, giving her a look she couldn't read.

"Yes," she said softly. She would have elaborated but she didn't trust her voice not to tremble.

"Good. I'm happy about that," he said, smiling, then he sighed. "But I'm also tired, so I need to go. Two things before I do. First, I think you're pretty safe to experiment a bit on your own. Do it more gently if I'm not around. Make sure you have an escape route and plan. Try not to do it at school. You should be able to find me in a few nights and we can talk about it more. Second, when I leave, I'm going to go through you, for just a second. It might help you recognize me in other situations, just in case you're ever in doubt. When we see each other again, you'll have to tell me what you felt. Whew. Okay. Gotta go."

H turned quickly and walked back toward the mall entrance. Once at the doors he turned, smiled, and waved.

She had just a second to see the businessman stop and put his hands to his forehead, before she was hit with something. It felt like a warm wind swirling around her body. It smelled like the ozone in the air when a storm was coming. She closed her eyes, hoping to see him. Instead, she felt him. Her brain was suddenly filled with a complex mixture of so many emotions and thoughts that she couldn't grab on to any of them. Fragments of feeling and abstract concepts whirled through her mind like leaves spinning in the air. She saw and felt a warm golden disk that burst upon her like rain. Her chest felt full to the point of exploding. This feeling spread out from her chest into her arms and legs. The center of her forehead began to tingle, and her eyes began to water. It felt like they were rolling up back in her head. So this was Clovis. He felt alien, completely alien, to any creature she had ever felt. He also felt wonderful. He felt like bliss. And then he was gone.

She opened her eyes and found, to her surprise, that the world had not changed. The sky was not pink. There were no new planets in the sky. The mall was still there, and so was the parking lot. A woman with two young kids walked by her and smiled. They apparently couldn't see the big TILT sign over her head. For a second, she felt like she might be dying—but what a way to go.

As she walked gingerly toward her car, not trusting her steps to be solid, she found herself so happy that she was crying.

Chapter Twenty

In the Hot Summer

The last week of Amelie's life had been different from any week since she had turned eleven.

On her return to school Monday, Amelie had tentatively tried sending out her energy at people around her. Each time she had waited until her target was talking to someone else and had aimed the energy in a short, direct blast. Each time, she hadn't been noticed, and the effect had been between the target and the person they were speaking with. There seemed to be no association with her, and no long-lasting effect on those she was targeting. But the impact of this on Amelie had been extraordinary. The energy that had always been straining to escape was now being released. Her shields, once so difficult to maintain and so easily shattered, were now flexible and firm. She found herself able to relax a bit at school for the first time ever. She was shocked by how easy it was to do this, and how different she felt.

Could something so simple completely change her life? Was Clovis right about that?

She wanted to wait until Friday night to find Clovis in the hallway, so that she would have the weekend to recover. Having to plan her life around the fact that she would be ill after seeing him probably didn't sound very healthy. Then again, how much different was it from people who went out on dates on Friday nights and got plastered? They vomited and slept too, just in a different order.

By the time Friday evening rolled around, Amelie could barely wait to get to bed. But rather than going up early, she made herself slow down, eat her dinner at a normal speed and clean up as she normally would. Her mother had been giving her very strange looks ever since the outbreak of the dog flu and had made several references to unwanted pregnancies among young people. To-night, Opal was unusually quiet, fixing Amelie with a stare that was uncharacteristically probing as she ate.

"Do you want me to run a load of laundry?" Amelie asked, as she finished cleaning up the table. It took a superhuman act of will to offer this. She didn't want to waste time collecting her brother and father's skid-marked underwear or her mother's stinky bra.

Opal gave her that strange look again before shrugging. "No. I figure the boys can look after themselves tonight. I'm a bit tired and goin' to bed early. Let them figure out the machine."

Amelie was shocked but simply nodded and went to her room.

She tried to read for another hour to calm herself and wait for the others to settle into their schedule. After that, she closed her eyes and was immediately pulled away.

#

Once in the hallway she found herself in front of a glowing white door flanked on either side by ornate golden light fixtures. In the center of the door was a large brass ring for knocking. The formality of this was offset by the screen door which had an iron push handle. Amelie reached out and had barely laid her fingers on the handle when she felt the familiar tug and a momentary blindness.

When her sight returned, she was standing in blazing sunlight, on a dirt path next to a glinting river. The banks of the river were a mixture of sandy dirt and dried mud. The sky above her was pale blue and filled with high, wispy clouds. Spanish moss dripped from the trees and the air was hazy with wet heat. The atmosphere was that contradictory Southern mix of boundless life and endless decay.

Amelie started down the dirt path, picking a direction at random. At a bend in the path, she came upon an old wooden bridge, which crossed a stream winding its way toward the river. Across the bridge was a small country fair. Not like the modern ones with the amusement rides, flashing lights, and commercialization. Instead, it consisted of small booths selling food, flower and vegetable competitions, as well as a few auctions. A fiddle band was playing folk music and a few people were dancing on the grass.

Crossing the bridge, Amelie spotted Clovis almost immediately. He was standing in the crowd watching the dancers. His back was to her, but she would know him anywhere. He had on a straw hat, a white, short-sleeved shirt, and tan trousers. His messy hair was sticking out from under the hat like it resented being confined. His shirt was untucked in the back, and he was wearing suspenders, like most of the other men in the crowd.

She slowed her step slightly. She had been so excited to see him, but now she felt shy.

Don't be stupid, she told herself. As she approached, he turned and smiled at her. She smiled back and, before she could talk herself out of it, gave him a hug.

This was normal for friends, right?

He tensed for a second, but then he put his arms around her waist and hugged her tightly, putting his face in her hair. Then, just as quickly, he pulled away.

"Someone's happy," he said with a smile, but his jaw was tight.

"It worked," she said. "I worked on it all week and it worked perfect."

"I know, I saw," Clovis replied.

"This was the easiest week I have had in years—" Amelie began, but Clovis cut her off.

"Let's take a walk," he said.

"So what do you think of Mississippi?" he asked as they made their way through old men buying pie and young children playing tag.

"Mississippi? That makes sense. Actually, it feels very homey to me." Amelie laughed. "Maybe I lived in Mississippi in some past life or something."

Clovis looked at her sharply, then turned and started walking in the direction of the bridge. His stride was more rigid than usual.

"Are you okay?" she asked.

"Sure. Why?"

"Are you mad because I hugged you?" she asked. He stopped and turned.

"No, of course not. Why would I be mad about that?" he asked.

"Well, that's when you tensed up," she said as they began walking forward again. Clovis gave her an odd little smile.

"Oh, I'm just worried about how it affects you," he said quietly. "You've done the reading, so you must know that it's dangerous to touch me too much, or for me to touch you too much."

"I saw that. But why is that exactly?" she asked.

They stopped at the bridge and Clovis leaned against the railing, looking out over the river.

"Because I drain your energy when I touch you. I'm glad you brought it up, because I haven't had the guts to ask you if I'm making you sick when you get back. Before I was afraid if I found that out, then maybe it would mean I should go. But it's better if I know."

"No, I've been fine," Amelie responded, too quickly.

"Don't lie to me, Ames," he replied, but then smiled. "But don't worry, I've already decided I'm not going to disappear. I'm too selfish for that. I just need to know where we stand on that … so I can figure out a plan."

Amelie sighed.

"Well, sometimes I vomit, but not always. The only time I got really sick was the time that you scratched me."

"That's it?" he asked skeptically.

"Yes. Mostly what's strange is the stuff I bring back. Like I found some straw in my hands after that time that we were at the racetrack. And then, after last time, I had sand in my hair."

Clovis's eyes widened.

A couple stepped onto the bridge. The man was blond with movie-star good looks. The woman was delicately boned wearing a powder blue dress and kitten heels. The man tipped his hat at them. Amelie turned back to Clovis.

"The weirdest time was after Disneyland when I came back with a picture in my notebook. It was the one we took but it wasn't you and me really ... but it was—"

Before she could say anymore, Clovis pulled her to him and kissed her. It wasn't an open-mouthed kiss, but his arms were around her waist and back, pulling her to him hard. He pulled his lips from hers and then whispered in her ear.

"Ssssshhhh. Don't say another word."

Amelie nodded. Another woman walked up from behind him and smiled at both of them. Clovis smiled back and took Amelie's hand, leading her down the dirt path away from the fair.

"Sorry," he said, dropping her hand. "I didn't know who those people were. Shit, if the wrong person heard what you said ..."

He stopped and looked around. A little further down the path was a smallish mud island with a few straggling trees and bushes, just a stone's throw from the riverbank. Clovis pointed.

"Let's go there," he pointed, not bothering to take off his shoes before stepping into the river.

Amelie nodded, taking off hers and wading across the shallow water separating the small island from the shore.

When they reached the island, Clovis picked up some rocks and began to skim them. Amelie sat down on an old, thick tree branch that was stuck in the sandy ground. A few people were walking by, but their voices were muffled by the sound of the water and wind in the trees. After a couple of seconds Clovis turned to her.

"Good. They can't hear us. Okay, you said you have brought back physical objects from the places we visited?"

He came and sat down in front of her, mindless of the mud and his trousers. "Yeessssss ..."

155

"Jesus, Ame. Tiny bacteria are crazy enough but those other things … that's just … it's incredible. Scary, but incredible," he said, leaning in toward her. "You're sure that they were actual things from those places? You didn't just sort of conjure some replicas of them?"

"Conjure? Like a witch?" she laughed. "No. I'm sure the things came back with me. That photograph in front of Sleeping Beauty's castle, the people didn't look like us, but they did, if that makes sense."

"But you brought that actual picture back with you? You didn't find it somewhere in a magazine?"

"Yes. It showed up in my notebook. Is this bad?" she asked.

"Honestly, I don't know," Clovis replied. "I've never heard of anyone doing that before. So, yeah, it's scary. It's hard to believe."

"You don't believe me?"

"Oh, I believe you. I'm just stunned. I'll need to think about it," he said, taking off his hat and hanging it on an offshoot of the branch she was sitting on. His body passed close to her, and she could smell his sweat, which should have been unpleasant, but wasn't at all.

"Listen, you need to be very careful what you talk about within earshot of other people in these places," he continued. "Most of the time it should be fine, but you don't know who they are or what they might do with that information."

"Oh, you kissed me earlier to shut me up," Amelie muttered.

"Of course. Was that wrong? It was the quickest way I could think of to stop your mouth from moving."

"That worked but—well, you know, friends don't normally go around kissing each other on the mouth," she said. Her voice sounded naggy and prim even to her own ears.

"Oh, right," he said dryly. "I was too busy being concerned for your safety and welfare to worry about social conventions in that particular moment. Which, of course, I should know about because incubi are famous for their friendships with humans."

He stood up again and walked to the edge of the water, rolling up his sleeves. She glared at his back for a moment before his words sunk in, particularly the "concerned for your safety and welfare" thing. How many people in her life had ever cared for her safety?

Why the hell did you say that? she thought to herself.

"Sorry. It's just that you startled me. I wasn't expecting that," she said out loud.

Clovis turned around, sighed, and shrugged his shoulders. Whatever annoyance he had felt had come and gone quickly.

"No. It's good. We're different, so we're destined to misunderstand each other sometimes. So I'm glad you told me."

He came back to sit next to her.

"Listen, I'm not making light of friendship. It's just that I don't know *anything* about it. I don't know the boundaries or the rules or the expectations and I'm not used to not knowing stuff. I've never had a human friend before. I don't think I've had any incubi friends."

He unbuttoned his shirt and sat back with his hands in the dirt behind him.

"Mostly people just want to fuck me, and that's about it," he said.

Amelie was shocked by his word choice and the coldness that had crept into his voice.

"That's horrible," Amelie whispered.

"Is it? I don't know. Maybe that's all I've wanted. But I'm saying this to tell you that if I mess up, it's not because I don't want to be your friend. It's just new to me. I'm very good at seduction, but I'm sort of lost about all of this. So, if I step out of bounds, you're going to have to cut me some slack."

He smiled at her briefly, then furrowed his brow.

"But I did fuck up in one way that I should have thought about, because we had been talking about it. I know that we need to try to avoid touching each other. So kissing should be right out. I could drain you without knowing."

"How does that work? I mean, in the books they say that incubi lay on women in their sleep and basically rape them," Amelie said, looking down.

Clovis laughed, then shook his head.

"That little piece of propaganda was started by women who took lovers and then got pregnant," Clovis said. "When they found they were pregnant, they blamed it on us. Sometimes it was a father raping his daughters who pinned it on us."

"That's awful."

"But that's not what incubi do," Clovis said. "We can't come into your physical world without possessing someone, and most can't do that. So we meet humans in dreams. Also, no one who has sex with an incubus complains about it *ever*."

"Oh, okay. But if you seduce people regularly in dreams, how does that draining thing work?" Amelie asked, changing the subject as fast as she could.

"Well, I can tell you how it normally works. Normally, I see someone in a dream state, and I seduce them. I get energy from this, and the person gets pleasure. They rarely know anything happened besides just a very sexual dream."

"Do you see the same people over and over?"

Clovis reached for another rock and examined it.

"Me? No. It's actually very hard for most incubi to find a person more than once in the dream space."

"What's the dream space?"

"Oh, that's the space where your world and our world touch," he explained.

"But you find me here. Isn't this the dream space?"

"Here? No! This is a completely different story. This is another world. The dream space is still part of our story. We live in the same story, you and me."

"I don't get it," she said.

"Hmmmmm. It's easier to draw."

He pulled out a stick and made a drawing in the dry mud. He drew a polygon with points at the top and bottom and long sides. He then drew circles at each intersection of lines and an additional line and circle at the bottom of each, like a tail.

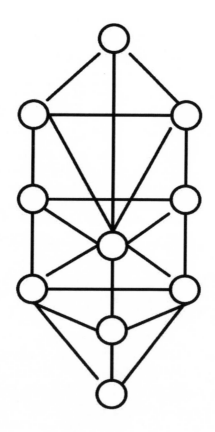

"This is our story. The one that you and I live in," he said, circling the entire image. "It goes from top to bottom. Each of these circles is a different layer and each one resonates at a different rate. We can live in the same universe, on the same planet, or even in the same room but be unaware of each other … like we superimposed on top of each other."

He stopped for a moment and tapped the mud with the stick, causing little bits of dirt to scatter. Some got caught in his hair, but he didn't notice.

"This is where you live most of the time," he said, pointing the stick to the bottom circle. "Incubi call it the Kingdom. It's also called Malkuth."

Then he pointed to a space just between the second and third circle from the bottom.

"And this is where I live most of the time."

"So you're saying you're more advanced than me, or something?" she asked.

"No, not at all," he sat back and shook his head. "It's not like that. As you go up, you just get less physical. As you go down, you get more physical. Or that's one aspect of it. As to which is better, it depends who you ask."

For a moment she saw his eyes darken and his jaw clench again.

"So I live in the most physical place?" she asked.

"Yes, but my world is fairly physical too. It's not as intense as yours, but we have form and sensation. The way we feel physical sensation is probably like how you feel physical sensation in dreams. When you go up further, you lose form and sensation … or that's what people say."

"That doesn't sound very nice," Amelie said.

"Yeah, but maybe that's because I'm shitty at explaining it. I'm pretending to be a lot more knowledgeable than I am," Clovis said, with a small grin.

"But where is *this* place on that chart? The place that we are in now?" Amelie asked.

"Well, that's the thing," Clovis said, lowering his voice, even though there was no one around. "We aren't in our story anymore."

He took his stick and drew an exact replica of his first drawing. Then a line connecting the two with arrows.

"We moved from this story to that story. It's a completely different reality," he said, pointing from one image to the next.

"But how could we do that?" she said, also lowering her voice.

"Not many creatures can. We came through the hallway. The hallway connects all stories, all different realities. Most of the time, to get from one story to another you would have to go all the way to the top of your story and enter another story from the very top," he said, pointing from the bottom circle in his drawing to the top.

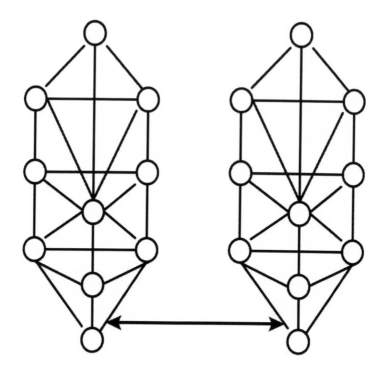

"But the hallway usually seems to enter somewhere here." He pointed to a spot between her bottom circle and the next one up. "Just slightly below the dream space."

"When we go through a door in the hallway, do we go into the dream space of other stories?"

"I think mostly yes, but you can never be sure. And you can't trust logic or rationality in these places. That's one of the ways that the doors in the hallway are dangerous."

"How do you learn to get in the hallway and then which doors you can go in, and which you can't?" she asked.

"You don't learn," he said sharply. "You either can or you can't. You either know or you don't. For a lot of people, their first time in the hallway is their last. They either die or they go crazy. So when I met you and learned that you came through the hallway, I knew how special you were."

His eyes caught hers.

"You're like me," he said softly.

"What does that mean?" she asked, feeling her heart begin to race. She had never in her life heard that phrase before.

You're like me.

"For one thing, it means that you're a Cambion."

"Cambion? What is that?"

"It's someone who's lineage is mixed. Your lineage isn't completely human, just like my lineage isn't completely incubus. We are mixed breeds, you and I," Clovis said with a gentle smile.

"I'm not completely human?"

"No. Does that surprise you? Do you see lots of people around you who can do what you do? Do you find that most other people think the way you think?" he asked.

Amelie just stared. She felt the faint outline of the TILT sign forming over her head again.

"Exactly," he said. "There are lots of mixed breed things around, but compared to the overall population, it's a small number. Usually, life is quite difficult for them. They think differently from other people. They often have autoimmune diseases because their DNA is mixed, and their immune system has to fight off diseases from both lineages, so it gets confused. They are also susceptible to viruses from other stories, which are about the only things in existence that can jump from story to story."

He stopped for a moment and turned to her.

"Also, you need to know that your susceptibility to these other-story viruses makes you a target for creatures out there whose job it is to prevent viruses from other stories getting to ours. The fact that you can get into the hallway AND bring things back. No—no one can know that."

"What? Wait. What creatures would target me?" Amelie asked.

"Creatures that would kill you if they knew what I know about you. No, they wouldn't kill you, they'd *unmake* you. They'd think you're a risk to this world and would throw you all the way back up to the top of this story. It would take you thousands of years to work your way back down to physicality. They would unmake me just for telling you this. So it's better to stay off their radar."

Amelie sat back and put her hands in the mud just to ground herself. Her head was spinning.

"Then what am I ... besides human?" she asked.

"I don't know. That's always one of the great mysteries for creatures like us—the discovery of exactly what we are. Although, I should warn you, you need to make sure that you really want to know the answer to that question before you go looking. You may or may not like what you find out," he said, then he was quiet.

Amelie was dizzy, and a bit nauseous. She wasn't sure if it was the heat, or all the information that had just been dumped into her lap. She and Clovis were the same type of creature. She was not completely human. She could travel to not just distant worlds but whole other—well, stories. There were things that would kill her if they knew this. She knew that she couldn't be making this up because she had *never* been this creative.

There were so many questions buzzing in her head that she chose a simple one, one that was closest her heart.

"Before you made a point of telling me that incubi are always selfish and vain. All the reading says the same … but you said you put yourself in danger to help me. Did you do this because we are the same?" she asked.

Clovis started a bit, then was silent for a moment.

"Yeah, and maybe by helping you, I can make up for some things I did in the past."

Amelie didn't understand this, and she could see so many emotions running across Clovis's face, she didn't want to pry. Instead, she took his hand.

"Thank you. This week at school, I was able to breathe for the first time since I was a little girl. So thanks for being friends with me and for … well, for everything."

He stood up, leaned over and gave her a little kiss on the head as he pulled his hand away gently.

No touching, remember.

"You're welcome," he said softly.

He grabbed a stick from the tree and tossed it long across the river.

"Still, you're right about one thing. I *have* been very nice to you. But don't feel any pressure or anything. I wouldn't want you to feel compelled to, like, let me win arguments, or flatter me. I wouldn't want you to do that," he said, grinning.

"Oh, don't worry. That's not happening. You certainly don't need any encouragement on the vanity thing," she snorted, stretching her legs out in front of her.

"Wait a minute. When have I said anything vain around you?" he asked putting his hand over his chest with mock indignation. "Can you think of one vain thing I've said?"

Amelie opened her mouth, and then shut it. Now that he mentioned it, she couldn't remember him saying anything specifically vain. She knew he must have, but she couldn't remember it with him standing there looking at her with

162

that cocky smile. He had taken off his hat and his hair looked like a rat's nest. His unbuttoned shirt was now painted with mud. Underneath, he had on an undershirt that was sticking to his body with the heat. His face was flushed, and the tip of his nose was getting red. And of course, even in this state, he was gorgeous. Just standing there, he was distracting.

Think, he must have said something, she thought, but nothing came.

"Oh, you don't have to say anything. I know you know you're—" she said before she could stop herself, and then clamped her mouth shut, covering her mouth with her hand. Clovis laughed out loud.

"What, handsome? Is that what you were going to say? It's okay, you can say that," he smiled.

"See?" she said, blushing. "Vain. Exactly."

"So I'm vain because I know I'm handsome?" He smiled but his voice took on a more serious tone. "Oh, this is that culture thing again."

He came and sat down next to her, running one hand through his hair.

"Look, all incubi are beautiful. It's how we're made. It would be like me accusing you of being vain because you said you had skin. You are expected to have skin. Without it, you are either dead or severely handicapped. It's like that with us and beauty. It's not really something we take that seriously."

"But you said that beauty is important to you … when we saw that woman in Hong Kong …" she said.

"Did I? If I did, then I expressed it the wrong way. We appreciate beauty as something more than physical. Even physical beauty we see in a broader spectrum than most humans. Humans put very strange boundaries around beauty. It has to be a certain age, shape, size, etc. We don't operate that way. Humans have fairly strict criteria … but it changes over time" he said, coming to sit next to her.

"Have you ever been to any of the bigger museums?" he asked.

"I've been to the one in Charlotte," she replied.

"Hmmmm, one day I'd love to take you to the Louvre, or the Met—or the National Gallery. It's really fascinating to see how the standard of beauty changes over the centuries. I've had the chance to see it over time, but you can see it by looking at the paintings. Humans are very changeable about beauty. Maybe I can sort out a way to take you."

Over the centuries …

"It must feel strange being immortal," Amelie said quietly.

"It's the only thing I know," he shrugged. "I could just as easily say 'it must feel strange to know you're going to die'. But that is the only reality you know."

Ouch.

Clovis sat up quickly.

"Shit. That was really insensitive," he said. "I guess immortality doesn't teach you tact, huh?"

He laughed a little and shrugged nervously.

"See, you can tell that I'm not seducing you, because I wouldn't be saying clumsy things like that all the time if I were."

Amelie nodded mechanically. She wasn't sure exactly sure if she was happy or upset about that whole "not seducing you" thing.

"I guess you were asking whether or not I experience existential angst?" he continued. "The answer is no—well, not most of the time."

He looked out over the river and was silent. She sat and just watched him. She wondered what sorts of things would go on inside his head. What wealth of experience he had to draw on when he was thinking. It was unimaginable.

After a couple of minutes, he looked back to her. She could hear the tree frogs singing to each other from the trees. A cool wind came up behind him. The feel of it was delicious on her skin. The smell of it was the smell of Clovis, which was intoxicating.

"I probably deal with immortality in the same way that humans cope with the prospect of death. I don't think about it. I live in the moment. If you live in the moment, or in the very near future or past, then life can be sweet."

Clovis was looking at her with a slight smile on his face. This smile, like most of his face, was subtle but not static. The corners of his mouth moved up and down ever so slightly while maintaining the smile. His eyebrows knit for a milisecond and then relaxed. The only thing not in constant motion were his eyes. They had a focus that was as visceral as a touch. Amelie felt his eyes on her skin like the heat of the sun. Suddenly she wanted him to touch her.

"Enough about me," he said quickly, breaking eye contact. "It's too hot here. Let's get wet."

Already there, she thought to herself and then blushed that such a thought had entered her mind.

He stood up and began pulling off his shirt and undershirt.

"Won't people stare?" she asked, desperately trying to derail her brain.

"Not as long as *you* don't remove any clothes. We can't do that here. It's the Deep South in the fifties, so that would be a big no. But we can get our feet wet and splash our faces."

He kicked his shoes off and rolled up his trousers. There wasn't much she could do with her dress. Clovis walked in up to his knees in the water, leaned down and splashed water on his face and neck. With a little grin, he splashed some back at her. When he leaned back down, she couldn't resist and splashed

164

his back. The ensuing water fight ended up as all water fights do, with both of them completely immersed.

The water was warm, barely cooler than the air, but it was a wonderful relief anyway. At some point Amelie tried to get out and Clovis pulled her back down into the water.

"This isn't completely kosher, so let's enjoy it while we can, before a policeman comes to take me away …" he said, throwing his hands out in the water. Amelie started laughing until she heard a familiar voice.

"Well, well, what a nice surprise."

A woman and man were standing on the shore. Not a policeman—no, much, much worse. The man was the handsome man from the bridge, but the woman had morphed into Rose. Clovis pulled Amelie toward him and put his arm possessively around her neck. She could feel his tension even in his forearm.

"Nice to see you, but I'm kind of having a moment here," he drawled lazily.

"Oh yes, I saw your little water game. She's quite the minx, that one. I swear, she looks familiar to me. You just seem to be attracted to people I think I know," Rose purred at Clovis, but her eyes were firmly on Amelie, and the expression was one of hate and hunger.

"Who's your friend?" Clovis asked her, looking at the handsome man.

"Let's go, Claire," the man said testily.

"Oh, just a minute," Rose said as she kissed the man on his neck. "This is Ben, my new husband."

Amelie was trying to look at Rose as if she were just another person here. However, Rose was wearing another silky-looking slip dress. The difference from the last one was that this one was even closer to transparent, revealing a body that could only be described as ripe. Of course, that wasn't what other people would see. Amelie's heart was beating hard. When she opened her inner eye, she saw green, black, and yellow light clinging to Rose's dress and hair. All the colors of poison.

"I'm glad to see you back in the game. You've kept yourself to yourself for way too long, my dear," Rose cooed to Clovis, twirling her hair with one finger.

"Well, just because you don't see me doesn't mean I'm not around," Clovis said with deadpan delivery.

Amelie tried to make herself small. She also felt herself getting thin. Would Rose be able to tell if she disappeared? She didn't know. She clutched at Clovis's shirt, mentally trying to relay this information to him.

"Claire," the handsome man said again, this time with an edge of serious hostility.

165

"Claire. Don't tell me that you haven't mentioned me to your new husband?" Clovis asked, as he moved to shallower water and pulled Amelie into his lap. A storm cloud formed over the man's face. Clovis's behavior now seemed calculated to offend this man. Amelie could feel his hand resting just above her breast in a way that was seriously pushing the boundaries of propriety for this era.

"Is this an old boyfriend?" the man asked Rose. Rose was actually beginning to flush.

"Yessss," she said softly, looking down as if ashamed, but her eyes were aflame.

"We were very close," Clovis said. "So ... well ... congratulations to you."

The look on Clovis's face was showing just the slightest edge of lust tinged with boredom. All this, everything he was doing, was designed. He was trying to make an impact on someone, but Amelie wasn't quite sure who.

"Ben, let's just go," Rose purred, but she didn't move as she continued to stare at Clovis.

"No," Ben replied. "I want a word with this fella. I'm sorry ma'am, but can I borrow your, uh, friend for a few moments?"

Amelie nodded. Rose's eyes were now completely flaming as Clovis unseated Amelie from his lap. He stood slowly and, shirtless and dripping, made his way to the bank without haste. Ben snorted, took Rose's hand and escorted her toward the other bank. Clovis was picking up his hat and shoes, but when he realized that Rose was otherwise engaged, he caught her Amelie's eye and mouthed, "Go."

I don't know how.

Suddenly, everything around her started to fade. Rose's eyes were not on her, but Amelie didn't want to take any chances. She made her way to the shore and sat behind a small clump of bushes as saw her skin begin to pull apart.

"Clovis, be safe," she said softly, as she felt herself pulled away.

#

This time she couldn't even make it to the bathroom before she started vomiting. Luckily, she was able to grab her trashcan just in the nick of time.

Chapter Twenty-One

Crossing a Shadowed Line

Phil Sawyer sat in his car, his hand shoved into his pants. He had parked in the teachers' lot, facing the student parking lot so that he could see Amelie as she arrived. In this way, he could watch her walk all the way into the school, rather than just seeing her cross the landing. He had tried this for the first time last Friday, and she hadn't noticed him. At that time, he had waited to touch himself until later on in the bathroom. But today, he was going to risk taking his pleasure while she was still in his line of sight.

A part of him knew this was dangerous. If someone saw him, he would be fired. Even worse, he would be exposed for what he was, but he was having a harder time caring about this recently. He wondered if his reduced inhibitions were because he had contracted dog flu. Last week he had had a fever for a few days and his sexual appetite had certainly become more accentuated in the past few days, but he couldn't blame all of this on the flu.

A shadow suddenly appeared in front of his car. He had been seeing more of these recently as well. Initially, he thought they were just floaters in his eyes, but now they had taken on more definitive shapes, and moved with purpose. That purpose seemed to be finding Amelie.

As he watched, the shadow began to slide down toward the parking lot. Sure enough, Amelie was pulling into the lot in her green Corolla. As Amelie got out of her car, she adjusted her books, put her keys in her purse, and made her way from the parking lot toward the cul-de-sac. She walked with that sensual swaying that he only saw when she thought she was alone.

Sawyer was about to unzip his pants, but something stopped him. She was alone. There was no one else in the parking lot. Looking around, he saw no one on the landing. He and Amelie were alone. He quickly grabbed his briefcase. He tried not to look like he was moving too quickly. He needed this to look casual.

"Ms. McCormick," he called. She hesitated for a moment, but then kept walking. He saw her stance change to a more rigid posture. It didn't stop him.

"How are your applications to gap year programs coming along?" he asked, catching up with her.

"Oh fine," she said.

Only a few seconds alone. Why hadn't he planned for this?

"Do you have any idea where you will go?" he asked.

"No, not yet," she replied. Was it just his imagination or was the sway back? And as she glanced at him out of the side of her eye, he wondered what that gaze meant.

"Perhaps you will let me know once you have decided. I like to keep up with what our students make of themselves. You will do that, won't you?" he asked, stuttering.

A human-sized shadow appeared out of nowhere and insinuated itself between the two of them. Through its dark haze, Sawyer saw Amelie turn and smile at him.

"Sure," she said. The blue-gold of her eyes wasn't dimmed by the thing between them, but accentuated.

"Thank you," he said, reaching out to touch her upper arm. So close to her breast, just a slight movement would put his hand there.

"Ames," called a voice from behind them. Sawyer turned to see Hudson Crowe approaching. "Can I talk to you a second?"

"Excuse me," Amelie said, but as she turned to walk back to Hudson, she caught his eye. There was something in her gaze that made his insides turn to water.

She wants me. She doesn't know it yet, but she wants me.

With this thought, he turned and almost skipped into the school building.

Chapter Twenty-Two

A Gift for Royalty

Amelie spent the next five school days trying to avoid any contact with Mr. Sawyer. The fact that he had approached her as she was walking into school bothered her in the extreme. She was going to have avoid all interactions with him.

If only Sawyer had gotten that memo. Every time she turned a corner, he was standing there. She had taken to altering her routes to all her classes every day. She had also started coming to school later so that she would never be alone in or near the school.

Despite the Sawyer issue, she was enjoying school for the first time in her life. Every day she gained more control over her energy. She discovered that she could direct energy into plants as well as people. This was an amazing discovery, as trees couldn't stalk her. They did rustle when she walked by, but that was lovely. All of this made her energy levels more stable and gave her the freedom to experience some normal emotions without so much fear. She felt like someone who had been released from prison. No, it was greater than that, she felt like she had been brought back from the dead.

It probably would have been unrealistic for her *not* to fall in love with the person who did that for her.

As if reflecting her own experiences, the school itself had lightened up in the past few weeks. The incidence of dog flu in the school seemed to disappear overnight. As if in celebration of spring, everyone she encountered was healthy and happy. There was a lot of laughter and smiles all around.

Even her friends had been unusually easy to get along with in the past few weeks. Elodie and Carter were in a stable place. Carter had stopped pestering Amelie for her homework and had even actually taken to chitchatting with her on the landing. Jack was back to ignoring her existence and was focusing his attention on Judith. This had taken Judith off guard and prevented her normal torturing for fun. Aidan had gone back to his obsession with his car.

She had also been spending more time with Hudson. The rumor mill had spun them as a couple. When she mentioned this to him, he had shrugged and said that it might actually work in their favor, now that Jack seemed to have lost interest in her. One of the greatest benefits of this was that she could go to lunch with Hudson instead of her friends because, if these girls agreed on one thing, it was that boyfriends came first.

The biggest downside of the week was her nervousness about Clovis's well-being. The last time she saw him, he was being hauled away by the sadistic Rose and her paramour. She was pretty sure he could handle himself, but the lack of communication since then had made her nervous. She told herself that she would wait until the weekend to try to find him, but it took every ounce of her willpower.

By the time Friday night rolled around, she could think about little else. That evening, she was so distracted that she told her mother that she felt ill and went up to her bedroom before dinner.

#

As Amelie stepped into the hallway, the very first door on her right gleamed at her. There was no question about it. It was painted a bright orange-red and was covered with golden figures. Looking at it triggered that déjà vu feeling.

When she touched it, the hallway seemed to crumble around her and she found herself sitting in a boat, docked in a muddy green lake in the heat of a summer day. In front of her was a Japanese pagoda, surrounded by flowering cherry trees. Clovis was standing in front of the pagoda. He waved and started toward her. He was wearing a black kimono with red cross stitching across it and a burgundy shirt underneath, but both of these things were loose, so there was a fair amount of his skin on display.

"Before you laugh at what I'm wearing, I think you should look at yourself," he said, helping her out of the boat. She looked down and saw that she was wearing a bright pink and orange kimono with a vivid yellow obi tied around her waist.

"It's pink," Amelie groaned, looking down at herself.

"No, it's bright pink," Clovis said with a laugh.

"Why do you get black, and I get bright pink?"

"Either because I got here first, or because you can pull it off. What do you think?" he asked, waving his hand around him.

170

"It's beautiful," she said. This was an understatement. This place would be envied by other beautiful places. The temple was set at the bottom of a mountain amid trees that were in full bloom. Everywhere she looked she saw cherry blossoms, plum blossoms, and blossoms from other trees she didn't recognize. There were even splashes of purple at the top of the mountain that for all the world looked like heather.

"I've been really worried about you after the last time. I mean, you just sort of let Rose take you away."

Clovis shrugged. "I know how to deal with Rose."

She was about to ask more, but when she looked at Clovis, his smile was tight. She thought it best to leave it alone for now.

"This is Japan, right?" she asked him as they began to walk up the stairs toward the temple.

"It's this story's approximation of it," he said. "But it's nice, right?"

He looked at her intently. They were standing just in front of the temple. His black eyes were completely unreadable, and his facial expressions were moving too fast to begin to follow.

Amelie nodded.

"Come on, I have something for you," he said, taking her hand.

They walked through the shaded pagoda. Inside, it was filled with tiny rock gardens, paintings, statues, and a few penis-shaped fertility sculptures. She waited for Clovis to comment, but he didn't. Instead, he led her outside and into a garden filled with bridges, ponds, trees, and flowering plants. Amelie had never been to Japan, yet everything around her felt vaguely familiar.

"This garden is huge," Amelie said as she hopped across some stepping stones placed strategically across the grass. This was harder than it seemed in a kimono.

"That's because it belongs to royalty," Clovis replied.

"Oh, are we allowed here then?" Amelie asked.

Clovis laughed.

"Remember, we're possessing people who belong here."

They came to a series of rocks that had been placed across one of the ponds. It bridged the distance between the shore and a small island located in the middle of the pond. Clovis jumped to the first stone and then held his hand out to Amelie, helping her across. The tiny island had three or four large stones, along with several bushes with bright pink flowers. On the other side of it was a stone bridge. Clovis sat down on one of the rocks and picked some flowers from one of the bushes and handed them to her.

"Wildflowers," he said, smiling gently. "You said they were your favorite flower."

For a second, she had no idea what he was talking about, but then she remembered that she had babbled something like that the time he was inside Carter. He had remembered this.

He put a flower behind her ear.

"How has school been?" he asked as they crossed the bridge and began walking down another path, getting lost in another section of the gardens. "What's happened with your creepy vice principal?"

"Oh, he watches me constantly—but other than that he hasn't really done anything out of the ordinary," she added quickly, seeing Clovis open his mouth to ask. She didn't really want to talk about Sawyer here. It was like pouring slime on a rose.

They walked toward a pavilion that was situated at the center of the gardens. It was larger than the others but made of the same red wood. There was a light breeze blowing and the soft sound of cicadas buzzing in the trees around them. The air was warm and soft against her skin. When Clovis's hand briefly touched hers, she felt a little electrical jolt.

"Still, if he's that interested in you, I should probably find out more about him, to make sure he isn't a problem," Clovis said, interrupting her thoughts as they approached the pagoda.

"How would you do that?"

"Seduce him, of course," Clovis said flatly.

Amelie felt a wave of revulsion.

"That wouldn't be a problem for you?" she said, with a little more edge in her voice than she would have liked. Clovis either didn't hear it or ignored it.

"Why would it be? I'm an incubus. Seducing people is what we do."

Amelie again felt the rumbling of anxiety in her stomach. Before she could stop herself, her stomach had taken hold of her vocal cords.

"Why have you not tried to seduce me, then, seeing as that's what you do. Am I not attractive to you?" she heard herself ask with horror. She sounded petulant and whiny even in her own ears.

Clovis spun to look at her, his eyes wide and mouth open.

"What? Jesus Christ. I explained that. I haven't seduced you because I don't want to hurt you. I actually *like* you."

Suddenly his expression darkened in a way she hadn't seen before. A small mirthless smile played at his lips.

"Or is that what you really want from me? Despite all you say … do you just want what everyone wants?"

172

Without warning, he pulled her into the pagoda and shoved her up against one of its wooden beams. He searched her eyes, his nose almost touching hers. Above them, the sun disappeared behind the clouds and all noise around them seemed to cease. All she could hear was her own heart and his breathing.

"Is that it? After all this, is it as simple as that?" He moved closer, his eyes still glued to her face. He was beginning to breathe hard. He put his lips next to her ear.

"Do you just want me to fuck you?" he whispered, then moved his face down to her neck. "Is that what you want? To let me know your body, know your taste. That what you *really* want, Ames?"

His lips were now at her collarbone.

She was trembling. She couldn't help it. There was some energy emanating from him that was washing over her. It brought a tingling, tugging sensation in her gut that was more than just pleasure—it was hunger. The intensity of it was indescribable. Something seemed to liquefy in the pit of her stomach and her knees buckled.

Clovis grabbed her around the waist and pushed her against the beam, supporting her by putting his leg between hers, pushing against the most sensitive part of her. He was staring into her eyes again. It felt like he was laying her heart bare, and she couldn't fight it.

"Having trouble with the knees?" he whispered. "You must have read about what bliss it is to be with one of us? You should know that the only ones who get written about are the weak ones. They allow it to happen to stroke their egos. The strong ones don't need the advertisement. I'm not one of the weak ones. In fact, I have a reputation even among my own kind."

His breath was warm on her face. He increased the pressure on the leg that he had between her legs, causing a friction that ensured she wouldn't regain the use of her legs. His hands were only on her waist but just this made her feel faint. She had no control over her own body. To her humiliation, she heard a small whimper escape her mouth.

"There's only one catch," he whispered as he delicately kissed her eyebrows. "If I come ... then I go and that's it. Not so bad though. You learned what I could teach you. There's no more reason to hang around with me and deal with all the bullshit that I don't know about humans. You can let me finally show you what I *do* know about humans, what I'm *really* good at. It would be much less hassle for you, all round. Is that what you want, Ames?"

He pulled back and looked at her, grinning with his whirly black animal eyes and smoky grin.

173

Then the reality of these words slapped her back to her senses. He was talking about leaving her. She felt her heart seize in her chest, and she pushed him away from her hard. Her legs were suddenly solid under her.

"No! Stop it!"

She wanted to scream, but it came out as a squeak. His expression hadn't changed, so she slapped him—hard. It hurt her hand, but the pain was good. It cleared her head. He looked surprised for a second, but his eyes were still whirling as he slowly grinned. But at least he had stopped touching her. And the energy coming off him was banked just a bit.

"I just asked you one stupid question," she said with a voice breaking. "I just suddenly got this idea that maybe I've got this thing I do to make up for the fact that I'm a troll or something. It was just me being stupid and insecure. That's all it was. That's all."

Then she hung her head and slid down to the ground, putting her arms around her legs and starting to cry in earnest. What she had just said to him had been both a horrific lie and a painful truth. She couldn't tell him she didn't desire him, because he had just seen her acting like she was in heat. But that wasn't why she was crying. She was crying not because she desired him but because she loved him, and she certainly couldn't say that. So if it was a choice between having the best sex she could ever have, or having him with her, she chose the latter.

When she looked up, Clovis's eyes were now wide as saucers, and he had stopped smiling. His expression was puzzled.

"Wait, Amelie. How did you? How could you? You shouldn't have been able to …" he began, but then stopped and backed away. He shook his head, and his eyes cleared.

"Oh god. I'm sorry. I just … I thought … I just thought something stupid. Goddamn it." He turned, took a few steps and then grabbed the rail of the pagoda with both hands.

"I guess you're not the only one who's insecure," he whispered, head down. He turned and walked back toward her. Amelie tried to press herself even further back into the wooden beam.

He stopped for a second, but then thought better of it. He sat down on the wooden floor of the pagoda and reached out for her, pulling her to him. She let him. He pulled her into his lap, put his arms around her and rested his chin on her head.

"I'm sorry, Ames. I didn't know. I just … I should be better at this stuff. I should have been able to read you better. Forgive me," he said as he stroked her hair. "I told you I don't understand—well, lots of things apparently."

Amelie was still crying but not for the reasons he probably thought. She was crying because she was a total impostor and liar. She was pretending to be his friend, and she was, but he was so much more to her than that. She was also crying because, when he said he would leave, she felt like she might die. Literally, she felt her heart stop. It felt like someone had stabbed her. That was what broke the desire.

"I'm sorry, too," she hiccuped. "I wasn't really thinking. I didn't know ..."

"You didn't know that I'm an insecure fuck up? How could you know that? Surprise!"

He pulled her closer to him. "But that was really shitty of me. Did I hurt you—I mean, physically?"

Amelie shook her head. She looked up at his face. He was trying for a smile, but it looked fragile and fleeting. She also saw fear. A fear she understood. This stopped her tears, and her fear. She touched the red mark on his cheek.

"You know, for the record, I care about *you*, not just about ... you know," she said. Clovis touched his forehead to hers.

"Well, for the record, I should tell you that I do find you desirable," he said. "Hell, there's nothing not to desire. But I'd like to think that you would already know that, seeing as how you're sitting on my lap."

Amelie had noticed, it would have been difficult not to, but she hadn't wanted to think about it. But now he'd acknowledged it in such an open manner she felt that tightening in her stomach and another wave of desire.

"The problem is that seducing you would put us on a path where I would have to leave you. And I like you too much to want to do that. Which is, by the way, completely against my nature. So what I said just now wasn't nice, but it was coming from a real place of frustration. I'm a creature designed to have sex. So not having sex with someone I actually like is intensely frustrating, and something I haven't felt before."

She almost said she loved him at that moment. It was on the tip of her tongue, but she knew desire and love were different. He liked her. He felt desire for her. But that obviously didn't equal love in his book. After all, he felt things differently than she did.

"And speaking of ..." Clovis said, picking her up and putting her on the ground next to him. "That feels too good to me to be good for you," he said, standing. He went and sat on the railing of the pagoda.

"Because I acted like an asshole, I need to ask you a couple of questions that might make you uncomfortable. But I need to know how bad I fucked up here and what needs to be done to make it right."

"Okay," she said softly.

"When I did that to you, just now, what did you feel?"

Amelie felt her heart jump into her mouth. There was no way she could tell him that. She must have looked as horrified as she felt because he immediately said, "I know you must have felt desire. That's what we do. But did you feel physical pain anywhere? Like a burning pain or a stabbing pain? Anything sharp?"

Apart from when you said you would leave me? she thought, but instead she said, "No. There was nothing painful."

Clovis's shoulders relaxed.

"Okay. Good. You're so susceptible that I need to be very careful with you. If you had felt pain, then I might have damaged you somehow. If not, you should be okay. I'm pretty sure you'll be sick, but it probably won't be too bad."

"Is that what it feels like when you seduce people?" she asked, wiping her eyes with her kimono.

"That? Oh no. That wasn't a real seduction. Well, it was like a mini seduction. Even if I was acting like an ass, I would never be that cavalier with you."

Oh my god. What would a real seduction feel like? she thought.

"Still, it was pretty amazing that you were able to push me away. Most people couldn't do that."

"Why?"

"They wouldn't have enough control over their senses," he replied.

But of course.

"So that stuff about having a reputation. Was that true?" she asked, looking at her feet.

He sighed and ran his hand through his hair.

"Did I say that? I did, didn't I? Wow, I must have been having a serious ego moment." He laughed a little.

"So it's true?"

"Yeah, it's true."

Amelie sat up straighter and looked up at him.

"What did you mean by that?"

He came down to sit beside her.

"You sure you want to know this?"

"Yes, I want to know you," she said.

Clovis smiled and looked down. He studied the floorboards. She just waited. Her tears were gone. The storm was over. She was calm now. No, she was happy now. Which was crazy, as she was now sitting here waiting for him to tell her about how he seduced other women. Still, none of that mattered somehow.

176

Clovis sighed. "I went through this period where I decided that if I was going to be an incubus, then I was going to be the best I could be at all the worst parts. So, I made a point of seducing those who were the most challenging."

"Like?"

"Oh, anyone who was difficult to seduce for whatever reason. Some were narcissistic celebrity-types, some were royalty, some were homophobic men, some were in love with god."

"And I guess you've been successful in seducing all these men and women who didn't want to be seduced?" she asked.

"Yep. That's how I got the rep."

"Do you still do that?"

"No," he said emphatically, catching her eye.

"Why did you stop?" she asked. He sat back and closed his eyes for a moment.

"I'd like to say that I had some great revelation and suddenly the evil of my ways was clear to me, but it was a lot simpler than that. I just stopped feeling anything from doing it. I kept having to do worse and worse things to get any sensation at all from it. Then I noticed that when I wasn't doing these horrible things, I didn't feel anything at all. So, I dropped my campaign to get consensual sex from the non-consensual and went back to behaving in a normal way for an incubus."

"That being?"

"Well, we seduce when we need to or when someone really needs us to. That's all."

"So you still seduce people?" she asked.

"Yeah, it's what I am. It's kind of like how I feed but not really. That analogy only goes so far, but it's good enough for now. Also, sometimes people need us, like when they are going to die, and we get drawn to them."

"Were you drawn to me?" she asked, then stopped and put her hand over her mouth.

"That's okay. It's a fair question," he said. "But no, you found me, remember? And I'm not planning to let you die on my watch."

Amelie leaned her head on his shoulder. She understood him a little better now. The sky above was back to blue with tiny, puffy white clouds and the air smelled of the cherry blossoms that floated all around them. The cicadas were singing again. She could see people walking on the paths near them but seemed to avoid the pagoda they were in. Clovis gently brushed a hair off her face.

"I feel like I'm going to go soon," she whispered. He scrutinized her.

"You don't look thin yet."

177

"No. But I've noticed that I get a weird déjà vu feeling about five minutes before I leave."

Clovis's eyes widened a bit.

"Do you get déjà vu a lot? Is that a normal thing for you?"

"Sometimes, but that's not the weird thing. The weird thing is that it's not like normal déjà vu. Like when we were in Disneyland, I didn't feel like I had been in Disneyland before. It felt more like I had been in a situation like that with you before," she said, smiling at him. "Or in Mississippi. I felt like we had walked by rivers like that before."

"And this time? It feels the same way?"

"No, today it *does* feel like I've been here before. I feel like *we've* been in this pagoda before. Except we haven't done or said the same things. Do you know what I mean?" she asked.

He nodded, but his eyes suddenly looked unfocused. Then he shook his head and stood up quickly.

"Okay, too much emotion for one day, right? So now that I've vented my sexual frustration in an incredibly stupid way, let me show you something nice before you get taken away."

They walked out of the pagoda and on to another walkway. The trees were swaying in a gentle breeze. A few couples walked by them and smiled.

This time, rather than wandering, Clovis seemed to be leading her. He stopped when they came to an area with five or six koi ponds arranged in a semicircle around a small cherry tree. Their path curved around and between the ponds.

"Have you been here often?" Amelie asked as she bent down to look at the fish.

"Yes. I like to come here. It's beautiful and makes me happy. No, not exactly happy. I know a place like this in our own story," he said squatting down next to her.

He put his fingers out to the koi and they nibbled on them.

"These were the very first carps in Japan. They were brought here as a gift to the royal family," he said.

The movement of the fish was hypnotic. They were beautiful in the way they seemed to dance with the currents of the water. Her head began to feel like it was filled with cotton. She closed her eyes.

"The emperor was enchanted by them," Clovis said. "He said—"

"That he rejoiced at them, morning and night," Amelie said. "He kept them in the pond of Ijishi. They looked different then, they weren't so colorful, but they were still so beautiful. Maybe we should just turn ourselves into fishes, so we could be together always."

Amelie had turned in time to see Clovis mouth her words as she was speaking them.

"Why did I say that? How did I know that thing about Ijishi?" Amelie asked. "And how did you know what I was going to say?"

Clovis didn't say anything, he just put his head in his hands.

"Oh god," he whispered, covering his eyes with his hands. "Oh god. Oh god."

"Clovis. Are you all right?"

He was rocking back and forth on his heels. He was so close to the edge of the pond, she was afraid he might fall in.

"Are you okay?" she asked, touching his arm. It was trembling.

"Yes. No. I don't know," he said into his hands.

"Did that mean something? What I just said—what just happened? Did it mean something?"

Clovis lifted his face from his hands, and his eyes were filled with tears.

"I think so, but I have to go somewhere to find out and I have to do it now."

"Is it that important?" she asked.

Clovis laughed but it ended in something that sounded a bit like a sob.

"Yes, Ames. It would be the most important thing that has happened to me in thousands and thousands of years. Maybe in my whole existence, but I have to be sure before I do anything."

"You're scaring me now. You're not leaving me, are you?"

"No. No. No. And hell no. But if I'm right about this, then everything has changed, I've been amazingly stupid for millennia and I have a lot of apologies to make."

"To who?"

"Almost everyone ... but mainly to you." Amelie saw transparent flower petals float by. She felt light in her skin.

"No. No. Shit. You're leaving." Clovis reached for her and took her face in his hands.

"Okay. Listen. Don't do anything dangerous until I can find you again in your world. It may be a couple of weeks, but don't go to the hallway. You hear that? DO NOT GO IN THE HALLWAY. Don't practice too much. Don't walk out in traffic. Don't eat too fast. Don't be alone with people. And please try not to get sick. I've put you at risk today already, so stay in bed tomorrow. Just rest. Just give me a week or so. Then I should be able to explain it."

He hit his head with his fists. "What else? Don't drive if you don't have to. Just don't … I just can't … I don't suppose I could talk you into staying in a bomb shelter for two weeks? That would be great. No? Too much?"

He laughed, but it had the edge of hysteria. Then he reached out for her, but his hands went through her. That seemed to stabilize him.

"Okay. Until you see me, you take care of yourself. Promise? Don't take chances. Promise? Don't let anything happen to you."

Amelie nodded, as the wind blew her whole world away.

#

Amelie woke sobbing in her bed but that ended as she felt bile rise in her throat. She tried to stand up, but her legs collapsed under her, so she vomited in her trashcan before crawling back in bed. She hadn't felt this bad in a while. She grabbed the thermometer that she had started keeping near her bed. She had no fever, but she was shivering.

She was frightened. Whatever had happened back there was apparently a very big deal, but she had no idea what it was. Another wave of nausea shook her, and she grabbed for the trashcan, retching. As she was vomiting bile, she heard the horrible whine of the coffee grinder downstairs.

At least it was Saturday. Amelie lay back down and took deep breaths. She couldn't let her family see her sick. She had gone to bed saying she was sick last night, and Opal had been giving her suspicious looks. If she was sick in the mornings too often, Opal might insist she go see an OB-GYN, because an un-wanted pregnancy wouldn't be allowed in the house.

Amelie got up slowly and gingerly put clothes on. She didn't have enough energy to be around too many people, but she didn't want to drive too far in her condition. So she decided to go to the local library. At least for a while, until she could stabilize herself, if that was still even a possibility.

Chapter Twenty-Three

Mouse Bugs

Amelie hadn't seen Clovis in two weeks. This hadn't been too hard the first couple of days. He had told her to give him a couple of weeks and not to go into the hallway to look for him. Still, she'd been expecting him to show up at school. After the first week, her impatience started getting the best of her. She read all the assignments in her classes. She read ahead on some of other assignments. She made the decision to accept the gap year program with the Sorbonne in Paris and told the school. All of this was accomplished in a vain attempt to distract herself. She missed Clovis so much that it was manifesting as a physical ache in her pelvis.

On day fifteen, she woke in the middle of the night from a nightmare. The only part of it she could remember was that Clovis was in trouble.

She lay back down and, without fanfare, her brain flew her to the hallway. It was dimmer than usual, and vegetation covered the ground and black doorways. She had never encountered vegetation here before and this stuff looked like the devil's attempt at ivy. It was dark purple, with a slimy sort of sheen. As she walked past doors, it snaked over her feet and reached out to her from the walls.

Why on earth did I end up here?

Her recent trips into the hallway had been very short and had led her immediately to a door, maybe because Clovis had been directing her. This time she had come on her own accord, so she moved carefully, treading between plant life as much as possible. When she accidentally stepped on one, it squished in an insectile way.

Clovis had told her, vehemently, that she should immediately leave if she sensed any danger in the hallway, but she wouldn't classify this as exactly danger. Of course, he had also told her not to come to the hallway AT ALL until she saw him again, so maybe she should just leave …

Suddenly she saw a faint glow further down the hallway. She moved quickly toward the door. Sure enough, it had what she now recognized as Clovis's signature glow. When she put her hand to the door, vines wrapped themselves around her wrist and pulled her through.

#

Directly above Amelie's head, the sky was black, but neither with night nor cloud. Instead, it was dark with smoke. There was a light on the horizon, bleeding out from this darkness in shades of red, orange, and fiery yellow.

She was standing in a narrow, rocky valley. Mountains with steep cliff faces rose up on either side of her. The smell of sulfur permeated the air and the valley before her stretched out for endless miles before ending in a final monstrous mountain. It was from this that the colors were emanating.

Volcano.

Shit, she thought. *I hope it's not going to erupt.*

Amelie looked around but saw no one. She was alone in this black and orange world. A hot wind blew through the valley and hit her face with a stronger smell of sulfur, and something else, something coppery and sweet. It was at that moment she noticed the dark grass on the valley floor in the distance. It waved as another gust of wind from the mountain blew through it. When this wind reached Amelie's ears it carried the sound of clicking. Her muscles tensed before her brain engaged. She had been too distracted by the colors of this world to see her inner eye's colors. Scarlet. Black. Green.

Danger. Danger. Danger.

That was when she noticed that the "grass" was moving—in her direction. The first "blades" of grass were just close enough to make out. They were not vegetation, but some sort of insect. One landed right next to her. It looked like a greenish-purple locust, but bulgy and bloated with obscenely large, liquid-filled nodules on either side of its head. Covering it was something that looked like a cross between rat hair and spider silk. One of the things hit her leg before she realized it and she felt a searing pain run up her sciatic nerve. She slammed the thing away and squashed it. It looked like the spawn of a grasshopper and a leprous rat.

A tidal wave of them was swarming in her direction. These first ones were obviously scouts. Amelie turned and raced for the cliffs. She knew she had little chance of making it there before they caught up with her, but she knew that whatever happened here would impact her physical body, so she ran for her life.

Suddenly someone was running beside her with a torch.

Clovis.

182

"Run for that cliff!" he yelled, pointing, as he swiped the flame at the creatures on the bleeding edge of the swarm.

She made it there faster than she would have thought possible.

"Climb," he yelled from behind her. "They can't climb very far, and they can't fly much further."

Fly, god, they can fly, she thought, as she reached the cliff face.

It was steep, but craggy, providing handholds. As she jumped on the first boulder, she felt one of the bugs hit her chest, near her breast. She felt another flash of searing pain, this time radiating through her heart and lungs. She gasped but kept her hold of the rock. Clovis was now next to her. He scrambled past her, up the rock, grabbing her by the hand and hauling her up over the ledge.

"Keep them off with this," he yelled, shoving her the torch, as he grabbed a rock above him and yanked himself up.

A small cloud of monsters flew at her. She swiped at them with the flame, and they all exploded. She wondered if they were filled with flammable gas.

Just then she heard Clovis land hard right next to her.

"This way," he yelled, pointing upward to his right. "Around the corner, you just have to climb up to the next ledge. It's just there."

Her leg was throbbing and trembling treacherously. She wondered if her heart would soon be doing the same. Clovis took the torch and motioned for her to go first. She tried to grab the first handhold but couldn't pull herself up. She felt herself roughly pushed upward by the butt. Two nasty bastards hit the cliff face next to her head and fell. She pulled herself up and over the edge of the next ledge. Clovis was up in a flash and pulling her around another rock and into a large cave.

"Are we safe?" she asked, but he shoved her toward the back of the cave. He grabbed debris that was littered on the floor and piled it at the entrance, lighting it. As it began to burn, he turned back to her.

"Find things that burn," he yelled. "They're repelled by fire. They won't be here long, but we have to keep them away until they move past."

Despite the growing pain in her leg and chest, Amelie scrambled across the floor, collecting weeds and leaves. She also found the dried-out carcass of an animal, about the size of a Great Dane. It wasn't time to be fussy. She dragged that to the fire.

"Here," she said.

"Good, good," Clovis said as he pushed it into the flame and poked at it until it caught. Outside, the swarm seemed to be thinning, but it was hard to tell.

"Thank god," Clovis muttered to himself.

183

"Are they almost gone?" she asked, just as he whirled on her.

"What the hell are you doing here?" he yelled. "Didn't I tell you NEVER, EVER to come into a place like this? The last time I saw you, didn't I try to convince you to stay in an actual bunker for two weeks? Did you not understand that? God!"

He turned around and set the torch down on a small boulder. Amelie's leg chose to that moment to give out and she hit the floor. Clovis was by her side in a flash.

"Oh god no. Tell me that you weren't bitten!"

He ran his hands over her legs and body. She weakly pointed to her leg. He ripped off the strange, soft leather pants she was now wearing. Her leg was swelling and turning a vicious green-purple color.

"Okay. Your leg. Not so bad." He looked up at her and she shook her head. Her tongue was starting to swell, and she was losing her words. She yanked her shirt down to expose a mark on her breast. His intake of breath was audible.

He squatted beside her and pulled her up to lean against the wall.

"Okay, listen to me very carefully," he said in a slow, controlled voice. "I can fix this, but you have to stay with me. You CANNOT go back. You've been badly poisoned and there is no antidote for this in your story. If you go back, you'll die."

She heard him, but he sounded very far away. She felt like she was falling down a hole in her own head.

"I have to go get what I need for the antidote, but you CANNOT fall asleep or go back while I'm gone. Promise me! Swear it."

He was right in her face. So strange that black eyes could convey so much fear and warmth. So strange.

She nodded.

Then he was gone, and she was left with her brain, which was malfunctioning. She began to tremble all over as a thousand black horses stampeded through her limbs. An unimaginable wave of panic hit her and pulled her under. She began to scream, tossing and twitching in an effort to get away from her own body. It felt like bugs had laid eggs in her body and they were hatching and crawling under her skin, behind her eyes, feasting on the most vulnerable parts of her brain, causing a chemical storm in her head. In a desperate attempt to calm herself, she began to concentrate on counting her own moans and screams.

At some point she became aware that Clovis had returned. He had a bag with him, and she could hear something scrambling in it. Probably more of those things, she thought.

Is he trying to finish me off? Is he that mad at me?

He dropped the bag to the ground and there was a crunching sound as he ground his boot into it. He then opened the bag, dropped in something that looked like oregano, and squished it up again. A few seconds later, he was sitting next to her with a noxious mixture of brown, purple, red, and green mashed up in his palm.

"You have to eat this, and keep it down," he said as he sprinkled some more herbs into the bag. "Do you hear me? Do you understand?"

She realized that her head had fallen to her chest. She managed to look up and nod. He held up two fingers to her mouth, on which was a heap of the most repellent stuff she had ever smelled. She opened her mouth and allowed him to spoon in portions. Each time she gagged, and each time he waited a few seconds to make sure it would stay down.

"You'll vomit this back up, but you need to keep it down for at least a few minutes."

Easy to say. Her esophagus now echoed her leg and chest, in that it was on fire. The muscles all over her body were spasming, as if she was having a seizure. Clovis grabbed her and held her tightly in his arms. He was whispering something that she couldn't make out, in a language she didn't understand, while she continued to shake for what felt like an eternity.

"Why aren't you vomiting?" he muttered. "You should be vomiting by now. You need to vomit now."

He leaned her back against the rock.

Her head felt like it was the size of a balloon. She thought she might be screaming again, but it was hard to tell. It could all just be happening in her head.

"Here, sweetheart. Just drink some water for me."

She tried to look up and him, but the world seemed so sideways.

Did he always have those wings?

She didn't remember that. Wings looked very odd with leather armor.

"Come on, just a bit, okay."

Wow, he sounded scared.

The storm in her head was starting to subside just a bit, replaced by a fiber-glass insulation feeling. Everything looked soft and pink, but she was fairly sure if she tried to move, she would be cut to ribbons.

She lifted her head to the pouch he offered. It was water and tasted good. She drank deeply. That was when her stomach revolted, and she vomited.

That was just the start. She vomited until she had nothing left to vomit. Then she vomited bile, then blood. Finally, everything just went black.

Later, when Amelie came to, she expected to be in her bed. Instead, she was lying on the cold rocky floor of the same cave, covered in sweat and stink, with her head in Clovis's lap. He was gently stroking her hair despite what was now in it. When she looked up at him, she was shocked to find him crying.

"Oh, you're awake," he said, wiping his eyes quickly. "You slept for a while."

She looked down at herself and her surroundings. She was covered with multicolored muck.

"Oh gross," was all she could say. He smiled gently.

"Well, that's one way to say it, I guess. Do you feel like you can sit up and drink some water?"

"I don't want to be sick again," she whispered. Her throat was tight and raw.

"No, just a sip," he said, as helped her up and put her back against the wall. Her brain was back to some semblance of functioning. The panic and horror were gone.

Amelie looked around as he went to get the pouch of water. In the midst of all this, he had managed to make another fire further back in the cave. She must have been out for a while because this second fire was filled with dark red embers.

Clovis came and sat next to her, holding the pouch to her lips. The water tasted good, but she only took a small sip. She didn't want it to come back up.

"Do you want to get out of those clothes?" he asked gently.

She nodded. Clovis helped her pull the leather coverings and linen shirt over her head. It was only after he took these off that she realized she had no underclothes, but this probably wasn't the time for modesty. If he had watched her vomit for hours, any hope of being an object of lust was long gone. He dressed her in men's clothes he found in his pack, using hers to clean up the mess on the ground around them, before tossing them into the fire. He then grabbed a blanket and tucked it in around her. There was a lot she should probably ask but she felt so tired. Finally, she asked, "Will I be okay?"

He had returned to poking at the fire.

"Yeah. You'll be okay," he said, coming to sit in front of her. "Although I won't lie to you. You almost died. These things are wicked poisonous."

"Why didn't they bite you?" she asked. He snorted.

"They did, but I have an immunity to them. I have an immunity to most things."

He took her hand.

186

"But you don't. So why did you come here?" His voice was soft, but his words were pointed. "This was exactly the sort of thing I was afraid of. That's why I told you never to go into a door that seemed dangerous."

"It didn't seem dangerous," she started, but he raised an eyebrow at her.

"Okay, it did seem dangerous. But it didn't seem scary." She stopped and continued more softly, "I just wanted to see you."

He put his head in his hands, as if she had just accused him of rape.

"Fuck. I'm making you do dangerous things."

"You didn't make me do anything," she responded. "I'm not stupid. I'm just …"

In love with you.

She stopped herself just in time.

"Reckless, is that what you were going to say?" Clovis asked.

"Yeah, that was it," Amelie muttered, but her voice chose this moment to crack.

"Wow, this has been a really stellar day," she whispered to herself as she closed her eyes, rested her head back on the cave wall and pulled her knees up to her chest. She felt tears welling in her eyes. Damn it, not now. This was not the time for a confession of love. She should try to hold on to whatever tenuous shred of dignity she still had.

She heard him move to sit right next to her, so that their hips and legs were touching. She said nothing, but she noticed how hot his skin was. She wondered if this was normal for him. The contact of his skin to hers felt purposeful on his part.

She turned to look at him and he smiled and ran his hands through his hair. He was wearing the clothes of a warrior.

She closed her eyes again. They were both quiet for a while, but he didn't move away like he usually did. She felt the pit of her stomach heating up, and it was not a result of poison. She felt tears well in her eyes again.

Why would someone want to have this feeling? Why feel this for someone if they don't, or can't, reciprocate? Is this what other people felt with her?

Great, now she felt guilty on top of everything else. Clovis moved and the spot where they had been touching felt cold. He turned his body to face her. She heard this rather than saw it, as her eyes were still closed. She felt him brush the hair off her face with his hand.

"Are you crying because of something I said, or just because you've been through—well, all of this?"

It was a direct question, so she should answer it. But for the life of her, she couldn't figure out how to do it. The truth was too humiliating but lying was not something she wanted to do with him. She lied with everyone else, but not him. So she said nothing.

"Umm, it was something I said," he said. "Open your eyes and look at me, because I have something you need to hear."

She tried but just couldn't do it.

"Please, Ames," he whispered. She opened her eyes and his were staring right into hers.

"You have to understand. Well, I need to tell you some things. About me." He sighed.

"First, I'm not a purely seduction kind of incubus. I am, or I'm supposed to be, what we call the 'transition' variety. I'm the sort of incubus that's called on to help people to their death. I haven't done this for years, but it's my great gift, and it's also why I'm so good at seduction. I can make someone want to go to death just to be with me. It makes it easier for people to let go of this world and go on."

He stopped for a minute and then sighed heavily.

Great. I have fallen in love with Death. Actual Death.

"Yeah, it's horrible in lots of ways, but that's another story," he said, mind reading again. "Of course, I also seduce for other reasons. But that's just it. Seduction doesn't mean love for us. It's kind of a cross between having a meal, doing a job, and creating art."

She was trying to maintain some level of eye contact, but it was very uncomfortable.

Clovis was sitting on his knees in front of her, and he had taken her hands in his. He had such an earnest expression, but she had no idea what he was trying to say. He came to her because she was dying? He wasn't capable of feeling love and sex at the same time? He wasn't capable of love?

He took another deep breath and started to speak again, but then stopped and sighed.

"This isn't really coming out right. And I shouldn't keep touching you," he said, dropping her hands.

Was this the seduction-with-no-love thing?

"I don't want to hurt you more. Fuck, fuck, fuck, fuck!" He stood and began pacing around the cave again. She tried to watch him, but it was hard to keep her eyes focused. She was coming in and out of mental clarity.

As he walked, he clenched his fists and his face had taken on that scary animal quality again. He turned back to look at her with an expression that, for a moment, looked like the paintings of fallen angels—beautiful and damned. Then his eyes softened, and he nodded to himself.

"Okay then, just wait a minute. I'll be right back," he said and walked out of the cave.

Is this the incubus version of "I'll call you"? she wondered, before the weight of her eyelids won over her will.

She must have fallen asleep for a moment, because she was startled when he walked back in the cave. She had no idea how long he had been gone but he looked more solid somehow.

He walked straight over and sat down in front of her.

"Come here," he said, shocking her fully awake by pulling her into his lap. He took her face in his hands and placed his lips on hers, but this was no kiss. Instead, he was breathing into her mouth and as he did so, she felt a rush of energy. His lips tasted of gin and honey.

Suddenly, Amelie was no longer sleepy. She felt like she had been given a strong stimulant. Her thoughts began erratically racing through her head. Her body, on the other hand, was not erratic. It was very clear in what *it* wanted.

Clovis pulled back and she looked down. He pulled her chin up again and looked directly into her eyes.

"This isn't seduction," he said. "You don't feel that, right?"

She shook her head.

"I need to be sure that I'm not seducing you right now. If that happens, I could drain you even more. You don't feel that, do you?"

Amelie shook her head again.

"Good, I just gave you a lot of energy. So that should put us on equal footing for energy exchange or even better," he said, as he touched her hair. She had no idea what the hell he was talking about.

"What is your name?" he asked quickly.

"Amelie."

"Your father's name is?"

"Brent."

"Who was the last person you fell in love with?"

"I don't fall in love with people. They fall in love with me," was her knee-jerk lie. Well, it was true in the past tense.

He laughed in spite of himself.

"You seem fairly clearheaded," he said, but then his eyes became softer.

"But could it be that I'm the first person you've fallen in love with in this lifetime?" he asked.

It was such a direct, and dangerous, question and yet he asked it with no hesitation or fear. His onyx eyes were completely open. She felt her words die on her tongue. After a second, he looked away.

"While you were lying there thrashing, I was terrified. If something had happened to you, it would have been my fault."

She started to say something, but he shook his head.

"No, let me say this. I don't feel things the same way that you do. Feelings provide sensation for me in the same way that the physical world provides sensation for you. So my feelings are stronger and broader. When I saw you out there, I had so many feelings at once that I was overwhelmed for a second. I wasn't expecting to see you here, particularly after pretty much begging you to stay in a bunker. So I felt the thrill of seeing you, but anger because you were taking risks."

He blew his hair out of his eyes and ran his hand through his hair, then laughed.

"You know, incubi who fall in love with humans are viewed like humans who marry their pets." He continued, "We're told that we're discouraged from relationships with humans because we're so much better, but that's not true. It's discouraged because it never works out well for either the incubus or the person the incubus loves."

"Why?" she whispered, unsure of where he was going with this.

"We drain energy from humans. You already know that. Loving someone makes all that harder because we aren't able to keep from touching. With an incubus, the sexual desire doesn't fade over time, it gets more intense. So this drains a human's energy away. It might start out as small illnesses, but eventually it wears them down to the point that it makes them susceptible to disease. So the human dies and the incubus goes crazy."

Clovis sighed. "That's what happened to me, and that's what got me in trouble. I fell in love with a Japanese princess. She eventually killed herself, and I went full tilt crazy. And when an incubus goes crazy, it ... well, it can be a really bad thing."

Clovis was quiet for a moment, then he got up and walked over to the fire again.

"That's why I took you to that story based on Japan," he said softly, not looking at her. "When we were in that garden, when you said those words, I knew it was you. So I went looking for answers about you, because coming back to me in this life is something we're told never happens. Looking for information like that is breaking all the rules, so I had to seek out some dangerous creatures, in less than desirable places, and that's why I was here."

He turned back to her.

"A place you should never have been," he said, his eyes getting stormy again before quickly fading.

190

"But I should have been quicker. If I had just moved when I first saw you, you wouldn't have been bitten. And if I had lost you again, it would have been *my* fault."

His voice broke, and he looked up at the top of the cave.

"All my bullshit about protecting you, and here I am, the one who almost lets you get killed and in one of *my* worlds. I'm such an asshole."

"No," she said, pulling herself up to her knees. "I did something stupid. I did the exact thing you told me not to do. That's not your fault. You've changed my life and in only the best ways. You've been my best friend and—"

Suddenly she stopped, her little speech had forced her to focus and had stabilized her brain. What he had been saying suddenly registered.

"Wait, are you saying you love me?" she whispered. He turned around from the fire and crossed his arms over his chest.

"Well, yeah ... of course. I mean, let's be honest, why would I have done half the things that I've done if I didn't love you? I'm not made to be particularly altruistic. So, yeah. I'm saying I love you."

"But you're saying it from across the room. Isn't this usually where you would kiss me or something?"

"Are you wanting me to kiss you?" he asked, but he uncrossed his arms and smiled.

"Well, yes. But it's not just that ..."

"Meaning you want more than just sex?"

"Yes. I want you."

"Knowing everything that I am, you still choose me?"

"Well, I'm not sure I have any choice in the matter, but yes."

She could have said that better. But all self-recrimination disappeared when Clovis smiled. It was his crooked, amused half smile, but his eyes weren't exactly smiling. They looked smoky.

"Well, then I think we have a problem," he said, coming over and sitting down in front of her. "My touching you is dangerous for you."

"But you said that doesn't hurt people in dreams," she began, but he put his finger to her lips.

"You're different. And I'm different. We aren't in a dream here. You take things back with you from here. I'm designed to drain better than most incubi, so I can help people die. If I hurt you, or if I drain your energy too much, I will make you very, very sick."

"So we love each other, but we can't touch each other. God, that sucks so bad," Amelie said, with tears welling in her eyes.

"Not completely," he said, coming to her and scooping her up in his arms. He held her close as she buried her face in his chest.

They sat for a few minutes like this. She felt his heat again, and the increase in his breathing and heart rate. She was breathing fast as well. When she turned her face up to look at him, he was staring at her with those crazy, whirling eyes, but she wasn't afraid. No, she was far from afraid.

She threw her arms around his neck and kissed him hard. He resisted for a split second, but then he was kissing her back forcefully. These were not light, playful kisses. He kissed her like he was consuming her—and maybe he was. Whether he pushed her on her back, or she pulled him down on her, was unclear. What was clear was that she wanted him. She wanted to be as close to him as she could be. She wanted him inside of her. Her legs were apart, and he was lying between them, breathing hard, with his hands on her body. Suddenly he stopped and pulled himself backward.

"No. No. No. I will end up killing you if we keep this up. I can't do this," he said through clenched teeth.

He stood up and started walking around the cave. A sound escaped her that sounded unnervingly like a whimper. She sat up and pulled her knees to her chest. She refused to cry again like a baby. This was as bad for him as it was for her. She wasn't going to make things worse by crying. She was thinking all this as the tears began to slide down her cheek.

Maybe he won't notice, she thought. But he did, and came back to sit in front of her ... not touching her.

"Yeah, okay, this definitely sucks. But we'll find a way. I'm smarter than most incubi," he said, with a slight smile.

"No vanity, huh?" She found herself smiling a bit, as she wiped her nose in a not-so-delicate way.

"Not vanity, we've screwed this up a few times before, so I have more experience," he said, with a dark little laugh.

"We have a few possible solutions," he continued.

Solutions. Solutions is a good word.

"The first solution is safe and simple, but unlikely to work. The second is questionably ethical and time limited. The last is the 'Clovis will be damned if anyone finds out about it' solution. I shouldn't even mention it, to be honest, but it's the most real solution, and I'm kind of desperate now."

He sighed and shook his head.

"What's the safe solution?" she asked.

192

"I do what incubi do and try to find you only in your dreams—only in the dream space of our own world. This is what we are meant to do anyway, and I wouldn't drain you very much."

"Well, it's not perfect but it sounds okay. Why did you say it wouldn't work?" she asked.

"Well, unlike most incubi, I *can* find people in the dream space. It requires dropping lower, but I can do it. The problem is more on your side. The dream space isn't like the hallway. Humans don't dream that much, and usually those dreams are very short. If I could find you, it won't be for very long and you might not even remember it."

"Okay, no. What about the second one?"

"I do basically what I did here. We meet in stories in the hallway. I collect energy from someone and then give it back to you. But with that, I could never get enough energy for us to be able to do much more than we have done here, and you'll still get sick."

"So, what is this damning solution?" she asked, looking at his beautiful, crazy eyes.

"Well, you know I can possess people in your world," he said softly. She heard her own intake of breath.

"Yes."

"When I do that, do you see them or me?" he asked.

"It depends on the person," she said. "When you were in Carter's head, I just saw Carter. But with Hudson, for a moment, I saw you."

"Right," he said. "So I could possess someone more permanently. If we found the right person, it could be for hours, days, or even months. He or she would need to be someone who is open to the prospect of possession. They don't necessarily have to agree to it, per se, they just have to not fight that feeling when it happens. It's also better if it's someone you don't know that well.

"But would you do that?" he asked suddenly. "Would that be good enough for you? Would you be willing to do something that immoral?"

"I know I should say 'no, no that's horrible', but I can't," she whispered, placing her forehead on his. "Yes, I would do that to be with you. But I don't like what you said about you being damned if you were caught."

"No. That part's my problem. Don't worry about that," he said, lightly kissing her lips. "I have experience avoiding capture. There are some very powerful beings out there who would love to unmake me, and I have kept myself out of their way for millennia. I just don't want you to do something you'll end up hating me for."

"I can't hate you," she said as she pulled him to her and kissed him again. For just a moment, he was kissing her back, his tongue meeting hers, twisting, consuming. Then he gently pushed her away.

"No, baby. We've done too much already, and I don't want to hurt you anymore. Plus, I think you're fading, so you'll go back soon."

"I don't want to." Amelie began to weep.

"I don't want you too, either. It's nuts, but this horrible place will now be sacred to me. But before you fade, I need to you to promise me something. You're going to be very sick when you get back. That's why I wanted you to stay here as long as you could. The longer you're here, the more time the antidote has to work in your system. But you have the combination of being poisoned and being with me, so you're going to be sick. Not life-threatening sick, but hospital sick."

Amelie closed her eyes and he reached out to pull her close again.

"When you wake up, the first thing I want you to do is go get your brother."

"Will?" she gasped. "Why Will?"

"Because I can't help unless there's someone easy for me to be in. Your parents are too difficult to possess. So it has to be your brother. Promise that no matter how you feel in the first moments, you will go to him first. Promise it."

"I promise," she whispered, tears still on her face. But now they were feeling less wet. She was going away.

"Go to Will," Clovis whispered, holding her in his arms until it was all blown away like dust and dreams.

#

When she woke in her bed, her pillow was drenched from her tears. And yes, she felt very tired and sick as a dog, but mostly she felt a hole where her heart was. She had heard people say things like that before, but she never realized it was an actual physical sensation.

When she remembered she had promised to find Will, she sat up. It wasn't until she tried to stand that she realized how sick she was. Her legs couldn't hold her weight. Try as she might, she couldn't stand. So instead, she crawled out of her bedroom and down the stairs, but slowly, as she felt light-headedness coming over her. By the time she had made it to the bottom of the stairs she was having trouble holding on to consciousness.

She managed to pull herself down the hall and knock weakly on the bottom of Will's bedroom door. At first there was nothing. She had just pulled herself up enough to turn the handle of the doorknob when the door opened. She fell against her brother's legs and was immediately picked up by strong arms.

She had just enough time to hear Will say, "I got you," and see his eyes turn from blue to black, before she blacked out.

Chapter Twenty-Four

Death by Interior Design

"You been gettin' sick a lot in the past couple of months, little girl," Amelie's dad said as he stood glaring at her from the end of her hospital bed.

Her father's big-boned frame had probably been muscular in his youth. Since then, most of his mass had moved to vacation spots around his belly. His round, reddish face was creased between his eyes from too much squinting at the TV. This morning he had dark circles under his eyes in addition to the perpetual squint, which spoke to lack of sleep.

Although Amelie's body felt like someone had tried to turn her digestive tract inside out, her brain was clear enough to hear the accusation in her father's voice—and to be shocked by it. What he said was true. This had been the third time in as many months that she had been sick. Of course, this one would be different in his mind because it landed her in the hospital, which meant a co-pay would be forthcoming, and co-pays were a sin.

"You sure you ain't pregnant?" he asked, giving her the redneck father equivalent of the evil eye. The depth of his paternal concern was deeply moving.

"Brent, leave her alone," her mother snapped. "She's been up to her damn eyeballs in that whole SAT, college stuff. Ain't no wonder she's sick sometimes. Stays up to all hours studying and all."

Amelie inhaled sharply, briefly choking on her own spit.

Opal had been sitting quietly by Amelie's bed that morning when she woke. They hadn't spoken to each other. Amelie had pretended to be dozing through all the poking and prodding of the nurses, and Opal had pretended to be reading *The Economist*, both of which were equally implausible. Her father had recently arrived. Amelie assumed that Opal's comment was probably because she was pissed off at being saddled with the brunt of the parental responsibility this time. Still, even knowing this, Opal's comment could have knocked Amelie over with a feather. Her mother was actually defending her. The number of times that this had happened before was … never.

"I'm just sayin' that sometimes people get sick when—"

"You're talkin' shit is what you're doing," Opal interrupted him. Brent's eyes went wide. Her mother was smart-mouthed to be sure, but even her father would be shocked she was siding with Amelie.

"You need to git to work, and *I* need to git to work," Opal snapped, emphasizing the "I" part. Opal then stood up and flipped her hand in the direction of the door. Before leaving she came to Amelie's bedside.

"The doctor said you can come home once the fever stayed down for twenty-four hours. You'll likely git out tomorrow night. So just rest up while you're here. Try to read, or whatever it is you like to do," she said to Amelie, actually looking her in the eye for once.

As her father turned to leave the room with a cursory nod, Opal leaned closer to her and said softly, "But don't sleep too much. It probably ain't good for you just now. And your brother won't be doing no more visiting here, that's for damn sure."

Now Amelie could have been knocked over by someone's extended exhale.

Her mother gave her a weird little smile, before turning to leave the room. After she left, Amelie promptly grabbed the vomit tray and retched. She could understand why her father suspected her of pregnancy. If she hadn't known her own sexual status, she would have suspected it too. As she lay back down, every muscle in her abdomen screamed for her to stop moving already.

What the hell had Opal meant about sleeping not being good for her? And what was that reference to her brother not visiting? Clovis had been possessing her brother in order to get her to the hospital quickly, but she wondered how long he had stayed and what he might have said. She began to feel dizzy and sick again, so she closed her eyes.

Amelie took deep breaths, trying to settle the nausea. After a few minutes, she sat up slowly and tried to stabilize herself by focusing on the room around her.

She was still in the ER, but she had been placed in an actual room, as opposed to one of the makeshift beds in the hall. The decor of the room was painfully colorful. The floor was royal blue with large yellow circles splattered across it. The uncomfortable-looking plastic chairs, where her mother had been sitting, were vibrant orange. This was bad enough, but the privacy curtain was in a multicolored rainbow pattern that looked like it had been designed by a five-year-old. She wasn't sure if it was her illness, the overwhelming smell of disinfectant, or the decor that was making her dizzy and nauseated.

She closed her eyes again and replayed moments of the night before. She could see the cave and Clovis watching her from his spot near the fire. She saw the look on his face when he held her.

He loves me.

She instinctively put her arms around herself and immediately regretted it as her stomach shrieked.

I'm in love.

Last night she had told Clovis that she was willing to try possession in order for them to be together, immoral or not. She didn't tell him that she would be willing to try even more immoral things. She tried not to think of those things, but they were coming unbidden to her mind. He had said something about *him* being damned by using possession to see each other, and this weighed on her mind, but for him and not for her. She wasn't all that concerned about being damned herself. She should have been, but she wasn't. She realized that this was probably a sign that there was something fundamentally wrong with her, but then again, she had always had something fundamentally wrong with her.

She was pulled out of her thoughts when she heard someone come into the room. She opened her eyes to see Dr. Diasil walking toward her bed. She remembered that Clovis had specifically told her to stay away from him. She pulled her energy in fast.

"Hello Amelie," he said, pulling up a chair and sitting next to her. "Do you remember me?"

"Yes," she said, breathing out and aiming energy at a potted plant across the room. She then smoothed her shields down around herself again.

"Indeed," he said. "And here you are again." His voice was completely neutral, but the words sounded like an accusation.

And what are you doing in the ER, Urgent Care doctor? she thought but she said nothing.

He took out a pen and pulled her chart from the side of the bed.

"What can you tell me about this illness. How did it come on?" he asked, his large brown eyes regarding her with a bit too much intensity. He didn't look nearly bored enough to be a real doctor examining a patient whose symptoms were a midrange fever and vomiting.

Her inner eye opened and she saw the room bathed in yellow and red light. Interest. Passion. Danger. She would need to step carefully, measure her words, and think of the downstream impact of each one. This was even harder given her shaky emotional state.

"I started feeling a bit sick yesterday afternoon," she said slowly. "It was just nausea, really. But I woke up in the middle of the night with dizziness and nausea."

"Yes. Your brother was *very* concerned when you were brought in. He said that you had to be carried to the car, and was insistent that you be seen immediately," Dr. Diasil responded. His eyes were scanning her face with intensity.

That would have been Clovis.

"I guess I had a fever," she said quickly, before she could stop herself.

Shut up. Don't offer conclusions. Don't volunteer information and only answer what's asked.

"Perhaps. But your fever wasn't high. We checked potential causes for your symptoms, but all of the normal ones checked negative. Normally, I would just conclude this was a virus but given your history—"

"What would be the normal causes for my symptoms?" she asked, interrupting him to buy herself time and supplemental information for lies she might need. He sighed and furrowed his brow.

"Well, you didn't have a cardiac incident," he said, tapping his pen on the paper. "You have no ear infections. Your blood glucose levels are completely normal. You have normal blood pressure. You have no anemia."

He stopped for a moment and looked at her.

"And you're not pregnant," he added.

"That's good," she said, with a forced smile.

"Yes. That is all good, but to be honest with you, the aggregate of your symptoms looks like poisoning ... by an animal or insect."

How could he know this?

"Why would you think that?" she asked, in as flat a voice as she could muster.

"Well, the symptoms that I mentioned, as well as your loss of consciousness, mental confusion, and the blue cast to your lips when you were brought in. There were some unusual substances found in what you vomited. You also had some strange marks on your chest that could have been stings from an insect, but that seem to have disappeared."

Shit.

"Do you know if you happen to be allergic to bee stings?" he asked, raising an eyebrow at her.

"Not that I know," she replied.

"Hmmm. I'll want to keep you for at least another twenty-four to seventy-two hours. I'll also have you moved to a private unit, just in case it's something contagious," he said.

199

"You're quarantining me?"

"No. I'm just giving you a private room. It's just a precaution," he said quickly. "Once you're stable, you can go home. In the meantime, we can monitor your vitals."

And take blood samples. Clovis had told her not to let him take blood samples.

"Don't worry, I'm sure it's just a virus, but this gets you out of school for a few days," he finished with a smile that looked unnatural on his face.

Amelie nodded.

"Get some rest and I'll check on you later," he said, as he patted her hand.

I bet you will.

After he left, Amelie examined the IV in her arm. It was basically chaining her to her bed. A short, petite nurse entered the room smiling. Her red hair was styled in a pixie cut and her name tag read *Bonnie*. She was carrying a tray with the implements required for a blood draw.

Great.

Amelie closed her eyes, so she wouldn't see the blood being drawn against her will.

"Don't worry, Psyche. No one will take your blood today."

Amelie's eyes flew open. The nurse came and sat on edge of her bed. For just for a second her form flickered, and she saw Clovis's face, black eyes, and his tousled hair.

"You're here," she whispered.

"Yeah. And I'm relieved. I was scared it would be a lot worse, but you're recovering fast."

He reached out and took her hand. She felt dizzy again but not from the illness.

Stop it. You need to tell him ...

"The doctor," she whispered. "He's the guy who saw me when I got scratched by the dog."

"I know," he said. "I saw him—and he's bad news."

"He's taking lots of blood samples. What if—"

"Ssssh," Clovis said, putting his finger to her lips. "I'll take care of that. I'll make sure nothing of any interest gets into the wrong hands."

"You can do that?" she whispered.

He smiled. "You forget, I can be almost anyone. At least for a little while."

"Will the nurse get in trouble?" Amelie asked, regarding the pixie face in front of her. This nurse was nice. She would hate to get someone in trouble, but if it was a choice between being safe and being nice, she would choose safe.

"No, but let's not talk anymore about that. I can't stay long, and other people will come in soon."

Amelie nodded. Clovis leaned forward and whispered in her ear.

"Listen, there is something I need to tell you to help keep you safe. You would have died in that place if I hadn't found you, but you can get out of stories anytime you want."

"I can't. I've tried."

"You control it with your heartbeat," Clovis said. "Your heart has additional beats—or it has that ability. You feel your heart beating super fast sometimes, right?"

"Yes," she replied. In a normal day her heart went off rhythm several times, all day if she had caffeine. Suddenly the fact that her first meeting with Clovis had been after her obsession with Red Bull began to make sense.

"You can use these extra beats to match the heartbeats you would need in different stories. If you can reset your heartbeat, you'll be drawn home," Clovis said.

"What? Why would I have heartbeats from other worlds? Is that common?"

"You have heartbeats tied to other worlds because of your parentage—whatever that is. I think that must be the thing that lets you get into the hallway to begin with. Most humans can't get in. Most Cambion can't. So there must be something about the nature of your parentage that gave you these additional heartbeats."

"But lots of people have weird hearts and weird heartbeats. Or that's what our doctor told us," Amelie replied.

"Sure, but those beats come from a physical defect. Yours don't, but the important thing you need to remember is that this can get you out of the worlds in the hallway."

"How?"

"It's easy. Just hold your breath. When your heart starts to run out of oxygen, your heart will default to one beat—the beat of your world. Does that make sense?"

Amelie nodded. Clovis kissed her forehead.

"But for now, I need you to take care of yourself while you're here and concentrate on getting better. You have to stay well for me. Okay?"

Her throat closed up. Flashes of images hit her brain. Flowers. Water. Firelight. She nodded.

"Good. I'll see you as much as I can, but I'll be around even if you can't see me. Maybe if you concentrate, you can feel me," he said with a little smile. "But don't worry. I'll take care of you."

She heard another nurse coming toward the room. Clovis got up quickly, took the tray, and threw the syringes in the biohazard trash. Just as the lid of the trash slammed shut, a middle-aged Latina woman with large hips and a larger smile stepped into the room. On her uniform she had a name tag that read *Sofia*.

"Hi, Amelie," she said, walking toward her. "You doing better?" Amelie looked over toward Clovis. He smiled and then he was gone. Amelie's heart seized.

The nurse looked between the two of them.

"Everything okay, Bonnie?" she asked, as the other nurse put her hand to her forehead and weaved a bit.

"Yes, I'm just getting tired. It's been a long shift," Bonnie said, shaking her head.

"Well, you can clear out. Amelie and I have got it under control here," she said, smiling at Amelie.

Amelie opened her inner eye and saw nothing but the color of good intentions. She relaxed.

"Have you done the blood draw?" Sofia asked.

"Yes. That's already done," Bonnie replied.

Amelie laid her head back down on the pillow and closed her eyes.

#

Sofia was filling up her pitcher of water when Amelie woke up. She turned to Amelie with a smile and was about to say something when another nurse roughly pulled back the curtain.

"We need you in room 12 STAT. Code blue," she snapped.

"What happened?" Sofia asked as she quickly followed the woman from the room.

From a distance, Amelie heard the other woman reply.

"It's Dr. Diasil."

Chapter Twenty-Five

Japanese Garden Groupies

Amelie was released from the hospital twenty-four hours after being admitted, with instructions to stay out of school for a week to recuperate. Dr. Diasil had experienced some medical emergency and a much less interested doctor had taken over her case. His interactions with her had been of the more regular, bored doctor variety. Amelie had considered asking the nurses about the condition of Dr. Diasil, but she was afraid of the answer she might get. Clovis had identified Dr. Diasil as a threat. Now that threat had been eliminated.

The hallway would be off limits for a week, until she had fully recovered. Her experience with the rat bugs had taught her something that Clovis had been unable to—the hallway was dangerous.

She managed to keep herself engaged and entertained enough for the first five days of her convalescence but by Friday she was going crazy. If she stayed inside, she knew she wouldn't be able to resist going to look for Clovis, dangerous or not. So she escaped to the public library.

When she arrived, the library was in its usual, mostly peopleless, state and that was just fine with Amelie. The old librarian must have had the day off, because a younger version was sitting at the desk perusing an old Marvel comic book. He didn't even look up as she walked in. Her energy was so well contained now that sometimes she could manage to make herself so uninteresting as to be invisible. It was blissful.

Amelie found a spot for herself and began to look up some books on Japan. Clovis said the garden they were in had come from this story, so she wanted to see if she could find some reference to it. Or maybe even find out about the story Clovis had told her about the princess and the koi.

As she wandered through the stacks, she picked up books and brought them back to her table. On her third trip to the stacks, a wave of fatigue hit her, and she dropped to her knees.

"Are you okay?"

A man appeared out of nowhere, crouching at her side. Her inner eye engaged, and she saw light bouncing off his dark skin, swirling, changing, and then being sucked back into him. She had never seen this before.

"I'm fine," she said, head down for a second, trying to close her inner eye down, which seemed to be malfunctioning.

When she looked up, the man was staring at her wide-eyed. But probably not as wide-eyed as she was. She hadn't taken in his full appearance at first. Now she did—and what an appearance it was.

He was tall and thin, but broad across the chest and shoulders. He had dark hair, full lips, high cheekbones, and a strong, sharp jawline. His almond-shaped eyes had a slight upward slant, making him look Asian, but the shocking blue color hinted at a mixed ancestry. But it wasn't his body that marked him odd, it was what was adorning it. On his head he had an unusually tall but dingy black stovepipe hat with a maroon band. Stuck in the band was a seven of spades Bicycle playing card. His trousers were black and tight with a rather ornate codpiece over his crotch.

"Oh, don't be worried, I'm in a play and this is my costume," the man said, shrugging. "I don't have time to change before rehearsal. Plus, I'm trying to keep in character."

The cadence of his voice seemed familiar. For a moment, she was excited. She quickly checked his eyes, but they were still blue. The energy coming off this person was weirder than she had ever encountered in a normal human person.

What the fuck?

"Are you sick? Do we need to call someone?" the man asked.

Amelie shook her head. The man reached out, but as his hand touched her arm, she heard him gasp. This gasp turned into a cough as he turned his head away.

"Here, let's get you to a proper chair, shall we? Are you able to stand up?" he asked. She nodded but she was breathing out of her mouth. She was suddenly severely nauseated.

"My stuff is over there," she said, indicating the couch near the stacks on her left.

The man took her to the couch and helped her sit.

"Do I need to call someone to take you home?" he asked.

"No, I'm just a little nauseated. It'll pass in a moment."

"Not pregnant, are you?" he asked. Amelie started and she suddenly felt an almost electrical buzz throughout her body, pushing against her shields.

"Of course not," she said, sending a small blast of energy toward the bird sitting on the windowsill and then slamming her shields down.

"I'm sorry. I shouldn't have asked that, it was very indelicate of me. But if you need anything, I will be right over there," the man said, indicating a couch against the wall. "I'm memorizing my lines."

He then smiled, returned to his couch, and sat down with a notebook.

Amelie nodded and closed her eyes. She scanned the man's energy but felt nothing amiss. Actually, she felt nothing at all. When she opened her inner eye again, she saw no color, no light, nothing. That, in and of itself, was weird. She closed her eyes and used her senses to scan the room. Everything seemed normal.

"I was getting myself some water. Would you like some?" she heard a voice say suddenly. She opened her eyes to find the man had brought her some water while her eyes were closed.

"Thanks," she said crisply, taking the water.

"No problem. Let me know if you need some crackers or something," he said. His voice was soft and unassuming, and she felt no glamour signs coming from him.

He turned to walk back to his seat.

"I'm sorry," Amelie said. "That sounded really snappy. Thanks for the water."

The man turned around and walked back, stopping at a respectable distance.

"I don't mind. I'm prone to low blood sugar myself, and it makes me dizzy and cranky," he said, shrugging. To her own surprise, Amelie heard herself laugh.

"Are you saying I'm dizzy *and* cranky?" she asked.

"Maybe," he said, then looked down at the book she had in her hands. It was the book on Japanese gardens.

"I see you are interested in Japanese gardening. I love Japan. It's one of my very favorite places."

"Have you been there?" she asked before she could help herself. The memory of Clovis standing next to the koi pond inserted itself in her head.

"Lots of times. I'm not overly fond of Tokyo, but I love Kyoto."

"Why?" she asked, her eyes scanning his face.

"I love the gardens and the history. Are you doing a report?" he asked.

She faltered for just a moment but quickly thought of a lie.

"Yes. I'm looking up myths and stories related to Japanese gardens."

"That's quite specific. Is this a school project?"

"Yes," she said, then hesitated for a second. "I wanted to include a story someone once told me, but I can't find any written record of it."

Stop talking about this. Right now.

But sometimes strangers were the easiest people to talk to.

"What's the story?" the man asked, sitting in a chair across the table from her.

"It was a story about a Japanese princess. She lived in a palace with her family. I think it was near a place called Ijishi," said Amelie.

The man's eyes widened again.

"Is that the end?" he asked.

"Apparently she killed herself," Amelie said softly. "I don't know anymore. I don't know if it's a myth or a story about a real person or just a story this guy made up."

"Who was the guy? Was he Japanese?" the man asked, his words touching her eardrums like silk threads.

Is this a glamour?

"No. He wasn't. He isn't," she said, pulling up her shields a bit more.

"Hmmm. It's an interesting story. It sounds more like mythology or an actual event rather than a literary story. Does this person like mythology?" he asked.

"He likes stories," Amelie said with a small smile.

SHUT. UP.

"Don't we all," the man laughed. "At least those of us that love libraries."

The room around her suddenly began to pulse with yellow and orange light.

Caution.

"Oh, look at the time. I'll be late for my rehearsal," the man said, bowing slightly to her. "I hope you have a lovely day, and that you find your story."

Amelie watched as the man left. The librarian was so consumed by his comic book that he didn't even look up as the man passed.

Amelie shook her head slightly. All that was weird but maybe everything just seemed weird to her today. Still, she should tell Clovis about it the next time she saw him. Tonight, she would try to find him tonight.

With that, she turned her attention back to her book on Japan.

#

Amelie didn't see the man in the hat stop in the parking lot outside. Nor did she see him approached by a stunningly beautiful woman with platinum hair.

Chapter Twenty-Six

Rochester Manor

That night, when Amelie went to the hallway, she planned to be particularly careful. She had seen how dangerous it could be and wanted no repeat of her rat bug experience. But when she touched down in the hallway, she was pulled directly in front of a stone door which was shining in that way that told her Clovis was behind it. When she reached out to touch it, it was with only slight trepidation.

The door, and the hallway, melted away and Amelie found herself in a brightness that blinded her for a moment. When her eyes adjusted, she saw she was in a garden, attached to a manor house. In style, it was similar to the garden where she first met Clovis. But while that garden had been sculpted and meticulous, this one was wild and untended. The stone paths were overrun by flowers she couldn't name. There were scraggly bushes covered with yellow flowers, blue flowers hanging from vines that crawled over the stonework, and clumps of small white flowers everywhere, pushing forth even between the stones of the walkway.

Amelie looked around for Clovis, but she was alone in the garden. She turned toward the house. It had probably been grand in the past, but now ivy was covering the lower floors and the stonework was beginning to crumble. Gargoyle waterspouts adorned the upper floors but were in such disrepair that they were no longer fearsome, unless you feared age. Amelie approached the nearest door, which had a large, rusty doorknob in the center of it that looked as if it hadn't been used in decades.

I wonder if I could get tetanus here? she thought, covering her hands with the cloak she was wearing before turning the doorknob.

Despite the rust, it was unlocked and surprisingly easy to open. The door opened into a narrow corridor that was dark and cool. She heard a cough and followed it to a large room off the central corridor.

The first thing that Amelie thought, when she entered this room, was that it had been decorated by a man with an unhealthy deer fetish—or her dad. Antlers hung from various spots around the room. The head of a stag hung just above an empty fireplace at the far end of the room. There were more antlers, minus their heads, at other points along the walls. In the center of the room was a circular chandelier made of iron, also set with antlers, sporting unlit candles. It reminded her of a richer version of her own family's living room. But once her eyes took in the couch in the center of the room, everything else became dim.

Lying on it, asleep, was Clovis. He was wearing a dark suit and some tie-like thing around his neck that Amelie thought was called a cravat. His feet, in riding boots, were propped up on the end of the couch. For a moment, she just watched him. She felt like she did the first time she had seen him, like she could watch him for eternity. The light coming through a less-than-clean windowpane across from him danced on his forehead and dark eyebrows. His complexion was slightly darker in this place, and his hair a little less wavy but mostly he looked as he always did. He looked like an angel. No, that was too tame and there was nothing tame about Clovis. Maybe he looked like an angel sleeping off a hangover.

He coughed again, and his soot-rimmed eyes fluttered. When he saw her, he came fully awake and his whole face beamed. His expression was more like a boy of her age than that of a man who would wear the clothes he was wearing.

"Hi," she said, feeling ridiculously shy again.

"Hi, yourself," he said back.

He stood up and was in front on her in a couple of strides. He took her in his arms and swung her around in a circle.

"God, I'm happy to see you," he said. "It feels like it's been forever since I've seen you where you could see me."

"I always feel like it's you. Even if you're in someone else's body," she replied.

At that moment, she caught a glimpse of their reflection in the mirror on the wall and gasped. The man in the mirror was old, haggard, and cruel-looking.

"What's wrong?" Clovis asked.

"You don't look like you. You know, in your reflection," she sputtered. Clovis laughed out loud.

"Of course I don't. I look like the person I'm possessing."

"Then why do you look like you when I look at you with my eyes?"

Clovis gave her a sideways smile, running his hands down her back.

"I thought you said you had read up about incubi."

"I did. Well, what I could find. But no one said anything about incubi looking different in mirrors. So why would you look like that in the mirror and like this when I look at you?"

"Hmmm," he said, "how do I say this?"

He was trying to suppress a smile.

"Well, you've heard of sirens, right?"

"The ones that sing people to their death?" she asked.

"It's not exactly their voices. Their voices trigger something in men so that when they look at the siren, they will see their heart's desire. That trait was stolen from incubi. When people look at us, they see their heart's desire."

Amelie felt blood beginning to rush to her face.

"So usually when people see me, they see me as their heart's desire. But when I met *you* …"

"I saw you as you are," Amelie whispered.

"Exactly. You saw me. No one sees *me*," he said softly.

"So you've known how I felt from the beginning?" she whispered, her cheeks burning.

"To be honest, I didn't know what to think in the beginning. But by the time we went to Disneyland, yeah, I knew."

"Why did you try to push me away?" She didn't really want to ask that question, but it popped out of her mouth.

"Because I'm fucked up," he said, taking her face in his hands. "But I promise you that I won't push you away again. I'm here for the long term. For our whole story … whatever way it goes."

He pulled her to him and kissed her.

She felt as though she couldn't get close enough to him.

He tangled his hands in the folds of her cloak, pulling her closer. She could feel desire wash over her. He yanked the clasp of her cloak and it fell to the ground. He ran his hands down her back, pulling her closer still. Then suddenly he stopped. He backed up, his eyes closed, breathing deeply.

"Okay. Enough now. I stole some energy before I got here, but if we keep this up, you'll get sick again," he said, stepping back and walking across the room to the window, taking deep breaths as he went.

Amelie felt a dull ache in her pelvis, as if she had period cramps, accompanied by a desire that made her feel like chewing on something. Clovis stopped at the window.

"It's okay," she said. "I don't mind getting a little sick."

"No, it's not okay," Clovis said, turning to face her. "At some point, my ability to stop will—well, I won't have one."

"Then I'll stop us," she replied, knowing what she said was a lie even as she was saying it.

Clovis laughed and shook his head. "No, you won't."

She crossed her arms over her chest.

"You're as frustrated about this as I am, so I don't think I can count on you to say no," he said.

He walked over to the couch, sat down and patted the seat next to him. Amelie went and sat next to him, his leg barely touching hers. Still, hers was trembling.

"What about the other thing you said. About a way we could be together. About possessing someone in my world ... you know, to really be together?" she asked softly.

Clovis looked at her intently.

"You would do that? You would be okay with that? Me being in someone else's body ... not looking like me?" he asked.

"As long as it's you ... yes, I'm okay with it."

He took her face in his hands and kissed her softly.

"That scares me more than a little, Psyche," he said. "But it excites me too. I'd have to plan it carefully. It would have to be just the right person. There're lots of ways that it could go really wrong."

"If you just possess them, and then I leave before you let them go, that shouldn't be too hard, right? You've done that before."

Clovis laughed. "Oh, it will be hard to hold someone under those circumstances, but I can do it. There are other things that worry me more than just the physicality of all this."

"Like what?"

He looked at her and brushed hair off her face.

"Amelie," he said softly, "this type of love, this thing we have together, it's hard for me to explain it over lifetimes, and you don't remember. But ... well, it isn't pretty. It isn't hearts and roses. It isn't holding hands in the park and eating romantic dinners in candlelight at some quaint little restaurant in Paris. Well, it can be all of those things, but it's much more. It's more powerful and much scarier. You're going to see that as time goes on. It can drive people crazy. It does drive people crazy. It drove me crazy. This sort of love is hard enough when the roles we are given are malleable enough to contain it, like lovers. But imagine what would have happened if you had been my mother, or we had been

211

siblings, or I had been an adult human who met you as a child. You can see how this could go very wrong, very fast."

Amelie crossed her arms over her chest. It was defensive gesture but damn it, she suddenly felt defensive. Clovis blew air and threw his hands in the air, and stood up, pacing the room.

"How do I make you understand?" he muttered. Then he looked up. "Look there was a book written in your world. It was about a boy who killed a bunch of kids in his school. Then he went home and killed his father and sister, but he let his mother live. The mother was cold and distant. The boy was dark, mean, and sadistic. Do you know it?" he said.

"Yeah, I know it. Charlotte wrote a book report about it."

"Well, the intellectualized question the story supposedly asked was whether the boy was born evil or if he became evil because his mother rejected him as a child. But to me, it was just a love story gone wrong."

"That's what Charlotte said," Amelie replied.

"Yeah, who do you think gave her that idea?" he said flatly.

"You were inside Charlotte?" Amelie asked, shocked despite the fact that she shouldn't have been.

"Of course, I have been inside everyone in your classes," he said. Amelie felt things go sideways again with the implications of that, but he continued.

"Charlotte not only read the book but watched the movie, so I did as well. All I could see was that these two creatures had this sort of powerful love between them. The kind we have. In the end, the boy went crazy. He killed his whole family, just so he could have her to himself. When I watched this story, all I could think was that they could have prevented everyone else's suffering if they had just gone off together as lovers. Yes, they would have been damned by society and themselves. Everything about that would have been taboo, but at least everyone would have lived."

"But we aren't in roles like that," Amelie said.

"Yes, we are!" he snapped. "You're a human. I'm an incubus. You're breaking no end of cosmic rules, whether you know that or not, by coming to the hallway to find me, including draining your own energy and making yourself sick. I'm hurting people by stealing their bodies in your world so I can be near you. I have physically and mentally damaged humans, sometimes just for looking at you. I steal people's actual life energy, so that I can touch you a bit when we are here. Does any of that sound remotely ethical?"

Then he stopped speaking, a look of pain suddenly flashing across his face.

"But all that doesn't matter. What matters is that we love each other, and we are here. And the further we go with this, the harder it will be to hold on to sanity … especially for me."

"You seem fairly sane to me," Amelie said.

Stupidly, she was feeling rejected. She didn't know why, and her brain knew better, but she felt it anyway. Clovis sat down next to her again, and took her shoulders, forcing her to look at him.

"Do I? Do I really seem sane? When you think of me, is 'sane' the first word that comes to mind? You saw what I did to your friend Jack. And I suppose you heard that Dr. Diasil died? You do know I did that? I seduced him to his death. You guessed that, right?" he asked, his face close to hers.

Amelie felt a moment of shock. She had guessed that Clovis had killed Dr. Diasil. The shock was from hearing him say it out loud.

Clovis leaned in to put his mouth to her ear.

"You know what I would have done, if I had been the son in that book?" he whispered to her, enunciating each word slowly, as if it were rolling off his lips. He ran his hands up her thighs.

"I would have waited until I was old enough and strong enough, maybe eighteen or nineteen. Then I would have chloroformed her and taken her to a hotel somewhere in another city. Not a creepy, isolated place, but somewhere nice and upscale, somewhere that, if she screamed or called out, people would have been right there to help her. That way, when I seduced her and her resolve broke, she would have to admit to loving me because she would know that she could have escaped. After that, I would have kept her in ecstasy for as long as it took to wipe everything and everyone else from her mind. Once she was mine, I would have taken her away forever. If I had to beg, borrow, steal, kill, or prostitute myself to earn money, I would have done it, it wouldn't have mattered. Does that sound particularly sane to you? Would you still think me sane if I told you that I have done all that I just said, and worse?"

You stole a body and did this to me, didn't you? her mind whispered, and she felt light-headed.

Amelie felt the heat from his breath in her ear. Her own skin was so hot that she was beginning to sweat, even in this cold place. Why did his words not disturb her? Why did she get pinpricks of memories in her brain and why did these memories not scare her? For once, it was like she could see a little bit inside his head.

Suddenly, he sat back from her and shook his head.

"But that's not love, Ames. It's the desire part of this love, for sure, but it's what happens when the desire part gets out of control and starts consuming everything else. I don't want that to happen to us, not this time, not now that I know. That's what scares me. I'm afraid that if we take the step into me possessing someone in order to have sex with you, then it will go there. I'm not sure that I can keep myself from going there. It's kind of how I'm made."

Amelie was trembling again. How often did he leave her trembling? She knew he was right. Everything he said made sense, but she was pissed off at him anyway.

This time it was she who got up, walking to the window and looking out at the rolling green hills in the distance. She didn't want to talk about this anymore. She loved him.

"Touching you feels too good to be good," Clovis said softly. She nodded. He was right, and she was being a petulant child.

"This stupid thing is pulling at my neck," Clovis said suddenly, as he pulled at the cravat. "It's hard to believe someone ever thought this was a good look."

Weird clothes. Also, you should tell him about that guy—

"Oh, right. I should tell you about this guy I saw when I was at the library the other day," she said, coming to sit beside him again.

"Your school library?" he asked.

"No, the public library," she replied. "But he was so odd."

"Yeah?" Clovis asked in a softer tone.

"Yeah. He was wearing these really weird clothes and he started asking me about the books I was reading."

"What weird clothes?" Clovis asked sharply, sitting up straighter.

"Really out-of-fashion stuff. Like stuff from another time," she replied. Clovis eyes were widening.

"What *exactly* was he wearing?"

"Well, this tall black hat, and a codpiece," she replied with a little laugh.

Clovis turned the color of a sheet and took her by the arm.

"He said something to you? And you answered?" he asked.

"Well, yeah. It would have been rude not to."

"What did he ask, and what did you say? Think carefully. I need to know exactly."

"What? You're scaring me."

"What did you say?" Clovis answered, his eyes wider than she had ever seen. He didn't look crazy or like an animal. *He looked scared.*

"Well, he asked me about books I was looking at. I said I was doing a report."

"What books did you have?"

214

"A book on Japanese gardens," she said softly. Clovis closed his eyes and clenched his fists.

"No," he whispered, squeezing his eyes shut. His lashes started to look a bit wet.

"But the guy didn't seem scary or dangerous," she said quickly, putting her hand on his arm.

"Of course not. He never does. That's his tactic," Clovis whispered, his eyes still closed.

"Tactic? Who is he? Do you know him?"

"Yes, but is that all? What else did he say, what did you say?"

Amelie felt her stomach turn.

"He said something about liking stories and libraries."

"Fuck. Fuck. Fuck. Fuck. FUCK!"

Clovis slammed his fists on the couch, got to his feet and began walking in circles around the room.

"What? What's wrong?"

"You know the people that I said were watching me. Looking for me. Well, that's one of them. His name is Dante," Clovis said.

"Why would he be talking to me? Because of you?"

"Oh, I wish it were that, but if he's talking to you about stories then they damn well must suspect that you can get to them," Clovis said. "And of course, the fact that you spoke to him means he knew you could see him."

"Why shouldn't I be able to see him?" she asked, her stomach beginning to knot.

"Because he's a ghost. Only Cambion can see him. No. Only really unique and really strong Cambion can see him. Goddamn it."

He walked in circles with clenched fists. Suddenly he stopped and let out his breath.

"Okay," he said, coming to crouch in front of her. "We have to slow things down. We have to get them off your scent. Maybe they found you through me … but now they've found you."

He stopped for a minute, and his eyes got even wider.

"Or maybe because they think you have brought a … oh no … oh shit." Clovis put his head in his hands.

Amelie touched his forearm.

"What is the name of that flu that was going around your city?" he asked, looking back up at her.

"Dog flu," she whispered, feeling the knot in her stomach tighten.

"And did that outbreak start just after we met the first time and you got sick after I scratched you?"

She felt the blood drain from her head.

"Yeah. That's what I thought. But they can't know that yet. If they did—" he stopped.

Clovis reached out and took her face in his hands.

"Listen, Ames, we can't do any of the physical stuff in your world anymore," he said. "Not for a while. If he was drawn to the energy we make together ... if we make that ... they would ... no, we just can't risk it."

"What?" She felt like she had been kicked in the gut.

Clovis was scared of something, but his words threatened her need for him. She jerked her head out of his hands.

"It's too dangerous," Clovis said. "You're already vulnerable with just what little we have done. If we have sex in your world ... it could make you even more vulnerable. It's not worth it."

Now she felt like she had been kicked in the teeth.

"I'm not worth it?" she whispered.

"No. Sex isn't worth it. It's not worth that risk. You have to keep your immune system as impenetrable as you can make it right now, so they don't see you as a threat."

"I see," she said, standing up and walking toward the window. She knew that something was going on. She knew that she shouldn't take this as rejection, but her need wasn't listening.

"Amelie. Don't act like a child about this. It's just sex. It's not worth you being unmade."

"Well, I wouldn't know, would I?" she snapped.

He stood up and came to stand in front of her, but he didn't touch her. She felt like she suddenly had the plague.

"Honey, these people have two lists. One is the kill list, and the other is people they are watching to see if they go on the kill list. No, it's worse than a kill list."

He turned his head up to the ceiling. She could see that his eyes were wet.

"They have an unmake list. If they know you, it means that you're on one of their lists. As he didn't immediately destroy you, it means that you're on the watch list. It also means they haven't tracked the viruses back to you, so they don't know you are a risk—not yet."

"What do you mean, 'know I'm a risk'?" she asked.

"You brought back a virus from another story, that's exactly what they believe they exist to prevent. They think that foreign viruses corrupt this reality that we live in. They've found that these sorts of viruses change the DNA of everything. They've even tracked these viruses to the rise in shootings, serial killers, sociopaths, and all sorts of other things. They have a whole organization designed to look for people who might be hosts for this sort of virus … and you seem to be."

"That's not my fault!" she said, sounding whiny even to her own ears.

"Of course it's not your fault, but it doesn't change the fact that you're vulnerable to such viruses, and that makes you too dangerous. Too dangerous means they unmake you. And if they unmake you, I don't know how long it will take me to find you again. Do you get it?"

Maybe what he was saying was logical, but that didn't matter. She felt like he was calling her Typhoid Mary and that he didn't want her. She knew she was being ridiculous, but she just couldn't help it. She laughed a little.

"What?" he asked sharply.

"Oh. I don't know. I was just wondering if maybe the only reason you considered having sex with me in my world was because I was willing. Maybe that's a first for you. You once told me you liked firsts. Maybe no one else in the past would do that for you."

She knew it wasn't true, and it was a mean thing to say, but her emotions were all over the place.

Clovis blinked hard. He looked like she had just slapped him in the face. Then he stepped away from her.

"What? You think what? God. No. I can't. Not now. Just no," he said. "We don't need this shit right now. And I need to be clearheaded."

At that moment, there was a loud crash above them. And the sound of a woman's voice laughing.

"Wait here," Clovis said sharply, and then turned and walked through the door that led to the hallway.

#

The minute he had left the room Amelie felt a wave of regret.

Now that he was gone, and the drug-like intoxication she felt in his presence faded, her brain woke up. It was then that his words began to sink in.

Kill list. Danger.

She couldn't believe she had stood there and insinuated that he wasn't trying hard enough to be with her when all he was doing was looking out for her well-being. She shook her head.

"Cloooovvvvissss," she heard a singsong voice calling from somewhere above her. She knew the voice.

Rose.

"Clovis, no," she said, as she got up and tried to run after him, but at that moment two things happened simultaneously. There was an explosion at the top of the house, and the world around her began to fade.

No. No. No. No.

#

When she opened her eyes in her own story, she was in her darkened bedroom. She flipped on the light and examined her body. For once, there were no marks on her. Then the nausea hit her, and she vomited in the lined trashcan that now had a permanent place by her bedside.

Afterward, she lay on her back. She worried about what she had said to Clovis. She worried about Rose showing up. But mostly, she felt waves of humiliation about how she had acted. Remembering her own words, her face burned with shame. She wondered how he could stand her when she could barely stand herself. With this thought, she began to cry.

She cried deeply but quietly until finally, exhausted, she fell into a fitful, morning sleep.

Chapter Twenty-Seven

Deals With the Devil

"Her name is Amelie McCormick."

Sawyer's head jerked toward the window at the sound of Amelie's name.

This was the earliest he had ever come to work. In fact, he had arrived when the sky was still mostly dark, and the birds were just beginning to sing for the sunrise. His window was cracked open to catch the early morning breeze, and it allowed him to hear the voices outside. At first, he thought it was just the gardeners, so he had ignored them, but now someone was talking about Amelie.

He snuck to the window and peeped outside. On the landing stood the strangest looking man and woman that he had ever seen. The woman was pale, blonde, and perfect. Her heart-shaped face held huge eyes and beautifully formed lips. She was wearing a white dress and her platinum hair was pulled up in a ponytail high on her head. Her sparkling eyes were locked on the man in front of her.

If she was striking in appearance, her companion was otherworldly. He was darker-skinned, tall and thin. On his head he had a black, stovepipe hat. His trousers were adorned with an actual codpiece. As the woman tapped her foot, he reached out to caress her arm. His movements were slow and languid, but occasionally jerky, as if frames had been cut from a film. Also, something in the way he stroked her arm radiated with sexuality. The woman stopped tapping and gave him a small smile.

"And Amelie, she goes to school here?" the woman asked, looking around her with unmasked disdain.

"Yes," the man replied.

"We were the ones to send her here?" she asked with a sigh.

"Yes. She's been tracked."

"Obviously not well, if it has taken this long to realize she's a threat," the woman said, tapping her foot again. "When did he contact you?"

"Two days ago."

"Did he contact you before or after we decided to come for her?"

"After," the man replied, "but I don't think he had access to that decision. I suspect that it's just coincidence. I saw the girl a few days ago. So it's likely she told him that she saw me."

"And why should I listen to anything he has to say anyway?" the pale woman asked of her companion. "He's dangerous and we both know it. If he's this close, why don't I simply unmake him and be done with it?"

"I don't think you could catch him, my love," the man replied. "We've tried to unmake him at close quarters before, but his thought patterns are simply too fast to latch on to."

The woman snorted.

"Well, one thing we know is that this place has a serious infestation," the man said, pointing toward the back of the auditorium. Sawyer followed the line of his finger and saw his black shadows creeping and rolling near the base of the building. The ones that we capable of leading him to Amelie.

"We'll deal with that later," the woman replied. "They've seen us. We'll come back later when they are less prepared."

Suddenly, as if out of nowhere, a third man appeared beside them. No, "man" was not the operative word. The creature in front of them was dressed like a high school boy, with a black T-shirt, khaki shorts, and black trainers. He looked about eighteen or nineteen, with pale skin and shaggy, unkempt hair, but that was where his similarity to any high schooler ended. The face and body of the boy were perfect. In fact, he was so beautiful that he was hard to look at. Sawyer felt a pang in his heart. This was the same sort of pang that he felt when an extraordinary student showed up, times one million.

The boy looked like an angel. The moment Sawyer thought this, large black wings appeared on the boy's shoulders.

"Looks like someone hasn't been doing their job," the angel said, with a dark, humorless smile. "This place is a viral pigsty."

"I don't think that's your business and I'm surprised you're concerned, given your disregard for hygiene, or even safety," replied the woman.

As she spoke, she moved closer to the angel. Her eyes were now glowing bright blue. For a moment, these eyes drifted up and toward Sawyer, who dropped to the ground, his heart hammering.

"So why did you want to see us?" he heard the man in the hat ask in a silky-smooth voice.

"Come on, Dante. I know why you're here. And you know that I know. You talked to Amelie, and you got enough information out of her to trace her back to me."

Despite his terror, Sawyer raised himself just enough to peek through the window.

He saw the creature called Dante nodding.

"I want to know what you know about her, and what you're planning to do," the angel said, crossing his arms over his chest.

The woman cocked her head.

"That's not really your business, is it?" the woman asked, voice sounding like tiny shards of broken glass falling on a metal plate. "You must think very highly of yourself to think that you have any right to know about our actions or our business."

The angel laughed.

"I don't know about that, Kara. But I do think highly enough of myself to believe that I can keep Amelie off your radar, for the rest of her natural life, if it comes to that. I suspect you might find that problematic."

There was silence then, but it wasn't static silence. Sawyer could feel rivers of tension pass by him even if he could see nothing.

"Yes, you probably can," Dante finally said. "But that begs the question of why you would and why you're here."

"I'm here because I *could* keep her off your radar, but it would be tiring. And it certainly wouldn't be any fun for me," the angel replied.

"And you are all about the fun," said Kara, her voice acidic.

"And who made me this way? But the reason I contacted Dante is because I think I can help you. You're searching for Amelie because you think she is the source of the recent viruses, am I right?"

Kara's face became stony, and Dante smiled ever so slightly.

"Yes, we do," Dante replied.

"Well, you're right. She *is* the source of them, or at least some of them. But what you may not know is that she brought one of these viruses back directly from the hallway."

"If that's true then you surely understand why she has to be unmade," Dante said softly.

"In theory, yeah," the angel said. "But if you unmake her, how do you know that she won't eventually be remade in exactly the same fashion? I know you'll say that you'll deal with that when it happens, but suppose you didn't have to? Suppose there was a fix?"

"If such a thing were possible, we would know about it, and we would have implemented it," Dante replied.

"Not necessarily. You wouldn't think about it if it went against your world's rules. You wouldn't allow yourself to, given your history," said the angel.

"And you know such a thing?" Dante asked quickly, his voice much less silky.

"Yeah, I do," the angel replied.

There was a flash and a sound, like lightning had struck the landing. Sawyer peeked outside. The angel was gone. Kara was standing with one arm outstretched, two fingers pointed. Dante took her arm.

"You see. He reads your thoughts before your actions."

"Was that really necessary?" asked the angel. He had reappeared behind them.

Just at that moment, there was the sound of a car pulling into the lower parking lot.

"Listen, I have a proposal that will solve your problem. If you accept it, then you agree to stop hounding me—forever. Will you hear it?"

Kara looked at him hard, but it was Dante who responded.

"Yes, we will listen."

"Good. Let's go somewhere else to discuss this. There are people coming, and someone has been listening," said the angel, looking up, directly at Sawyer. The angel's eyes were black and merciless.

Sawyer threw himself to the ground. At the same moment a gust of hot wind blew over him. It smelled of ash and burning plastic and was strong enough that a few books were knocked from the shelves of his bookcase. And then, all was silent.

#

Sawyer stayed on the floor for a long while, afraid to move. His heart hammered and his head felt like it would split. It wasn't until he heard the sound of adult voices on the landing that he was able to sit up.

When he looked outside, he saw Ms. Hartness and Principal Scales walking into the school. He stood up and moved to his desk.

His brain was whirling. Amelie was special. He had always known that. In recent weeks, he had let his desire show. Now, when he caught her eye, her glance revealed her own desire of him. He knew that she was ready, but now it seemed she was the consort of an angel.

Sawyer felt a sharp pain in his head, then an idea grew from that pain. What if the beautiful creature wasn't an angel but a demon. Demons were, after all, fallen angels who lusted after human women. In that case, he needed to make his play for her before the demon did. He would need to do it soon, while she was still receptive.

"Phil. Would you like a doughnut?" Hartness called from the outer office.

"Absolutely," he called back, grimacing slightly. "You're my angel."

Chapter Twenty-Eight

The Lights Go Out

Amelie had heard nothing from Clovis for a week. She had accused him of choosing her because she was his only choice. It was stupid and she had known that as it was coming out of her mouth. It wasn't until afterward that she realized exactly *how* stupid it had sounded. He had just told her that she was in danger, and all she could think about was her own insecurity. She had acted like a whiny, insecure teenage girl with someone who was thousands, if not millions, of years old. While she believed him when he told her that he loved her, she still wondered why he was willing to put up with her. Maybe he had decided that he wasn't.

On top of that, she had no idea what Clovis had encountered when he went up the stairs. She knew he could take care of himself with Rose, but she hated that her actions had put him in closer proximity to a creature that horrible.

At school that week, Amelie tried to act normally. She even tried to muster enthusiasm when Hudson approached her about going to prom. She hadn't planned on going, but he made a convincing argument that it would help cement their relationship in the minds of others. Their fake relationship had worked out incredibly well for both of them. There was significantly less sex teasing, and she had the freedom to eat lunches with him rather than her friends.

On the night of the dance, Amelie and Hudson didn't show up until 10 p.m. When they got there everything was already in full swing. There was a band at the far end of the auditorium and numerous round tables sporting white tablecloths were scattered around the periphery. In the center of the room was a dance floor, with an actual, cheesy disco ball above it. The air was already thick with the smell of alcohol, with a slight undertone of vomit that Amelie knew would become more pronounced as the night went on. The lights were dimmed and, although it was hard to see the faces of the people in the distance, that didn't seem to stop her friends from spotting her immediately.

"Amelie, Hudson," Sophie greeted them as they walked up. At the table was Jack, Judith, and Carter. Everyone had weird smiles on their faces.

"Hi," Hudson said, holding out a chair for Amelie.

Amelie sat down. Her friends were staring at her expectantly—everyone but Carter. Carter had a glazed sort of look in his eyes as he stared into the distance.

"Where's Elodie?" she asked, to break the tension. All eyebrows went up at once.

Sophie pointed to Carter and then to the table.

"How classy," Hudson mumbled. It took Amelie a second longer than Hudson to catch on.

Elodie's working on her blowjob-in-public badge. Great.

Amelie put her head in her hands, and everyone laughed.

"Don't worry, it'll be over soon, if his face is any indication," Judith drawled, her eyes crawling over Amelie's face like flies.

"Well, let's not be present for that," said Hudson, standing. "Amelie, want to get a drink?"

"Yes. That would be great," she muttered. The others laughed again as they walked off.

"They do enjoy treating us like virginal geeks," Hudson whispered to her. Amelie nodded but said nothing. That was a topic she really didn't want to open. To end the conversation, she used a well-rehearsed and well-loved female strategy.

"Can you grab me a drink? I need to go to the restroom for a moment," she asked, as they approached the bar.

"Sure," he replied. Amelie nodded and headed in the direction of the restroom. As she got there, two girls came stumbling out. From the look and smell of it, the effects of the evening's alcohol consumption were already being felt.

Amelie swallowed her gag reflex and entered the restroom. It was mercifully empty for the moment, and, despite the smell, there were no obvious signs of vomit. She checked herself in the mirror. Her face looked okay, but her eye makeup was beginning to smudge. She wasn't used to wearing this stuff.

She grabbed a paper towel and was leaning forward to wipe the black from under her eyes when she heard something behind her. In the mirror she saw a person enter the bathroom. It took a millisecond for her to realize that the person was none other than Mr. Sawyer.

He closed the door behind him and switched off the lights.

She was alone in there.

The bathroom was now pitch black.

He's coming after me in a public place. If he'll do this, it means he doesn't care if he gets caught. He'll try to get away with as much as he can before that happens.

All those years of avoiding this, of planning and preparing in her brain for something like this happening, paid off. She didn't scream—not yet. She didn't want him to know her location. Before she screamed, she wanted to be closer to the door so she would be sure to be heard.

Instead, she crouched on the floor. She took off her heels and moved quickly and silently away from the spot she had been. She didn't move directly toward the door, because he would be expecting that. Instead, she moved in a counter-clockwise direction, in order to get to the door from behind him. She couldn't see him; her eyes hadn't adjusted to the dark yet. She didn't know if he could see her, but she was trying to be as quiet as possible. Just as she made it past the line of sinks, only a few feet from the door, Sawyer reached out and grabbed her by the hair.

She screamed and grabbed at his hand.

He pushed her down on the tiled floor. Her nose was assaulted by the scent of Pantene conditioner. She struck out at him, but he grabbed her arms and pinned them to the cold wet tiles.

"FIRE!" she screamed as loud as she could, but Sawyer smashed his lips against hers. His breath smelled like old coffee and his sour, sticky tongue pushed at her lips as she jerked her head from side to side. She turned her head to the side and opened her lips long enough to scream again. Sawyer used that moment to grab her head and force his tongue inside her mouth.

Suddenly the lights came on, and Amelie saw Mr. Sawyer's face. His eyes blinked with shock and then his face twisted with a combination of lust, pain, and rage as he was abruptly yanked off her. For just a moment, Amelie saw Hudson's face. It was a mask of fury. Hudson dragged Sawyer across the bathroom and threw him out the door. For a moment, Amelie was frozen where she was.

He came after me in public. In public.

There was a commotion just outside the bathroom. Amelie stood and made her way to the door on shaky legs.

As she reached the open door, she saw Phil Sawyer lying on the floor, with Hudson standing over him. Sawyer was protecting his head with his arms, as though expecting to be kicked. Students standing nearby had frozen and were staring. Hudson was breathing hard, his hands clenched into fists.

At that moment Ms. Hartness appeared in the gathering crowd.

226

"Phil, what's wrong? Are you okay?" she asked, crouching next to him. Sawyer curled himself into a ball and pulled his head down to his chest.

Ms. Hartness looked at Hudson with fire in her eyes.

"What have you done to him?" she snarled.

"He was attacking Amelie," Hudson snarled back. Mr. Scales was approaching from the other side of the auditorium.

"What? Don't be ridiculous. He would—" Ms. Hartness began but then her eyes found Amelie, where she stood swaying in the doorframe. When Ms. Hartness looked back at Mr. Sawyer, he curled up tighter. Hartness's eyes went wide.

"No," she whispered, turning a pale green in the dim lights.

"What's going on here?" said Scales as he walked up. The sound of his voice acted like a trigger on Sawyer.

He instantly scrambled to his feet and ran for the fire exit.

Chapter Twenty-Nine

Clovis Plays to the People

The commotion that followed Mr. Sawyer's sudden departure allowed Amelie to escape the scene. Hudson had intercepted Scales and was being questioned by him. She didn't know how Hudson knew that she needed time to compose herself, but he did.

She was still shaky and didn't want to answer questions yet. Sawyer had taken her by surprise. This should never have happened. She should have sensed him before he came into the room. Now that she could control her gifts, she needed to use them better. She should have scanned her environment before she let herself be left alone.

Amelie sat down at an empty table. She wiped her mouth repeatedly with the back of her hand. She couldn't believe that asshole had kissed her. That kiss had told her more about him than she had ever wanted to know. She saw his violent fantasies about girls in the school, about boys in the school, about her. All of that was bad, but it was nothing she hadn't seen or experienced before, during her dark days. What was new was that there was something underneath all of that. There was a presence in him that had energy patterns that she didn't recognize, colors around him that she had never seen before. Colors that were totally foreign to the human brain. She shivered a bit.

You're just wound up, she told herself. *An asshole kissed you. It's not the first time and it won't be the last. Brush it off and shut it down.*

She would deal with this later, when she was better prepared. With her new-found control, maybe she could make him fall in love with someone else. Too bad Ms. Pryll was out of the picture.

She ran her hands through her hair as she sat up straighter and shook out her arms. In the background, the band started playing again. The music had a strong backbeat. It sounded like Motown, but more seductive. She breathed in time with the backbeat. She felt it pulsing in her hips.

"Just fyi, Scales is on Hartness now," Hudson said, sitting down next to her.

"What?"

"Ms. Hartness. After talking to me, Scales cornered Hartness. I've never seen him so angry. If you don't want to be grilled about it right now, I'd stay out of his way," Hudson said, leaning close to her.

"Where is Sawyer?" Amelie asked, looking around.

"He bolted out the fire exit. Scales talked to one or two teachers as well as the security guards, so I'm guessing they're searching the grounds for him."

"Have they called the police?" she asked.

"I don't know."

"What did Scales ask you?" Amelie asked.

"Just the basics about what I saw. But man, he's furious. There's serious rage potential hiding in there. I think he might have—"

Hudson was cut off by Elodie, who had appeared suddenly at the table and pulled a chair up next to Amelie.

"Oh my god, you have to help," Elodie said in Amelie's ear. "She's out of control."

Apparently, the news about her and Sawyer hadn't made it to her girlfriends yet.

"Who's out of control?" Amelie asked.

"Look!" Elodie said, pointing to the stage. Amelie looked—and the energy hit her like a body slam. The air coming from the direction of the stage smelled like incense and sex. Her head was throbbing in time with the music.

The stage was overrun with people. Strike that, the stage was overrun by dancing girls—seductively dancing girls. The band, Charlie Danos's band, was playing an extended version of "Mustang Sally". Charlie was playing guitar and singing, which must have been difficult as one girl had her arms around his neck from the back, another one was leaning up against one side of him, and Sophie had wrapped herself around one of his legs.

"I know she has a crush on him, but we need to get her off that stage," Elodie said. "She's making a fool of herself."

This was a bit much from a girl who had just given her boyfriend a blowjob under their dinner table, but whatever. Amelie wasn't interested in that. She wasn't interested in Sophie either. Her eyes were locked on Charlie. Charlie Danos didn't like Motown. The person on the stage danced with his hips in a languid, earthy, sexual way that Charlie couldn't have pulled off in his wildest wet dreams. He certainly couldn't provoke whatever was happening on that stage.

"Let's go get her," Elodie said in Amelie's ear, but didn't move to stand up.

Amelie nodded, standing. She started to make her way through the crowd to get closer to the stage.

Wait, there was a crowd.

Crowds don't gather around bands playing at a prom. On top of that the crowd was predominantly female. They were all dancing, playing with their hair, touching their lips and swaying their hips. The air around her felt like an orgy waiting to happen.

When she got about ten feet from the stage, she stopped. As she watched, Charlie turned his head and touched foreheads with the girl leaning on him. The girl clutched him harder. He grinned. Amelie knew that grin. Charlie caught her eye and held her gaze. Charlie's blue eyes were black. He sighed into the microphone, grin still on his face. Sophie now had one arm *and* one leg wrapped around his leg. She was gazing up at him with her lips parted. She looked like a porn star. To complete this picture, she reached up and brazenly ran her hand over his crotch. Charlie's grin widened slightly but his eyes never left Amelie's face.

Amelie turned and pushed her way back through the crowd. She was relieved to see him, to know that he was all right, but she hadn't expected to see this. She wasn't sure if she was hurt, angry, disappointed, frustrated, or some combination of all of the above.

Was he trying to punish her for her stupid behavior?

Hudson was suddenly at her side.

"What's all that about?" he whispered. She was saved from having to answer that question when the music stopped suddenly.

"Psyche," Charlie Danos's voice whispered into the microphone. Amelie heard the name circle around her like a blanket. She stopped but refused to turn around and look at him. Hudson put his hand on her arm.

"Okay then, it seems like she's mad at me," Clovis said, "Amelie, this next one is for you."

All eyes turned to stare at her. Even in the darkness of the dance hall, she felt naked in the scrutiny of their collective gaze. She also felt the intensity of their hostility.

What the fuck was he doing?

Continuing their Motown groove, the band then launched into a version of Martha and the Vandellas' "Heat Wave". This had always been a favorite song of hers, in a dark-humor sort of way. How Clovis had known that, she would never know. Now she turned around. Charlie/Clovis was standing at the microphone, hands gripping it, lips touching it and eyes closed.

The Motown version of this song had always sounded weirdly upbeat and perky, given the subject matter. The cover the band was now performing had the same peppy arrangement, but the vocals were grittier, darker, and more desperate-sounding. Clovis still stood at the microphone, looking down and barely moving. Occasionally he would grab his head or handfuls of his hair, but that was the only movement. There was nothing else to distract from the intensity of his voice.

No one was dancing, despite the catchy tune and beat. Everyone was just staring, some with their mouths hanging open like trout. Clovis was pushing up against the microphone in a stance that was both sexual and desperate, also possibly painful.

Amelie found herself moving back toward the small stage, almost against her will. People stepped aside to let her pass. Something was happening in the room. Amelie opened her inner eye and saw a rose-colored mist, radiating from the stage and creeping like smoke through the crowd. Couples began to draw closer to each other. Others began to look away from the stage and toward someone else in the room, with wide-eyed longing. Heidi Stack and Charlotte Ives came together on the dance floor and began to kiss passionately.

By the end, the *yeah yeah yeah yeah* and *burning burning burning* vocals were less sung than growled. *Right here in my heart* was a scream.

At the end of the song, the auditorium was quiet for a second, then there was a full round of applause. That, in itself, was unusual for a band at a school dance. Songs were supposed to be the soundtrack for the rest of the activity, and no one claps for a soundtrack, but this was different. Everyone had been riveted by the antics on the stage for the last couple of songs. And this last song, it had been a love letter—to her.

Clovis stepped away from the microphone and did a little bow, then jumped from stage and began to make his way toward Amelie, who was rooted where she stood. The bass player looked shocked but quickly grabbed his microphone.

"Thanks everyone. We'll be taking a fifteen-minute break now."

#

People were still staring as "Charlie" made his way over to her. She briefly wondered if he would kiss her in front of everyone now. She found herself wanting him to, despite her previous annoyance or the inherent danger, but he stopped at a polite, respectful distance.

"Hi," he said, a bit shyly.

231

He tried to shove his hands in his pockets before he realized that his leather pants didn't have pockets, so he put them behind his back. She still felt eyes on her, but less obviously so. People's attentions were being directed elsewhere and Amelie suspected Clovis was encouraging that.

"Well, that was subtle," said Hudson, who was still at Amelie's side. She had forgotten he was there, but he obviously recognized Clovis.

Clovis shrugged.

"Sometimes subtle doesn't work. It's better just to put yourself out there. That's why men starting writing songs. You can let out what you feel easier when you sing."

He turned to Amelie.

"Are you mad at me?" he asked as he took her hand. She wanted to be mad at him. She felt like she should be mad at him for something, but just at that moment she couldn't remember what she should be mad about.

"Nope, looks like she isn't," Hudson replied for her. "I'm gonna go get whatever passes for punch and leave you two to—well, to whatever. Come get me when you want to go home."

With this Hudson headed off. Amelie turned to watch him go and her head cleared just a bit—enough to remember why she was annoyed.

"What was all that about?" she started, indicating the stage. As she looked in that direction, she saw Sophie sitting on the edge of the stage. If looks could kill, Amelie would be sleeping under a tombstone.

"What was what about?" Clovis asked, moving closer to her.

"That stuff on the stage, with the pack of ravenous females."

Clovis was about to answer when he was interrupted.

"Mr. Danos!" a voice called. Clovis turned but didn't let go of her hand. Mr. Roberts was striding toward them.

"Uh, yeah," Clovis replied. Amelie felt his hand tighten on hers.

"I know you're not one of my students, but I'm a chaperone here, and while many of the other teachers didn't seem to notice, I *do* know the words to the Nine Inch Nails song you played earlier this evening. While it was a surprisingly good performance, and you did a nice job of slurring the lyrics, I cannot stress strongly enough that it isn't appropriate for a high school dance."

Clovis pulled Amelie up next to him but relaxed his hold on her hand a bit.

"Yes, sir. I guess that song was over the top."

"Sir", uh-oh, Charlie would never say "sir". For that matter, neither would Clovis under normal circumstances.

"It wasn't just the music that was over the top, Mr. Danos," Mr. Roberts said. "Your behavior on the stage was also far from the PG-13 expectations of our community for a student event. The last song you played was a very age-appropriate song, which I personally love. I love less watching high school girls, some of whom are my students, simulate intercourse, fellatio, and a host of other sexual acts on a spoiled, would-be musician who knows that he doesn't have to work for a living because his daddy will always pay for him. No, I don't enjoy that at all."

"Yes, sir," Clovis said.

Mr. Roberts looked at him oddly. Amelie squeezed Clovis's hand. Charlie would never ever be this polite, particularly after being openly insulted. Amelie thought she should intercede a bit but before she could speak Mr. Roberts stepped in closer to them, looking intently at Clovis.

"So do you mind telling me, Mr. Danos, why exactly you decided to create that Dante-like situation for sexually frustrated male teachers? Surely you knew that we wouldn't approve."

Clovis narrowed his eyes for just a second.

"It was because of her," he said, nodding at Amelie.

"What? Me? What did I have to do with all that?"

"Yes, do tell," Mr. Roberts responded, with arms folded over his chest. Clovis, for his part, seemed to be trying to suppress a smile.

"Well, I really like this girl." He shrugged a bit. "But we had a fight a few weeks ago. It was a long and complicated fight, but basically she said that the only reason I was interested in her was because I couldn't get anyone else. I took that as an insult to both me *and* her. So I wanted to show her that I don't have a dearth of options in that department."

"Is that so?" Mr. Roberts said dryly. Clovis locked eyes with him.

"Yes, that's so," he said firmly. He then turned to Amelie. "And if I choose her, it isn't because she's my only option."

Amelie grinned in spite of herself.

He turned back to Mr. Roberts.

"But you are completely correct, sir. I didn't need to be that blatant and it was probably a stupid, egotistical thing for me to do. So, I won't be playing anymore for the rest of the night. The rest of my band can fill in and I'm sure they'll be more conservative in what they do and play."

"Very well," Mr. Roberts said, the beginnings of a small smile playing at the corners of his mouth as well. "But perhaps you should make yourself scarce before another teacher sobers up enough to notice your behavior."

Clovis quickly took Amelie's hand and led her toward one of the side exits. Just as they were about to walk out the door, Mr. Roberts came trotting up behind them.

"Oh, a couple more things, kiddos. Amelie, behave yourself tonight, I don't want any unplanned pregnancies in my class. It is a bad reflection on me as an authority figure."

Mr. Roberts then looked at Clovis and said softly, "Please keep Ms. McCormick away from Mr. Sawyer, as I believe there was a bit of an incident this evening."

Amelie felt her heart skip a beat. Clovis raised his eyebrows but nodded.

"And one last thing," Mr. Roberts continued. "Whoever *you* are, would you make sure that you leave Charlie Danos's body in reasonable condition when you go. His father will notice and will certainly complain if anything untoward happens to his son."

Amelie's mouth hung open, but Clovis just nodded and pulled her out the door and into the night.

Chapter Thirty

Exchangeable Form

Outside, the night air was cool and fresh. The lights in the parking lot illuminated shapes well enough to see forms but not details. Clovis had a firm hold of her hand as he led them from the auditorium.

When they were a respectable distance away, Amelie pulled Clovis to a stop. "Oh my god. Did he just say what I thought he did?" she asked.

"Yes, he did," Clovis said. His hand tightened on hers. Amelie faced him.

"Does he know what you are?" she whispered.

"I'm not sure if he knows exactly what I am, but he clearly knows I'm not Charlie."

"Is that a problem?" she asked. Her eyes had adjusted enough now to see Clovis's brow furrow.

"I don't know," he replied. "Some people are very interested in things they consider 'occult'. He may be one of them. He didn't feel particularly unusual the times that I possessed him, but something about him was odd tonight. He felt … I don't know, 'full' somehow. Probably not a problem but we should still be careful around him. Don't give him too much information."

He shrugged and gave her a little smile.

Amelie felt that dopey rush in her gut again. She hadn't wanted to admit how badly she had missed him or that she had been afraid that she had scared him off for good—at least not out loud. It was such a relief to see him, even when he was surrounded by girls on a stage.

Suddenly the jealousy flared, and she dropped his hand.

"Oh, and you never answered my question, what the hell was that all about in there? What exactly were you trying to prove with the whole faking sex with all those girls?" she snapped, crossing her arms over her chest.

"I did answer it. It's pretty much exactly what I told your teacher," Clovis responded, a bit dryly. "Do you still think that I'm only with you because I don't have access to anyone else?"

"No," she said, "but—"

"Then I made my point. That's what I wanted to show you. You aren't the only one who can have whomever you want, whenever you want them. And you aren't the only one who's had people want you, but not know you. That's been my whole existence."

Amelie felt the anger rush out of her, like a deflating balloon. That last sentence, and the flat way that he said it, hit home. To never be known, for however long he had lived. It took her a while after meeting Clovis to realize that she had spent most of her life knowing no one and being known by no one. He had saved her from that, with the things he taught her and with his presence. How horrible it must have been for him, to feel that for so many long years.

Clovis looked at her silently. He was facing her and the light from the auditorium was behind him. It created a halo effect and obscured his features a bit. She reached out and took his hand again. He gave it a gentle squeeze and started walking her in the direction of the parking lot. Amelie wanted to say something, but she was at a loss.

"I want to know you," she said finally. "I've always wanted to know you, but sometimes I think you don't want to let me."

"You wanting is enough," was all he said.

They found her car and he sat down on the hood, scooting back until he was leaning against the windshield. Amelie joined him. The night was clear, and the stars were bright for being in a city. Night creatures were singing to each other, and an occasional breeze rustled the new leaves in the trees. One of Clovis's legs was touching hers. She was acutely aware of the touch.

"I'm sorry about walking away the last time I saw you," he said, looking up at the sky. "I ... there's a lot I needed to think about. And your comment about—well, what you said about me choosing you because you were my only option. That's *really* insulting to an incubus. I know you didn't mean it that way. You don't know our culture and I know I overreacted to it. But I was already wound up after you told me about meeting Dante. And some things are just sort of knee-jerk, you know?"

"I know," she said. "I acted like a baby. I'm also sorry I didn't tell you about seeing that guy, Dante, earlier. I just forgot about it. I know you're trying to protect me ... and us."

Clovis nodded.

"Is he going to be a problem?" she asked.

"No, we'll find a way around that problem," Clovis said, turning to look at her and brushing some hair off her face.

She couldn't see his face very well, and that was better. In the soft light, she could almost see him as himself.

"Did Rose find you? I was really worried," she asked softly.

Clovis shrugged.

"Rose is Rose. She found me, then she died. Or her character died. That's what happens to her character in that book, so I just had to wait once the fire broke out. I knew you had escaped because I felt you leave. And I knew you were okay because I have been watching you."

He's been watching me, she thought, feeling herself flush with pleasure.

Clovis's face grew stern.

"Listen. You're more vulnerable and exposed when you're in the hallway. With Dante and Kara knowing about you, you can't afford to do anything else to attract their attention when you're vulnerable. So you can't go into the hallway for a while, not until I tell you it's okay."

"How will I see you then?" she said, feeling the panic rising in her stomach.

"I'll come here," he said.

"But you said that takes a lot of energy for you."

Clovis moved closer to her, his face close to hers.

"I'll find a way. I'm a big boy."

Amelie felt her heart racing at his proximity. But he pulled back again and leaned against the windshield of the car.

"So your weird teacher said we should stay away from Mr. Sawyer. Did something happen?"

Amelie sighed. She didn't want to dwell on this. "Oh, he just tried to kiss me."

Clovis sat up straighter.

"Did he manage to do it—kiss you, that is?"

"Yes, but just once." Clovis sat up and turned to look at her. "He grabbed me in the girls' bathroom and—"

"Look at me," he said, taking her face in his hands. His eyes searched hers. They were not swirly or soft, but sharp and intense.

"What?"

She saw his eyes widen as his jaw clenched. Then he closed his eyes and let out a sigh.

"It's okay. I'll take care of it."

She started to say something, but he didn't let her.

"He did this without your permission?" he asked slowly and with emphasis.

237

"Yeah, but Hudson saw him. I got out of there before I had to answer questions. Hudson told Scales, so I guess they are looking for him. I haven't seen him since."

"Right," Clovis said, fists clenched. "It'll be dealt with."

"What are you doing, marking him for death or something?" she asked with a little laugh, trying to lighten the mood.

"Something like that," he said, not laughing.

"Clovis, you can't do anything crazy," she said, taking his arm. He turned to look at her. Yes, there was definitely something about the dark that made it easier to see Clovis behind Charlie's face. That was scary and intoxicating in equal parts.

He said nothing. Instead, he lay back down, put his arm out, and beckoned her with his hand, closing the subject with body language, as he often did. She lay down with her head on his shoulder.

"Lie down on top of me," he said. She felt her insides liquefy. But she also suddenly felt painfully shy.

She draped one leg over his body.

"Nope," he said softly. He then moved her body so that she was right on top of him. She could feel all of him. Her face was inches from his.

"I thought you didn't want to get too physical right now," she choked out.

"I changed my mind," he whispered. "I will go as far as you want to take it."

"But you said—"

"Forget what I said and kiss me."

She had kissed him before, but never in a situation like this. This was intensely intimate. Ten minutes ago, she would have said that she couldn't do this with Clovis in Charlie's body, because she despised Charlie. But now she didn't see his body anymore. It was just a vehicle for Clovis.

She leaned down and put her lips to his. At first, he smelled like Charlie's cologne, but when she closed her eyes, she could smell Clovis, the way he always smelled when she saw him in the night—like grass and flowers and something more animal.

He put his arms around her and leaned up to kiss her hard. He pulled her body upward slightly to get her closer, and she could feel a bulge in his pants. He inclined his head to the side and kissed her more deeply.

She let herself fall into this. The smell of him, the taste of his mouth, his hands on her body. Clovis had been worried about her reaction to him using another body to touch her, to be with her. To be honest, she had worried about it too, but she would never have admitted it to him. Now she found that she didn't care at all whose body he was in.

238

He rolled her onto her side and ran his hands up her legs and under her dress. She was momentarily glad that she had bucked tradition and had worn a shorter dress. His hands had easier access and she loved the feel of them on her bare skin. She had her hands in his hair. She wrapped one of her legs around his waist. She knew that she should stop, that they should stop, but she just couldn't. She wanted him to touch her. She felt him hard against her.

"Amelie!" she heard a familiar voice exclaim.

Will?

She sat up quickly. Her brother was standing in front of her car with Aidan and Carter. Judith was standing to one side of them, looking amused.

"Charlie? Really?" Will laughed. "Charlie's the guy? I never would have guessed that."

Her brother looked unnaturally happy. Amelie wondered if he had been taking something. Clovis sat up.

"Hi Will," he said coldly. "Nice to see you again and all, but your timing kinda sucks."

"Sophie called him because she was worried about you," Judith said flatly, "and Charlie's band was asked to leave by the principal. So they want to pack up and go."

As she was saying this, the bass player from the band walked up behind them, took in the situation and glared at his bandmate.

"Charlie, come on man, we wanna go," he said.

"Yeah. Okay. I'll be there in a minute," Clovis said, looking at Amelie with pained eyes.

At that moment, Hudson walked up. Her car seemed to have become a social magnet. Hudson surveyed the situation quickly. Clovis slid off the car hood.

"Hey Amelie," Hudson said. "I thought maybe you might be about ready to go home."

"Yeah, I guess I should," she said. She looked at Clovis. She was pissed off at everyone around them, and particularly herself. She should have suggested that they get into her car to avoid being seen. She felt her eyes well up. She caught Hudson's eye.

"Let's go," he said. "I'll drive."

Amelie nodded and turned to look at Clovis. He did that little wave, and her heart felt like it was ripping apart.

When Hudson put his hand out for her keys, she gave them to him, then buried her face in her hands. She was starting to cry and needed to pull everything in now. She didn't want to affect Hudson. Besides Clovis, he was the only friend she had ever had.

Once inside the car, Amelie pulled her feet up and cried into the folds of her dress as Hudson pulled out of the parking lot. She felt like an idiot. It wasn't like she wasn't going to see him again. Maybe not tonight, but she was sure she would seem him in the next couple of days. But having him in her world, in her arms, in the flesh … every time that happened, she felt more and more connected to him. Every time she was with him, she fell more in love with him. She realized that she wanted him in her world. She wanted it more than she had ever wanted anything. She wanted it in a way that made her afraid she would do anything to get it.

#

Suddenly the car stopped, and Hudson pulled the brake. When Amelie looked up, she realized they were at the golf course.

"Why are we here?" she asked, turning to Hudson.

"Because I can't bear to watch your heart break like that," he said. "I don't know what everyone interrupted back there, but I think it must have been really bad timing."

"There's no good time to leave him," she said softly.

"Well, maybe you can have a softer goodbye then," Hudson replied as he crawled to the back seat.

"What are you doing?" she asked.

"I know I asked that your friend never possesses me. But I guess I meant not without my permission. So I'm giving my permission. As long as he doesn't do it for too long, and never without my okay."

Amelie put her hands to her mouth, realizing what he was saying.

"Hudson, are you sure? I think it hurts when he takes over people. And I know it's exhausting when he leaves. You said so yourself."

"I know. That's why I'm putting a limit of fifteen minutes on his visit. Can you promise me that? Can you make sure?"

"Yes," she said.

"Okay, how do we call him?"

"I'm sure he's listening," she said softly as she crawled into the back seat as well. Hudson's eyes closed and when they opened, they were black as night.

"Tell your friend thank you," Clovis said. "He's a good one, this guy. I'm glad he's your friend."

Amelie crawled into his lap. She was vaguely aware of Hudson's smaller frame, but it didn't matter. Clovis took her in his arms.

"It gets harder and harder to be away from you," Clovis said, as he whispered into her neck. He ran little kisses over her neck. "But doing this drains me too. I have been in someone else's body for way over two hours now. I'll have to recuperate a lot after this. Still, right now I can't make myself care."

He took her face in his hands. She was sure that her nose was red, and her eyes were swollen, but he didn't seem to care. He kissed her lips tenderly.

"I love you. I love you. I love you," she said over and over as they kissed. Clovis pulled her to him as if he were trying to crush them together. She let herself fall into him, into the sound of the heart that was not his, the beating of the blood that he was borrowing. But that didn't matter, the essence of him was there and it was enough to blind and intoxicate her. When she came to her senses for a moment, she glanced at the clock. It had been seventeen minutes.

"It's been fifteen minutes," she whispered into Clovis's mouth.

"Okay." His face was wet. "I'll find a way to be with you at your class beach trip next Friday … if you want."

"Yes," she managed to whisper.

"You probably won't see me much between now and then, but I will do what I can. Look for me in little ways. I'll talk to you a bit every day though. I promise," he said, smiling into her mouth.

Then he picked her up and sat her on the seat next to him. She wasn't sure if Hudson would have been able to do that. He smiled wistfully and waved. She waved back. He closed his eyes.

When his eyes opened, they were blue again, and Hudson was there. He put his hands up to his face.

"Jesus," he said softly and wiped his face. "I'm not sure if I should envy you, or feel sorry for you."

"Maybe both," Amelie said, wiping her eyes. "Thanks Hudson. I know we stayed a bit long, but we won't do that again with you. It's too dangerous for you, and I would feel horrible if you got hurt."

"But you wouldn't feel horrible if Charlie or Aidan or Jack got hurt?" he asked.

"Honestly, no," she said with a slight shrug. "I guess that makes me a horrible person."

"Well, if it does then I'm a horrible person too," Hudson said, then stopped for a second.

"Jesus," he said suddenly, putting a hand to his head.

"What?"

241

"It feels like someone is driving a nail through my eyeball. I didn't feel that when he did this before."

"He wasn't in you very long before. Aidan was sick for a few days after Clovis left him. But I think he might have been in him a bit longer and he wasn't trying to be gentle with him. Still, let's get you home," she said as she crawled up to the driver's seat. Hudson crawled into the passenger's seat and cradled his head.

It was good to have something else to concentrate on besides the fact that Clovis was gone again.

They drove toward Hudson's house in silence.

"Thanks for going to the dance with me," Hudson said suddenly.

"Why should you thank me? I should thank you," Amelie said. "You're my friend. Maybe a better friend than I deserve. I owe you big."

"You don't owe me anything. Like I said before, it actually feels really good when he takes over. At least while it's happening. And I know a couple of things that I didn't know before."

"What's that?"

"I know what he is. I know that he loves you. He loves you like … well, I can't even describe it. I can't imagine what it would be like to have something love me like that. And to be honest, I'm not sure I'd want it. It makes me scared for you. It's actually scarier than if he didn't love you. Love like that isn't gentle. It's a battering ram."

Amelie pulled up just in front of his house. Hudson turned to her and took her hands off the steering wheel, holding them in his own.

"Look. I know I said that I didn't want him to use me, but I think you both need to be careful about who he chooses to possess. I don't know why I think this, but I do. So, if you have a need, it's better to ask me than to take a bigger risk. Okay?"

"Okay," she replied, and, looking at his earnest face, she knew what he was saying. He knew the next logical steps for this relationship, and he knew where that would lead. He also had some idea of what Clovis could do to him. What he didn't know was what *she* could do to him which was why she would never put him at risk that way. For some reason, he was more immune to her than most and, at her most selfish, she didn't want to risk losing that.

"Bye, Hudson," she said, as she leaned over and kissed his forehead. He nodded and gave her a small smile before he got out of the car and walked up the walkway without looking back.

She waited to make sure that he got in safely and then she put the car in gear and pulled away.

She didn't see the dark shadows that were collecting in the spot where Hudson had just been standing.

Chapter Thirty-One

Ley Lines Cross Time

A week later, Amelie found herself in the unenviable position of driving down to their senior beach trip with a hungover Sophie.

The past week had been difficult. Amelie missed Clovis horribly. He had been true to his word and had spoken with her in tiny ways every day. One day a man at the 7-Eleven winked at her with black eyes, grabbing her hand briefly as he handed her a drink. Another day, Heidi Stack had started singing "Heat Wave" as Amelie was walking past. In these ways, Clovis let her know he was around. And while these things were comforting and reassuring, they did nothing to bank her need to be with him. She thought about him constantly. To keep herself placated, she kept a mantra running through her head.

You'll see him Friday. You'll see him Friday.

When Sophie suggested that they ride to the beach together, Amelie had agreed without much thought. Had she been on her game, she wouldn't have agreed to this, particularly given Sophie's behavior at the dance. Luckily for her, Sophie seemed to be too hungover to think about past grievances. Through the four-hour trip, she did little more than grunt at Amelie and demand stops to procure caffeine.

Given this, Amelie should have been relieved when they finally pulled up to Judith's parents' beach house. Instead, a cold chill ran down her spine for no reason. It was a beautiful house, three stories with a light-yellow exterior, white columns, and windows that reflected the sunlight. But rather than looking welcoming, Amelie thought it looked like the deceptive glow of an anglerfish.

She shook her head and eased the car into the driveway.

"Hey, thanks for driving," Sophie said suddenly. "Sorry I was bad company."

That's weird. Sophie never apologizes.

Amelie looked at Sophie and, for just a moment, her blue eyes turned black, and she smiled. But it was gone in the next instant, making Amelie wonder if she had really seen it at all.

"Were you up really late last night?" Amelie asked.

"Yeah. I went out to see a band. But you might already know that ..." she said, with a strange look.

"Why would I know?"

"It was Charlie's band."

"Oh."

Uh-oh.

"Listen, I'm cool with it. Charlie's a musician. It's not like I expect him to be monogamous. I mean, I'm not, so why should I expect him to be?"

"You're involved with Charlie?" she asked and then winced. She shouldn't have said that.

Sophie snorted.

"What? He didn't tell you? Well, isn't that just like a man? I hope you aren't too devastated."

"No. I'm fine. I'm not that interested in him really."

"That's not what Judith said. And he certainly seemed to be into you at the dance."

"Well, looks can be deceiving," Amelie found herself snapping back.

"Yes, they certainly can," Sophie said.

Sophie then leaned over and kissed Amelie full on the lips. It was a short kiss, but not a chaste one. Amelie was so shocked at first that she simply sat there, frozen. Sophie pulled back looked at her expectantly, her eyes still blue. This was Sophie.

"I ... listen ... Sophie," Amelie began.

"Oh. Don't. It's not a problem. I have bigger fish to fry," Sophie said, flipping her hand as she got out of the car. She then pulled her case from the trunk.

"Thanks again for the ride," she called, as she mounted the stairs to the door of the beach house.

Did I forget to let out energy? Did something slip out? What the hell just happened? Since when does Sophie like girls?

Amelie let out her breath and put her head against the steering wheel, letting her energy out toward the sea oats as she checked her shields.

When everything was in place, she took a deep breath, grabbed her bags from the trunk, and started up the stairs herself.

She could already hear something that sounded like screaming coming from inside.

The noise that she had heard from outside became clearer as she entered the house. It wasn't screaming, as she had initially thought. It was earthier than that, which made her even more surprised to find Elodie standing in the kitchen. Elodie looked tanned and windblown, but not happy.

"Hi. When did you get here?" Amelie asked, to cover her obvious surprise.

"Carter picked me up early, so we've been here a couple of hours already," she said. "He went out to pick up some food and beers."

"He should have been back by now," she muttered as she pulled her cell phone out of her pocket and walked through the living room to the back porch facing the ocean.

There was a banging sound from the street side of the house, followed by a moan.

"Who knew Jack would be that good, or that Judith was human enough to have orgasms?"

Amelie jumped. She hadn't seen Sophie lying on the couch.

"That's Jack and Judith?" she sputtered.

"Oh yeah. They've always been the secret item. Bet you thought it was me, but I was just the decoy." Sophie laughed. "There's a lot you don't seem to know, huh?"

"Apparently," Amelie replied. "Is my room upstairs?"

"Yeah. We gave you the room with the single bed. We thought it wouldn't be a problem because Hudson's not coming but let me know if you want to share a double."

"No. No. It's fine," Amelie said, as she retreated upstairs.

Once in her room, she threw her backpack on the bed. The walls of the room were painted mint green. The bedspread was yellow and mint. It was probably meant to have a calming effect, but it looked a bit too much like someone vomited ice cream for Amelie's taste. The floors were wooden, like every other room in the house. Above her head was a ceiling fan made of chrome.

Amelie didn't want to think about her exchanges with Sophie, downstairs or in the car. So she buried it with all the other things she didn't want to think about: Sawyer's kiss, Mr. Roberts's recognition of Clovis, Hudson's offer.

It was already hot, so Amelie switched on the ceiling fan. She had a door that led to a balcony with a gorgeous view of the dunes and the ocean. Looking out at the waves with the sea oats swaying in the salty breeze, she could almost believe she was the only one here. The beach was empty but for seagulls and sandpipers. She lay down on the bed and closed her eyes. She didn't want to go back downstairs and hang out with Sophie, so she decided to rest until the others got back. She closed her eyes.

When Amelie opened her eyes, it was fully dark. She could hear voices coming from the beach. She got up slowly and walked to the balcony window without turning on the lights. Outside, in the water, she could see Elodie. At first, she thought she was playing in the waves, but that seemed unlikely at night. Then she realized that Elodie was pulling off articles of her clothing and throwing them into the sea. Amelie opened the door of her balcony and walked outside in the dark. She could hear Elodie yelling, but she couldn't tell what she was saying.

As she watched, Carter ran to the beach. He jumped into the water and grabbed Elodie from behind. After some struggling, he managed to throw her over his shoulder and carry her back into the house.

Amelie heard the downstairs door open and Elodie's drunken voice.

"Why do you care? You don't love me anyway. Because there has always been someone else, right?"

Amelie heard Carter's voice say something, but it was unintelligible. That was when she noticed the other voices, and there were a lot of them.

A house party on the first night. Great. I will need to block off my room somehow if I don't want people having sex on my bed.

Amelie had closed the balcony door and was about to go downstairs when, out of the corner of her eye, she saw a different figure walking down the beach. It was a grown man wearing a T-shirt, black shorts and running shoes … but for a moment she saw a boy with messy black hair. She opened the door to the deck and ran outside onto the widow's walk. The man looked up and waved at her.

Clovis.

With a little shock, she saw that the person he had chosen to inhabit was none other than Mr. Roberts. She laughed to herself. He had a wicked sense of humor, her Clovis.

She waved back and immediately ran back inside, starting down the stairs. She had taken only a few steps when she realized that her earlier assessment had been correct, the downstairs living area was filled with people. She peered around the edge of the stairs to get a sense of who was attending this little soiree. She saw Carter and Jack sitting at the bar in the kitchen. Carter had his head in his hands and Jack was throwing back a can of beer. Amelie could hear the sound of girls' voices in the back room, and Elodie sobbing loudly. The house reeked of pizza and alcohol, which might have explained some of the melodrama.

Amelie breathed out, targeting all her energy toward a potted plant sitting at the bottom of the stairs. Once she felt completely drained of her energy, she moved quietly down the stairs. She pushed her way past a few guys she didn't know, who were nursing beers and watching basketball on the widescreen TV in the living room. She froze when she heard Judith's voice, as she stormed into the kitchen. Amelie quickly moved behind the two guys, so that she was out of line of sight.

"Elodie wants to talk to you!" Judith snapped at Carter.

"I can't right now. I just don't have the energy," he mumbled into his beer.

"Well, given the circumstances, you better find the energy," Judith snorted.

Amelie's eyes widened.

Carter sighed and got up. He looked about ten years older. Amelie wondered what the hell had happened. As soon as Carter had gone, Judith rounded on Jack.

"We need to have a talk as well," Judith said, in a flat, conversational tone that belied her defensive body stance.

"Look. I understand how you feel about me. I just don't feel the same. I can't help that," Jack said in a weird, distant voice.

"Yeah, I got that," Judith snapped. "But I didn't want to talk about my little confession. I wanted to talk about yours."

Jack pushed his chair back from the bar and got up.

"I'm not talking about that. I shouldn't have told you." He turned to leave the kitchen.

"Well, you did," Judith growled, following him.

They were now facing away from her, so Amelie used the opportunity to push her way through the crowd. She didn't know most of these people. She suspected that they were the university crowd. But, to her horror, she caught site of a guy with shaggy dark hair, who she recognized as Charlie Danos, standing with his hands in the pockets of his dark shorts. As she watched, he yanked his hands and the seams of his shorts split down the sides. There was laughter all around.

What the hell is he doing here?

His presence gave her even more reason to want to escape. She moved to the door, opened it quickly, and quietly stepped out into the night.

Thankfully, no one was on the porch. The night wind was warmer than she might have expected for early June. It sang as it caressed the sea oats like a lover. The ocean spray threw moisture and salt into the air, making everything smell both primeval and newly born.

Amelie ran down the long wooden boardwalk. When she reached the end of the walkway, she saw the figure of Mr. Roberts standing at the bottom of the stairs.

He looked up at her and his smile was brighter than the full moon above them. Once again, she saw him as he was for just a moment. His large black eyes and pale skin. Then that image disappeared, and she saw the face of her teacher Mr. Roberts, but with Clovis's eyes.

"Ms. McCormick—Psyche—would you like to take a little walk on the beach?" he asked as he bowed to her.

She laughed and ran down the stairs. It took every ounce of her willpower not to throw herself into his arms, but that would look very bad if someone happened to see them from the house.

"Yes, let's go for a walk," she said, as she came to stand next to him.

They walked together down the beach, not holding hands but with their arms touching.

"Your friends seem to be going crazy," said Clovis.

"Yeah. I guess you saw Elodie on the beach, huh?"

"Yep." He smiled an odd smile.

"I think she is freaking out because she's plastered."

"No, she's freaking out because she's pregnant," replied Clovis.

"What? She's *what*? How do you know?"

"I can smell it," Clovis responded, shrugging his shoulders.

"Jeez. Well, that explains all that. But it doesn't explain all the people I didn't know in the house."

"I think they're swarming," Clovis said. "It'll pass when the virus passes."

"What are you talking about?"

"The last virus you came back with, the one they are now calling 'mouse flu'. It developed from the poison of the cthaivailles."

"The rat bugs?" Amelie asked.

"Yes, they are called cthaivailles. They gave you the mouse flu but apparently bits of their poison merged with some local viruses to make one hell of something contagious. It's been starting to infect people in the last few weeks. Being drawn to groups and swarming is one of the symptoms. Another is being attracted to light and fire."

Amelie felt her throat begin to tighten. Another virus coming from her.

"I haven't heard about any of that. My mother hasn't said anything," Amelie said.

"That's because it looks like a normal gastro. The weird symptoms aren't that noticeable. It's only been noticed in some infectious disease circles. Also, the media just jumped all over the dog flu thing because it made people fuck each other," he said with a little snort.

By now they were further down the beach, where the lights became fewer and further between.

"You think we are out of sight yet?" Clovis asked, changing the subject.

"Almost."

"Then catch me," he laughed, taking off running down the beach. She ran after him. It was strange, but empowering, to be chasing him. She wondered if this was what it felt like to be a man. As she gained on him, he looked a bit fuzzy and indistinct to her. He stopped suddenly and turned.

Amelie ran straight into him. Off balance, he grabbed her and pulled her to him. Tottering, they both fell to the wet sand, laughing.

Clovis took her face in his hands. He kissed her gently, and then not so gently. She pushed herself up on her knees and he did the same. He pulled her into his arms, and she pushed her body against his. She could feel his heat even through damp clothes.

"Come on, I have a private spot just up there. I'm not sure how your class-mates would feel about seeing you make out with your teacher?" He smiled.

For a moment Amelie got a sick feeling in her stomach at his words, but it faded quickly as Clovis smiled at her and took her hand, leading her up the sand dune.

Chapter Thirty-Two

Beyond the Outer Banks

As they walked up the sand dunes, Amelie watched Clovis's face. He wasn't a bad fit for Mr. Roberts, whose face could adapt to some of Clovis's more subtle expressions.

"Why did you pick this guy?" Amelie asked.

"Because I found him in a sporting goods store yesterday," he said, smiling and pointing. There was a large beige and green tent pitched in the sand dunes, surrounded by sea oats. The wind from the ocean had pulled the entrance flap open and it was fluttering in the breeze.

"You picked him just so you could buy a tent?" she laughed.

Clovis shrugged.

"I thought it would solve a lot of problems." Clovis led her to it and held the flap back.

"Welcome to your castle," he said.

Inside, the tent was big enough to hold six people. Clovis had put electric candles around the perimeter and some pillows in the center, along with an air mattress and some blankets.

"You bought all this?" she asked, sitting on a blanket. He smiled and shrugged.

"You're ever surprising," she said.

Now that she was alone with him, she felt strangely nervous. Conversation usually came easily between them, but she was having a hard time knowing what to say.

He patted the mattress next to him for her to come lie down. Amelie's shyness intensified almost to the point of paralysis. She came and sat on the edge of the mattress, pulling her knees up to her chest and putting her arms around

251

them. She wanted to be in Clovis's arms more than anything, but she didn't know how to start that.

"Have I scared you?" he asked suddenly.

"No," she said. "It's just ..."

"You aren't having second thoughts, are you?" he asked, then his face froze.

"Wait, this isn't your first time, is it? No, I know this isn't your first time because—" he stopped, closed his eyes and grimaced.

"It's my first time voluntarily," Amelie whispered, realizing this truth only as she said it. Her first time had been with her brother.

This was why she was hesitating. Desire had always been her enemy, not her friend. Clovis looked like she had just kicked him in the stomach.

"How could I have forgotten that?" he asked, sitting next to her. He ran a hand through his hair. "I can be such a fucking idiot. I'm so sorry. Are you sure you want to do this? We don't have to do it now, you know. We can wait ..."

"I just ..." Amelie felt tears welling up in her eyes and her traitor throat closing up.

Being here with him was overwhelming. She looked up. Clovis had opened the tent flap on top, so they could see the stars. He had thought to do that. How could she tell him that she couldn't believe that someone so incredible could love her? How could she say that she was crying not because anything was wrong, but because everything was so right that it scared her? That her feelings for him were so strong that it felt like insanity?

Clovis was looking at her intently.

"It's just that I love you," she whispered. "I just ... sometimes I don't know what to do with that. I don't even have the words, but when I'm with you, I could leave everything else behind. But I should be more independent, shouldn't I? I should know more about what you are. I haven't even asked that many questions, have I? Shouldn't I be asking you more questions?"

She was just babbling now, using words as another mask.

"There are a lot of 'shoulds' in what you just said," Clovis said softly, brushing a stray hair off her face. "But I'll answer anything you want me to answer. And I promise I'll do only what you want me to do."

He then leaned into her and kissed her very softly. The smell of him was as intoxicating as always. Funny how he smelled the same no matter what body he was in. The kisses were also always the same, but right now they were gentle.

His reserve helped her lose hers.

She wrapped her arms around his neck and kissed him harder. His kisses tasted sweet but with a kick, like whiskey. She pulled him down to the mattress and put her leg around his waist. He was breathing fast but keeping his touches to the strictly G-rated parts of her body: hair, arms, legs. Amelie could feel his restraint, and through that restraint, his love for her. The simple joy of being next to him put paid to whatever shyness she felt. She wanted this. She wanted him. She may have even wanted him more *because* of her past. How wonderful to be able to replace those awful memories with this one.

Her desire to feel his bare skin against hers eclipsed any insecurity she might have had. She sat up and pulled off her sundress without hesitation. She was left with exposed breasts and underwear. Clovis made a noise in the back of his throat that was something like a growl, but he made no move. Amelie wondered again how much he was holding back for her sake. She guessed a lot. This gave her a feeling of power. She changed position so she was seated on top of him. What she felt between her legs was rock hard and bigger than she expected. She wondered for a second if he would fit inside her. He gave a sharp intake of breath, but then purposefully put his hands above his head, grabbing one wrist with his other hand, keeping his eyes locked on hers. The gesture was unmistakable. She would have to initiate, but it was requiring a lot of control on his part. She heard a noise escape from her that was not unlike the one he had just made.

She leaned forward and began kissing him again. She deeply wished that she could see him for him, but his eyes were still his. She closed her eyes and his flesh seemed to change under her hands. His skin felt softer and his muscles harder. He sat up as she pulled his shirt off, and then lay down in the same position. She ran her hands over his outstretched arms. He trembled but kept himself still. She began to kiss beneath his arms and down his biceps but when she got to his wrists, she saw that he was grabbing them so hard that a ring he was wearing had cut him and he was bleeding.

She sat back and looked at him. His face seemed to change and for a brief moment, she saw the boy she knew, with the huge dark eyes ... but they were closed, and he was biting his lip hard. She lay down and began kissing him again. He seemed to strain against his own hands, leaning up to return her kiss. Her insides had seemingly turned to liquid and were leaking out of her.

She kissed him and pulled his arms down and around her.

"I need you to hold me. I need to feel you need me," she whispered in his ear.

He immediately pulled her tight and rolled her over with one leg between hers. He kissed her without restraint. His hands traced her breasts and then ran down the sides of her body. He used his leg to push between her legs, hitting a pile of nerves that made her body jerk. She grabbed him and began to push his shorts downward. Without breaking the kiss, he removed his clothes, and repositioned himself between her legs—but he didn't enter her.

He was holding himself on his arms, not putting his whole weight on her. She could feel him, hard and just at the entrance to her, but he went no further. She was so wet that the insides of her thighs were slick. If she had been less insane right now, she might have been embarrassed, but all she wanted was for him to be inside her. Right now, it didn't matter what body he was in. She knew his smell, his kisses, and his movements for his own.

"Now," she whispered. "Now, now, now."

"Are you sure?" he whispered.

She was more than ready. She wanted him. She wanted whatever body he was in. She wanted his lips, his tongue, his soul. She wanted his babies.

That thought shocked her.

"Could I get pregnant?" she asked suddenly. "From you, could I get pregnant from this?"

Clovis stopped, a bit shocked. He looked at her deeply and pulled back.

"Yes, you could."

"Would it be yours or his?" she asked.

"It would be both," he said softly. "Do you want me to do something to prevent that?"

"No," she heard herself say as she pulled his head down to hers. "No, I don't."

She kissed him without reservation, her body screaming for his. When he slipped inside her, she gasped. Everyone had told her that this would hurt, but it didn't. She just felt full, and an increased desire for him to be further in, to get as close as he could.

He moved in and out of her, but kept his body connected to that bundle of nerves that was making her thighs shake. An electrical current was now flowing between her womb, her heart, and her brain. It pulsed and throbbed, running a circuit around her body, making her arms and legs tingle. This current was feeding on Clovis's energy, feeding on itself, feeding on her sanity. When she felt that she could no longer bear it, something exploded inside … lifting her, pushing her higher. She heard herself scream. She heard him moan and felt his body began to tremble. She was shaking all over as he slowed his movements to gentle rocking motions. He gently kissed her face and her eyelids.

She never knew that anything could feel like this. She had spent so much time mocking this sort of thing in her head—what an idiot she was. She was going to have to rethink that whole *Lady Chatterley's Lover* thing.

When she opened her eyes again, her soul sighed in bliss.

Clovis's eyes met hers, but not just his eyes, his face was now his own, the pale skin, the large black eyes, the straight nose, the quirky, off-center smile, and messy hair. Her heart skipped a beat and then produced a surge of heat that spread to her whole body. Her eyes filled with tears.

"It's you," she whispered.

"Yeah, it's me." He smiled.

He was still inside her, and she felt bliss. She reached up to trace the lines of his face with her fingers. His skin was pale and soft. He took one of her fingers in his mouth for a moment, and she felt the extraordinary heat of him. He kissed the palm of her hand and leaned down to kiss her mouth. But as she began to put her arms around him, they encountered an obstacle. She pulled back, and gasped.

"You have wings!" She laughed. "I thought I had imagined it in the cave."

"Oh, so you see those now?" Clovis asked teasingly and stretched them out so she could see them fully. His wings were mostly pitch black, but with an occasional tiny white feather on the periphery. The wings were large enough that they pushed against the sides of the tent.

"So does this mean that you're really an angel or a demon or something?" she said with a smile.

"Well, that depends on who you ask," he said. "Some religions say that we are angels that fell in love with human women and fell from grace. Some of my kind interpret this to mean fell down the resonances into a more physical space. Some think that's bad. Some don't."

"And you?"

"I don't worry about that … or I didn't," he said, then changed gears. "You know, I had to let you think that I was a klutz all those times the wind pulled on my wings."

Amelie reached her hands out and touched them.

"Like when?" she asked, as she caressed them. They felt like silk and glass.

"Pretty much every time we saw each other. Like when I almost fell over at the horse races because my wing hit one of the bleachers. Or tonight when you ran into me. It's easier if I can use them for balance, but I have to act as if they aren't there if people can't see them, which throws me off."

"But why can I see them, and you, now?" she asked.

"Because our energy is completely connected now," he said. "So my resonance pulls you up and yours pulls me down. So we are in our own space. We are one person right now, in body and energy, so you can only see me as I am."

"And do I look the same to you now?" Amelie asked, feeling strangely shy, given their position.

"Mostly. Maybe you look—well, more you."

"Is that good or bad?" she asked.

"Good, it confirms what I already knew—that I will have no regrets."

He drew her tightly to him, folding his wings around her. A draft of cold air was ruffling her hair, chilling her, but his skin was so warm. They kissed. He was still hard inside her. And weirdly, she was not uncomfortable. She felt that she could stay like this forever.

"So are you okay with doing this now?" she whispered to him.

"'This' was never the problem. 'This' is nothing but good, as long as I'm not draining you. It's what comes of this that's the problem. For me and for you."

"So what comes of this?" she asked, expecting reassurance, but he just gave her a melancholy smile.

"I need to tell you a story now, one that I have been putting off telling," he said with a sigh.

Amelie felt her heart tremble.

He kissed her again, gently, on the lips. He was silent for a moment. She could hear the wind coming off the ocean and the sound of the tent flapping in the breeze. She could also hear the soft sound of the wind in his wings ... it sounded like a whisper. Her hand was over his heart, it was beating strong and solid under her fingers.

Finally, Clovis sighed and began to speak.

"I told you I was a transition type of incubus. I seduce people and make their death pleasant and painless. I told you that, but I didn't tell you that after the person dies, the incubus takes the person to the upper winds. The winds then carry them to rebirth. But we were always told to keep ourselves emotionally distanced from humans ... even as we seduced them.

"When I was a young Cambion incubus, I kept falling in love with humans. Every few hundred years, I'd fall desperately in love with someone ... once it was with a Japanese princess."

Clovis gave her a sad little smile.

"Every time it happened, it made me a bit crazier. I'd follow the person through their life and then spend several hundred years grieving the loss of them after they died.

"After a couple of thousand years of this, an older, and supposedly wiser, incubus told me that I needed to stop. She said what I was feeling wasn't real love. When an incubus loves someone, it's forever, so she said that what I was feeling couldn't be love, because I was feeling it for different humans. She said what I felt wasn't love but a different desire, coming from my father's lineage. At first, I was excited about that ... until she told me exactly *what* my father was."

Clovis stopped. Amelie could feel his heart beginning to beat hard in his chest.

"What was your father?" she finally asked in a whisper.

"It's too horrible," Clovis said in the smallest voice she had ever heard him use. He was silent for a moment, then he took a deep breath and began again.

"I've already told you what I did after that. My campaign to seduce without consent and how I stopped because I stopped feeling anything. I pulled away from humans except for the very basic feeding needs. Around this time, my half brother fell in love with a human. And things went really wrong ...."

"What do you mean?" Amelie asked in a voice she could barely hear herself. Clovis closed his eyes tighter.

"There were two people that were supposed to die. One of them was a young slave girl, and the other was her unborn child. Two incubi were called to take these souls to the upper winds. The girl was supposed to be taken by a very powerful, but unstable, incubus. I was called to take the soul of the unborn child. Unfortunately, the mother and daughter were part of a cult that practiced human sacrifice and were scheduled to die by flame."

"That's horrible," Amelie whispered.

"Yeah, it was. I had pulled away from doing this by that time, so the call went to my brother. And all of that might have gone fine ... but Rose got involved."

At the mention of Rose's name, a numbing feeling crept into Amelie's bones, like Novocain.

"What did she do?"

Clovis sighed.

"She tricked my brother," he said. "Rose's greatest desire is to be a part of the physical world, so she wanted to scar their souls and steal their bodies."

"How? How could she do that? How would that be possible?" Amelie asked.

"She couldn't and it wasn't," Clovis said, his jaw tight and twitching. "Or at least, she couldn't capture their bodies, which died in the flames, but she did manage to shred both souls. My brother went mad with grief for the soul that had been in his charge, that he had fallen in love with—and called me."

Amelie could see tears in the corners of Clovis's eyes. She touched his arm. He smiled briefly but kept his eyes closed.

"I did ... I tried ... well, I did the best I could," he said, in a voice deep with grief. "I can't explain it exactly, except that her soul survived. But I knew that she was going to be permanently delicate … permanently vulnerable from that life onward. I'm not a god, so I can only fix some things."

He was quiet for a moment. Amelie had a thousand questions, but she didn't want to push him. Finally, she whispered, "So the girl lived?"

Clovis opened his eyes and turned to her.

"Yes, I'm looking at her," he said, tears staining his face.

Amelie felt no shock, instead, her heart felt like it was unfolding in her chest.

"I became suspicious when we were at Disneyland, and you mentioned having déjà vu. As there is no such thing as déjà vu, there is only memory, I went to see a ghoul, because they can see past lives. He told me you were the girl that I had saved. The girl that my brother fell in love with. So, as if I didn't have enough reason to hate myself, I realized that I was falling in love with my brother's love."

Amelie's world suddenly tilted sideways.

"That was why you tried to push me away … on the beach that time?" she whispered.

"Yeah. I mean, I know I can be a shit, but I decided that seducing the one great love of my brother was too much even for me. Then, when you told me about your history, I thought that I could help you. I thought that this might be why I was drawn to you … so that I could redeem myself."

"You did help me," she whispered.

Clovis smiled at her.

"I'm glad, but it didn't change the real reason I was helping you. I was in love with you. I knew that really early on … and I knew that you loved me. But it was such a betrayal of my brother that I tried to keep it platonic and be your teacher … your friend. Still, I knew deep down that it was just an excuse to stay with you. I kept asking myself why I was doing this again.

"Then I began to notice little things. The way you smile, the way your energy flows just before you move. All sorts of little things. I started having déjà vu myself. So I made a point of taking you to specific places that were recreations of places where I had fallen in love before, just to see how you would react."

"That was what happened in the Japanese garden?"

"Yep, that's when I knew."

He pulled her tighter to him. His arms were trembling.

"So I went to the ghouls again and paid their price to learn all your past lives, and you know what I found?"

Clovis turned to face her, tears on his cheek.

"I discovered that all those humans I had fallen in love with had always been the same human. The same soul over and over. The one I had fallen in love with only once, millennia before, and had never gotten over it … in the true incubi way."

Amelie's heart felt as if it would burst from her chest.

"I loved you in all your lives and brought you to your death thousands of times. But when Rose told me about my father, I abandoned you because I stopped believing in anything."

"So that older, wiser incubi *was* Rose then?" she asked.

"Yes. And because of the shit she fed me, and because I believed it, you were left to fend for yourself in your life and your death for hundreds of years. And in one of those deaths, you ended up with my brother, who fell in love with you and let you go to the flames. I saved you, but what you have been through makes you vulnerable and unique. And all that was my fault."

Clovis took her face and turned it to meet his.

"But I swear to you, that ends now. From now on, I will protect you. I will make sure that nothing can touch you. I will do what I have to do, no matter how terrible, no matter how painful or dangerous, to make sure that your soul is protected and whole. If it is, if you're safe from the wrong kind of infections, then Dante and Kara can have no problem with you."

Amelie closed her eyes and touched her forehead to his.

"I know this is a lot to take in," he said softly.

Amelie just ran her hands through his hair and down his shoulders. His body felt tight as metal. It was all she could do to breathe at this moment. She could feel his heart beating wildly against her hand. Hers was beating just as fast.

"I love you," she whispered. "I can't do anything but love you. But I'm also terrified … a bit."

To her surprise, she felt his body relax and he smiled.

"Of course, you are. You'd be a fool if you weren't. This thing between us is like an unending avalanche, a crushing, unyielding, relentless thing. It doesn't care who gets hurt or betrayed."

"Is that another reason why you tried to scare me away that time on the beach?"

"Yes. And probably several times since then, before I understood. I know I might have hurt you in those moments but, even without our history, you have to understand what this means for me—and for you."

Clovis bent down and kissed her again. This kiss was different. It wasn't a kiss of passion, there was something more profound about it.

"In the past, the very best scenario that could come out of this is that you and I have an affair in life, for as long as you can stand the frustration. When you can no longer stand it, you find a lover who reminds you a little of me. You get married, you have children, and you have a normal life. You try to be happy and maybe a lot of times you are. But what you have will never match up to what you've had with me, and a part of you will pine for me all your days … but you will have a real life."

"And what happens to *you* in that 'best' scenario?" Amelie asked, tears threatening.

"Oh, I saved the best part for last. I get to watch all this. I get to be there on your wedding day, and see another man love you night after night in a way that I can't. I get to see the children I didn't father. At the end of your life, when you die, I'll still be there loving you just as much as I love you now. I will take your soul to the upper air and let you go, knowing that I am giving up the only person I will ever love, and that I might not be able to find you in your next life. The very worst part is that, even if I find you, you won't remember me."

"Oh god," Amelie whispered.

"Actually, it's even worse. Incubi aren't altruistic … or masochistic. So, when we see every kiss of another, when we hear every endearment you whisper in the night, we won't enjoy it in some sort of 'at least she is happy now' way. Nope, we aren't that perfect. The longing, the anger and jealousy, can claw out our souls."

"But why would you do that then? Why would you stay?"

"Because I don't have a choice. When we fall in love, it is soul-altering, that's our nature. That's the real reason it's so discouraged. It's beautiful and horrible in equal parts. I can't explain to you how it feels for me to love you. There are no words strong enough. But I would bear all these things, just to be near you."

"Well, okay, what if I just had a life with you here?" Amelie asked, turning to look in his face. "Just like we are now. I could do that. I could have a job and a day life, but then I could be with you at night, in someone's physical body. Why wouldn't that work?"

"Well, it's wrong for me to steal bodies, but that's not the real reason. The real reason is because I know what it would do to you. It will pull you away from physical life. Eventually our bright midnights will outshine the sun for you. You will forget to live in this world. Without care, your body will fall apart. You'll get sick and you'll die. You'll think you're coming to me, but you'll just forget."

Amelie buried her face in his chest.

"So it's hopeless," she whispered. "I won't put you through that hell and you won't let me just stay with you."

Clovis pulled back and pulled her chin up to look at him. There were tears on his cheeks, but he was smiling.

"No, my love, it isn't hopeless. I wanted to explain why I tried to pull away, before I realized who you were. Now that I know, I will never again be the one pushing you away from me. You may not know this about me, but I don't give up when I want something. I might fuck up, and I might fuck up over and over, but I will never give up. And what I want is to find a way for us to be together— in a real way. I want to find a way to bring you to my world or me to yours. What I told you just now was the best, most commonly accepted scenario for incubus-human love stories, but it won't be ours."

"What can we do?" she whispered.

Clovis took a deep breath and let it out slowly. When he looked at her the crazy whirling was back in his eyes.

"We have to break out of this cycle, and it won't be easy. It will mean breaking rules that have existed since the birth of this story. I've always been a risk taker, but I can't commit you to that. You have to know anything we do is a huge risk. Whatever comes of this will require you to be strong. Remember, in the end, Psyche had to be much stronger than Cupid. Much of their fate was due to her strength. I will do whatever I can to spare you that kind of path, but there is no doubt that you will have to be strong—at least for a while."

"I can be strong," she whispered as she buried her face in his neck. "If you love me, I'm not afraid. I don't care what anyone thinks. I don't care what I do. I don't care where I live. I don't even care *if* I live ... if dying would mean being with you, then I will walk straight out to the ocean now and drown myself."

"No!" Clovis said forcefully. "You've done that before, and it doesn't work. Remember what I told you. If you die now, then I may not be able to find you in your next life. That's the way you have to be strong. You have to live. No matter what happens, you have to live. This won't work if you just survive, you have to learn from life, promise that!"

She nodded. She could feel that his words had many layers, but she was too lost in sensation to read it well.

"That's our challenge," he continued. "Yours is to adapt to your life here. Mine is to find a way to keep us together after this."

"What do you mean, 'after this'?" Amelie asked but Clovis just shook his head.

"I'm an incubus, and whatever else may have been said of our kind, we play the long game."

He stopped and kissed her eyes. Then he smiled a tight, fleeting smile.

"Knowing all this, can you still love me? Knowing how I have failed you before and the horrible things that I have done?"

"I don't know how to not love you," she said, and he smiled openly.

261

"Then enough of all of this for now. For now, we don't have to worry about the long game. The short game, the right now, is that I'm inside you and I plan to stay here as long as I can, and as long as you can bear it."

With that, he kissed her hard on the mouth. She felt dizzy to the point of fainting but let herself just fall into it.

#

She didn't know how long they made love after that. Time stopped functioning in any normal way. She did seem to hear herself at times. She knew she screamed and wondered if someone might have heard her. Her body was lifted by wave after hormonal wave. Eventually her nerves were so sensitized that the feelings were almost painful. But still, even sore and sensitized, she didn't want him to stop. Clovis kept her in this state for what seemed like a small eternity.

When Amelie came to her senses, she was in Clovis's arms and wings. The feathers felt like a silk blanket. He sighed and pulled her in closer to him, wrapping her tighter in his arms. Then he lay still. She felt his breath coming hot against her neck.

She could see the stars above her through the open tent flap. Time seemed to stop. She sensed this was a defining moment in her life—no, in all of her lives. It was, without a doubt, the best moment of her current life. She wondered if it was the best moment any human had ever experienced, and with that thought came a sense of foreboding. What price would be demanded for this level of bliss? Looking down at Clovis's sleeping form, she found that she didn't care. Let fate take its pound of flesh.

She felt herself drifting into sleep. Clovis held her close even in sleep. He was hard inside her, even asleep. She wondered if he ever wasn't hard. But she was now having difficulty maintaining consciousness. She fell into a soft sleep, surrounded by the smell of his breath and the silk of his wings. The blackness of the night kissed her skin, making promises of perpetual bliss.

But when she woke, it was to cold water, harsh sunlight, and the sound of screaming.

Chapter Thirty-Three

Meeting the Maker

Phil Sawyer was waiting, crouched in the bushes, next to a Victorian mansion on Arbor Lane. He had been hiding out in various places since his attempt to seduce Amelie. That had been almost a week ago, and yet he had evaded both the school and the police. They'd naively expected him to return home, to his wife, his life. He'd watched them raid his home from the window of a neighbor's house. He knew that the police would go there, just as he'd known the neighbor's house would be empty. He knew this because the shadows led him there.

He didn't know what these shadows were, but they were protecting him. They helped him hide. They alerted him to the presence of dangers, both from authorities and from people on the street. But they had also led him to Amelie on the night of the dance, and that had gone disastrously wrong.

He'd been sure she wanted him. He had seen it in the way she moved when he was around her, the way she cut her eyes at him. He had given her the chance to have him that night at the dance, but she'd been repelled by him.

He had been wrong. The shadows had been wrong. Or maybe not. He had wanted to find her, and they had taken him to her. Maybe that's all they could do. They couldn't make her want him. The pain of that was excruciating, because he still wanted her. His desire had not been eased by that night at the dance. That brief contact with her lips had inflamed his passion to such a degree that he was forced to masturbate five or six times a day now. If he didn't find a way to release this, he would go crazy.

Sawyer had been thinking these thoughts this afternoon, sitting behind the dumpsters at the McDonald's, when the shadows had appeared again. He had followed them, and they led him here. He had nowhere else to go, so he had crawled into a thick clump of bushes that separated two houses, and had fallen asleep.

It wasn't until he woke to the sound of a car door slamming that he realized where he was. As he peered out from his little hiding place, he saw Hudson Crowe walking up the drive of the house next door. A few minutes later, Hudson appeared at the back of the house with a small backpack. He sat down in a lounge chair next to the pool and pulled a book from his bag.

The sun was fading behind the trees that encircled the back yard. As Sawyer watched, Hudson lay down his book and grabbed a remote control that was sitting on a small patio table next to him. He pointed it toward the pool and lights came on, illuminating the water. Hudson then took a small black game console from his bag. Sawyer recognized the design as one of the very new, very expensive games on the market.

Hudson. The rich kid who had alerted the school to his activities. His other desire.

Maybe he had been led here for a reason. The pool was separated from the main house by a line of small Cypress trees. If he was quick, he could make this happen. Of course, it was likely he'd be caught, but eventually he'd be caught anyway. This way he would have his moment with Hudson, at Hudson's expense.

So he waited as the sun sank on the horizon and the shadows grew longer, meeting and dancing with the shadows that always accompanied him now.

As he waited and watched, his desire for Hudson grew. It merged with the longing he felt for Amelie. It squirmed in his belly, wrapping around his testicles until he felt he would go mad with it. When he could bear it no longer, he scanned his environment for objects. If he had known about this earlier, he would have found a way to get some chloroform, but he wouldn't find that here.

What he did find was a brick.

He had a momentary hesitation. This would certainly hurt Hudson and it might kill him. Sawyer decided he didn't care. As long as he had enough time to enter him, to own him. He couldn't bring himself to care what happened afterward.

As the shadows began to move toward Hudson, Sawyer advanced slowly, brick in hand. Hudson must have sensed something because just as Sawyer was upon him, he turned. Sawyer brought the brick down hard on the side of his face. Hudson's head snapped to the right and his body fell from the chair with surprisingly little noise or fanfare.

Sawyer was quickly upon him. Hudson's face was bloody. His nose might have been broken. None of that mattered. Sawyer wasn't interested in his face.

He quickly turned his body over and grabbed at the waist of the Hudson's sweatpants. He pulled down both the sweatpants and underpants using both hands to drag them to Hudson's knees. Hudson's beautiful ass was white and muscular.

Sawyer was breathing hard. He unzipped his own pants quickly and moved on top of Hudson's prostrate form.

Just as he was positioning himself between Hudson's legs, he noticed movement out of the corner of his eye. For a second, his brain had trouble processing what he saw.

Standing there, next to the pool, were the platinum blonde woman and the dark-skinned man that he had seen on the landing a few weeks ago. The ones named Kara and Dante. Kara was standing with her hands open in front of her, palms up. The shadows that had been present were being drawn toward her. As they neared her body, they were stretched and pulled until they were nothing but small pools of liquid at her feet. He didn't know how long she had been there but there was a stream of dark liquid circling around her.

"You decided to visit the boy?" asked Dante. Sawyer pulled himself up and turned to run but his legs went numb, and he fell to the ground.

"Uh-uh," said Kara. "You're going nowhere."

The veil of desire dropped from him, and Sawyer looked back at Hudson. The blow to his head would cause swelling and damage, maybe death. He did this. Phil Sawyer. How could he do this? He didn't take risks like this. His eyes fell on the shadows at Kara's feet.

"Please. I don't know why I did this. I couldn't control it. It's not my fault that I'm different."

"Killers and sociopaths always believe they're different," Dante said. "They believe they're special. Sometimes they're right."

He was smiling, but his eyes were flat and expressionless. It was the most horrible thing Sawyer had ever seen.

"I know I have a problem. I know I'm sick. They made me sick," Sawyer babbled, pointing to the shadows at Kara's feet. Kara was staring at him coldly.

"If you let me go, I promise I'll get help. I promise. The boy will be okay. We just need to call an ambulance."

"How do you know? You hit him on the head with a brick," said Dante.

"But—"

"Hudson will be fine," said Kara. "We'll take care of him."

"Oh. You came for him?" Sawyer said. "I'm sorry. I won't go near him again. I won't bother anyone anymore. I'll leave here. I'll never come back."

"Yes. You'll leave here, but you will leave with us," said Kara, her voice soft. She extended her hands to him, as if in welcome.

Feeling suddenly came back to Sawyer's legs. He looked up at Kara. Her look was unreadable. She radiated an energy that he couldn't even begin to describe. He felt himself become erect again. He wanted to kiss this woman, to hold her, and to run away from her as fast as he could.

"But before you can be near any other living creature, we need to fix you," Kara said softly, moving toward him.

Sawyer fell to his knees in front of her. She knelt and put her arms around him.

When she let go of him and stepped back, much of Sawyer's skin fell from his body, following her.

He shrieked. His muscles, fat, blood and organs were spreading, pushing outward, reaching for her. His screams were cut short as his lungs filled with fluid and his mouth lost form. His last visual was of his own arm, reaching out on the ground and stretching like chewing gum before liquefying in front of him. Then his eyes, ears, nose, and all his other senses, failed him.

Yet he was still awake, aware. He was aware when she slowly and methodically began shredding his soul.

Chapter Thirty-Four

The Storm After the Calm

Amelie woke to cold water hitting her face. Instinctively she scrambled backward, grabbing for the nearest article of clothing she could find, which turned out to be a man's shirt. A girl was screaming something at her, but she couldn't make out the words. Then she heard a man's voice.

"Oh my god. Amelie. What the hell?"

Amelie's eyes were watering, her vision blurred from the salt water, but she knew the man next to her. She'd been with him all night, and he was no longer Clovis. He was turned away from her, facing outside the tent, but she could read the shock and horror in the angles of his body.

"You fucking slut!" the girl screamed.

Amelie now recognized Elodie, who was squatting at the entrance of the tent, holding a bucket in her hands. Her long hair was hanging in stringy clumps in front of her face. She looked a like a baboon. Her arms were shaking as she crawled into the tent toward Amelie. Amelie backed further away, pulling the shirt in front of her naked breasts.

Mr. Roberts grabbed Elodie before she could get further in.

"Fuck you, let go of me!" Elodie screamed. "It's not enough for her to have Hudson! No, she has to have Jack and Charlie and Carter! *My* Carter!"

Elodie's voice hitched at his name.

Now that Amelie's eyes had cleared, she could make out the wreck of Elodie's face. Her face was red, puffy, and severely scratched, as if she had had a good cry and followed that up with trying to claw her own face off.

"Ms. Rogers. Calm down. Come out here with me and we can talk about it."

Mr. Roberts turned back toward Amelie. Their eyes met. The look of horror in his was soul shattering. He looked destroyed. No, he looked damned.

Clovis, what have we done?

Mr. Roberts held her gaze.

"Go," he mouthed.

Then he forcibly pulled Elodie away from the tent.

Amelie grabbed her sundress and threw it on. Her underwear was around here somewhere but she didn't have time to look for it.

"She got you too!" Elodie screamed from outside the tent.

"Calm down, Ms. Rogers," he said. "Whatever ... what ... whatever might have happened here between me and Ms. McCormick doesn't concern you."

Elodie uttered a high-pitched, shrieking laugh.

"Doesn't it? It doesn't concern me that she's a witch? I was too stupid to see it before, but now I do. All last night, all those stupid boys could do was fight about who loved her most. Carter got in a fight with Charlie Danos over her. Can you believe that? Her face is plain, and she has a fat ass."

Amelie listened to this with dawning terror. She'd thought she was free of her curse. She had to get out of here before people went crazy. She looked around for her purse which held her car keys and realized with horror that she had left it in the house. She would need to go back to get them—and it would be better to do so before Elodie got back.

Mr. Roberts was still with Elodie at the entrance of the tent so she couldn't escape that way. The only other option was the window on the other side. Amelie ripped it open and crawled out, falling hard on the sand. She stood quickly. Elodie and Mr. Roberts were standing across from her, with the tent between them. Luckily, Elodie was facing away from her.

Amelie darted to the left, going up and over the nearest sand dune, rolling as she did. Then she got to her feet and ran at full speed toward the space between the two closest beach houses. There she stopped for a minute to catch her breath. She couldn't see the tent from where she was, which meant that they couldn't see her.

She had no idea what had gone on at the house, but something had gone wrong—something had gone terrifyingly wrong. She needed to get back to the house to get her keys so she could get out of here, and she had no idea what the situation would be when she got there.

Elodie had said that Carter, Charlie, and Jack had expressed love for her. She knew that she had glamoured Jack, but she thought that was over. Carter and Charlie had never exhibited any signs of glamouring. Before she had learned control, they had dismissed her completely. And since she had learned control ... what? They had been friendly but nothing weird.

What happened?

268

Her heart was beating wildly in her chest in a rhythm that was all its own. She heard screaming again, coming across the dunes on the winds from the ocean. At least Elodie was still with Mr. Roberts.

Amelie made her way between the two houses and to the street. She hadn't had the presence of mind to take her sandals with her when she had left the house last night, and now the sharp stones by the side of the road were cutting into her feet as she walked.

Amelie walked quickly down the street toward their beach house. It was walking toward danger, but she had no choice. She needed her car. As the house came into view, she opened her inner eyelid and saw what she was expecting—and what she feared. The house was surrounded by a noxious combination of yellow, green, and red swirling mists. These mists seemed to squirm and pulse as if teeming with living things—living things she didn't want to see. Something had happened there for sure. The one good thing was that her car was still in the driveway, and it seemed to be intact.

Amelie slowed as she approached the driveway. She wondered if there was any way for her to sneak into the house unnoticed. She had just stepped onto the driveway when something struck her arm painfully and bounced off onto the ground in front of her. With a surge of relief, Amelie saw it was her keys.

She heard a singsong voice from the balcony above her. "I'm guessing you'll be wanting those right about now."

Sophie was there, leaning over the railing with a manic look on her face.

"You missed a lot of fun last night!" Sophie laughed. Then she reached down and picked up Amelie's backpack, which she then slung at Amelie as well. Amelie jumped back just in time, or it would have hit her head.

"Did Elodie find you?" Sophie asked, with a weird giggle.

Amelie nodded. She crouched slowly, picking up her backpack and keys, her eyes never leaving Sophie. The colors around Sophie were the same as the house, but redder and with a little added pink for flavor. Sophie leaned over the railing alarmingly far, her feet obviously off the ground behind her.

"I don't know what's worse," she said, pitching her voice softer, so that it could barely be heard over the sound of the wind through the sea oats, "knowing that you fucked with every single guy I wanted is bad enough. I mean, you fucked *with* Jack and Carter without fucking them. Then you half fucked Charlie, leaving him with a serious case of blue balls, which I had to hear about in great detail last night. And you spent the night with the one teacher that I wanted to fuck. All that's bad. But you know what's worse?"

Amelie shook her head as she edged her way toward the door of her car.

269

"What's worse is that you're so obviously not interested in me. Fuck, I can't believe I even said that. I didn't even know I wanted you until yesterday. But I do, and I don't like it when I don't get what I want. So, watch yourself, sweetie."

Even from this distance, Amelie saw that Sophie's eyes were red and swollen. Then Sophie disappeared from the balcony.

Clovis. Clovis had been in her yesterday for just a moment. And he had been in Jack, Carter and Charlie as well. This was the common theme. Oh shit! What if he left some of his desire for her in them?

Amelie moved quickly, opening the trunk of the car and throwing her backpack inside. Then she went to the driver's door. Just as she put her keys in the lock a blur flashed over her head and she ducked. Behind her a dark bottle hit the ground. The smell of alcohol accosted her nostrils as shards of glass exploded all directions. She felt a sharp pain as some of it hit her calf. It had been a bottle of Crown Royal.

"Hey, I thought you might need a drink for your drive." Sophie cackled. Then she crossed her arms on the balcony. In her right hand, she held a gun.

She's gone crazy.

"You know, they said I should kill you," Sophie said, cradling the gun.

"Who's 'they'?" Amelie asked, backing toward the car, her keys behind her.

"The voices—in my head. The ones that seem to be talking to everyone these days. That nutty flu," said Sophie, with a little giggle.

Yes, she's gone crazy. But maybe they've all gone crazy.

Amelie's hands were trembling so badly that she could barely get the keys into the door. Just as she got inside and slammed the door, Jack came barreling out of the house. He vaulted over the railing, landing hard on the sand twenty feet in front of her.

Amelie managed to get her keys in the ignition the first try. She threw the car into reverse and pulled out into the street without even looking behind her. Jack had gotten to his feet and was stumbling toward the car. Amelie hit the gas and the car moved forward, engine screaming between gears. She only remembered to breathe when Jack was a small dot behind her.

Her leg was throbbing, and she could see a thick shard of glass embedded in her calf. She needed to find a safe place to bandage it, collect herself, and try to figure out what the hell had happened last night.

Most of all she needed to find Clovis.

Chapter Thirty-Five

Untouchables

Despite spending two days in a Motel 6 doing little but flying, Amelie had found nothing in her flights but the usual scenery and stars. She hadn't even managed to find the hallway. On Monday morning, she got in her car to return home and she cried the whole way.

She wasn't sure exactly what she would do, given what had happened with Mr. Roberts, but she had nowhere else to go. Besides, at home she could shower, change, and collect necessary belongings before her parents or brother got back.

Just as she was pulling into the parking lot of her family's apartment complex, her phone rang. She didn't recognize the number and hesitated a moment before answering. On the third ring, she picked up. Even if it was Elodie or Sophie, it was better communicating by phone than in person.

"Is this Amelie?" asked a familiar male voice.

"Yes."

"Amelie, this is Principal Scales. Where are you?"

"I'm sorry I'm not at school, sir. I was late getting back from the beach weekend—" she began.

"No, no. I'm afraid your tardiness isn't why I'm calling. I wish it were that simple," he began, and Amelie felt her stomach drop into her groin.

"What's wrong, sir?" she whispered.

"I'm not sure exactly how to say this, Amelie. But let me start by suggesting that you don't return to school today."

"Why?" she asked, already knowing the answer.

"It has come to the attention of the school that one of our teachers might have had inappropriate contact with you during the senior beach trip."

Amelie felt blood drain from her head.

271

"Who called you?"

"We've been informed by several students. We were also called by the parents of one of your classmates. I'm afraid we'll need to investigate the situation, and the authorities may need to be called. We've already had a conversation with the teacher in question, and he has admitted to the accusations."

Oh god. Mr. Roberts was going to be in trouble because of her.

"It's not his fault. It's my fault," Amelie blurted. "I'm seventeen and it was with my consent."

"Amelie, what he did to you was statutory rape."

"But I'm seventeen, I'm old enough—" she began, but he cut her off.

"Amelie, you're a student. He was your teacher. In that case, your age doesn't matter in the eyes of the law. So it will have to be criminally investigated."

Amelie felt tears welling in her eyes again.

What have we done? What have I done?

"What will happen to Mr. Roberts?" she whispered into the phone.

"I don't know, but the authorities will want to talk to you."

A sob escaped Amelie's throat.

"I'm so sorry, Amelie. This should never have happened. And I'm afraid I have to ask you about something else. You know Hudson Crowe?"

"Yes."

"You two are dating?"

"Yes, we are," Amelie said.

As she looked out of her car window, her inner eye opened and she saw a cloud of black in the distance, rising from the earth toward the sky. It looked like a black tidal wave, filled with shadowy figures twisting and rolling in a gray mist.

As she watched it began moving toward her.

"Have you seen Hudson recently?" Scales asked.

"Not since before the beach trip," she replied. A numbness was spreading in her brain. The wave of black mist was now cresting over her head.

"I'm afraid Hudson is missing. No one has seen him since last Thursday. His parents are, of course, frantic."

The wave crashed over her.

Oh god no. Hudson.

"Has anyone found Mr. Sawyer?" she asked.

The phone went silent.

"No, he is missing as well," Scales finally said. "That's another reason why it would be better for you to stay away from school. It is also inadvisable for you to participate in your graduation ceremonies. We will, of course, mail you your high school diploma."

"Okay," Amelie managed to choke out. She hung up, put her head on the steering wheel of her car and sobbed.

It was an hour before she was able to calm herself enough to go inside.

#

Once in her bedroom, Amelie tried again to get into the hallway to look for Clovis, but with no success. She wasn't even able to fly. After a time, she gave up, put her head into her pillow and cried. She sobbed until her throat was raw and her head was pounding.

After a time, she turned over in her bed and stared at the ceiling. The house was quiet. She didn't know how long she had been crying, it could have been minutes or hours, but the light outside was changing. She took a deep breath, wiped her eyes, and sat up.

I need to think this through before I have to explain anything. I've likely destroyed one person's life. People are missing. God knows what happened if Sawyer got ahold of Hudson … and there isn't a thing I can do about it. But someone will be here soon, so I need to pull myself together.

It wasn't easy. Everyone thought that she had slept with Mr. Roberts. She had, but only his form. Clovis, the real person she had slept with, was missing. Her classmates were now affected by her in ways that she could never have guessed and for reasons that she was just now beginning to suspect. They hadn't been glamoured by her. When Sophie had thrown the keys at her, she had been hurt and angry, but acting in Amelie's best interest, not her own. This was not what happened with a glamour. No, it seemed like somehow they had adopted some feelings Clovis had for her while he was possessing them. This was why she hadn't caught it. None of them exhibited the signs and symptoms of obsession. What they had exhibited were symptoms of love.

She heard a sound from downstairs and sat up rigidly in her bed. Instinctively, she threw shields around her when she recognized the footfall as that of her brother.

"Amelie, you home?" Will called from downstairs. His voice sounded tight and edgy.

"I'm upstairs," she called, wiping her eyes and getting up. It was better to meet Will on his own turf, so she got up and started walking downstairs.

Will was standing in the kitchen.

"Are you okay?" he asked as she descended the stairs. As Will looked up at her, Amelie saw dark circles under his eyes and an expression that would have indicated concern, had he been a normal brother.

"I'm fine," she said, as she walked past him to the refrigerator to grab a bottle of Diet Coke.

"You don't have to do that. I already heard," Will said softly. He was way too close to her for comfort, and they were alone in the house.

Oh shit. Clovis had been in him too!

"Listen, Will. Whatever you *think* you know about whatever you *think* is going on with me, I don't want to talk about it," she snapped at him, as she turned to walk out of the kitchen.

Will put a hand on the doorframe, blocking her path.

"Amelie, listen. I know you're smarter than me. I know you're smarter than most people," he said with a weird calm. "But you might not know everything there is to know about the situation you're in."

"What do you know about the situation I'm in?" She was starting to get angry. Her emotions were boiling just under the surface, splashing memories, impressions, and word choice into her brain randomly.

"Jack called me," he said.

"I said, I don't want to talk about it." She ducked under his arm and headed back up the stairs.

He followed her. This was forbidden and disturbing. She did a mental checklist of things that could be used as weapons in her room.

"You may not want to talk about it, but I can tell you that Mom and Dad *will* want to talk about it. You think they won't want to play this out to something that can benefit them?"

This wasn't Will's normal voice pattern, nor his words. She whirled quickly to look at him. He was standing at her bedroom door with his arms crossed over his chest. He stepped back quickly as she approached him, searching his blue eyes for signs of black. But his eyes were his own. No one else there. It was just the words that were wrong. Suddenly the meaning of his words sunk in.

"What do you mean, 'benefit them'?" she asked, stepping back.

"You think they won't try to sue your teacher, or the school, or both?" he asked softly. "They may not be smart, but they can smell money."

She sank down hard on her bed and put her head in her hands. Of course, he was right. With their whole "the man has been holding us down" mentality, this would be the perfect opportunity for them to screw "the man".

Clovis, where are you? Where are you? I need you, she thought for the thousandth time.

Tears welled up in her eyes again, and she was tempted to just let the sobs come out until she remembered she was not alone. She was dangerously not alone.

Will was leaning against the doorframe of her bedroom. The look on his face was one of concern—and something else. His arms were folded defensively across his chest, and his jaw was clenched, but his head was slightly bowed. The stance was unlike him. Amelie sighed and wiped her eyes.

"You're right. They will do that … and I should have thought of it. Thanks for the tip," she said, trying not to let bitterness color her words. She was thankful for the heads-up, no matter who it came from.

He crossed to her and gently put a hand on her shoulder. She reacted instantly.

"Don't touch me," she snarled, as she jumped up and pushed him backward.

"I'm just trying to help," he said, his hands held up. The stance was like Clovis in the field where they first met, which seemed like a hundred years ago. But this wasn't Clovis.

"You don't always have to be alone, you know. You don't have to be so fucking closed off. You can let people help you," Will snapped.

Suddenly a chasm appeared in her shields, and anger stepped out of it.

"No, I can't let people help me," she snapped back, advancing on him. "And yes, I always have to be alone. I have to be alone all the time."

Will was backing out of her room, toward the head of the stairs. The look on his face was one of dawning horror. She didn't care. She was sick of it, sick of all of it.

"I've had to be alone my whole life. And you, of all people, should know why," she snarled at him.

Will took another quick step back as if slapped and his eyes began to dart. His jaw muscles were twitching.

He turned to head down the stairs, but Amelie had had enough of everything, the family silence, the resentment of her parents, the protection of Will's amnesia above all else.

She felt an inkiness well up in her heart. Not anger exactly. Not even hate. It was something worse, something darker. When she spoke, she was no longer raising her voice.

She grabbed Will by the arm and pulled him around to face her. They were standing on the landing of the stairs, just as it turned toward the kitchen. She was much shorter than him, but she felt suddenly felt huge.

"What? You mean to tell me you don't remember? You don't remember being thirteen and raping your eleven-year-old sister?" she asked silkily.

275

Will's eyes began to roll up in his head. She didn't care.

She grabbed him by the shirt and shook him. "Oh no, you don't," she said. "You don't get a free pass this time."

"I don't know what you're talking about," he said, pulling backward. "You're fucking crazy."

Now this was Will. The calm, concerned creature inhabiting his body was now gone. Good riddance. She preferred the truth. He pulled back from her and she just let go of him. He lost his balance and fell backward down the remaining three or four stairs, smacking his head on the kitchen floor. Amelie stood on the stairs, breathing hard, waiting to hear him yell or cry or something. But what she heard was silence. Suddenly her anger was gone.

Will was still on the floor, but he had put his hands up to his head. At least he was conscious. Amelie came down the stairs and sat next to him. He turned over and looked up at the ceiling.

"Are you okay?" Amelie asked him.

"No," he whispered.

"I should call an ambulance then," Amelie said, starting to get up, but Will grabbed her hand.

"No, I'm okay physically," he said, voice tight.

"But … but … I remember," he choked out. "I remember what I did to you. I remember you screaming and not being able to stop myself."

Amelie felt the need to pull her hand away from him, but as she looked at him, he raised his eyes to hers. He looked damned. She seemed to have that effect on everyone around her.

"I remembered it for the first time today," he whispered. "I had gotten the call from Jack. I finished my last class and was on my way to the car when all these images … well, I remembered all of it. I had to run over to a trashcan to puke. I couldn't believe I did that. I can't believe I forgot it. I must have psychological problems. But I haven't felt that about you since then. Not even once."

He turned his head and tears fell from his eyes onto the stained linoleum of their kitchen floor.

"I always wondered why you hated me. I thought you were just a bitch. But you were just protecting yourself. I'm a monster," he sobbed, his eyes tightly shut and his body shaking.

Amelie reached out and put her hand on his head. He winced at her touch, but he didn't pull away.

"You're not the monster, Will," she whispered, running her hands through his hair. "I'm the monster."

As she said this, she knew it to be true.

Will hadn't been able to control his actions anymore than anyone else who had interacted with her. Whatever she was, she had been dangerous for everyone around her from that year to this. Without the blonde woman, she would have not survived what she was. Clovis had taught her how to have a life being what *she* was. But *she* was the problem, not other people.

Just at that moment, her cell phone rang.

More good news?

Amelie got up and pulled her phone from her bag, which she had dropped on the floor in the hall.

"Amelie?" asked a familiar, clipped voice. "It's Colin Roberts."

Amelie felt her legs give out from under her and she sat down hard in the middle of the floor.

"I don't think you're supposed to talk to me," was what came out of her mouth.

Mr. Roberts laughed a mirthless laugh.

"I'm sure that's what you were told, but you and I know that the story isn't what they think. Am I right?"

Amelie said nothing. Her heart was beating fast in her chest.

"Amelie, I *remember* what happened. I remember that your friend took control of me, and I let him do that. I was curious, but I made a mistake. I didn't know what he and you were going to do. And I'll have to pay for that mistake for the rest of my life."

"Oh," was all Amelie could say. She was horrified by the thought that he might have been hiding inside Clovis during their time together. Had he seen what they did? Had he heard the secrets they had told?

"But that's not why I called," Mr. Roberts said in a cold, tight voice. "I seem to remember you were planning to go to Paris for the next year."

"Yes," she whispered. She was breaking out into a cold sweat.

"Would you consider leaving early?"

"I don't have a place to stay yet," she replied.

"That's not a problem. Do you have your passport yet?"

"Yes."

"Well, I have a friend in Paris who has a small rooftop apartment, a *chambre de bonne*, that she's willing to rent to you for a very reasonable price if you can come now."

"I don't have tickets."

"I'll get them for you—if you leave tonight."

"Why would you do that?"

277

"Well, for the altruistic reasons, I think it would be good for you to get out of this town sooner rather than later. A lot of your classmates aren't very understanding about what they think happened between us. They would be even less understanding if they guessed what really happened. We live in a very Christian state, you know."

"Okay."

"But you want to know the more selfish reasons, yes?" he asked, his voice turning tight. "My hope is that if you leave, things might blow over quicker. You've already made a mess of my life, and I don't want it to get worse. My girlfriend packed her stuff and left this morning. I won't see her again. My career is in shambles, and I suspect that I will no longer be able to continue as a teacher. My reputation as human has also taken a bit of a hit. But I can't very well come out and say that I was possessed by a demon, can I? Who would believe that?"

"He's not a demon," Amelie whispered.

"Is that what he told you? And you believed him? What proof did he give you? None, right? So why would you put your trust in a creature that was willing to take over someone else's body? Does that sound like an ethical, trustworthy creature? No, that sounds like a demon to me."

"You don't understand."

"I may understand better than you think," Mr. Roberts snapped. "I understand that you were lonely, and you found something to fill your loneliness. His affection became addictive to you, and you eventually lost any grasp on morals, ethics or implications of your behavior. And now we will all suffer for it. And where is your friend? I'm betting he has disappeared, hasn't he? Because that's what demons do, Amelie! They use us then they leave."

"How do you know?"

"That's not important," he said. "What's important is that _you_ leave."

Amelie felt the tears running down her cheeks. She didn't believe him, but the words still stung.

Clovis, where are you?

"I'll go to Paris," she whispered into the phone.

"Tonight?"

"Yes."

"I'll text you with the number of a locker at the airport and the code. In the locker will be your tickets, the phone number of my friend, the apartment address in Paris and some cash. Your flight leaves at 8:15 p.m., so you'll need to leave for the airport now. When you get to Paris, you can email the school and tell them that you left early because you couldn't stand the pressure."

"Okay."

"If you tell anyone I did any of this, I will deny it. But you should leave now if you want to catch the plane."

"Okay. And, for the record, I'm sorry. I didn't think it would hurt you," Amelie said softly.

"No, you didn't think at all. That was the problem," Mr. Roberts said with a sigh. "I don't ever want to see you again, but I wish you well. And I feel very sorry for you."

Then he had hung up.

Amelie walked back to the kitchen to check on Will. He had fallen asleep on the floor. She should probably wake him up, because he could have a concussion. She reached down and poked him, and his eyes fluttered for a moment before closing again. She closed her eyes and opened her inner eye. The energy surrounding him was in the same patterns that it always was. He was fine.

She then went upstairs and quickly packed as many things as she could into a medium-sized suitcase. She grabbed her passport and dragged the suitcase downstairs. Before leaving, she went back into the kitchen, bent down, and kissed Will on the forehead. She had never done that before, and it felt both good and sad.

Then she grabbed her purse and suitcase and walked out the door, leaving a path of destruction in her wake.

Chapter Thirty-Six

Not to Touch the Earth

Amelie's flight to Paris was a night flight, but she didn't sleep. It wasn't until she was in a taxi from the airport to her new apartment in the 7th arrondissement that she fell asleep. She woke in tears when the driver banged on the glass behind him to alert her that they were at her destination.

She had dreamed of Clovis making love to Rose and it made her heart bleed. *Where was he?*

She was saved from extended human interaction by a surly *guardienne*. When Amelie rang the bell and introduced herself, the woman shoved an envelope with keys into her hand and announced that Madame was gone for the week but that she had left instructions for her in the envelope.

By the time Amelie had dragged her suitcase up the tiny spiral staircase to her flat under the eaves of the Haussmann-style building, she was exhausted. She dropped her bag and let herself fall onto the unmade single bed.

At first, all she saw was the darkness behind her eyes, but then she found herself standing at the edge of a pond filled with koi. Most of the fish were swimming listlessly in circles but a few were belly-up in the water. The sky was dark and cloudy above her head, and the trees looked barren and lifeless. As she began walking toward the pavilion, the grass underfoot crunched, its colors pale and faded, as if dried by drought.

As she got closer to the pavilion, she heard something behind her.

She whirled around but saw nothing and no one.

This is a trap. You didn't come by the hallway, and you aren't in a story now. This is a dream.

"Not exactly a dream. We're a bit below the dreamscape," said a voice from the pavilion. Amelie whirled again, only to be faced with the creature she least wanted to see.

"So have you found him yet?" Rose purred.

She was wearing a modest blue dress, but it was still clingy enough to show her perfect figure. And, of course, she was wearing high-heeled sandals.

"Excuse me?" Amelie replied coldly. Her anger was rising, which was a nice change from longing and fear.

"Have you found Clovis yet?" Rose asked, index finger to the side of her lip.

"How do you know I'm looking for him?"

"Because you're here."

Amelie began backing away.

"Oh, you don't need to be afraid of me. I just wanted to see how you're doing, after being dumped."

"I'm fine," Amelie said stiffly.

"I'm sure you are, honey. I'm sure you'll get over him quickly enough. Twenty or thirty years should do it," laughed Rose.

The words cut Amelie, and something must have showed.

"Oh no. Honey. You aren't still expecting him to come back, are you? You don't know? Didn't he tell you? He's a seducer, and he brings death. That's what he does. He seduces people slowly until they love him. Then he leaves, and they can't stand it. So, they kill themselves. And *voilà*, death accomplished."

Rose laughed again. Amelie felt each word piercing her heart.

"I must admit, I'm a bit surprised he didn't tell you. He usually does. It's the final blow, and the emotion that comes from it is delicious. How badly did he make you love him before he fucked you? Would you have died for him? Killed for him? Abominated the natural order of things for him?" As Rose said this, she was moving toward her.

"Clovis didn't share it with you?" Amelie asked as coldly as she could manage, backing away. In this moment, Amelie wanted nothing more than to kill Rose.

Kill her. Clovis had said that she should kill Rose if Rose every found her alone. But with what?

"No. Clovis didn't tell me," Rose continued, biting one nail. "I haven't seen him since—well, in a while. I thought he might just be resting after such a long seduction, but I can't feel him either."

Then she seemed to catch herself, and she laughed.

"Of course, he is probably enjoying my concern as well. I wonder if he could be tempted to show himself if—"

Rose stopped, her brow furrowed then, without another word, she launched herself at Amelie.

281

When Rose's hand grabbed hers, Amelie's brain exploded with images of Clovis. Clovis seducing people. Clovis with Rose in multiple sexual positions. Clovis whipping a chained man. Clovis laughing as a young girl jumped out a window. On and on. More and more. The images filled her head, piling on top of each other, each one worse than the last. Clovis's face, beautiful as always, but cold and cruel.

"I've always been so proud of my son," Rose said softly.

Her son?

A sharp pain shot through Amelie's head. And she heard Rose laugh.

Something in Amelie's head snapped and everything went black.

Chapter Thirty-Seven

Like Daughter, Like Mother

Amelie woke gasping and crying on her little bed. She sat up and wiped her eyes. It had been a dream, that was all. She had dreamed about Rose because she was worried about Clovis.

You don't really believe that.

No, she wasn't going to fixate on this. It was just a dream.

But didn't Clovis tell you that incubi usually meet people in their dreams? It might have been a dream, but that didn't mean it wasn't Rose or that what she said wasn't true.

Amelie shook her head. She stood up quickly. No, she wasn't going to think about that right now. Right now, she had to unpack and get some food. She opened up her suitcase and began to unpack when she remembered that she hadn't taken everything out of her landlady's envelope.

She picked it up off the end of the bed where she had dropped it. In it were another set of keys and a small Post-it Note.

Welcome Amelie. We were pleased Colin told us you wanted to rent our chambre de bonne. I hope you enjoy it. There are quite a few other students on the same floor with you, so I'm sure you will make friends in no time!

Your mother called last night and wants you to call her back. She said that you can call collect. We're going out of town tonight and will be gone for the week. I have left you the keys to the front door, and to our apartment. Feel free to use the phone downstairs, as long as you are calling collect. Of course, you can use the apartment as well, just within reason. Have a great weekend, Laura.

Her mother called? What the fuck now?

Amelie had texted home from the airport and left her landlady's address and number in case of emergency. She never had the slightest expectation that any member of her family would call her—especially not her mother.

Opal probably wanted to sue the school. But suppose there was some information about Hudson? Damn it. Looking at her watch, she realized it was already 4 p.m., which meant it would be morning at home. Her mother would be at work, so maybe she could just leave a voicemail. Even if she had to talk to Opal, the day couldn't really get any worse, could it?

Amelie went to her landlady's apartment downstairs and let herself in. The place was clean, neat, and almost sterile. She sat on a couch next to the phone and called the international operator. When she heard her mother's voice on the other end of the line accept the call, she almost choked.

"Amelie? That you?" Opal asked.

"Yes. What's wrong?" Amelie asked sharply, waiting for her mother's tirade. She didn't know what the tirade would be about, but she knew there would be a tirade. Her mother was home on a workday.

"Nothing's wrong. You just got something that you might want to know about, is all," her mother said.

Her tone was off. Amelie had expected serious hostility, given that she had left home without notice and before her parents could file that civil lawsuit that her mother was probably keen to file.

"What is it?" Amelie asked tightly.

"Well, your papa and I was talking about getting a lawyer to sue the school. You know, for what happened to you with that teacher and all."

Will had been right. She had to give her brother credit.

"But we didn't have to," her mother continued. "The school system sent someone by yesterday. A nice man in a very expensive suit. He brought a check. If we accept it, then we have to sign something that says that we won't talk about none of this and we won't sue the school system. You have to sign it, too."

Of course. This was a money issue, and her mother was all about the money.

"Was the check made out to me or you?" Amelie asked.

"It was made out to you. You're an adult now, so it's in your name. It's a lot of money, Amelie. Enough for your brother's college and yours. All you have to do is sign."

"Oh, it's enough for Will to finish college, is it?" she snapped. She shouldn't bother but she couldn't help it.

"Amelie, ain't no need to be like that," her mother started. "You already got scholarship offers for three schools here at home, three good schools. Plus, the money is enough for you to go to one of those fancy Northern private universities without a scholarship, even if you pay for all your brother's school. You got no reason to be—"

Opal stopped. The line went very quiet, and Amelie thought they had been cut off. She was about to hang up when her mother spoke.

"No, the truth is you got every reason to be however you want to be," she said quietly. "Hold on a second, I want to go to the other room."

You could have knocked Amelie over with a feather. Her brain told her that this must be a whole lot of money, and Opal would say whatever she had to in order to get her hands on some or all of it. Her instincts told her otherwise. Whatever was going on with her mother, there was an honesty to it.

She heard a door close and an exhalation as her mother apparently took a seat.

"It's time for some truth between us, girl," her mother began. "I was about to say that you got no reason to be nasty with us. But I don't feel like lying, not now that I know."

"Now that you know what?" Amelie asked.

"Quiet girl. I got a lot to say, and I probably wouldn't say none of it if I wasn't already drinking. After we got the check yesterday, we all went out. I took today off work to be here if you called. But I couldn't figure out what I would say to you, you know, so you would let us keep some of the money. So I started drinking early. Sometimes you need drink to realize that the only thing you can say is truth. If you tell your papa or your brother what I tell you, I will swear on my grave that you're a liar, but I'm gonna say it anyway."

She stopped for a moment. "I wish I had known about you before all this happened. It might have made things better between us. Not good, you know, but better."

"I have no idea what you're talking about—" Amelie began, but her mother interrupted her.

"I don't rightly know where to start. I guess I'll start with meeting him," Opal said. "I was never smart like you, but when I was young, I was more beautiful than a woman has a right to be. I was movie-star beautiful. By the time I was a teenager, men started asking my parents to marry me. Not date me— marry me. My mama and papa were dirt poor, but they didn't want me to marry too young. They wanted me to finish some schooling. But that's not what I want to talk to you about."

She stopped and Amelie felt a sense of vertigo, as if she were standing on the edge of a cliff.

"One night, when I was about seventeen, I met this boy in my dreams," her mother began quietly. "He was tan, blond, and the finest thing I had ever seen. I met him in a castle. He was dressed just like a prince, and I was dressed like a princess. We laughed and danced, and all the girls were jealous of me, just like Cinderella. When I woke up, I thought it was the best dream I had ever had, and I didn't forget it. I just couldn't forget that boy. Days went by, and I couldn't get him out my head, you know?"

"Yes." Amelie breathed softly.

"Well, he came back after that. Not every night but maybe every week. And we did things. I had never had sex yet in real life, but I did in my dreams, and it was wonderful. I wanted to go to bed earlier and earlier every night. Finally, after about a month of this, I met Brent. He was awful handsome too, but once I started dating him, I didn't see my golden boy anymore. Brent and I had dated for a year when he asked me to marry him. I said yes."

She sighed.

"I was happy, but I was also sad. I missed my golden boy," her mother said, with a voice that sounded much further away than a mere ocean. "And then— well, I was expecting too much of Brent come our wedding night. I thought it would be like with *him*, but it wasn't. It was sweaty and smelly and over so fast. I cried that night, but in the bathroom where Brent wouldn't hear. After that, I didn't want to have sex with him. I did, but I didn't enjoy it.

"When I got pregnant with your brother, I was happy. It was a reason not to have sex anymore. So Brent and I didn't have much sex during the pregnancy, and none afterward, while I was nursing. I nursed until Will was a year old. Just after I stopped nursing, Brent got called to work at a new construction site for two weeks. That was when my golden boy come back."

Amelie heard Opal take a sip of something and cough.

"The first night, I had just gone to sleep after putting Will down," Opal continued. "He was here in my dream, standing next to some old car and dressed like Robert Redford from *The Great Gatsby*. He looked so handsome … but he was angry 'cause he thought that I had picked Brent over him. He told me that he couldn't be with me if Brent was there. But he said that he was going to have me, completely, for the two weeks Brent was away. And he did."

Opal's voice was a bit slurred. Amelie wondered if she even remembered she was on the phone. She suspected not.

"For them two weeks, he was there in my dreams. He did things to me. It's a good thing Brent wasn't there 'cause I know I was moaning in my sleep. And every morning when I woke up, I was wet, like I had been with a man."

"He raped you?" Amelie asked.

"Oh no, it wasn't rape, girl," her mother said, with a dark laugh. "I was hot for him in every way. But by the time Brent got back, I was used up. I got flu and was down for two more weeks. Brent was mad but got his mama to come and help out. My golden boy was gone by then."

"Did you ever see him again?" Amelie whispered.

"No. I never did. And I was never the same. I had sex with Brent a few weeks after that, and it was like trying to go back to eating bad hamburger after you'd gotten used to steak. But damned if I didn't get pregnant immediately. This time with you."

Amelie heard her sigh.

"I guess it don't come as no surprise to you that I didn't want you. I wanted Will. When he was born, with his fat little face and his blond hair, I loved him from the get-go. With you, I never felt that. I guess people would say that I was bad mother 'cause I couldn't love my own daughter. But I just couldn't. Even when you was little, you felt different. When you got older, and was so smart, it made it harder. If I hadn't seen you comin' out me with my own eyes, I would have thought you came from someone else. I used to worry myself at night about it. How I couldn't love you. But I was never good at pretending."

Amelie heard the strain in Opal's voice. She probably should have felt distraught. Her mother just admitted to not loving her. Instead, she felt relieved. If it was in the open, they didn't need to pretend to emotions neither of them felt. Because, truth be told, she had never loved Opal either. She had needed her at times, but she had never loved her. Opal coughed and Amelie heard her swallowing. Probably more booze.

"Look, we don't have to go into this. If you want—"

"No," Opal said harshly. "This is my time to talk. Only gonna do it once. Where was I? Oh yeah. So, there we were, a little family. Like everyone says you oughta be, but none of it was right. I didn't want my husband in my bed, I didn't love my daughter. The only thing that kept me going was that I did love Will. Then, all that shit started when you was about eleven."

"No—" Amelie said, but her mother cut her off.

"Hush girl. You need to hear this bit. When that thing happened with your brother, I knew what had happened. I saw the look coming in his eye. I saw the look coming in your papa's eyes too. You wasn't beautiful like I had been—no, it was like you had some kind of spell you were puttin' on the menfolk. The womenfolk hated you, but when we put you in that hospital, when I put you there, I didn't do it 'cause I hated you. I did it to save your brother. After I sent you away, he forgot what he did. He still don't remember. He don't understand why you hate him. I know you look at him a lot to see if he remembers, but he don't. I know that, 'cause I'm his mama."

He does now, Amelie thought, but it was not what came out of her mouth.

"Okay. Fine. What am I supposed to say to that? He doesn't remember, so it's okay?" Amelie heard herself say.

"No. I'm sayin' that if you blame anyone, if someone has to take the sin for that, it should be me and not him. I should have seen it coming. I'd seen that kind of crazy before. I had felt it. I should have known. But when you came back, you was different. It was like livin' in the house with a ghost. You were there, but you weren't there. We couldn't talk to you. You didn't talk to us. But I knew when you started having the dreams. You changed." Opal said this as a whisper.

"You stopped being so mousy, and I saw there was something wild in you. You were holding a rage inside, and I saw the craziness too. For the first time, I saw a part of me in you." Her mother said this with something like admiration.

"If I had known that you had that wildness, that strength, that anger in you, then I might have known how to be your mother. If you had come back from that hospital, and slapped me, or yelled at me, or called me a fucking bitch, I could have started there to work back to something, but you gave me jack shit. But when I knew that you had met someone out there, I knew you was like me. At least in some ways. You knew what it was like to be loved by someone who really knows how."

"Do you regret it?" Amelie whispered, in spite of herself.

"My time with him? Not for one minute. My time with him was the best time of my life. I would drop everything to go back to him. Well, maybe everything but Will. But when I'm old and Will has a family of his own, I hope he comes back to me. I would be happy to just sleep with him till I die. Or find some other way to be with him."

Her mother paused again, and Amelie heard her gulping.

"But you did that, didn't you?" Opal continued. "You were smart enough to find a way to really be with your boy, even if for just a little while. I wish god had given me the smarts to do what you did. So don't you be cowardly. Don't you regret it. Most folk will never get to feel what you and I got to feel. Don't you dare regret it."

Amelie heard tears in her mother's voice. She had tears in her eyes as well. She hated them.

"Back to the check," Amelie said, as coldly as she could. "You can have what you need for Will. What needs to happen?"

Opal was quiet for a moment. She coughed and cleared her voice.

"Well, I guess you heard enough then. We need to mail the paper to you, and you need to sign it. Then we can deposit the check in your checking account here."

"And then?"

"You take what you want and give us what you want. No, give it to Will. I don't want nothing—don't deserve it."

Amelie heard Opal sigh.

"You know, you could also come home. You and I got bad history, but this is still your home. And no one gonna understand what happened to you any better than me. You don't have to talk about it. You don't have to do anything but what you've always done. And you don't have to hide no more. You can stay here till you decide what college to go to."

Amelie was trying to keep her tears from wetting the phone.

Why now? Why have this conversation now, when it does no good? Why not years ago?

"Okay," she said, trying not to sniff. "You can FedEx the check to me. I can deposit it from here, just include a note with your account numbers."

She wanted off the phone badly.

"All right. But you think about coming home. It might not be good for you being by yourself in a strange place just now," her mother said, also making an attempt to sound cold and factual, but failing.

"Yeah, okay. I'll let you know when I get the papers. Bye," Amelie said, as she abruptly hung up. She put her head down on Laura's couch and sobbed.

"Clovis, where are you?" she said, but there was no answer.

After some time, she got up and walked to the window. The sun was beginning to sink down in the sky. It was probably about 5 p.m. Amelie got the keys and went back upstairs toward her room where she lay down on her bed and cried herself into another uncomfortable sleep.

#

Amelie woke near sunset. She left her room, meaning to go downstairs to the street to find food, but instead she was drawn to a little door that led to the roof. When she tried it, she found it unlocked, and she climbed the rusty metal stairs to a door that opened onto the roof.

Now, standing on the rooftop of her building at sunset, Amelie pulled her sweater around her against the moist chill in the air. She could hear an orchestra playing somewhere below. It must have been far away because she could only hear brief phrases of the music, drifting across the breeze. The sun was setting behind the city skyline. This was the time she would usually begin her hunt for Clovis ... but never again. The time for that was over.

289

She closed her eyes against the beauty of her surroundings, tears tracking softly down her cheeks. Clovis wasn't coming back, but she couldn't hate him. Even if everything Rose had said was true, she couldn't hate him. He gave her the greatest gift anyone had ever given her. He had given her the skills to control her abilities, and therefore the freedom to walk unhindered in the world. She could have a life now, for whatever that was worth. So her brain could never hate him. But her heart ... well, her heart would never love another. This was not some schoolgirl feeling of drama. It came with dimmed colors and symbols that confirmed this suspicion. Her love for him would never go away, and it would never stop hurting. It would stay with her like a chronic disease.

In the fading light, she slumped to her knees and began to sob. She rocked back and forth, keening, as the moon chased the sun from the sky. She cried his name over and over again, as if trying to eject it from her body. She fell over to her side and curled into a ball, shaking and gasping. She went on like this for what felt like an infinity.

Just when she was beginning to wonder if her heart would just burst, a numbness crept over her. A beautiful blankness that felt like morphine. Her tears subsided.

"Enough now," she whispered to herself, sitting up and hugging her knees to her chest. She had to give up on him or she wouldn't survive. She might not be able to forget but she could bury. She had lots of experience with that.

She closed her eyes, visualizing herself stepping outside of herself. She saw her own body sitting on the rooftop. She also saw a strange, transparent black cocoon of energy was surrounding her body. That had never been there before. It looked like some sort of shield.

Amelie shook her head. She looked closer into herself, at the rivers of energy than ran up and down her body and the little bundles of light that collected them. She saw her heart. Not the organ that pumps blood, but the energy center that lived within it. She saw it glowing gold, purple, red, and pink. Running through the light were cracks. She saw rivulets of gold and pink light bleeding from the cracks.

She reached gently into her own body and took her heart in her hands. It felt delicate and fragile. She felt the overwhelming desire to protect this injured little thing. She conjured a box with one hand. The box was made of crystal ice and lined with white silk. She laid her own heart gently in the box and closed the lid. She surrounded it with golden chains and silver barbs. Around that she wrapped golden wool, softening the barbs and edges. She then placed it back into her own chest. And it was done. She could still feel her heart beating, but dimly, like the music she heard in the distance.

Around her, the world was still the same. The sky was now a flame-blue canvas reflecting the city lights. Nothing had stopped or died as a result of what she had just done. She stood up, wiping her face. Across from her, a little girl was staring from the window of an adjacent building. Amelie gave her a little wave. The girl smiled and was starting to wave back, when a woman came up behind her and quickly pulled the girl back from the window. Amelie wondered what the woman had seen. Had she seen a girl or a woman? Had she seen someone suicidal or homicidal? Had she seen a sorrowing angel? Or a recovering monster? Amelie knew she was all these things.

She looked down at the city around her. She needed to find a way to survive here. She wasn't ready to go back, at least not yet. It was strange but this city might turn out to be what she thought she had always wanted. It was a place she could be alone.

With this thought she left the roof and made her way to her tiny little room, where she would sleep ... and only sleep.

Chapter Thirty-Eight

Amelie Opts Out and In

The next morning Amelie woke with a mouth full of cotton and eyes sealed shut with mucus. Whatever endorphins had been coursing through her bloodstream as a result of her cry were gone. She woke feeling empty and dead.

The sun was shining through the tiny window of her room. She stood and looked out. The sky was blue with puffy white clouds and the air smelled of flowers and sugar. Once again, the sound of music drifted across the rooftops. Someone was practicing piano, with the occasional charming mistakes. It was all so perfect that it could have been from a movie. The young, daring girl coming to France on her own to face the quirky challenges of being an American in Paris … only to eventually find love, on the grass in front of the Eiffel Tower.

Amelie hated it—all of it.

Despite all the horror of the past few days, she felt better physically than she ever had in her life. She had no headaches, no stomachaches, and no intestinal distress. Her muscles weren't tight or spasming. Her neck and spine felt completely relaxed despite the lumpy bed.

Maybe this is the payback for emotional hell. I get physical perfection.

She looked in her purse. She still had enough cash to eat for a couple of weeks. But then she would have to sort out a bank account and transfer some money. She had planned to sort that out before she left, but things had gone to hell in a hand basket.

Why spend your own money when you can get someone else to spend theirs? asked a new, cold part of her.

This made Amelie smile. The thought of using other people for once, instead of them using her, amused her.

292

She threw on the blue-and-white striped T-shirt that she had bought months ago for this occasion, and a pair of jeans. She left her room and went out, making her way toward Champ de Mars. She would find a victim to buy her breakfast there. She hoped it would be someone she could easily despise.

As she arrived, a perfect target was standing on the grass of Champ de Mars staring up at the Eiffel Tower. He looked bored. He was wearing nondescript dark pants and a polo shirt. His blond hair was combed in a side part. She guessed he was a foreigner here. She opened her inner eye, which had become stronger now. She saw his sexual need and the shame he felt from his need. He reminded her a little bit of Mr. Sawyer. She felt a dark joy surge in her.

Amelie approached the man and targeted a beam of energy toward him. When he turned to look at her, his blue eyes widened like a cartoon and his mouth dropped open. The energy she had sent was purely sexual. There was no love in it.

"Hi," she said. "Do you speak English?"

"Yes, I'm Canadian," he said, smiling at her and briefly catching her eye. There was a faint sheen of sweat on his upper lip. Flashes of black and green jutted out from his eyes as she watched with her inner eye.

"Are you American?" he asked.

Okay, this one might be dangerous. But who cares?

"Yes. I'm here on a study program. I just got here. Are you visiting?"

"Yes, I'm here on a business trip," he replied.

He's here away from his wife and family—and looking to get laid. Well, he's going to be disappointed.

"I'm Amelie," she said, reaching out her hand.

"Andy," he replied, taking it.

At his touch, pictures began flashing into her head. None of them were pretty. The pictures were of war, battles, and dead bodies. That was strange coming from a businessman.

He's not a businessman. He's something else. He's military or government.

"Hey, I hope I'm not being too forward, but can I invite you to breakfast? Maybe a crêpe?" he asked.

Amelie laughed out loud.

"What's funny?" Andy's eyes narrowed.

"It's just that that's exactly what I was wanting," Amelie replied, catching his eye and holding his gaze. She let out another minuscule pulse of energy. Andy shivered, then smiled.

"Excellent," he said, reaching out a hand as if to touch her before catching himself and drawing it back.

With her inner eye, Amelie saw that all the colors had disappeared. She saw only black.

You shouldn't go anywhere with this guy.

Why not? After everything else, I think I can handle it, she argued with herself.

It didn't ring true even in her own head. She *wasn't* sure she could handle it, but she also wasn't sure she cared.

They walked together to a small market a few streets away. Instead of crêpes, they bought some strawberries, cheese, and bread. As they walked out of the market, the sky overhead turned darker. They were almost to Champ de Mars when the skies opened, and a cool, early summer rain doused them.

Andy grabbed a newspaper and put it over her head.

"My hotel is just a block away, we can eat there," he said, grabbing her hand and breaking into a quick trot.

The touch of his hand brought another wave of blackness, along with the sound of a woman crying.

Do not go anywhere with this man. The voice sounded like Clovis, but it wasn't. It was just her mind mimicking his voice.

Why the hell not?

They came to a small hotel on Avenue de la Bourdonnais. She and Andy breezed through an empty reception area and into a tiny elevator. He still had hold of Amelie's hand. The elevator was so small that there was barely enough room for both of them and the bag of food, so she ended up pressed against him. The energy radiating off him felt like psychic Novocain.

"Don't worry, we're just about there," he said, looking at her with a smile that should have been consoling but wasn't. After all, what would he think she would be worried about?

They came out of the lift and into a long corridor.

"My room is at the corner, it has a great view," he said, taking her hand again. His grip was a little too tight for comfort.

She was just about to pull away, when he brought her to a door and unlocked it with one hand.

Then he held out an arm to her, motioning her inside.

"It's not too bad for a three-star hotel, right?" he asked, and his slightly embarrassed demeanor reassured her.

The room looked corporate and unobtrusive. The bed coverings were cream, beige, and black. There was a desk on the wall near the windows. It looked like any chain hotel in any city. The one anomaly was a vase filled with white roses.

White roses ... like they use at funerals.

The door clicked shut behind her.

"So where should we put the food—" she began, collecting her energy, when Andy backhanded her across the face.

#

Amelie fell onto the bed, her face throbbing, and scrambled to move backward, but Andy was immediately on top of her. He straddled her, his knees on her upper arms and his hand over her mouth.

Suddenly, and uselessly, the images in her head became clear. The flashes of dead bodies and war. These things weren't some memories of trauma. They were simply his interests.

He doesn't care what I look like living. His interest is what I look like dead.

He grabbed her around the throat and began pressing. He was cutting off the blood to her brain. She fought him, but this was the natural reaction of her body. Deep inside her, in that place below the here and now, she was starting to feel a sense of calm.

Things began to turn black around her as she struggled. She knew the man would do awful things to her dead body, but that wouldn't matter, she would be gone. In fact, he might be doing her a favor.

Her weird sense of internal calm was broken by a rumbling sound, like a large train headed her way, and with it came a wind that whipped around her. It was dry and soft and lifted her up and out of her body.

Amelie was now hovering over herself. The man on top of her was pulling down his trousers. The room around her began to shake. Light spilled in from the windows, the doorframes and all the tiny cracks in the plaster. Whatever was making the train sound was getting closer.

In the center of the room, the light was beginning to collect into a humanoid form, when a tall woman burst through the bedroom door, yanked the man from Amelie and threw him to the floor.

She pulled out a gun with a silencer and unceremoniously shot Andy in the back of the head. The woman then turned her face upward, looking straight at Amelie. She had blonde hair that was lowlighted in black and a face with features that looked Japanese. Her almond-shaped eyes were strikingly blue. These eyes found Amelie's and caught them.

"Not leaving so soon, are you?" she asked her, the corners of her mouth turning up ever so slightly.

The woman moved to her limp body and put her lips on Amelie's, beginning CPR. Amelie felt herself jerked downward toward her body and resisted.

What was there to go back to? And why would she want to?

These thoughts were wiped away when she felt the fire in her lungs. She sat up instinctively, her body racked with coughs. The woman was sitting next to her on the bed, regarding her with strange eyes. Her face was beautiful in that way that can only be seen in mixed races. A thick, ugly scar that snaked across her left cheek, but rather than tarnishing her beauty the contrast enhanced it. She had a full mouth and pale skin with light freckles splayed across her nose. Her nose was straight and fine. She was tall and thin but not delicate. She looked like she could have been a tennis player or a gymnast.

"Lie back down," she said, pushing Amelie gently back down. "I'm not letting you kill yourself today."

She gave Amelie a look that might have been disdain but wasn't.

"Who are you, and what are you doing here?" Amelie managed to croak out. Her throat was painful.

"My name is Majo," the woman said. "I'm here saving your life."

"Suppose I didn't want to be saved?" Amelie whispered. The woman rolled her eyes.

"You gave in to a moment of weakness, that's all. It happens to the best of us. Besides, he was one of ours who had gone off radar, so I had to take him out anyway, for obvious reasons."

"Is he? I mean, did you?" she asked, pointing to the body.

"Did I kill him? Yeah, he's gone. No problem there."

"But won't someone come for him?"

"They already came," she said, then stopped herself suddenly. "Oh, you mean the authorities? No, not until we're long gone. I just erased all records of us from their video surveillance."

Amelie was shocked in spite of herself.

"You can do that?" she asked.

Majo gave her a tiny smile.

"You can rule the world from a laptop," she replied, reaching into her backpack.

"Put these on," she said, handing Amelie clothes. "There is a car waiting downstairs. Can you stand up?"

Amelie nodded and Majo helped her to a standing position. Majo's touch was cold but solid and steadying. Her inner eye flew open, and Amelie saw the other woman surrounded by halos of pink, red, blue, and gold. Odd colors for a woman who had just killed someone.

"What if I don't trust you or don't want to go with you?" Amelie asked. Majo shrugged.

"You can stay here and explain the dead body when the authorities do show up. But do you really want to continue in the mode that you were in when you decided to go to the room of someone that I'm sure you would have known was a psychopath?"

Amelie was taken aback—but she wasn't quite sure what she was most taken aback by. Finally, she looked Majo directly in the eye.

"No, I guess I don't," she whispered.

"Good. Admission is the first step to recovery," Majo replied softly.

#

Less than ten minutes later, their car pulled up in front of the strangest door Amelie had ever seen. It was statement to the blatant weirdness of the thing that she noticed it at all, but this door was something that would be hard not to notice. The wooden door and the decorative ceramic molding surrounding it were created as if straight lines were a sin. Both were ornately decorated with peacocks and lizards, flowers and vines. On top of the door were two nudes— a male and a female. The panes on the door itself consisted of two round panes at the top with three sideways rectangular panes beneath it. From a distance, the structure of the door looked like a giant alien head.

As Majo helped her out of the car, Amelie swayed a bit on unsteady legs.

"You, okay?" Majo asked, putting her arm around Amelie's waist. Majo's touch steadied her and made her head feel clearer.

She's a Cambion, too, Amelie thought, before pushing the memories that came with those words from her brain.

"Come on, let's get past the penis and let a doctor have a look at you."

"The penis?"

Majo smiled and pointed to the door. It took a moment but suddenly Amelie realized that what she had seen as an alien head was really the carving of an upside-down phallus.

She almost smiled—almost.

Majo took her through the front door and into a dark interior. The inside of the building was the polar opposite of the exterior. It was stark, cold, and smelled like antiseptic. It also looked a lot bigger on the inside that it had seemed from the outside.

Majo led her to a dark-haired woman reading a book behind a reception desk.

"We have a check-in," Majo said. The woman nodded, barely looking up.

"And I will accompany her through her day," Majo continued. The woman's head snapped up.

"Really? You will stay?" she asked in English, with a thick French accent.

"Was that somehow unclear?" Majo asked. The woman blanched and shook her head.

Majo led Amelie upstairs to the first door of many she would go through that day. Behind each one she was met by white-coated people who bandaged her, took blood, performed tests, and wrote notes. And at the end of each, she came back to sit with Majo. After what felt like days, Amelie came out of a room to find Majo standing instead of sitting. She had a small smile on her face.

"Am I done?" she asked. Majo smiled softly.

"Not quite. You have one more conversation."

"And then someone will explain this to me?"

"Yes."

Majo took her to the top floor of the building. The first door on their right opened onto a room that looked vastly different from the sterile, white-and-silver rooms she had been in. This room looked like it had once been a recreation room, maybe fifty years ago. At one end was a ping-pong table and a foosball game. At the other was a large-screen TV attached to the wall, with two old, brown leather sofas flanking it. A young man was lying on one of these, tossing some sort of ball in the air while staring at the TV.

"Your last interview," the Majo said with no inflection, indicating to the young man.

Amelie went in and sat down on the other couch. The man didn't look up or indicate that he saw her in any way. So she openly studied him. Something about him looked familiar and became more familiar the more she looked.

He was not good-looking. He had pasty skin and a nose that was too large for his face by a good fifteen percent. It also had a bump on it that suggested that he had been in more than a few fights in his life. His hair was unkempt and that ash color that her mother used to call "dishwater blond". It was actually closer to brown, but either way it was nondescript. His clothes didn't help. He was wearing khaki pants, a cream shirt, and a crumpled brown jacket. He was so beige that he could have disappeared by standing in front of a paper sack. Until he sat up, turned to her, and caught her eye with the brightest, non-augmented blue eyes she had ever seen in her life.

"So," he said, with an accent that was some variety of British. "I'm your final interview?"

"Yes," she said, adding nothing more. He laughed out loud and smacked his knee.

"Oh, so prim. I love newbies," he said with a smile.

His teeth were like his eyes. They were whiter than they should have been, but the whiteness didn't look like the result of cosmetic intervention. There was a chip in his front tooth and slight gap between a canine tooth and a molar that no respectable orthodontist would have allowed to remain. No, she suspected the white teeth were natural.

"What is this part of the interview about?" she asked, annoyed with his smile, his eyes, and his attitude of superiority.

"It's the part where I warn you what it means to go forward," he replied with a shrug.

"Okay. Warn me then."

"Well, if you're like most people, you have been brought here under *dire* circumstances." He drew out the word "dire" and there was a slight rolling of his eyes that made her want to strangle him.

"Most have either gone off their heads, killed someone else, or tried to kill themselves. You?" he asked.

She said nothing, she simply ground her back teeth together. She wanted nothing more than to smack the shit out of this guy, but it was good to feel that. It was good to feel something besides numbing despair.

"Ah, you don't want to talk about it. That means you tried to kill yourself," he said, leaning back down into the couch.

"The point I'm making, or that I'm supposed to be making, is this. Right now, if I tell you you'll be required to give up the rest of your life and your identity to be a part of this, you aren't likely to think that's a bad thing. It's like depressed people joining the Army or the Foreign Legion. But sooner or later, you'll start to feel better and when you feel better, you may want things that you aren't allowed to have here."

"How about we start with what I *can* get here," Amelie said. "Or do here. I don't have a clear picture of that."

"No, and you won't for a while. But I can tell you that you will want for nothing in terms of your physical needs. Your food, housing, clothing, medical, and all the daily needs of life will be provided. Actually, it's much more than your needs. We provide most of your wants as well. If you want the newest computer, you'll get it. If you want to buy a five-thousand-dollar kite, it will be provided for you."

"So, what do I have to do?" she replied. She could feel her eyes throbbing. She sat up and threw a small blast of energy at an ant she saw crawling in the corner. It began crawling in crazy circles. The man turned his eyes in the direction of the ant—and smiled.

299

"We know you have talents," he continued. "All you have to do is use them when you're asked to use them and in the way that you're asked to use them."

This sounded like a cult.

"Now you have the 'oh my, I've fallen in with a cult' look, but that's not quite it," he said. "Cults are usually religious. We are actively *not* religious. Cults are also usually willing to recruit almost anyone. We only recruit people with particular gifts—and very few people make it through the process here. And all real cults are known and tracked by governments. But we are known by only the people involved."

"What happens to people who don't make it through the process or who don't want to stay?"

He just looked at her and raised an eyebrow.

"So I join, or I die?" she asked. He just shrugged.

"You were planning to die anyway, right? We make it painless, if that's your choice."

"What do you do here?"

"Me in particular?" he asked with another smile and a wink.

"No, you the plural," she snapped.

"We are all about infrastructure—human infrastructure. We clean up the infrastructure of society from the inside out. If we know that there is an incompetent president in South America who threatens the nature of the world, we find a way to get his people to dispose of him. If there is a serial killer murdering kids that the police can't find and that threatens the order of things, we eliminate him. If someone unsuited for religion takes over some country, we get rid of them. At least sometimes."

"You can do that?"

"You have a talent, but we have people with much greater talents than yours, so yeah, we can do that."

She had to admit that this sounded good to her right now. It sounded like a purpose.

"All that probably sounds good right now, but you have to realize that if you join us, you give up a normal life," he said quietly. "And I mean you give it up immediately, completely, and forever."

"And if you have a family?" Amelie asked, thinking of her mother and the money she had been given.

"We arrange for your death, for which they will be generously compensated," he replied.

Generously compensated. Her mother would like that.

"From this moment forward, your life will be in our world," he continued. "You give up all those things that people think make life worth living. You give up relationships. You give up kids. You give up love."

"Love is horrible," she said flatly.

He laughed—a barking sort of laugh.

"She speaks the truth," he said, standing.

He held out his hand, and she took it. It wasn't moist and clammy, like she was expecting it to be. It was actually dry and firm.

"Well then, I guess the interview is done," he said, using the handshake to help her to her feet.

"Welcome to the Ghosting Academy. I'm James. Come this way and let me show you your new life," he said, as he escorted her out of the room and into yet another hallway.

And, just like that first one, this hallway felt like it might go on forever.

Acknowledgments

As always, my heartfelt gratitude goes out to everyone who helped in the creation of this book. So big thanks to Tessa, Addie, Myra, Hassy, Leo, Laila, Valerie, Charlotte and Ian, for all their insights, help and support.

Most of all, thanks to my family: Sebastien, my son and lovingly merciless dev editor, Lucas, my dreamer, who knows what I really meant to say, and Julien, my husband, best friend, and partner for all life's adventures.

* * *

For Those Who Enjoyed this Book

Amelie, Majo, James, Caio, Clovis and Hudson will return in "The Ghosting Academy".

As most people know, reviews make or break authors, so if this book made you feel anything, do please share it, and connect with me at the following…

Webpage: Lsdelorme.com
Insta: lsdelormeauthor
Twitter:@lexyshawdelorme
Facebook Page: LS Delorme
Tiktok:@lexyshawdelorme